RETURN
OF THE
WHITE DEER

For Howie... my
gambling buddy —
enjoy the read until we
can enjoy the casino again —

Robert Sells

Rvl

Martin Sisters Publishing

Published by

Sky Vine Books, a division of Martin Sisters Publishing, LLC

www.martinsisterspublishing.com

Copyright © 2012 by Robert Sells

ISBN: 978-1-937273-24-8

Science Fiction/Fantasy

Printed in the United States of America
Martin Sisters Publishing, LLC

DEDICATION

For my wife, Dale, without whose gentle prodding, infinite patience, and perceptive critical analysis, this story never would have left my mind.

ACKNOWLEGEMENTS

My first thanks must go to my children whose expectant eyes helped conjure so many stories. During the difficult process of writing, Margaret Duff was my ever enthusiastic supporter. Her kind words pulled me over rough waters. Astute suggestions came from Karen Weidman, a good friend, and Caressa Sells, my English major daughter. My son, Rob, badgered me about the title and eventually we agreed upon *Return of the White Deer*. My writing was polished by Nancy Luckhurst. The staff of Martin Sisters Publishing was helpful and gentle with my naïve questions. Aaron Lazar was both my inspiration and guiding light in this new world of writing. To all, a heartfelt thank-you.

Finally, my thanks are extended to you, the reader, for taking a chance on new author with an old story.

SKY VINE BOOKS

Science Fiction/Fantasy

An imprint of Martin Sisters Publishing, LLC

PROLOGUE

Last and tallest of the Pennines range in England, Cross Fell Mountain loomed above the forest called Markwood. Getting to the wooded plateau near the peak of the mountain was challenging for even the most experienced mountain climbers. The king of Mercia, Cearl, precariously positioned just below the plateau, wedged his toe into the slight crack reluctantly offered by the steep cliff and raised himself higher. His foot slipped, but strong, sure hands maintained a grip on a rock. Fierce eyes bore into the unforgiving mountain. In one fluid motion, he swung himself up to a ledge leading to the plateau. He had beaten it. For a moment, the king lay on the ground, taking in great gulps of air. The remaining climb to the peak would have been short and easy, but reaching the peak held no importance for him. Here was his quarry. He raised his head, dark eyes slowly scanned right, left, and back to the right. Between two large bushes he glimpsed the movement of something white in color...and then nothing. Could just be the fog, he thought. Or, could it finally be the end of his hunt?

The king, crouched low, crept stealthily from the ledge onto the level ground. Hidden behind a solitary tree, he shifted his quiver of arrows to the ground. There were four long arrows, each sporting golden feathers, each with a shaft engraved with a unique animal symbol, tipped with a large, jagged head. Three of the arrows had been successfully used before: one sporting the image of a wild boar, one a bear, and one a mountain lion. Brushing the blond hair from his face, his long fingers reached out to the fourth arrow, bearing the unimpressive form of a deer. Back at the castle, late the night before, he had carefully painted the humble form stark white. Now, on the mountain, he caressed the perfectly straight arrow and silently notched it in the tight string of the great bow.

Cearl was an accomplished hunter. He was considered the best swordsman in the kingdom and one of the best archers. Many slain

1

animals were silent testaments to his skill with the bow, the heads of which adorned the Great Hall. The graves of many men, both good and bad, were evidence of his ability with the sword. To him these encounters were nothing more than sport, even the killing of men. Today's effort, however, was of a more serious nature.

After the Romans departed England, the land fragmented into dozens of small kingdoms. The success of these small kingdoms depended upon strong leaders. The white deer, a strange creature approaching the status of myth, had a long history of choosing able and caring leaders for Mercia. Cearl's father, King Jared had not been chosen by the white deer, at least not in the typical manner. The old king claimed to have communed with the animal in a dream, but most were skeptical of his account. Regardless, it was validation enough for a nation mired in civil war. After his coronation, the white deer disappeared from sight; many took it as a sign of her disapproval. The next year a famine wasted the country. The year after witnessed a terrible plague. Many whispered it was not coincidental that dark times had befallen the country.

Upon the death of his father, Cearl assumed the mantle of king, without being chosen by the deer. Those who challenged his legitimacy succumbed to his sword. Brave advisers in court urged him to invent a connection with the mysterious animal just his father had done. Cearl retorted that if indeed the white deer lived, its head would be mounted above his throne. If it did not live, why bother with any charade?

But, he was not blind to the discontent of his subjects. So he resolved to hunt down the animal and neatly eliminate the problem. He was on Cross Fell Mountain because it was the last place the deer was sighted years before.

Movement again. With grim satisfaction, he realized this was no fog. Cearl followed the ghostly motion in the waning light. From behind a holly bush, the white deer emerged. Astonished at her very existence and then her beauty, he gaped at the specter. She stood calmly, almost regally, on the edge of a cliff and looked over the vast expanse of Markwood forest below. Cearl regained his composure and deliberately pulled the string back, aiming at the heart of the animal. At that moment, she turned her head to look at him. Not more than twenty paces away, her startlingly blue eyes pierced into his very soul. He felt fear for the first time. He shook his head free from distracting thoughts and released the missile. It sailed harmlessly past her neck.

She continued to stare at him, unperturbed by the arrow that had just barely missed her. Cearl was stunned; he had never missed before. So confident was he in his abilities only one arrow was dedicated for each prize he sought and only one arrow was ever needed. Yet the deer still stood directly before him, alive, aware, and unfazed.

Looking down he found another arrow, frantically strung it, and turned back in the deer's direction, but there was only empty ground. Cearl ran to where his arrow had passed into the bush, but in the last light of the day, he could not find the treasured shaft.

He stayed there on the mountain, huddled under the tree that neither blocked the rain nor sheltered him from the cold wind. The next morning he searched in vain for the spent arrow. Miserable and hungry, he returned to the castle.

For an entire year, he returned each month to challenge death on the cliff. He searched the plateau for some sign of the white deer or his arrow, but both seemed to have vanished. On that cursed mountain he did find two other things: frustration and its child, anger. Not the flickering anger which makes a brief appearance and then politely leaves, but the deep, abiding anger that alters the very essence of a person. As one maddening year passed and then another, his visits became less frequent yet his obsession intensified.

3

After his mountain visits ceased, he invited hordes of hunters to search Markwood for the deer. Some were true hunters, but most were former soldiers or criminals willing to do the bidding of whoever paid them the most gold coins. Cearl rewarded them well as they searched both forest and mountain. They found no white deer, so their arrows wreaked vengeance on other animals, thinning the numbers of both large and small beasts. Mercia became a land made harsh by a bitter king and barren by heartless hunters.

After many years, he withdrew most of the huntsmen from the fruitless search, but still retained their services. The mountain was declared off-limits to all but the very best hunters within that dark group. Any rumors of the white deer were thoroughly investigated by those cruel mercenaries.

Despite the king's brutal efforts to eliminate the white deer and her influence, the legend grew.

CHAPTER ONE

Two travelers, a boy and a girl, traversed a road that ran straight as an arrow through the countryside. The girl, tall and slim, laughed. Though unaware of it, she was growing into a beautiful woman. Liana had convinced herself that her gray eyes were an unacceptable color, her nose too small, and the flowing chestnut hair, now loosely secured at the back of her head, was far too unruly for anyone to find appealing. Were she pressed to name her best feature, she would admit that her teeth were rather nice which explained the ease of her laughter with the boy.

The boy's given name was Penda, but everyone called him Pen. He was the same height as the girl, but his young body displayed a greater stature. His frame, once lean and wiry, had filled out with muscle. His pleasant face was not yet burdened with lines of worry. Like many twelve-year-olds, he thought he knew almost everything, except death, which had not yet visited friends or family. He also did not know that his life would soon change. Within a month, certainty would be replaced by doubt, pride by humility, and life by death. For now, though, the most troubling matter of his innocent existence was trying to focus on the embarrassing question Liana posed.

Astride a finely muscled brown horse, she stopped, turned to her companion, and asked once again with exasperation, "Pen, why do you hide it from your father?"

Pen found it difficult to concentrate on matters so disconcerting and Liana's questions were often such; his mind had drifted to the horse. The old horse had carried him even at the tender age of three and now dutifully helped his father plow the fields. But he ran so slowly…. Pen's ruminations dissolved away as Liana pushed him and tried to dislodge either rider or answer.

Firm in the saddle, he shook his head free of his musings, squinted his blue eyes, and focused on his companion. "What did you ask?"

Liana glowered, a clear sign she was about to chastise him for his inattentiveness.

"Pen! You must listen better! What's wrong with simply telling your father?"

"You don't have to yell, Liana. I hear perfectly well."

Eyes rolled, Liana looked away as her hair whipped around. Pen knew he had better get to the answer or suffer her acerbic words, undoubtedly being framed right now.

His mouth formed a rare frown as he struggled with the explanation. "Father is a farmer, Liana… just a farmer. That really explains it all, I guess. Not only has he no weapons, he doesn't want any around. Though he was of age, he didn't fight in the war. Songor did, but not my father. Father… well… he is what he is." Pen continued; his face strained with the effort of explanation. "He wants me to be a farmer too, but that's not what I am, Liana. A soldier perhaps. Maybe a huntsman."

"You, a huntsman?" She laughed. "You walk around ants to avoid hurting them. I can't see you as a huntsman, Pen."

He smiled. "No, I guess you're right, I couldn't be that. However I end up, I must be able defend myself. I need to know how to wield a sword, Liana." His voice dropped to a whisper: "I must be ready."

"For what?"

"I don't know!" he snapped, startling her. "I just know I have to be ready... for something."

Liana glared at him, more angered by her own surprise than offended by his harsh tone. She shot back at him, "You sneak away to Thatch to have that old soldier teach you how to use a sword. And, what is worse, you tell your father you were with me! All I can do is nod and smile, nod and smile. So, I become part of the lie! Wrong! Wrong, in so many ways, Pen! And I am wrong to let it continue. If you won't tell your father, maybe I should!"

The earlier eruption of anger vanished with Liana's threat. Panicked, he quickly begged, "Please don't, Liana. Father doesn't suspect anything and I don't want to upset him."

She shook her head resolutely as her steel-gray eyes drilled into him.

"You don't want to upset Pen! By telling him you were with me, you not only lied, you put me in the middle. I don't want to be involved in this anymore."

Tears welled in his eyes so he looked away. At twelve, tears formed quickly, but they were no longer allowed to fall in front of friends. Seeing his discomfort, she stopped pressing the point. Their horses carried them along, bodies and heads bobbing with their steady gait. After a few moments of silence, Liana added in a softer tone, "All right, Pen. I won't tell him. You can stop crying."

Pen struggled to compose himself and blinked away the tears as he continued to look away. Pretending to look at an abandoned hut, he waited until the evidence of his distress had sufficiently disappeared.

"I wasn't crying! I was... thinking." Then, quick as a snake strike, he turned and fired at her. "And you may be older than me, but I am taller! And you're just a stupid girl, anyway."

Instead of retaliating, she laughed at the outburst.

"Girl or not, you still need me to be part of your lies, don't you?" He started to protest but she held up her hand to silence him, eyebrows upraised, her head slightly tilted; her expression gave warning. "I will keep playing your game, but understand at some point you will have to tell him."

He knew she was right, so he turned away and ignored her.

Liana was his best friend. Not that he would ever admit it to other friends, especially Jack, who was nearly his best friend. She was not like other girls. She would climb a tree, casually brush away wet leaves and even squirmy slugs, and step over the occasional snake without shuddering like he did. She was also skilled in matters boys considered important, like archery. Once, one of his friends brought an old bow from his father's hunting rack. He and his friend shot arrows at a not-too-distant tree for the entire afternoon, getting progressively closer to the crude target they had erected. Liana came by and watched them show off for a few minutes. Then she snatched the bow from Pen and effortlessly placed the arrow directly in the center of the target. No, she was definitely not like other girls.

A few farms they passed bustled with men planting crops. In the woods between the fields were dilapidated huts, depressing reminders of the recent deterioration of the country.

Two rough, barefoot men approached them with faces turned downward.

Liana no longer attended to Pen's idle talk, her hand slowly moved toward her knife.

In silence, the poorly attired men passed. Looking back over her shoulder, she noted their determined walk did not change. Relieved, Liana glanced back to Pen who still was complaining about his numerous, but simple chores, oblivious to the possible dangers on the road. She interrupted his incessant chatter.

"Your father let you have Mirus today. I thought he was going to plow the west field with him this morning."

"He and Songor were fixing the barn today. Tomorrow they might plow."

"Well, rider of the plow horse," she taunted, "let's see if you can beat me in a race to the farm." She looked at him with a grin and was about to spur her horse forward.

"No fair", he whined, "you have Brill and she is your fastest horse."

She held up, turned to her friend, and smiled.

"Why Pen, I'm just a stupid girl, don't you remember?"

She leaned over in the saddle, nose-to-nose with him. "But the girl always wins, doesn't she? Now talk to my backside, boy!" With that she whipped the reins back and forth; a cloud of dust trailed behind her and Brill.

No horse his father owned was a match for Brill, certainly not this one. The boy urged the large animal forward, bringing him to a lackluster canter. When the animal finally reached a respectable speed, he urged him into a gallop. The horse grudgingly complied. The distance between Mirus and Brill grew wider. Pen refused to spur the horse or whip its flanks. Someone, long ago, had left scars all over the poor creature's body, so he did his best to encourage him with words as he leaned over his neck and spoke into his ear.

"Onward, great steed. Faster, Mirus!" And the horse continued his indifferent gallop. Liana looked over her shoulder and laughed.

Pen recalled a word he heard Thatcher say when he wanted two boys to rush together to practice sword fighting. The word was "adgredi", a Latin word meaning to advance swiftly. In desperation, Pen yelled, "Adgredi!"

The horse came to an abrupt stop; Pen was nearly unsaddled. Well that didn't work. He was about to build up to a canter again, when the horse snorted, reared, almost dislodged him again and, in the blink of an eye, broke into a sudden, furious gallop, his black eyes fixed on the brown horse. The boy gripped tightly with his knees, praying he wouldn't fall. He had never known such speed. Shoulder-length hair flew back exposing an uninhibited grin. When Liana looked back again, her smile dropped away and was replaced by an astonished stare. They were only a few horse lengths behind and closing fast. Shocked, she spurred Brill faster as Mirus closed the gap.

At last they were neck and neck. Pen hazarded a sideways glance at the girl. She stared at him in amazement, her reins snapping right and left as Mirus slowly coasted past. When they splashed into the wide creek, water spraying away from the great horse, Pen pulled gently on the reins. When the horse finally stopped, knee-deep in water, the boy hugged him around the neck. Another splash sprayed behind them. Liana looked at Mirus for a few moments, watching him bob his head up and down, great blasts of air and water exploding from his nostrils. Squinting her eyes, she turned toward Pen.

"How did you do that?"

Pen, smiling broadly, looked at her. "Mirus said he didn't like looking at your backside."

Exchanging playful banter the two walked a short distance to Pen's farm. They failed to notice Pen's father waiting for them at the barn, arms folded. When they turned to lead the horses in, they were met with a dark scowl and their smiles wilted.

CHAPTER TWO

With a flip of his hand, Larmack silently ordered his son down. He stepped up to the boy, one eyebrow raised.

"Is there something you want to tell me, Penda?"

One of the tallest men in the village, Larmack's imposing height was complemented with well-developed muscles from years of hard farm work. The portion of his face not covered by thick, peppery beard was deeply lined, suggesting a past familiar with pain and suffering.

Pen had a sinking feeling his father had discovered his clandestine visits to Thatcher, but he silently prayed his secret was still intact.

He hoped to distract his father with what he thought was important news. "I finally won a race, Father."

Under his farmer's tan, a red hue filled his face. Pen grimaced, turned his face slightly, and cringed as he waited for the verbal attack that was sure to follow.

"I care nothing about a silly horse race; I care everything about your safety! Why didn't you tell me about your sword lessons?"

The boy, wide-eyed, just looked at his father.

"You think you can keep secrets with so many wagging tongues about?" Then, turning from his son, he lashed out at the girl. "Liana, I am disappointed in you."

"Sir, I...he..."

"No more lies, Liana! You are three years older and should know better."

Liana's head hung low. Larmack had never scolded her; he was more like a doting uncle than a neighbor. She wanted to scream that she had told Pen again and again to tell him, but she would not put her friend in a worse predicament, though he richly deserved it. Besides, she admitted to herself, she had indeed lied with her silence.

Guilt outweighed fear as Pen blurted out, "Father, I am at fault. I begged her to go along with my lies. Liana told me many times to tell you, but I didn't listen."

The father spun around to face to his son. "She gave you this advice and still you didn't tell me?"

The bowed head nodded.

"Leave us, Liana. I must speak to my son alone."

She wasn't sure if it was Pen's bravery in exonerating her or the pain she felt watching him being verbally thrashed, but tears came to her eyes and would not stop.

She pulled Brill away and rode off, wiping her nose and eyes.

Larmack realized his son had put himself in jeopardy by defending Liana. Softly he queried, "Why didn't you tell me, Pen?"

Pen watched Liana leave and then turned to his father.

"I was afraid you would forbid me to do it."

"Better to ask forgiveness than permission, eh?"

"Yes. No. I don't know! I just wanted to learn how to use a sword. You always tell me to avoid fights because you don't know how to use a sword. I won't do that."

Amused, the tall man put a foot on the fence rail, folded his arms, and raised an eyebrow. "Ah, you think your father a coward, then?"

Pen finally looked up, relieved to see a twinkle in his father's eyes.

"No, you are...wise. It would be foolish for you to challenge someone with a weapon."

The father could not suppress his smile. "So now I am a fool?"

"No. No sir."

He recalled how his father had many times advised him to listen first, think carefully, and, if absolutely necessary, speak. It was certainly necessary now. But what was the best way to say it?

His father waited patiently and finally the boy continued with a firmer voice, eyes holding his father's.

"We are different, you and I. If I stay on the farm, I won't be afraid of anyone! I mean to protect myself and that is only done with the sword. You can't teach me swording, sir, so I had to learn from Thatch."

Larmack was quiet for a few moments as he looked away from his son. He understood the lad's concerns.

"Perhaps you are right, son. I probably don't know as much as you or Thatcher about sword fighting, but I do know this. If you think having a sword makes you less afraid, then I am fearful for you. When violence is born, it grows up mighty fast and it's an ugly beast."

Larmack looked away, paused for a moment, and spoke so softly that Pen barely heard the words.

"Not everything is as it seems, son."

Pen stared at the tall man scanning the fields. He knew his father would protect him even if he had to match shovel against sword.

"I'm sorry I lied. I'll never again lie to you."

"At least as long as this memory is fresh, eh?" Larmack said good-naturedly, turning back to his son.

"No. Never again, sir, never."

He put his arm around the boy's shoulder and pulled him closer. "Good. I know you mean what you say, Pen."

As they walked to the barn, Pen endured the rare show of affection. Pen wanted to be considered an adult and this last year he had cast off any hugs his father had given him.

"Songor and I have to help Eldrick cut a new barn door." Larmack leaned to Pen's ear and whispered, "I told Songor our work would not give him time to make us dinner and that we would eat at the inn."

Pen smiled. Songor was a terrible cook, but they would never hurt his feelings by suggesting his meals were anything but tasty.

Father and son walked over to the wagon where Songor had just finished loading wood.

Larmack climbed onto the wagon and released the brake; the wagon inched forward as the mare slowly pulled it. Settled on the buckboard, he looked back at his son. "So, you got the old horse to run, did you? Knowing you, it wasn't by whip or spur, so how did you do it?"

Leading Mirus by the reins, he walked beside his father as the cart, moaning and creaking, moved toward the road.

"It was strange, sir. I just kept talking to him, trying to find something that might get him moving. I guess I just said the right word."

"The right word," mused Larmack, winking at Songor. "Let me guess... adgredi." The large black horse suddenly stirred and stared at the farmer.

Pen, a puzzled expression on his face, looked at his father.

"How did you know?"

His father laughed.

"He's been my horse far longer than yours, boy. I got him from an army officer; he was in many battles, son." The man snapped the reins and the cart careened off. Pen waved goodbye as Songor leaned back over the buckboard and smiled at the lad.

As the weary steed contentedly munched on the thick grass that lay near the barn, Pen wiped him down. His hand crossed over the scars Mirus had carried all these years. Pen spoke into his ear. "When I fully master the sword, I will seek out your previous owner and thrash him for you, dear Mirus. No one should ever have allowed you this pain!" Mirus looked at Pen, whinnied, then snorted and nuzzled his head close to the boy.

Leading the old horse to his stall, he thought once again about his father. He loved the tall, taciturn, gentle man and respected him in most things, but felt acutely embarrassed whenever he avoided confrontations. The previous week, Pen overheard the blacksmith, Griswold, curse the soldiers, right to their faces. He almost backed them down, but they got what they were after. When the soldiers came to collect taxes from his father, the man only stared into their eyes and handed over what they insolently demanded.

Pen long ago decided he would never quietly accept the soldiers' slurs and insults that accompanied the tax collection. He would soundly rebuke them as the blacksmith had done and, if necessary, punish them with his sword. Pen smiled at the thought. He looked down the road toward the village and the inn; his stomach growled.

CHAPTER THREE

Pen, Larmack, and Songor, lived on a farm just outside the village of Kirkland. The largest structure in the small village was the Three Decker Inn.

The three men dismounted upon arrival at the inn; their talk was light and jovial. Larmack surveyed the long porch in both directions before following his son and servant inside.

Songor burst into the room hailing one friend after another. Wide as he was tall, he waddled more than walked. He constantly wiped sweat from his ruddy face with a rag from his pocket. The hair he still had circled his pink skull like a white halo. If he wasn't talking, he was eating, and if he wasn't eating, he was drinking; often he tried to accomplish all three tasks at the same time. As Songor happily contributed to the general din of the tavern, Pen nodded to a few farmers and one of his friends.

Larmack scanned the clientele and the free tables that dotted the inn. The tavern was built over one hundred years earlier by a retired sea captain. He fashioned a series of three decks, each three steps higher than the one before it. Larmack preferred the highest one, and a table there was free. The trio climbed the steps to

17

highest level and claimed the table. The tall farmer sat in the corner facing the rest of the tavern.

Once seated, Songor immediately popped up and leaned over the railing (it sagged perilously with his weight) and chatted with a group of men right below him on a lower level. He chose this group because the aromatic steam from their pork stew reached his nostrils and excited his palate. Turning to Pen, his face was contorted with both confusion and concern. "Where be our dishes, Master Pen?" Just then three wooden bowls were slapped down in front of them.

The waitress shook her finger at Songor whose arms encircled the sumptuous treasure, eyes closed as if in a trance. His nose uplifted slightly as it inhaled the fragrant stew so delightfully close now.

"Don't you be expecting extra helpings, Songor. Last time you was here we had to kill two extra pigs!"

"Sally, this be me fav'rit. Come 'ere, lass. Let me give thee a kiss fer ye kindness to me." He reached out toward her.

Sally frowned and lightly tapped his hand with a small loaf of bread.

"Get on with you now. Here's your bread. Eat as much of that as you want, Songor." She huffed off to another table. Pen had already begun to eat the stew. Songor delayed his start for only a moment as he once again sniffed the steam from the mixture of small purple carrots, onions, peas, and chunks of pork in thick gravy. He attacked the stew and quickly surpassed both Pen and Larmack in his consumption.

He raised his hand to the waitress.

"Sally, Sally. Could you favor me with another bowl, dear?"

The waitress rolled her eyes and stomped down to the kettle. Later, their supper mostly done, Larmack rested with his back against the wall, watching the antics at one of the tables while he listened to Songor's ramblings.

"So, I walks right up to the bartender…"

Florid from the drink and sweat dripping from his forehead, Songor interrupted his tale only to take a draught of honey-laced mead. Before he continued, he leaned into Pen who seemed most interested in his words.

"… I looks him straight in eye, I did. And I told him just what I thought of his drinks."

Another gulp. An appreciative smile formed on his face; apparently he had a more favorable impression of this drink than the one in his story.

"Then he looks at me, grabs me cup…"

Songor giggled in anticipation and only allowed himself a quick sip so that he could finish his story.

"He said, he said," Songor chuckled, "'then you won't be missing it' and poured it on me head!" An explosion of laughter followed and Pen couldn't help but laugh with him. Larmack grinned and raised his cup to the storyteller.

"Sally, dear, we needs another cup of this fine, fine mead." Songor yelled over the clamor of the other patrons.

Songor kept talking. "'Minds me of the time we traveled to Lindsey. So many taverns and the mead there… oh, the mead. Sir, you remember when they threw Higgins into the vat. His head came out and he asked if he could have another drink."

Pen looked up from his plate, swallowed quickly, and asked, "You and father were in Lindsey, Songor?"

The fat man stopped talking and nervously looked at his master whose narrowed eyes glared at Songor.

"Well, yes, yes…but long ago. Long, long ago. Twas nothing, just a trip." He looked about uncomfortably for some distraction.

"Sally, dear, dear Sally. Songor be dying of thirst. Save him girl," he bellowed.

"But to get to Lindsey," persisted Pen, "you had to have gone through the Markwood Forest. Tell me about it."

19

Avoiding the stare of his irritated boss, Songor pondered the question for a few seconds and then responded. "Weren't much, Pen. Not much in Lindsey either." Songor quickly began another story, about a drinking contest he won handily, boring Pen into a daze.

The three were essentially finished with their meal, though Larmack had just started nibbling his almond cake which was covered with honey.

Upon Sally's delivery of the drink, Songor was about to extol the virtues of the Three Decker Inn's mead when two soldiers entered. The jovial din dropped immediately to absolute silence. Two men, both wearing bright red tunics with black trousers and boots, looked for a table. The locals put their heads down and silently studied the flat, wooden surfaces in front of them. Soldiers in these parts were sometimes like mean dogs and a stare could excite them into snapping and attacking. Larmack alone watched the two men saunter through.

Gorm and Eusibius were well known in the village and not much liked. They acted as the local police force, collected taxes (usually a bit more than what the books required), and ostentatiously practiced swordplay as they laughingly crashed into stores and bumped and pushed into people and obstacles in their way. Eusibius was older and consequently a bit more polite. Taller than his young comrade, he had a pockmarked face. Gorm was short, rash, and devilishly handsome. It was Gorm who noticed Larmack staring at them. Gorm led Eusibius toward the farmer. All talk had ceased and all that was heard was the noisy rattling of the swords as the soldiers climbed the last few steps. Larmack did not take his eyes off the two men as he casually placed a morsel of cake into his mouth.

Gorm stood over Larmack who cut another small piece of cake with his spoon.

"We want this table, farmer. Move on and let us eat."

Pen started to get up, but a stern glance from Larmack sat him back down. What was his father doing? It was for situations exactly like this that he wished for a sword at his side. The old farmer slowly brought the morsel to his mouth, closed his eyes and shook his head, making a show of enjoying the dessert.

"Gorm, you really should try this cake. It's quite delicious."

Incensed, the muscular soldier kicked his chair and repeated his order.

Larmack looked around and then back to the soldier.

"I see many empty tables."

"Well, we want this one, you impertinent trash. Get up and get out." His face matched the red of his tunic.

Songor slowly backed away from the table and stepped down past Eusibius, who watched the proceedings with a smirk on his face. Pen would have only been too glad to follow Songor, but his father had given him no sign to leave.

Larmack ignored the command, picked up the spoon, and cut off another small piece.

"Insolent pig! Now I will thrash you!" Gorm reached for his sword. What happened next was such a blur that even the boy who watched the entire incident could not say for sure what took place. But a moment later, sword cast aside, Gorm was face down on the ground as Larmack twisted the man's arm behind his back, head pressed into the floor. Then, just as abruptly, Larmack released his hold and casually sat back down on his chair. The enraged soldier immediately turned over, lunged toward Larmack as he reached for his knife.

The same knife Gorm futilely reached for was at his own throat. Somehow Larmack had extracted it during the struggle.

Eusibius reacted by reaching for his sword only to find it too gone. Then he felt the tip of a blade in his back. Songor pressed the point just enough to be uncomfortable.

"Ye mustn't move, Eusibius, sir."

Larmack held the blade close to the kneeling man's throat. "Now you will rise very slowly and sit down on that chair." As Gorm got up, he stared down at his blade touching the exposed fleshy part of his throat.

"Hands to your side... ah, very good. Sit there until I tell you to get up."

Gorm sat across from Larmack who had laid the knife down beside his plate. Larmack slowly finished the cake. Finally he pushed himself up from the seat. Stepping closer to Gorm, Larmack leaned down, close to his ear, and whispered, "Try to hurt me or mine and you will die."

The soldier turned defiantly toward the farmer, but went pale as he met with his cold, unblinking gaze.

Larmack stared until Gorm turned away. Then he calmly picked up the sword and handed it to Gorm, along with the knife. "Now you may have the table."

He walked down the steps, and Pen, stunned by the events, found himself momentarily alone with Gorm who breathed heavily and stared at the table. Quickly the boy got up, knocking his chair down and followed his father. Songor placed the blade of Eusebius on the table by the door as they left.

On the short ride home in the darkness, Pen was too astonished to say anything. Larmack offered nothing and even Songor was quiet. Pen repeatedly twisted his head to listen for approaching horses.

"Don't worry, Pen," Larmack said quietly, "they won't be bothering us tonight."

During the moonlit ride home, the boy looked sideways at the man riding beside him. This man who steadily worked from dawn to dusk, this man who tenderly cared for him when he was sick, this man who avoided confrontations, this man who was his father, was now a mystery to Pen.

When they reached the farm, Songor mumbled goodnight and walked quickly to his room in the barn. Pen returned the horses to their stalls. On the way out, he paused at Songor's door and knocked.

"Come in, Master Pen."

Songor was sitting on his rumpled cot. "I 'spected you might be visiting tonight."

Pen sat down on a chair facing Songor. "I've never seen anything happen so fast. How? What... Songor, was my father a soldier?"

No laugh, chuckle, or smile emerged as his face contorted into frown lines so rarely used. He worried a piece of thread out of his bed sheet and shook his head.

"Pen, I promised your Da' not to talk... to you or anyone. He says to me 'Songor, ye mustn't tell what we done.' How did he say it... wait, let me think..." the man winced and closed his eyes.

"I gots it now... he says... 'The past be dead, it canst have no part of now.' That's what he said, Master Pen. Or sumtin like that. So I canst talk about us soldiering. Canst, Master Pen, I simply canst." Songor looked pleadingly into the boy's eyes. Pen held his stare for a few seconds, thinking about Songor's inadvertent admission. Then he focused on his friend. Whenever the large man worried, sleep would be denied him. The boy patted him on the shoulder.

"I understand you can't tell me anything, Songor. You go to sleep now."

Relieved, the portly man lay down on his bed and promptly started snoring. Pen covered him with a blanket, patted him again, and walked out of the barn. His father had been a soldier!

Upon returning to the dark farmhouse, he found the farmer sitting on a chair by the fireplace.

"Son, don't ask me questions about tonight."

He looked at Pen with a piercing stare that brooked no question and demanded full compliance. Pen looked down and simply bade him goodnight. An hour later Larmack retired to his bed.

By the time Larmack finally found sleep, his son had lost his. Pen's sleep was plagued by strange dreams. He awoke, startled, and sat up in bed, sweating. He found himself breathing hard, but could not clearly remember the last dream. It had something to do with the white deer. Then, as he reclined on his cot, his eyes wide open, his mind recalled the odd events four years earlier...

CHAPTER FOUR

Eight-year-old Pen, excited about nearly everything (except chores), and Liana, just emerged from the cocoon of childhood, spent most of their free time together.

Though the young boy enjoyed spending time with Liana, he was frustrated. Paths well-trodden were paths too familiar for Pen.

A particularly sunny morning found eight-year-old Pen arguing with Liana. Invincible in his cloak of youth, he yearned to seek new adventures in the mysterious forest just down the road... Markwood. He issued another of his dares to enter that foreboding realm of impossibly tall trees and impassable thorny bushes. Such taunts usually resulted in a diatribe from the girl, but she was intent in coaxing a chipmunk to feed from her hand.

He pestered her with another challenge to enter the unknown woods; his raised voice scared off the timid creature. Liana pointed her finger like a stabbing dagger.

"Your own father told you never to go there, Pen! Why don't you ever listen?"

Exasperated, she once again warned him of the wild, dangerous animals and the mysterious green men who inhabited the inner part of the forest, never seen until they surrounded you. Dismemberment and death followed their manifestation.

"So what? I could fight them off, Liana." He jumped up and waved a stick in a menacing manner. She gave him a disgusted look and tried to coax the chipmunk back.

Pen stopped thrashing about, watched the chipmunk hesitantly reappear, and then blurted out, "You don't really believe that stuff, do you?"

The chipmunk darted off into the woods again. She turned slowly and glared at him. Eyes squinted tightly, she stabbed him with her stare.

"Yes. Everyone says it's true, even your father. He told you not to go near those woods."

"Come on, Liana. He wouldn't find out."

"We must not go into the forest. Ever! Bad things happen there." As usual, when she was this adamant, Liana got her way. She rose abruptly, deciding for both of them that the conversation and their time with the chipmunk had ended. They spent the rest of the morning walking along the creek. At the end of their trek, they saw the creek wind slowly until it disappeared in the thick forest. Cross Fell Mountain loomed behind the green wall. Pen turned to Liana, head tilted, and looked at her hopefully. She firmly shook her head and walked back along the creek, away from both mountain and forest.

As she mounted her horse to return home, Liana told Pen she would be gone for over a week. In the spring and summer, she was often absent for week or more. She refused to tell him where she went or what she did and it annoyed him immensely. Mother Hebron, Liana's mother, would also leave. It was all some kind of girl secret. Even Songor didn't know what was going on. Not allowed to ride a horse alone, eight-year old Pen was stuck at the farm and forced to amuse himself. As he waved goodbye to her, he looked in the direction of Markwood Forest. An idea came to mind and he smiled.

The next morning, Songor and Larmack trudged out under a sky still black with just a streak of lavender on the horizon, a silent promise of a new day. By mid-morning, chores done, the boy was packed with cheese, bread, and a rusty knife from the barn, all essential ingredients for his quest.

Pen darted to the creek. After looking over his shoulder to make sure no one saw him, he ran along the bank to where the churning waterway emerged from the tall, green wall of the forbidden forest. He hesitated a moment, his heart racing as much with anticipation as with trepidation and before impulse could be bested by reason he ducked under branches and followed the creek into the new world.

It was a world without sun, the diminished light a monotone green. He smelled the rich aroma of grass, ground, and dead leaves, all still damp in the perpetual green shade. Small creatures scurried here or slithered there, surprised by his entry. Birds tracked his progress with scolding chirps.

Though he had no fear of animals large or small, he was concerned about those mysterious green men. Liana insisted they could change from bush to person and back again. Though he didn't believe the story, the boy carefully scrutinized the bushes near him. They seemed normal enough, but he felt it necessary to check often.

After nearly an hour, he came to a small meadow, neatly bisected by the stream, lush grass on either side of its banks. Here he saw bright blue sky instead of the monotonous green canopy. Far away, on the other side of the meadow, circled by wild flowers, was a small pond. Settling on the thick grass, he took out the cheese and bread and commenced to eat. Before long, scurrying squirrels, rabbits, darting chipmunks, and fluttering birds surrounded him. They wanted the bits of his snack, unsure of how to safely extract the food once offered. Hunger overcame fear as they darted to the boy, plucked a morsel of food from his outstretched fingers, and ran away with their tiny treasure. When the food was finally gone, a few of the animals were enticed to accept his gentle caresses. Liana had tried this, unsuccessfully, during all their outings; he couldn't wait to tell her. She's going to be so jealous, he thought happily.

When evening began to inhale the sun's light, he sadly rose, waved goodbye to his new friends, and followed the creek out of the forest, getting home before his father and Songor ambled back from their labors.

He repeated this visit over each of the next few days. More and more animals of every type would visit him in the grove. Soon he was able to coax even the wary fox to allow his gentle touch.

He bounced out of bed early on the fourth morning, packed a lunch for himself, and put tidbits of food in his bag for his new friends. Arriving at the meadow, there were no animals to be seen nor could he hear any sounds, save the rustling of leaves in the wind. Puzzled he scanned the entire field.

At the far end of the meadow, she appeared. Perfectly proportioned, pure white, the deer walked purposefully toward Pen. The boy stood still, watching. The graceful animal slowly approached him, stopped within a few feet, cocked her head and stared. His mind seemed to be gently pried opened and faint ideas bubbled in his consciousness. A moment later, he was both shocked and delighted to clearly "hear" her thoughts as distinct words.

"Pen, I am so happy to finally meet you. You have taken good care of my friends. Thank you."

The deer's large blue eyes stared deeply into his blue eyes. "Don't be alarmed. Walk with me."

Although it had to be nearly two hundred yards away, it seemed it took them only a few steps to reach the other side of the pond.

Looking back, he saw the animals had emerged from hiding. Lined along the edge of the trees, all watched.

Oddly, he felt somewhat tired. His mind was fuzzy, as if in a dream.

The white deer stopped at a small outcrop of granite. In the shade of a tall tree, she continued the conversation.

"I am the caretaker of this forest, Pen, and all the forests in the land. Without a king to model goodness, to show kindness, to give mercy, balance always suffers. So the forest has suffered, so the land has suffered, and so too do your people suffer."

He wasn't sure what she was meant by "his people". Father, Songor, Liana, and Mother Hebron? The villagers? Caressed by a soft, cool breeze, Pen began to nod off.

"Balance must be restored, beyond the forest. There is only one who can do this, Pen." He looked at her carefully while she gazed at her animals on the edge of the forest. Unlike other wild creatures, her coat was untainted by dirt or brambles, no sores or wounds compromised her body. Her profile was perfect and beautiful. Her next message conveyed a deep melancholy as she turned toward the boy.

"I am sorry, young Pen."

She placed her head closer and he tentatively petted it. So soft was her hair. She gently brushed her jowl against his cheek.

Though enraptured by her closeness, he was concerned about her words. What was she sorry about?

As though answering his question, she explained. "I see your heart, Pen and I know you are good. But you will have to be brave and strong as well. You will need all of those qualities, and luck."

She abruptly backed up a few steps to a large, flat granite slab embedded in the ground. She struck it with her hoof and Pen heard a sharp crack followed by a stream of sparks emitting from the rock. He stiffened in fear, ready to run.

"I am about to tell you a secret. Forget this and you may forfeit your life, Pen, as well as the lives of others."

Blood drained from his face as he anxiously stared at her.

"In all this land, only one person knows my name. Repeat my name to only him so he will know you are the one chosen by me. He will be wearing a pure white robe, and when he requests the word, say "Angelus", for that is my name. Now close your eyes and whisper it back to me."

He squeezed shut his eyes and murmured her name, over and over. Her voice grew fainter as the deer repeated a hypnotic mantra:

"Only the one in white, Pen, only the one in white."

He didn't know how many times he'd chanted her name but suddenly he opened his eyes. Though it seemed like only a few seconds had passed, it was now almost dark. A few stars dotted the sky above. The forest animals had disappeared again and the deer was gone. Alarmed at how late it was, he ran through the meadow and returned home just before his father and Songor trudged in from the fields.

The next day, with Liana still gone, he decided to return to the meadow. After a few chores, he asked his father if he could play in the woods. Busy fixing the axle of the wagon, his father agreed. Pen wove along the creek bed and snuck back into Markwood forest. When he reached the meadow, no animals waited for him.

He sat in the middle of the meadow totally alone, save for the ever-present bees. He felt abandoned. Where were they? Why did they leave him alone?

He was alone and lonely where he once enjoyed so many new friends. Somehow he knew they would never return. The loss was too much, too sudden. Perhaps Liana was right after all. He should never have entered this strange forest, not because it was dangerous, but because it was enchanted. Shaking his head angrily, tears falling, he realized enchanted places don't follow the rules of the outside world. Sad and angry, he sprang up and ran out of the meadow.

He had wanted to share his experiences with Liana and all his friends, but the dream had turned into a nightmare. Perhaps it was best not to tell anyone, he thought. Who would believe him, anyway? Even if Liana believed him, she would certainly scold him. Upon hearing of the animals, she would gloat over his loss. He could hear her now. "I told you so, Pen! Don't go in Markwood. No good will come of it!" No, he thought, best not to tell anyone.

Pen emerged from the dark forest into the sunlight. He found some solace in the realization that his life could return to normal. He didn't like lying to his father about his excursions, so he would be relieved of that irritating guilt. He missed his friends and looked forward to some games in the nearby, thankfully un-enchanted woods. Liana would be home in a day or two. As he walked away from the mysterious forest, he was not half as sad as he might have been.

*

Liana returned a few days later and Pen was delighted. The pair ran across the fields, not stopping till they reached the cool woods. As always, Liana did not discuss her absence and Pen did not share his recent adventure with her.

The afternoon passed in conversation and exploration. The two friends again endeavored to coax small animals to eat from their hand, and, much to Liana's delight, they achieved instant success. She assumed they'd simply found the right food, but Pen knew it was because of his new ability to communicate with the animals.

Others, however, noted that Larmack's son had an unusual ability with animals. During a thunderstorm the blacksmith was trying to get two frightened horses into his barn. Pen walked up to the stomping animals, grabbed their reins, and led them into the barn without incident. The blacksmith just shook his head.

One winter morning, Liana came to the farm and helped Pen feed the animals. A duck waddled over to Liana quaking loudly. Liana threw it some meal, but the duck ignored the feed and continued her annoying harangue.

"Stupid duck," she muttered and started to walk away. But the duck followed, noisily quacking all the while. She threw more food. The duck looked at it, and again commenced quacking. Liana entered the barn where Pen threw hay to the horses.

"This silly duck refuses to eat, but she insists on quacking." She threw more meal down, but the duck ignored the offering and continued noisily after her.

Pen tilted his head as though trying to hear.

"No, she's trying to tell you...wait." And off he ran. The duck looked at him for a moment, then turned back to the girl and continued its insistent squawking. A minute later, Pen returned with a duckling cupped in his hand. He kneeled and laid the shivering baby by its cackling mother. She quickly inspected the squeaking offspring, nodded her head with some sort of approval, and proceeded to eat the meal on the floor, quiet at last. Pen gently petted both duck and duckling as they ate.

"What? How?"

"She was telling you that her baby had slipped through a crack in the floor and was trapped under the planks."

"But how did you know?" the astonished girl inquired.

He shrugged.

"I don't know. I just did."

Liana stared at him, wide-eyed.

"You talk with animals?"

"Well, it's not really talking..."

"You are a communicator!"

"What's that?" Pen asked.

Liana cocked her head and looked at the ground, puzzled.

"I'm not really sure. But mother does. She knows so much; you have no idea. We must tell her so she can explain things to us both."

So off to Liana's home they went.

As Liana and Pen entered the warm cottage, a smooth-faced woman with prematurely white hair greeted them. She was shorter than Liana and wore a blue apron, dusted with brown flour that covered a body nearly as slim as her daughter's. The kitchen was filled with the keen fragrance of cinnamon in the morning and the rich, pungent aroma of garlic in the evening. Nearly noon, both scents battled for prominence in the small kitchen.

Seeing her daughter's look of excitement, Mother Hebron wiped her gown clean from the flour, and sat, motioning for the children to sit on the other side of the table.

Liana related the story of Pen and the duck.

"Mother, could he be a communicator?"

Mother Hebron stared at Pen a long time before she responded.

"Pen, do you communicate with animals using your voice or through your thoughts?"

"I speak words to them, but I hear their thoughts."

Mother Hebron nodded, her eyes down, considering his response.

"One more question, child. Did you ever see a white deer?"

Pen's eyes widened a bit. He told no one of that time in the forest. How could she have guessed? He hesitated slightly, then answered in a voice he hoped was convincing.

"No...no deer."

Mother Hebron squinted and tilted her head quizzically. Why the hesitation, she wondered. Her eyes pierced into Pen's eyes. She could not discern any deception. No, she concluded, he was just a farm boy.

Hands folded on the flour-dusted table, she looked at the two children.

"All right. I am going to tell you about the past, but knowledge of the past can be dangerous. Don't share this with anyone, even your friends."

Wide-eyed, both children quickly nodded their heads in agreement.

"First, your ability to communicate with animals. It's a power no man has ever possessed, Pen, though a few women have it. It is good to have, but you mustn't let others know."

Pen frowned, confused.

"Let me explain, Pen. All of this has to do with Cearl and the White Deer."

She chuckled for a moment.

"First a lesson about religion. The Goddess was first in this land. All worshipped her long, long ago. Then the Saxons and Angles came from across the sea and brought their own gods, the cold gods of the North. The Goddess was pushed out and only a few remembered her. Not long ago the new god, the Jesus god came to England. It was told that Jesus was the son of the Goddess. The Christians called the Goddess, Mary. So those who still worshipped the Goddess followed her child, Jesus. Some became nuns. Jesus and the Goddess grew strong."

She smiled triumphantly. "Now Odin and Thor are being pushed out. Jesus and the Goddess will take their place. Soon."

Pen nodded. He knew the stories about these gods. Mother Hebron leaned toward the two children.

"When the Goddess alone was worshipped here, the White Deer chose one special man in each generation to become king. During those times Mercia remained strong. Cearl and his father followed the gods of the north. They were not chosen, and since they have reigned, the White Deer has all but vanished. A few say she is dead, killed by Thor, but most believe she is alive and ready to choose again. Cearl was jealous of the power the White Deer.

So, he had the nuns... driven out. He also killed the abbot and those who followed him. A dark time."

She squeezed her eyes shut to block her memories. After a time she returned to the present and the warmth of her kitchen.

"The women who communicated with animals are hunted by the king. He wants to use them to find the white deer.

"Now, have you told anyone else of this ability?" she asked Pen.

"No, just Liana."

Mother Hebron's expression softened a bit.

"Don't show your powers to anyone." Pen, pale and uneasy, agreed.

Mother Hebron shook her head with a rueful sigh. "King Cearl is obsessed with the myth. He has ordered that any sightings of the White Deer be reported immediately. Then his hunters are sent to investigate the sightings, and if they find the deer, they are to kill her."

She saw their horrified expressions and frowned.

"It's not a good king we have and these are not good times, children. With the exception of reporting a sighting, all talk about the White Deer is forbidden."

She stood and stared out the window as though she was looking for someone or something.

"More and more people whisper about seeing the Deer these days. Something is going to happen."

She closed her eyes and shook her head wearily.

"You were right to come here and talk with me."

She raised the two children from their chairs and put her arms around them, hugging them both.

"You have lived a wonderful life in this quiet little village, my children. But things are not always as they appear. When you grow up, the world changes. For the worse, I am afraid. Pen, heed my words. Don't attract attention and keep quiet, at least for the time being."

Pen agreed. After a slice of warm cinnamon cake dripping with honey, he and Liana went to the barn where the horses were stabled for winter. Liana blithely chatted about the revelations while Pen thought about the White Deer. Was it real or just a dream? Hadn't the Deer said something about him being the "chosen one"? Pen did not like to worry about things, so he framed it as a dream, not reality.

Still a boy, Pen did not know when you lie to yourself, it was the worst and most dangerous lie of all. Nor did he know that the grinning face of everyday life had a snap-jaw mouth which could rip a person apart without warning. Soon he would know both unpleasant facts.

CHAPTER FIVE

When Pen woke up, only disconcerting fragments of his dream and   recollections remained. Never one to dwell too long or too seriously on perplexing matters, his mind focused on friends, fun, and fencing. Nearly thirteen, he was puzzled only by his father's violence at the inn the night before and the revelation that he'd been in the army.

An hour before noon, having completed his chores, he walked to the barn. The sounds of pounding followed by his father's cursing... all accompanied by Songor's laughter. Looking up he saw the pair perched on the center beam of the barn.

The part of his father's face not hidden by his beard was beet red, not just from exertion, though profuse sweat on his forehead gave ample evidence of strenuous efforts. "If I have to bore this hole one more time, by God, I will chop this timber in two, four, and eight pieces!"

A broad smile on his face, Songor pointed to the corner of the barn, "Thar's the ax, sir. Have at it, 'cause, thar be more boring."

Shaking perspiration from his eyes, Larmack glared at his companion.

"I will have no more of your mirth at my expense, Songor!"

Pen waited for his father to control his breathing and Songor to control his stifled chuckles before he made his request.

"Father, I'm done with my chores. May I take Mirus to Mother Hebron's? I'll be back before sundown."

Larmack looked down at his Pen.

"Yes, but don't run him hard today, son. He's walking slowly from yesterday's race. He's old, but the best plow horse we own. I can't have him lame."

Pen agreed and quickly went to saddle the horse before his father could think of more chores for him. Quietly he led Mirus to the barn door when he heard his father's voice.

"Will you be going to Thatcher?"

The boy lowered his head for a moment, turned, and replied, "If that would be all right with you, sir."

Larmack glared at the boy.

"No, it's not all right, but you don't seem to care about my thoughts on the matter. Just don't get yourself killed when you play at swords." He turned back to bore a hole in the crossbeam which Songor, who winked at Pen, held in place. Fearful his father's wrath might fall on him, he quickly mounted Mirus and rode away.

Pen first stopped at the large barn that anchored one corner of the small village. Door ajar, in the barn's dark recesses, a sudden glow appeared. The smithy, a large man named Griswold, smudged with black soot, brought a large hammer down on a glowing horseshoe. His son, Jack, a slightly smaller version of the large man, steadily worked the bellows keeping the embers red hot. All work stopped and the two men approached the boy with broad smiles.

Happy to be released from their labors, the powerful pair sat on a bench by the door and shared village gossip. After they dispensed their interesting tidbits, Pen was peppered with questions about the incident at the Three Decker Inn the night before. His father's actions were apparently the talk of the village.

After ten minutes of talk Griswold stood up and wiped his hands on his clothing. He bade Pen good-bye and sauntered off to lunch as he joined a growing number of men and women in the dusty streets. Pen and Jack chatted a bit longer. The pair strode out together, Jack to lunch and Pen to continue his ride to Thatcher's. On the way, he thought about the time Jack and he became fast friends.

Pen was often sent on errands to the blacksmith's shop. Griswold was boisterous and pleasant with the villagers. However, all Pen could pull out of his son, Jack, was a grunted, terse, sometimes unintelligible response. The boy often wondered why the physical similarities Jack shared with his father didn't extend to personality; the father was gregarious, the son introverted.

One day Eric, the son of the owner of the town's general store, intercepted Pen as he left the barn. Surrounded by a number of friends, the older, taller boy chided Pen about how he addressed his father.

"Sir, this... sir, that. He's just a farmer. A 'yes' or 'no' would do just fine, boy."

Pen didn't know why Eric kept badgering him. He also didn't know why he addressed his father as sir. Maybe it was because nearly everyone else did. And, he didn't know why people were so respectful of his father who was, admittedly, just a farmer. But, he did know he was embarrassed anytime someone referenced the act. Pen gritted his teeth but kept walking to the wagon.

Frustrated he didn't get a sufficient reaction from Pen, Eric aimed a sharper barb at someone dear to the boy.

"And you are always with Liana. My father says her mom is a witch and a whore, so she knows..."

Pen charged at Eric, his head butting his chest. Both boys hit the ground and Pen's fists pounded him. The other boys recovered from their surprise and pulled Pen off, securing his arms. The smaller lad, barely restrained, still lunged at Eric.

"Don't ever say that, Eric, don't ever!"

Eric punched Pen in the chest. He was about to strike again when Jack appeared in his leather apron, covered in soot.

"Don't seem much like a fair fight to me; you and two others taking on a smaller boy. No, not fair at all."

"Stay out of this, Jack," sneered Eric.

"Nope, don't think so."

Without warning, he swung his large fist into Eric's face. Eric flew to the ground and landed on his rump, both hands covering a bloody nose. Jack turned toward the other boys who promptly let go of Pen and ran. Jack turned to face the bloodied Eric.

"You're lucky I don't have a blade, Jack."

Jack laughed. "Come visit me any day with or without a blade, Eric. You don't scare me."

He lunged at Eric who ran away following his two friends.

From that point on, they were best of friends. Whenever his father didn't need him at the barn, Jack would ride over to the farm and the two boys would hike or fish or swim. Self-conscious around most people, Jack found it easy to talk with Pen. At first, Liana was jealous of the time Pen spent with Jack, but she heard about the altercation with Eric. From that day on, she looked at Pen differently and regarded Jack as a friend.

His smile broadened when he realized he had finally reached Thatcher's house. It was large, but not ostentatious, and it was within an arrow's shot of the Three Decker Inn. Pen walked through the great room, adorned with tasteful tapestries and well-constructed, expensive furniture. He continued to the slate-covered courtyard where the heavy odor of sweat ruled over the fragrances from flowers which defined the perimeter. Two younger boys used wooden swords to batter each other while Thatcher upbraided one and praised another.

40

"Thrust hard, Jeremy…he's left you an opening. Darn! Darn! Darn! You've got to be quicker or you'll be dead once again."

Pen smiled at his mentor's mild rebuke. Thatcher was known as a man who never used foul language. Indeed, Pen had never heard him utter a vulgar word or expression.

A small man with graying short-cropped hair, "tightly packaged" as Mother Hebron would say, Thatcher was the kind of man with whom people avoided arguments. As he watched the two boys thrash about, he repeatedly shook his head and rolled his eyes upward in what appeared to be a silent prayer. He walked over to Pen as the pair continued their haphazard flailing.

"If they don't kill each other soon, I will," he growled lowly.

Seeing one make a gross mistake not capitalized upon by the other, he visibly winced, his eyes tightly closed. It took him a few seconds to control his temper.

"Enough, worms! Take a break, get some water, then watch Pen and me. Please learn something children!"

The younger boys waved eagerly at Pen who had acquired the lofty status of Thatcher's best student. The older man walked briskly over to a cabinet. Withdrawing two iron swords, old and relatively dull, he threw one to Pen and yelled, "Adgredi!"

They came together with quick, precise strokes. Pen effectively blocked a few of his teacher's blows. They slowly circled each other; jabs tested each opponent but did not compromise their defense. Thatcher attacked Pen with four separate moves designed to leave him open to a "death blow", but Pen had seen them before and adroitly avoided each trap.

Smiling, Thatcher slowly circled his opponent, taut muscles rippling.

"Not bad, Pen. Not bad. Now, let's see what you can do with a new test."

With that, the older man crouched a bit and tried to sweep his leg under Pen's to trip him. Pen jumped up and held his blade in position to block Thatcher's quick blow. The older man pressed forward with one new combination after another and Pen perfectly countered each of them. He successfully eluded all tricks his teacher offered. Pen had never beaten the old man. He once came close, only to be cleverly turned and "stabbed" in the back, fortunately with a wooden sword. The resulting superficial wound was with him for a week. Today, he vowed silently, would be different.

Thatcher attacked again. Pen knew the older man hated the defensive position. He slid beneath the slice of the blade and deftly moved to the side where the blade had momentarily stopped its swing. Slashing downward, he knocked it from Thatcher's grip. The boy quickly raised his sword to the master's throat.

Save for their hard breathing, absolute quiet replaced the clanging of swords. The two boys stopped chatting and looked on with dropped jaws, mouths open in astonishment. Never had they seen Thatcher beaten. In fact, they had never heard of anyone having beaten him.

The blade remained at his throat while Thatcher said, "Well, it seems that you are no longer in need of my lessons with the sword."

"Yield, sir."

The old man inclined his head with a sigh; Pen's stance relaxed a bit. Then, lightning fast, Thatcher slapped the blade from his throat and lunged into the boy. A moment later he was pressed in tight against Pen with his knife blade held against the lad's throat. The two combatants were nose-to-nose, their eyes locked on one another.

"Today," said the smiling old man, "we teach you how to fight with a knife."

CHAPTER SIX

Walking beside Mirus, Pen was pleasantly distracted as he made his way through the busy, dusty road leading home. A smile to old lady Beth and she educated him far more than he cared to know about her bunions. Stopped by Farmer Leland, a discussion regarding the merits of different wagon wheels ensued. One encounter after another found Pen a welcome sounding board.

It wasn't until late afternoon that Pen finally crossed the threshold of Mother Hebron's cottage. After hugging him, she pulled Pen to a seat at the table and promptly placed a large bowl of apple slices laced with honey and cinnamon before him.

Mother Hebron smiled as she watched him scoop up the dripping dessert and pop it in his mouth. The boy was always famished, she thought. He was tall for his age and strong, equal to most men. Though he was still "her boy", he became increasingly engaged in the things men seemed to enjoy like riding and fighting. Unlike his peers, Pen conjured no swagger, displayed no bravado. Each day he seemed to find a hundred reasons to smile and numerous reasons to laugh. She couldn't imagine him being serious in a sword fight, yet others claimed he was quite capable with the blade.

"How did it go with Thatcher today? Any luck in fighting him?"

"I won and I lost." He eagerly explained the tricks Thatcher showed him.

"I still have much to learn, Mother Hebron. Where is Liana, anyway?"

"You eat my cakes and fruit, barely speak a word to me, and all you can ask about is Liana!" Mother Hebron feigned exasperation. Returning to her dinner preparation, she threw a pinch of thyme onto the lamb she would roast for the next day. Doctoring the meat before returning it to the cold cellar, she told Pen that Liana was herding sheep into the barn for shearing the following day.

Pointing to the large chunk of meat on her table, she smiled and said, "This one will be relieved of that burden."

Eager to join his friend, Pen had jumped up from the table and flew toward the door, laughing at her joke.

She yelled at his back as he opened the door to leave.

"Come back here, you inconsiderate whelp!"

Pen, smiling broadly, stopped, returned, and leaned down to kiss her on the cheek.

"Thanks for the fruit, Mother dear."

She shooed him out with a smack on his rear from her large wooden spoon. "Out with you."

He laughed and raced out the door. As the door banged shut, she went to the window and watched him ride Mirus toward Liana and Brill. Her daughter deftly darted between the white puffs of sheep. Mother Hebron chuckled, realizing they would be a long time getting them into the barn.

She returned to the kitchen and sat down, thinking about the farm boy. She had helped raise the lad and watched the friendship between Liana and Pen grow. Perhaps her proud girl would marry

44

him. No one knew what the future held, she mused. One can only truly know the past. Hands folded, she thought about her own past, before she was Mother Hebron. She closed her eyes in the pleasant cottage and…

CHAPTER SEVEN

...opened them on a gray afternoon in a city. Her parents were both dead, victims of the plague. Now just five-years old, she stood wordlessly watching a cart bump down the cobblestone street carrying the two people who were the center of her world. Standing beside her was a muttering, short, hawk-nosed man who was her uncle. She had met him only once when her mother had fussed over him at supper one night.

Now her mother was dead, never again to fuss over the uncle or the child. Once the cart turned out of sight at the corner, the thin, gray-haired uncle grabbed her roughly and pulled her through dark winding streets, forcing her to run to keep up with him. All the way to his shop, he complained about the extra mouth to feed. Slamming the door shut upon their arrival, he immediately put her to work pounding leather with a wide, flat hammer. So began her new life.

She recalled no play of any sort while living with her uncle, but she had vivid memories of dozens of different tasks put upon her by the grumpy guardian. To be fair, the uncle provided daily sustenance. But he never fed her affection or praise, perhaps the most important food of all. Indeed communication was limited to the uncle giving gruff orders and instructions. In the time she was with him, he never addressed her by her name... Mary.

Though a naturally inquisitive child, it took Mary a week to hazard a question.

"Why is this leather so brown and this leather nearly white?"

The old man stared at her for a long moment and she feared he might hit her. His answer was a dismissive snort. The precedent safely set, Mary asked many questions. Occasionally the uncle provided answers in short sentences as though he was marshaling his words as carefully as he did his coins and food. Much to his frustration, the child kept asking questions, undaunted by his terse responses.

The work day started early for the child: cleaning the shop, sweeping the front, softening the tough leather, going through Tamworth to buy and deliver whatever her uncle requested. Only at nightfall did she and the old man sit down together to eat bread and drink soup. After the modest meal, the uncle would then lay down on a worn mat and go to sleep while Mary would put a blanket on the hard wood floor and pull her mother's shawl over her to keep her warm. Weary from the day's work, sleep came quickly as did the shivering dawn.

When she went on errands to purchase leather or string, there were times when the excessive weight of her load burned her muscles so badly that she had to stop and move into an empty doorway's safety. No one ever helped the waif as she panted for breath, huddled in the doorway. Indeed, no one even took notice. Such was the hustle and bustle of the city.

One morning, Mary rested against a door seldom used, as evidenced by a collection of autumn leaves at its base. Suddenly, she was propelled out into the street as a storekeeper charged out, hurrying to some task. The bolts of leather and skeins of yarn scattered and were kicked progressively farther away by rushing pedestrians. Weaving in and out of the crowd towering over her, she scooped one bundle after another. She knew she was missing the bag of yarn and frantically looked for it, her vision blurred by tears. The brown bag materialized in the hands of a pretty woman sporting a clean, light blue robe, her head protected by a hood of the same cloth. The ethereal creature moved gracefully through traffic, avoiding the frantic onslaught of the mob. The woman smiled as she offered the bag to Mary. She was about to place it on top of the pile Mary precariously carried when she hesitated and looked at the little girl.

"Where are you going, dear?"

"To Lamebrook, Miss."

The woman paused for a moment and considered the matter. The destination was far out of her way and in a part of the city that was unpleasant and dangerous. The lady in blue looked at the child, momentarily distracted by the task of juggling the objects she carried. The pathetic sight moved her deeply.

"Here," the pretty lady offered, "let me carry some of those."

Mary led the way through some twisted alleys to her uncle's establishment. After gathering up the merchandise from the kind lady, she placed it inside the door and turned to wave goodbye, but, nervously looking right and left, the kind lady was already scurrying away.

On subsequent trips Mary noticed other ladies dressed in light blue robes. All were quite pleasant. Once, she secretly followed one of the ladies through the city. The trail led to a large, domed building, walled in by smooth granite stones. The woman knocked on the door and was admitted by another blue-robed figure. The two hugged and laughed at the door before it closed.

Whenever Mary could spare a few minutes in her busy day, she would make her way back to the building referred to by others as "the convent".

One frigid night, after grumbling about too much firewood being used, the uncle went without heat as he worked with numbed hands, futilely trying to sew leather flaps together. Mary would peer into the workshop from the slightly warmer bedroom and watch the man do his best to continue his labor as he shivered. Finally, she went into the workshop, the tattered shawl pulled tight about her shoulders. She gently led the complaining old man back into the bedroom and eased him onto his mat. After covering him with his blanket, she stayed by his side, holding his hand, waiting for the shivers to abate, but they did not. A day later the uncle lay dead.

She arranged for the burial, using the last few coins in the shop. The coins went into the callous hands of the gravedigger who came by the shop early the next morning and, without ceremony or care, threw the body in a wagon. As the rickety wagon creaked down the street, Mary carefully closed the door behind her and walked away forever from the shop.

Soon she found herself at the door of the convent. On tiptoes, she banged the knocker as hard as she could. A minute later the door was slowly opened by a pair of blue-robed sisters who looked out into the street in puzzlement; they saw no one. Mary tugged on one of their robes. They looked down and saw the waif before them. The little girl smiled brightly and innocently declared, "I am going to join you."

As they considered the beaming creature who stared up at them with innocent blue eyes, they realized she was sincere. Soon other women, similarly clad, joined the group. While a few distracted Mary with questions, the rest stood to the side and quietly discussed the dilemma. The girl was far too young to admit into the order. Yet to cast her outside was unthinkable.

A tall, older woman in a simple white robe held tight with a thin blue belt walked over to the group. Immediately all talk ceased and the sisters collectively bowed their heads.

"Ladies, why the congregation in the sitting room?"

The sisters slowly parted to reveal Mary as she looked up from her chair by the fire, her legs curled under her.

"I've come to join you, Miss."

The leader of the order, whom the girl had addressed, was Mother Lena. Her etched face bespoke both age and wisdom. Seeing the child so unabashed with happiness, Mother Lena could not suppress her own smile. She pursed her lips together as she pondered the problem. She knew both the depths of depravity and the astonishing goodness of humans. Which for this child? The old lady reached out to caress the child's cheeks.

"Well, my little scallywag, I'm afraid you are too young to join."

Gasps from the sisters spoke to their affection for the girl. Mother Lena looked sharply at the congregation. Heads lowered again and silence ruled.

Turning back to the child, Lena smiled and offered her hand.

"We could use some help in the kitchen, though. First, however, let's get you a bath."

As the pair walked away, a sigh of relief rose from the group of sisters as they watched. This time Mother Lena did not turn around to admonish them.

The sisters took Mary in. She worked as hard as she could at her new job in the kitchen, but she was relieved of the most arduous tasks, as the sisters would hasten to help her at every turn. If Mary had dishes to wash, Sister Melody rolled up her sleeves and worked with her, telling her stories about the wild barrens in the west from where she came. If she had to light candles in the convent, Sister Francine would lift her up so she didn't need to carry along the heavy ladder. Some of her time was spent learning to read, write, and work with numbers; ancient Sister Sophia helped with that task. With a face like a wrinkled prune, she would sputter and mumble, raising her eyes to the heavens when Mary made an infrequent mistake and hugging her when she was correct. There was a great deal of hugging with the sisters and Mary began to feel like she had found a home.

When Sister Sophia fell ill and the other sisters feared for her life, but not her soul, it was an anxious Mary who attended her with Mother Lena. The little girl cared for her both day and night, giving her soft caresses with a cool towel and warm tea with honey to drink. Whether from Mother Lena's medicines or Mary's loving attention, Sister Sophia awoke one day, bright-eyed and ready to tutor.

Sensing that the little girl might have an inborn talent for healing, Mother Lena began to instruct her in healing herbs, nourishing roots, and beneficial oils. On long walks in a nearby forest, Mary was introduced to a multitude of different plants each with their own aptitude for health or healing.

The years passed and the beguiling child grew into a beautiful young woman, inside and out. When of age, she was admitted into the order. Naturally intelligent, she soon became one of the most respected healers of the order, and in turn, she trained the younger novices.

After twenty years of being protected and guided by the sisters of the order, Mary had become a strong, confident woman. By twenty-seven, she was the second in command of the order.

After old King Jared died, his indulgent reign was replaced by King Cearl's iron fist. Some of the older nuns were formerly priestesses of Astrid, the goddess who supposedly gave powers to the White Deer. Suspicious of any group connected to the White Deer, Cearl initiated a ruthless campaign to undermine the priestesses (now Christian nuns).

A few days before the winter solstice, Mother Lena, her once limber body now compromised by age, limped as quickly as she could into her rooms. The setting sun denied her the light she required, so the old lady hobbled over to light a few candles. Mary knocked at the door, and Mother Lena greeted her warmly, leaning down to embrace the smaller woman.

"Please, sit down, Sister Mary."

When agitated, the old woman repeatedly pursed her lips; Mary noticed the behavior as they sat. Mother Lena still took the time to fold her hands, straighten herself as much as possible, and present a composed image.

Though her body was failing, her mind was alert and clear thinking. Mother Lena knew the information she was about to impart would be devastating to any in the order, but in particular to Sister Mary. Nevertheless, she believed Mary was the best one to handle the information and take them beyond the crisis she saw as inevitable.

"I have been warned the King plans to physically remove us from the convent as early as tonight, but no later than tomorrow."

"What? He can't do that! He wouldn't dare!"

The old lady shook her head wearily, her eyes fixed on the young woman.

"Oh, he can do it, and he will do it, or possibly one of his followers. Perhaps Baron Glock."

Mary blustered about the impending travesty. As Mother Lena listened, she thought about the young woman. Without question, she was a gifted sister. A quick learner, a devoted disciple, she was all that as well. But, such a temper she had! Mother Lena raised her hand to silence the fiery condemnations leveled by the younger woman.

"Don't refuse to accept the inevitable, child, plan for it. That is what we will do tonight. You must shepherd the sisters out of the convent. Divide the money from the treasury so that each has enough to establish herself somewhere far away from the city. They must go without their robes, as I fear Christians will be persecuted or imprisoned. I don't know how much time we have left, so do it without delay."

"But, Mother, this can't be happening…"

The older woman rose, took a few steps closer to Mary, leaned down, and put her finger to the lips of the younger woman.

"It can and it is happening. Without delay, Sister Mary, without delay. Now go."

The younger priestess grudgingly rose as she was ordered and walked to the door. She stopped and looked back at her friend. "What about you, Mother Lena?"

"Other matters require my attention. When all have safely left the convent, meet me back here." Mother Lena was fumbling with a lock on a long, wooden container. Sister Mary remained at the door, watching the older lady try to undo the clasp with gnarled hands. It pained Mary to see such her struggle with the simple task. She ran back to the matron, opened the latched, and hugged her. Mother Lena looked at Mary, surprised at the sudden show of affection. She kissed her on the top of her head and then gently held her at arm's length. She smiled and patted her cheek.

"Off with you now, my little scallywag."

Sister Mary fought back tears. She managed a smile, turned right and left, giving orders to the nuns whom she met along the way.

Just before dawn Sister Mary wearily guided the last two novices down the tunnel that burrowed under the wall and emerged inside a hidden area of the forest.

She gave them each a small bag of gold coins and helped them onto horses. After they had gone over the hill with a young farm boy who acted as guide, she returned to the passageway and the long walk back to the convent where only a few sisters remained, gathering the last of the relics.

As she pulled the door open, screams erupted. Mary charged inside and witnessed two men in black tunics and pants roughly handling one of the sisters. She yelled for them to stop and, pulling her robe up, ran to intervene. Leaving the unfortunate woman to his partner, one of the soldiers turned towards Mary and restrained her by holding her arms down and pushing her against the wall with a painful thump. Meanwhile, her friend was dragged screaming into an adjacent room. Mary herself was roughly hauled toward a different door. She began to panic and fiercely tried to wrench herself free. Suddenly she felt the firm arms of someone behind her holding her still. The soldier released her and backed away. She looked over her shoulder and recognized the Baron.

"Oh, Baron Glock. Please, help. This man was beating a sister and now he... with me... oh, I don't know! Please, sire, help."

"James, I will take care of Sister...?" He looked at her, urging an answer with a cock of his head and a raised bushy brow line.

"Sister Mary."

"I will take care of Sister Mary, John. You can go." The soldier seemed disappointed, but smiled as he went into the room his cohort had entered just moments before. The sound of a struggle escaped as the door opened and silence followed as it closed.

"Come. Walk with me, Sister Mary." Taking her arm, he firmly guided her down the hall. Mary looked over her shoulder at the closed door, worried about the silence.

The Baron was tall, though well rounded by too many cakes and epicurean distractions. A black, neatly trimmed beard outlined his handsome face.

"The King has decreed the services the priestesses of the white deer...ah, pardon me, the sisters of Jesus... are no longer needed in Mercia." He momentarily frowned, and then cast an appraising look at the expensive tapestries on the walls. Still admiring the wall coverings while holding her close, he continued. "I always enjoyed coming to your services; so many girls and women to distract a man. I found the services quite stimulating."

He looked at Mary. His last words and appraising stare left her suddenly frightened; her heart began to beat wildly as he led her down the halls.

When they reached Mother Lena's dimly lit office, she looked for her mentor but saw only a white robe on the floor just beyond the chair in which she'd sat only hours earlier. A step closer and she recognized the crumpled body of Mother Lena, a pool of blood flowing toward her desk. A burst of anguished energy enabled her to rip away from the Baron. She knelt and gently turned Mother Lena onto her back. The old woman's eyes stared at the ceiling, but they were no longer soft and loving. Sister Mary's head sank to her chest and tears filled her eyes, drops falling on the prostrate body.

The Baron's strong hands pulled her to her feet. She resisted, trying to elbow herself away from the grip, but he was too strong and she too distraught.

Reaching inside his pocket, he withdrew a soiled handkerchief and gently dabbed away her tears. "No need to go on like that. We spared the others; be happy for that. Mother Lena was too old to be of use to us, anyway."

"Now, my men are rather occupied at this moment and here I am all alone with you. How fortuitous for us both." He leaned into her, his thick lips pressed against her face. Mary shifted her face away and tried to extract herself, but strong hands commanded the situation. He pushed her down onto the floor.

Already overwhelmed with sorrow and shock, Mary stopped resisting. She didn't scream or cry as he painfully defiled her and robbed her of her innocence. Her eyes, like those of her dead friend, stared without purpose at the ceiling as he grunted above her. Minutes later, tired from his exertions, he remained on top of her. She simply closed her eyes, shutting out the room. Neither saw the tall, red form approach them. Suddenly she heard the Baron call out and felt his weight lifted from her. As she opened her eyes, she saw that another man, large in stature, had yanked him off her. He handled the Baron easily as though he were a rag doll.

"What kind of vile man are you, Glock? To hurt this woman?"

The Baron sneered. "Don't worry, General, I made sure she enjoyed it."

The man backhanded the Baron, knocking him down. The Baron glared up at him, blood seeping from his nose.

Dressed in a soldier's uniform, red tunic, black pants, and boots, the tall man also wore the gray cape of an officer. The General looked at the Baron in disgust.

"Get out of my sight before I kill you. Take your men and be gone."

The Baron rose slowly, covering a broken nose with his handkerchief now stained red.

The officer pulled out his sword and the Baron scrambled away.

"The king shall hear of this, General!"

"You can count on it, Baron."

As the Baron backed into the hall, never moving his eyes from the menacing sword, he directed his voice to his men instructing them to cease their activities and meet him outside.

Still prostrate on the ground, Mary watched the exchange between the two men. When the officer returned, she noted peripheral movement; other red-shirted soldiers came into view. Self-conscious, she pulled her ripped gown together to cover herself.

The General knelt next to her, unfurled his gray cape, and covered her with it. He ordered his men out of the room to assist the many other women who were crying in the halls.

When he turned back to Sister Mary, she too was sobbing, her head turned toward Mother Lena. The General walked over to the body. He gently closed the old woman's eyes and carefully lifted the body onto a nearby bed. Taking a blanket from another chair, he covered the frail body.

"She was a good woman; I'm sorry this happened."

Mary stared at him and said nothing. He offered his hand to help her up. With the cloak wrapped tightly around her, she walked to the bed and gently stroked Mother Lena's cold cheek. Tears returned as she closed her eyes and shook uncontrollably.

The tall man protectively wrapped his arms around her; she flinched. Not again, she thought. Oh, please, not again. His grasp was firmer than the Baron's, yet somehow gentler. She sank into his arms, nearly collapsing. He carefully walked her to the door. "I'm taking you to a friend. Don't be afraid."

The General walked the shaking woman out of the large building, placed her onto his horse. Sister Mary's tears ceased, but her teeth chattered uncontrollably on that winter night. She noted with resignation that they approached the castle. What other shameful happenings lay before her, she wondered. At this point she no longer cared.

The General quickly hurried her through the castle's labyrinth. Down a hallway, he stopped in front of a door. After looking both ways to ensure no servants watched, he knocked. Moments later they were ushered into a large room by a beautiful woman in regal dress. The woman immediately knew Mary had suffered some grievous injury to body and soul. Reaching for the girl's hands, she gently led her inside the spacious apartment.

An hour later, the young sister lay sleeping on a large bed with heavy comforters to keep her warm. Having washed herself in the chamber's bath, she was dressed in a clean, white sleeping gown, borrowed from owner of the apartment. Even in sleep, her brow was knitted in consternation attesting she was still a victim of the night.

Standing above her, the woman watched her sleep. She was taller than most men. Dark auburn hair flowed down her back that shined so brightly it competed with the light from the fire. Her face made men stare in appreciation and woman glare with envy. Her eyes were deep green pools into which many a man had drowned.

"I still can't believe my brother ordered this travesty."

The General paced back and forth, like a caged lion. A head taller than the woman, his face was clean-shaven, deeply tanned, and far too lined with worry for a man who had not yet reached thirty years. Some women found him ruggedly handsome. Unfortunately, the ugly white scar running across his jawbone and the close-cropped brown hair scared away most of the fair sex.

"You can't believe it, Princess Elen? You know how worried Cearl is about the deer and anything associated with her. He ordered this raid. Believe it."

She looked at the General, astonished by his words; it was the most he had ever said to her.

"But why, General Petronius, would he assign the task to that vulgar Baron?"

"I think he knew the Baron would act reprehensibly. I think he may have even encouraged or perhaps ordered the nuns to be...to be..." He stumbled as he tried to find an acceptable word, not wanting to offend the princess.

Never one to mince words, she finished his sentence. "Raped. That is the correct word. Raped. He ordered the priestesses to be raped and murdered."

She looked again at the sleeping form on her bed. "This poor woman. Petronius, we don't even know her name."

He closed his eyes and shook his head, his knuckles white as he gripped the handle of his sword. "I should have killed Glock when I had the chance."

From behind them, a soft, but resolute voice sounded.

"Someday I will kill him."

The pair turned and saw the woman stare at them.

Princess Elen returned to sit beside the bed. Gently, she took the sister's hand.

"Shh... dear woman... rest now. Kill him later, if you must. Lord knows you have good reason."

The sister directed her eyes to the General and weakly smiled. "Thank you, General, for saving me and the other sisters. I am forever grateful to you."

"I wish I could have done more."

He stood beside the princess.

"I must leave, Sister. Princess Elen is as good a woman as ever there was in this city. Even here, though, you are still at risk. We must get you out as soon as you are able."

The woman struggled to rise, but Elen gently restrained her. "Sleep is what you need now, dear. Petronius will make the necessary arrangements. Rest." The girl smiled at the Princess and General before she closed her eyes.

"Mary," she said as she drifted off. "My name is Mary."

The pair watched the woman sleep, her face now relaxed.

Petronius walked to the door, Princess Elen beside him. "I fear the worst, Princess. I am sorry to say that your brother, my friend, perpetrated this evil action. That does not bode well for that poor, unfortunate woman. Nor does it bode well for you and me if we should be found to have helped her."

With that said, he left. The Princess closed the door behind him and leaned back against it, eyes closed.

He was right, of course. The situation was indeed dangerous for them, but strangely, she felt no fear. Her brother favored her above all people, but that was not why she remained calm. He would show no leniency or mercy if he suspected she challenged his authority and harbored the enemy. She felt no fear because of the strength and character of the man whom she could still hear walking down the hall.

Princess Elen feigned illness the next day and kept even servants away from her apartments. After the sun had set, a pass of safe conduct was delivered to her. Both she and the Sister understood its portent. Elen went to her closet to look for appropriate apparel.

A few hours later, two women, dressed in working-class attire, slipped unseen out of the castle and city. Far from Tamworth, at a crossroad, the Princess turned to Sister Mary.

"I must return now. The letter will allow you to use the road and pass freely through checkpoints. Here is some money which will help you secure safe lodgings. Use whatever is left to set yourself up in a new home. The coast might be the safest place for you, Sister. Take this road to the right." Mary nodded and embraced the Princess, holding her tightly for a few moments.

"Thank you for all that you have done. I know by helping me you have been placed in great peril."

Elen eased her horse toward the city and looked back over her shoulder. "God speed; may the White Deer protect you."

"And you, milady."

Sister Mary weighed the bag of coins in her hand; it was a generous gift. She waited until she was sure the Princess could not see her and urged her horse in the direction opposite the coast. She was going to the village of Kirkland. Known only to Mother Lena and herself, the convent's treasury (a fortune that would impress even a princess) was buried in Markwood Forest. Mary would claim it for the sisterhood and raise the order back to its former stature. She knew she had to be secretive about such an endeavor. Patience and preparation would be her ally.

Were any of the sisters to present themselves as devotees of Jesus, the King would surely kill them. Hopefully they would heed her warnings about blending into communities as anonymously as possible. Since she was well known as Sister Mary, second in command of the order, a new name was necessary. Perhaps it was just as well, she thought. Mary had been so deeply befouled by the brutality of Baron Glock that she needed a fresh start. Hebron, she decided, would be her name.

There was something else she had to do, something Mother Lena would never have sanctioned. Indeed, something the church would certainly frown upon. She must train the sisters to use weapons so they would never again be defenseless. Travesties she and others suffered would not happen again. Not without a fight, anyway.

She was near Kirkland when the sun peeked over the eastern hills. To the west, darkness commanded the horizon as a winter storm rolled in. A bad one, she thought. A different type of storm was also slowly moving into the small country. The oppressive taxes and the absence of any help from the King created both deep despair and simmering anger among the common people. Yes, she thought, there was another storm coming to Mercia…a war, a civil war…and soon, possibly in a few years. As she prodded her horse forward, it began to snow.

The next day, a fine lady mounted on a large brown horse trudged through the snow and into Kirkland. Before sunset she had visited a number of establishments and homes. By nightfall, everyone knew a woman had purchased a cottage and, much to the delight of the merchants, considerable furniture and goods to stock it. A single woman living alone was always viewed with raised eyebrows. A single woman with money, however, was different. The eyebrows would be raised, of course, but only after she turned her back.

She gave the story that her husband was killed in the war and she had been granted compensation from General Petronius who was known to be magnanimous with widows.

Money cannot buy respectability. However, a natural devotion to others usually demoted a questionable background to insignificance. As the days stretched into weeks, Hebron's friendliness became well known. When illness or injury sidelined one of the villagers or farmers, she would be at their side helping them with their responsibilities and healing them with her considerable knowledge of herbs and potions. Women appreciated her skills and soon depended on them. She made clear to the men, married and unmarried, that she was not interested in any dalliances.

Folks began to visit her cottage seeking medical attention. She charged modest fees and if payment wasn't forthcoming, she was tolerant and flexible. If peasants were particularly poor, she was also conveniently forgetful. Children, having a natural and accurate appraisal of most adults, loved her.

Her beautiful blond hair had turned white after her ordeal so at a relatively young age, she carried the mien of an elderly lady. Soon everyone simply referred to her as Mother Hebron. When she first heard the appellation, she chuckled. Since she was the indisputable head of the order, her title would certainly be Mother Hebron.

After five months of village residence, her life radically changed as she realized she was pregnant. Once she detected the faint stirrings of life inside her, she walked deep into Markwood Forest and sat in the shade against a tall oak tree. A life, innocent of the vicious acts of the Baron, grew inside her. She caressed her belly and recalled her own childhood, devoid of love and care after her parents died. She vowed this child would be hugged, praised, and loved every day. Resolved to face whatever rebukes the conservative village would throw at her, she resolutely walked back into the sunshine of the day.

Indeed, the pregnancy would normally have started tongues wagging and fingers shaking, but by this time she was universally recognized as Mother Hebron, a soul beyond reproach, a doer of good deeds who never uttered disparaging words about anyone, and, of course, willingly shared her money.

Months later, a servant burst into her cottage and begged her presence at the largest house in the village. The wealthy owner of the general store met her at its door. Disheveled and frantic, he led the pregnant Mother Hebron to the birthing room where his wife had just started labor. Shoving him out, she quickly attended the woman who screamed in pain. It was a breech birth, usually a death sentence for both baby and mother. Mother Hebron worked through the long night, applying her vast knowledge of medicine to reduce the pain and gently shift the dangerous position of the child in the birth canal. Morning brought the happy sound of a new life wailing; she had miraculously saved both patients. A relieved father held the tiny infant, crying in protest about his rude delivery from his mother's womb. He named the child Eric and returned to his wife without a word to the savior of his young family. Mother Hebron simply packed up her medicines and wearily returned to her horse.

As she walked out into the growing light of the day, she felt unmistakable pangs which announced the imminent birth of her own child. Unable to ride home, she frantically knocked on the door she had just left. When the father opened the door, she begged admittance. The father, frustrated by her untimely return, grudgingly showed her to a storage room and then returned to his new family. Mother Hebron was too tired and in too much pain to condemn his behavior as she gave birth to a baby girl.

Alone and uncomfortable in her surroundings, she left as soon as she regained enough strength and hurried home on her horse, pale and bleeding. Once home she placed the babe in a cradle and gently rocked her to sleep. She wanted to name her baby Lena after her dear friend and mentor, but was afraid someone might associate the name with the former nun. So, she named the baby girl Liana, as close to Lena as she dared.

Liana was active and precocious, a perpetual challenge to Mother Hebron's patience. At night when Liana fell asleep after nursing, Mother Hebron would contentedly sigh and relax as she knitted in her chair.

One dark, rainy night when Liana was barely three, a loud, insistent pounding at the door startled Mother Hebron. Grabbing a knife from a pocket in her dress, she cautiously opened the door. A bedraggled man with an unkempt beard stood clothed in a battered old coat. One arm rested at his side, but the other arm was missing, perhaps a casualty of the war, she thought. Rain had matted his straggly hair. Beside him was another man, shorter and considerably rounder than his partner, brown and gray hair circling his head like a wreath.

She motioned the two men into her home and out of the rain.

The taller, bearded man spoke. "Pardon the intrusion, ma'am, but I have a problem that maybe only you can help. My name is Larmack, ma'am. A simple farmer am I. This be Songor." Tears welled in his eyes. "I tried," he whispered, "but I can't feed him anymore."

She looked at the companion and understood his plight. He was rather formidable around the girth. But, what was she to do? Put a plate of stew before him? Or maybe two, she thought, considering his ample stomach.

The bearded man wiped his nose and tried again to speak. "Yesterday, I asked around and everyone said that Mother Hebron could help."

He opened his coat, and Mother Hebron saw that his other arm had been tucked inside holding a young babe, sound asleep on his chest, protected from the rain.

"My wife...she died and I tried to care for little Pen, but I can't. He cries, ma'am. He cries terrible."

He teared up again. "We've tried to feed him goat's milk, but he spits it out. He cries when he wakes, he's so hungry. Please help my child, Mother Hebron. Please."

Mother Hebron stared at the two men for a moment, her mind raced with the implications of her next move. She gently picked up the baby who, upon being woken, promptly cried. She judged that he could only be a week or so old. This poor man, she thought. She tenderly hugged the child to her breast. Though mollified by her touch, he hiccupped sobs. As the men watched, she carried the child to her chair, sat down, and opened her robe. Aware of their presence, she modestly turned away from their view. The men, in turn, averted their stare. The child cooed softly as he nursed and Mother Hebron gently touched his face. "Pen," she said. "I think that we will be good friends, you and I."

It was decided between them that Mother Hebron would raise Pen for a few years. She asked for no compensation, but the two men insisted they help with her farm that suffered as much from neglect as from ignorance.

Larmack and Songor worked both farms, rising before dawn to feed and care for their own animals and then make the short ride to Mother Hebron's farm. There they repaired the dilapidated barn, cared for the animals, and tended the fields. After lunch they returned to their own farm to work their crops until sundown, then wearily trudged to Mother Hebron's cottage for supper. The food, casual conversation, and Liana and Pen's frolicking always raised their spirits and spurred them on to continue their arduous tasks the following day.

When Pen reached the age of four, Larmack carried his son home. Larmack and Songor continued to occasionally work Mother Hebron's farm to help her (she always seemed busy with healing and other matters that took her away from the farm) and thank her for saving Pen's life. They continued to sup together, on occasion. Pen grew up with an intimate knowledge of two farms, two homes, and three caring adults.

CHAPTER EIGHT

The present rushed back to her as she shook her head. So many memories, she thought, and now so many new responsibilities to face. People were burden by the yoke of heavy taxes; some were starving. She sensed a civil war was near. It would demand her undivided efforts and perhaps her life. As Cearl's reign grew increasingly oppressive, discontent was fermenting. All that was needed was a spark...and a leader, of course.

Petronius, the brave, wonderful man who saved her, was the obvious choice. He had married Princess Elen and everyone spoke of their happiness together. Then tragically, wife and baby died in childbirth. After the great loss, he had disappeared. Most likely he was dead; grief, she knew, was as powerful a killer as the sword.

A leader was needed, but whom?

The next day, in the dim light of the early morning, Liana and Pen held the sheep for the two men as they quickly cut away the fleeces. They had all performed the same job months before and each knew their particular task, so the fleecing went smoothly. On that morning, all tacitly believed the cycle would repeat itself the following year and for many years thereafter. None suspected this would be the last time.

Just as the last animal, smooth-skinned and frightened, ran from Mother Hebron's barn, twelve-year-old Pen turned to Larmack.

"Father, can I go into the village? I have a few things to do."

"And I know what those things are, boy," grumbled Larmack. "You spend more time with that old man than you do with me or even Liana."

Pen started to protest, but Larmack silenced him by continuing.

"Yes, go on. I'm sure I don't need to tell you to be at Mother Hebron's by dinnertime!"

Pen strode out of the barn, intent on meeting Thatcher as quickly as possible. As he emerged from the barn, Liana, who had silently followed him, grabbed his elbow.

"I was thinking we could go down to the creek, this morning." She smiled prettily.

Pen pulled his arm free from her grasp. "No, I've got to meet Thatcher."

Her face darkened. "Your father was right! You spend more time with Thatcher than any of us. All this playing with swords; you have to grow up, Pen!"

"It's not playing, Liana, it's work! I don't want to go down to the creek. We've gone there a thousand times. Go help your mom cook or clean the house."

Pen had foolishly incited Liana. Hands on hips, she gave the boy a tongue-lashing. Her fury spent, she trudged off to the corral to pet Brill.

Pen was wounded by her words. Angered, he stomped into the corral beside her to saddle Mirus. His temper had cooled by the time he prepared the horse. He wondered if Liana was upset. Sometimes when they quarreled, Liana's eyes would water. He turned to look at her and she glared at him. All right, he thought, if she wants to be stubborn about this, he could be too. He turned to grab the bridle when Mirus nudged his back and he found himself a few steps closer to Liana and Brill. Startled, he looked behind him as the black horse again pushed him toward Liana. The boy started at the animal.

"Hey, what are you doing, Mirus?"

The horse nodded his head and pushed him so hard that he ended up face-to-face with Liana. They stared at each other, trying to maintain their frigid facades. Then laughter erupted. Seconds later apologies followed. After a short conversation, Pen said goodbye to his friend with a promise to visit the creek in a few days.

CHAPTER NINE

Pen listened carefully as Thatcher explained how to best use a knife in combat and showed him how to throw it. The knife sunk into the wood with a thunk, just below the neck on a crude outline drawing of a man, riddled with splintered wood from countless arrows.

"You missed the head," observed Pen.

"I didn't aim for the head, boy. It's too small a target. Aim for the torso. Always."

Following Thatcher's advice, Pen spent the next hour throwing the knife at the same target. When the blade stuck, it was usually nowhere near the body's outline. By the time the sun had neared its peak he was more successful.

"All right, lad; that is enough for one day. Take this dagger home and practice. Will I see you tomorrow?"

"Yes, sir, unless my father needs me in the fields. We didn't get to cross swords today."

Thatcher responded jovially. "No, I decided to give you one more day to bask in the glory of beating the old man."

He patted the boy's shoulder and walked him to the door where he nodded goodbye and watched him ride down the road past the inn. Pen was good with the sword, he mused. He's almost as knowledgeable as me and certainly quicker. Ah, to be young! In my day I could match his speed. Thatcher shook his head with a smile. No, this boy was very fast, faster than he ever was.

His best student was a farmer's son. Who could have guessed? Where might these skills take him? Certainly not into the employ of the King! Perhaps the boy would take his skills away from Mercia.

*

When Thatcher was a bit older than Pen, he considered hiring onto a ship to visit strange and faraway places. Then war broke out and he joined the army. Respected by both his fellow soldiers and his commanders, Thatcher found a home in the army. General Petronius was in charge in those days. Now there was a leader, he thought. Skilled in all weapons, demanding yet considerate of his troops, Thatcher would follow him through the gates of hell. He thought back to the day he first met the General...

The two men found themselves suddenly surrounded. Without a word, they went back to back, swords drawn. The pair wore red uniforms, dusty and ripped, the tattered product of the daylong battle. A sea of brown-shirted Northlanders circled them, yelling at them. The pair held off attacks by all who dared to come inside their own circle of death. Within a minute, seven bodies clad in coarse brown tunics lay before them, staining the sandy ground red.

Suddenly, four enemies simultaneously charged from four different directions. The two soldiers jumped apart to take the offensive against the rushing tribesmen. Clouds of dust cloaked the exchange as Thatcher lunged forward and ducked under the broad sweep of the first blade, his short brown hair slightly clipped. Too close to use his sword, he quickly pulled out his knife and sliced forward, striking his assailant below his heart. Before the slain man collapsed to the ground, Thatcher rolled and raised his sword to meet the metal from the other, larger man who sliced downward with all his might. Thatcher pulled to the right with his sword and, in a blur, brought his it to the center before his body, stabbing the man in the heart. His adversary showed more shock than pain, and a second later, he lay dead on the ground too.

"I count nine, sir," Thatcher said as he backed into his partner, his eyes scanning the jumble of men darting back and forth before him.

"Eleven," came the flat response.

A tall warrior with a bushy black beard and a matching head of hair pushed through the brown tunics. His clothes were much finer, suggesting he was an officer or nobleman.

"I need you attacking the enemy out there, not playing like ladies here. You and you, come with me, and let's have done with it."

Before he could take a step, the din of battle suddenly grew louder as Mercians broke through the brown line. Red soldiers rushed to the aid of the two men. The hunted became the hunters as Thatcher and his partner led a charge against the Northlanders, who rapidly gave ground to the Mercian surge. The tall warrior, who had just chastised his men, was the only one who stood firm, refusing to give up ground. He cocked his sword, determined to defend the position, but his men grabbed him and pulled him back to safety. The line of Northlanders continued to retreat, and in only a few minutes, it had turned into a rout.

As the cavalry pursued isolated groups of fleeing tribesmen, Thatcher found no enemy to engage. He knelt, exhausted from the battle, the energetic fight in the circle, and the subsequent chase. His comrade-in-arms, General Petronius, appeared invigorated as he shouted orders to each of his captains. One by one, they dispersed. The General saw Thatcher and briskly walked to meet him.

"Thatcher!"

Thatcher wearily pulled himself up, leaning on his bloody sword. He looked up into the eyes of his much taller leader, careful not to stare at the ugly white scar on his jaw.

His stern demeanor broke into a rare smile as the General placed a hand on his shoulder and said, "I will have you at my back again."

Thatcher was quiet for a moment, his eyes locked with the other man's focused stare. "And you at my back as well, General Petronius."

Without another word, the General turned and strode towards another group of men to organize another task. Thatcher merely collapsed on the ground, thankful for a few minutes of rest.

This, the third battle of a long campaign, was a devastating defeat for the Northland tribesmen. In the aftermath of the battle, at the request of the Northland leader, a young and proud warrior called Bruder, General Petronius was invited to the Northlander's capital city.

Hearing of the invitation, first captain Astible asked for and was granted a conference with Petronius. As he strode into the Petronius's tent the younger General took stock of his first captain, a large man whose face sagged from age and battle. Astible saluted his general and wasted no time speaking his mind.

"Sir, this could be a trap to capture or kill you. Don't agree to it."

Petronius smiled, aware of that Astible's concern for his safety had compelled him to offer this unsolicited advice. "This is necessary Astible. It could bring this war to close".

"At least take your bodyguards with you. They will protect you with their lives, Petronius."

"I will take just one man. Thatcher. He and I stood off a good many of the enemy when we were surrounded and alone. If danger awaits, he is a man I can depend upon."

"I am not happy about this, but take Thatcher then. He is a bit of a character, general, but, you are right; he is good in a fight."

A day later, two men in red uniforms, considerably cleaner than a few days before, rode between the high-banked hills that channeled them toward the Northlands. Breaking the long silence, Petronius mentioned casually, "Well, Thatcher, you may not have thought I was going to have need of your sword so soon."

Thatcher had scanned the crest of the hill, Every now and again brown-shirted riders could be seen as they followed a rocky path parallel with the two soldiers.

"I'm always willing to be at your back, sir, though I hope we settle on peace. I get mighty tired killing those Northlanders."

Petronius smiled at the smaller man.

The hills were smoothed by a cold wind that blew away everything but the rocks, stones, and long-rooted weeds and bushes. The few houses and even fewer barns they passed were all made of stone. It was a poor land and a poor people, thought Thatcher.

Finally the two men came to a green expanse near the stream just outside a large village. Soldiers were packed between this isolated green patch and the village.

The General and Thatcher got off their horses and walked over to Bruder who stood at a long, crudely made table directly in front of the soldiers. Thatcher recognized him as the tall warrior who had scolded his men for not killing them in the battle. Bruder who was willing to stand and fight an entire army by himself.

"So, the two swordsmen who delayed my troops. Too bad I didn't arrive earlier. We could have met sooner, General Petronius." Bruder smiled as he extended his hand.

The General returned the smile, firmly shook the hand and said, "Had we had met earlier, I have no doubt my comrade and I wouldn't be here today."

Bruder chuckled.

The negotiations went on for most of the day. The General, given authority by King Cearl to fully settle the dispute, insisted that the tribes no longer graze their livestock in the disputed hills and valleys between the two countries. Bruder, in turn, firmly expressed the need for more grazing land for his starving animals.

"Those valleys are not well populated, general. We disturbed only a few farms."

"Burning field and house is more than a disturbance, King Bruder. That we can't have."

Finally the two leaders agreed those areas not yet populated by Mercia farmers could be used, but not controlled by the Northlanders. Furthermore, the Northlanders were not to harass the Mercia farmers.

After they signed the treaty, Bruder pulled the General aside.

"I am not certain your King will honor this treaty, General."

"You have my word, King Bruder."

The King offered his hand to bind the agreement.

"That is enough for me, Petronius."

Returning to camp, the General was quiet. Thatcher was used to his reticence as he typically spoke only when necessary. He studied the great man, young, but admired by both his officers and his men. The neat uniform did not hide his well-muscled body. As well as being skilled with the sword, he was an excellent horseman, perhaps the best in the army. And, of course, he had that long scar on the side of his chin. A brawl wound? Unlikely. As Thatcher looked away, he decided he would not be the one to ask him about the scar.

The two men returned safely to camp later the next day. The General smiled at Thatcher and went off with his captains to discuss the army's withdrawal. That was the last time Thatcher saw him.

Petronius returned to the capital while Thatcher, now a captain, found himself stationed in the port city collecting tariffs from ships. When he finally returned to Tamworth a few years later, the General had married and retired.

Thatcher went west toward the barrens and the sea with another army to quell some disturbances perpetrated by a vicious tribe. Baron Glock was the new general. Dressed in black, this sycophant of the King bumbled the mission so thoroughly they never engaged the warring tribe. Upon his return to Mercia, Thatcher decided army life might not be as interesting or rewarding as it had been in the past. A month later, he walked from Tamworth, no longer a soldier.

*

Having served in the army for all his adult life, Thatcher retired with enough coins to buy a small farm. Unfortunately, he frittered away the money on drinks and women. As his last gold coin was spent in the small village of Kirkland, he decided to settle there. He took odd jobs to pay for cheap food and drink, and he was more often drunk than sober. Occasionally he had enough money for a bed, but more often than not, he could be found sleeping outside the Three Decker Inn.

That was where Mother Hebron found him one brisk autumn morning. She saw the sleeping form, noisily snoring. Well, at least he's not dead, she thought. She tried to wake him, pushing him with her foot. Only the tone of the snoring changed.

Mother Hebron went inside the inn and returned with a bucket of water which she dumped on the reclined body. He sputtered and squinted at her.

"Is it day or night?"

"Day. Morning, actually."

"Then, gosh darn it, leave me alone, woman. I have a few hours of sleep left and hopefully the dagburn rain has stopped." With that said, his head fell back down and he promptly returned to snoring.

Gosh darn it? Dagburn? Had he really uttered those silly words? Hadn't she heard something about this quirk? It was said that he never uttered a foul word under any provocation, unlike some others in the village.

A point in his favor.

She also recalled that no one would ever call him on this unusual quality. His temper was as swift as his sword and no one would challenge either. Perhaps he could be of some assistance.

She kicked him again, harder and said, "I may have a job for you."

Not bothering to raise himself up, he opened blood-shot eyes, trying to focus on the ground. He rubbed his face and looked again at the ground.

"Money or beer?" he queried the hard earth.

She looked at him with a puzzled expression.

"How are you going to pay me, woman? With money or beer?"

"With gold. But perhaps I have the wrong man." She started to walk away in disgust.

Suddenly he was walking jauntily beside her. "Gold you say. Well, I'm your man, dear lady. What is it you want me to do?"

Astonished, she stopped, looked at the spot where he previously reclined, and looked him up and down as he smiled at her. How could he have moved so quickly?

She considered him for a moment. A short man, only a bit taller than her, but strongly built, with a spring in his step. She knew he'd been in a few fights in Kirkland, all with soldiers. Everyone, soldiers and villagers, considered him an excellent swordsman. She hoped he might also know something about other weapons.

"Follow me and please don't speak…your breath alone could make me drunk!"

She mounted her horse and led him to her cottage. At her home, she dismounted, handed him the reins, and told him to take her horse into the barn.

He stood still for a moment watching her as she walked into the house. Thatcher didn't like any civilian giving him orders, but gold was gold, so he swallowed his retort and simply burped loudly, hoping she heard.

He'd been a farm hand before. The work was not to his liking but it usually paid well and he got a decent meal every now and again.

When he returned from the barn, she waited at the door and pointed to a bucket of water. "Clean yourself up over there and come inside."

Hmm, he mused, now this is getting interesting. The wench wants me clean! He watched her go inside. Pleasant face. Hair of pure white, but she didn't look old at all. Well put together. Yes, there might be other benefits besides gold and food.

The man who entered her house minutes later was clean-shaven (knives have many uses). Mother Hebron noticed that his brown hair, streaked with gray, retained natural tight curls after he washed. Clean, the man possessed a roguish charm.

"Sit here," she commanded, pointing to a chair opposite her's at the kitchen table.

The man flipped the chair around making it bang loudly on the floor and straddled it. He smiled as he faced her, his muscular physique obvious to the woman as his tunic hung partially open.

His abrupt and unusual actions unsettled her. Stammering, she began, "How do I start this... I... I have need of a man. I am told that you did some soldiering. Is that true?"

"Yes, ma'am. Some."

"I am also told that you served with General Petronius, not Baron Glock."

"Not quite true, that. I am proud to say that I did serve with General Petronius. Unfortunately, I served with the Baron on one campaign and then quit the army. Glock is a bloody idiot, ma'am, pardon my words."

She looked at him, considering the import of what he said.

"Everyone says you are very good with a sword. Do you know how to use other weapons?" she asked hopefully.

He puffed out his chest, jutting out his chin.

"There is no one better with a sword than I, 'cepting General Petronius. I am passable with bow and knife as well."

She measured his answers for a moment, weighing whether or not to commit money and secrets to the man before her. Really, there was no other choice. He was the only person in the area who knew how to use weapons and was not in pay of the King. She sensed the coming war and the sisters and others had to be trained and ready. Time was running short. Thatcher it is, she concluded.

Mother Hebron sighed in resignation. "I know some women who wish to be trained for self-defense. The sword would not be an acceptable weapon for them, but a bow and arrow might be, as skill matters more than strength with those weapons. Could you teach us how to use the bow?"

Thatcher rubbed his chin, tilted his head, and leaned away from her a bit. Eyes narrowed, he reflected that this could very well be an amazing stroke of luck: a business opportunity with an inexperienced female.

"Could I teach them the bow? Well, that depends, ma'am. First we need good bows and many arrows, and they don't come cheap. But, I know this man…"

Mother Hebron interrupted him. "I already have the bows, Thatcher. They are Verdon bows."

Thatcher stared at her. This woman was on top of her game. Verdon bows were the finest made.

"Then I need ten sessions to work with them…"

She interrupted again. "I will require your services for at least twenty sessions."

Thatcher stared at her again. Twenty sessions? Was she worried about simple defense or training them for the army?

"I can do it, ma'am, but its skilled labor. And twenty sessions...twenty sessions at least, you said. I will require twenty gold coins." Twenty gold coins for teaching a few girls even twenty lessons was far too much, but he could masterfully argue her down to ten coins and that would still be generous pay for his time.

"I am prepared to pay you one gold coin."

Thatcher was truly insulted. She was trying to out-trade him on his most marketable commodity, his skills!

"Well, miss, I must stop you right there. One gold coin is not near enough. Before you now stands one of the best soldiers the army has ever had. Skilled labor, ma'am, skilled labor."

"One coin, Thatcher. For twenty sessions."

"Four coins or I walk now, woman."

Without blinking or hesitating, Mother Hebron responded, "Two."

"Three coins and we have a deal."

Mother Hebron flashed an angry look.

"Two for each woman is quite enough, Thatcher. If you won't take it, then there's the road. Start walking!"

When she said it was for each female, his eyes widened. Here he was haggling with her to gain three coins total when she had already conceded a great deal more than he had even hoped for. There were probably four or five ladies he thought...that meant eight or ten gold coins! Best not show how eager I am for this deal.

"Ma'am you drive a hard bargain. I must say you have the better of me. Deal," he finally answered, head lowered. A smile flickered across his face, unseen by Mother Hebron. "Two coins."

"Done."

Thatcher put out his hand to shake on the deal. She ignored it. "Meet me here tomorrow at high noon." She stared at the man, waiting for him to withdraw as the discussion was clearly concluded.

Thatcher graced her with a roguish smile, got up slowly with a noticeable swagger, and leaned toward her. "Now that we are done with business, maybe you and I can get a bit better acquainted." His hand went to stroke her face.

Mother Hebron's eyes flashed. She slapped away his hand, and from her pocket she drew a knife and threatened him with it.

Thatcher watched the blade in front of him. His hands a blur, he quickly grabbed her wrist, twisted the knife out, bringing her painfully to her knees. He pushed her down on her back and picked up the blade. Mother Hebron stared at him wildly, ready to slash his face with her fingernails if he moved closer.

"Three things, lady. First, don't bring out a knife unless you use it quickly, 'cause it's too small a weapon to threaten with. Second, learn how to use a knife properly...you don't even know how to hold it! Third, get a real knife, not this toy." And with that he snapped placed the blade on the table and snapped the blade from the hilt. He offered his hand to help up from the floor.

She realized he could have been easily overpowered her if that was his intention. Cautiously, she took his hand and was pulled to her feet.

"Know this also, Mother Hebron, I meant you no harm. I read you wrong and I apologize. You want this to be just business? Fine. Just business it is." He looked at her angrily.

"Three," she replied.

"What?"

"Three gold coins," she repeated with a smile, "if you train us with the knife as well."

The next day he appeared at her cottage, sun high in the sky. He was in a very good mood, as he knew he really got the best end of the deal: three gold coins for teaching some sweet young things a bit about the bow…and the knife. Mother Hebron greeted him with a polite hello and offered him a horse. They galloped to the edge of the forest and tethered the horses. He followed her as she walked briskly through twists and turns in the thick woods. After nearly an hour of walking in the dark green shade, the pair emerged into a large, bright meadow. After Thatcher brushed off his tunic and pants, he looked up and saw his students. Not three or four as he had expected, nor even ten as he had hoped. Before him, clustered in groups, were over one hundred women adorned with blue robes loosely covering their bodies. All eyes were on Thatcher.

"So many," he whispered in amazement.

"Two hundred and twenty, to be exact. But that number will vary a bit every day. I expect there will be more."

He looked at her dumbly then back at the women who were now starting to encircle him. His mind quickly calculated the enormous fee.

"Well," he said with a grin, "I will just have to manage, won't I?"

"And here are the bows." Mother Hebron stood by a graveled area near the stream and unfurled a large cloth covering hundreds of bows. Thatcher looked in amazement. The Verdon bow was the best; not even soldiers could afford such a weapon.

He let out a long whistle and turned to his employer. "That wood there represents a small fortune. What you are paying me is another small fortune. Where does a farm woman get that much gold?"

Eyebrows arched as she pierced the man with her stare.

"You are paid and paid well to teach these women how to use bow and blade. You are also paid to be silent about these bows and this activity. Are we absolutely clear on that point, Thatcher?"

He returned her angry stare, his face turning red.

"Absolutely, ma'am. Absolutely!"

Darn, the woman acts so high and mighty! Thatcher gruffly barked out orders to the women surrounding him and the work began.

The meadow was quickly transformed into a training field. Arrows soon flew through the air in all directions. Thatcher ducked a number of times, loudly chastising the offender who would either weep or hold her hands to her mouth. Frustrated and not knowing how to handle either reaction, he would comment, "Quite unfair, young lady, quite unfair", and quickly walk away to escape the whines and tears. The first session ended. A few came close to hitting the assigned targets while none had yet hit Thatcher.

The results of their efforts were noticeable each time they met in the woods. In subsequent sessions, the women progressed from always missing the targets to usually hitting the targets to nearly always hitting the head-sized circle in its middle. The high grass was stomped down by the footfalls of the women as they retrieved arrows over and over. Meeting a few days every week for months, plump matrons and soft maidens had slimmed down; under their blue robes were tight muscles, strong enough to easily string a bow and walk or run miles a day.

Some of the women were former nuns, but most simply knew of the order and embraced the general tenants of the now illegal cult. All were sworn to secrecy, even from their husbands and fathers.

Though all the women were adults, there was one necessary exception. Liana had been insistent in accompanying her mother on those "special" days. Only six when the lessons began, she watched as the women honed their skills. She was a welcome sprite on the training field and even gruff Thatcher smiled at her enthusiastic contributions.

One day Thatcher brought a small bow for Liana. Between her self-appointed tasks, she practiced with the bow and became quite proficient.

After the twentieth session, Mother Hebron walked Thatcher over to a deserted area in the glen where she had thrown a blanket to cover something. She unfurled the blanket and he saw a small chest conveniently placed in a stout wheelbarrow. She motioned for him to open it. Inside were hundreds of gold coins. Thatcher marveled at the amber glow emanating from the chest.

During his return to his dingy room at the Three Decker Inn, the elated veteran had to slowly maneuver his treasure through the forest in the wheelbarrow Mother Hebron had thoughtfully supplied. The return trip took an hour longer than normal, but Thatcher didn't complain. Mother Hebron had provided a wagon and they rode back to the village together. Though often annoyed with Thatcher, Mother Hebron respected him. Ironically, he felt the same way about her, and at times they conversed almost civilly. Such was the trip home that day. She stopped suddenly, standing outside a large vacant house and pointed to the money in the wagon. "Now you are paid in full, Thatcher."

Thatcher looked at her, his bushy eyebrows reached over his eyes menacingly. He had already roughly tallied the coins in the chest and knew that she had given him considerably less than the agreed upon amount.

"No ma'am, this is just a bit more than half of what we agreed on. A tidy sum, to be sure. But not what we agreed upon…three coins per girl."

Mother Hebron looked at him steadily. "No, you are paid in full."

Make no mistake about Thatcher. He knew he'd been far overpaid for his services. Nevertheless, he felt it necessary to at least make some show of discontent. He wouldn't want her to ask for any of the money back! He stepped off the wagon, threw down his own Verdon bow (a gift from Mother Hebron) and with hands on hips, yelled loudly at her. "A deal is a deal, lady! I have fulfilled my part of the bargain. I took you on your word, I did."

Mother Hebron smiled. She nodded to the large house behind her. "You are paid in full... most is in the chest and the rest is there behind me."

Thatcher looked beyond her and saw only the stately house recently vacated due to a young merchant's untimely death. Thatcher looked back to her smiling face and back at the house again.

"You can't stay in some shabby room in the inn, Thatcher. I need you to finish the training and you need roots to stay here. It's yours, Thatch."

"Well, 'pon my word." He just stared at the house. He nodded to Mother Hebron and loaded the chest back onto the wheelbarrow. Inside the front door, he noted that the house was already well furnished; expensive tapestries accented the walls. Clearly she had bought not only the house, but the tasteful trappings as well. As he walked through the large center room he came to the courtyard, laid with slate so smooth that he figured someone must have polished the stones. It was a perfect house, he thought.

Perhaps he might put that courtyard to good use, he thought. He was almost always free during the week. Why not train young men as well? After all, they would have to know how to defend themselves against these women!

The next day a crude sign hung in front of the house: "Sword Master and Weapon Instructor".

Weekly sessions with the women were reduced to monthly sessions. Years passed as they learned all the subtle tricks of successfully using the bow and arrow as a weapon. They also learned how to wield a knife as well as how to throw it. He even taught the women how to effectively use swords. All the while he added still more coins to his chest.

In her eleventh year, Liana was given one of the Verdun bows and a knife. Possessing a natural talent for archery and unusual dedication, she was soon the best archer of all, even at such a young age.

*

Thatcher spent most of his time and money transforming his home into a training hall for young men. His old sign, long discarded, was replaced with a finely painted one: "Weapons Instruction for Young Men.." The village knew he was indeed a sword master. Securely established in his new home, he was a respected member of the community. Many boys and men sought his expertise, not just with the sword, but also with weighty decisions of home, family, and business. His secret was in not giving advice, but listening and telling a story about one of his many adventures. Most figured out what to do on their own and it usually worked out favorably. Their success was attributed to Thatcher. The old soldier had become a paragon of wisdom in and around Kirkland.

Thatcher himself was frustrated, though. Some were adroit with the blade, but not intelligent in their handling of it. A blade was not unlike a quill...anyone can write with a quill, but only a poet can scribe a good story. So far, he had no poets. Of what use were his considerable skills if he could not share them with one who could truly benefit?

One day, a young boy knocked on his door. He recognized him as Pen, Liana's friend. He stood a hair taller than Thatcher.

"Sir, my name is Pen. You don't know me. I am Farmer Larmack's son."

Thatcher couldn't resist playing with the lad. "Ah, and you wish to sell me some eggs. No, I don't eat them, don't want them. Goodbye!" With that he began to shut the door.

"No sir, no sir. No eggs," the boy yelled from behind the door. A moment later, the door opened a bit and Thatcher stuck out his head.

"No eggs? Then it's milk you be peddling. Yes, I certainly could use some milk. Fetch me some, boy."

Pen, confused, frowned at him, shook his head in frustration, and ran away. Thatcher was both surprised and mildly disappointed. He was going to stop the tricks, but the boy had given up too soon.

An hour later, he heard a knock at the door. Pen had returned. He handed Thatcher a jug, sloshing with milk.

"Your milk, sir. But I am not here to sell anything. I want to buy something. I want to purchase your services so you can train me to use a sword."

"Ah, young master Pen, you want to be a soldier, then?"

"No, I don't think so. I just want to know how to use a sword."

"Well, young man you said that you wanted to pay me for your services. Where is your money?"

Pen carefully extracted a worn bag from his side, dumped a handful of copper coins into his hand, and gave them to Thatcher. The man solemnly took the pittance offered and looked at the boy who stared back in earnest.

"When do we start, sir?"

Thatcher again looked at the assortment of coin in his hand. Obviously it was all the boy had. Not enough for Thatcher to even hand him a sword, let alone give him one lesson. To the boy, however, it measured a considerable fortune...all he owned. How often was he paid like that, he wondered.

"Let's find out whether I should take you on as a student, first."

He gave the lad an old, battered weapon he had considered discarding just a few days before. Pen handled it as though it was Elinrod, the beautiful and powerful sword of the King. He instructed the boy on how to care for the tarnished weapon. He put Pen through various lessons, each more demanding than the next. Surprisingly, this farmer's son seemed to have a natural talent with the blade. He learned quickly and his body easily mastered even complicated sets of moves. And he was fast, very fast. By late afternoon, Thatcher was exhausted. He sat down on a chair, catching his breath.

"Enough for today. I am sure you are too tired to continue," Thatcher commented, breathing heavily.

"Will you teach me the sword, sir?"

"Yes, yes. Tomorrow. Off with you now."

Pen thanked the master and ran off with his treasure wrapped in an old burlap bag.

Thatcher was still asleep the next morning when he heard banging at the door. He stumbled from his bedroom, opened the door. Pen's smile rivaled the new born sun Thatcher could see over his shoulder. His blade had been thoroughly cleaned and annoyingly reflected the light.

Thatcher scratched his head and yawned. "Come in. Give me a moment, young master."

The second day found him just as keen as the first. Thatcher agreed to meet with the boy once a week in the afternoon to train him. Each meeting found Pen as eager as he was talented.

Weeks turned into months and months into a year. The boy had grown much taller than Thatcher. The combination of strict training and farm work filled Pen out; he became a well-muscled young man. He was the best student Thatcher had ever trained, the "poet" he hoped to find. The only request the boy ever made was that their meetings be kept secret. That was impossible, of course, as so many students came and went while Pen was about, but Thatcher did not speak to anyone about his most remarkable student.

Nearly two years since he had first met the boy, Thatcher watched him look over his shoulder and wave goodbye as he rode out of sight. A proud smile formed on Thatcher's face as he recalled the boy beating the man.

While eating at the Three Decker Inn the night before, a friend told Thatcher about the altercation between old Farmer Larmack and Gorm. He was not surprised. Though he never met Larmack, he had watched him from a safe distance. Always watching, balanced on his toes, ready to move, this was not an ordinary farmer. He knew this was a dangerous man. Gorm found this out the hard way.

Now he watched Gorm mount his horse to follow Eusibius. The two men galloped in the direction of Tamworth. Something must be burning their tail feathers, he mused with a grin.

CHAPTER 10

Two days after the humiliating encounter at the inn with the farmer, Larmack, Eusibius suggested a few soldiers should accompany them to teach the entire family a much-needed lesson. A sullen Gorm repeated the farmer's words, "Try to hurt me or my own and you will die." Eusibius was sober enough to realize such an action might be risky. He had known men like Larmack...quiet, but deadly. After much discussion and a considerable number of encouraging drinks, the two men agreed upon a plan. As they stepped onto the inn's porch, they saw the farmer's son ride past. Gorm looked at Eusibius and smiled. They mounted their horses and rode toward the castle.

When the two soldiers arrived, the capital was filled with merchants and ministers of all shapes and sizes who walked about with airs of self-importance. The two soldiers galloped towards the castle, scattering the aforementioned who stared indignantly at them.

The castle had been deliberately built on a rise so it loomed above the city buildings, standing watch like a silent sentinel. It was tucked against the outer wall on one side of the bulging capital, its large courtyard a link between king and people.

The pair left their horses in the cobble-stoned courtyard and walked up wide marble steps. Guards opened doors for them as they approached.

"Gorm, don't tell him of the altercation, just speak of the rumors about the boy."

"You think he doesn't already know about it? The man has spies everywhere. No, I will tell the King of how these men trapped us, and then I will tell him of the rumors."

They passed through hallways well lit by hanging torches and sunlight piercing the gloom from the many embrasures. As they reached the great hall, two more guards wordlessly swung the great oaken doors open.

The large room was dark as all the windows were boarded. The walls stood bare and clammy; occasional drops splashed into small pools of dark water, echoing through the chamber.

In the dim light offered by smoldering embers, a robed figure sat in a large chair. Closer still, the shape could be seen bent toward a short man who nervously bowed repeatedly and then quickly left by another door. Two tall, well-muscled black men flanked what was now revealed as the King. The two soldiers stopped and kneeled.

King Cearl was a tall man, his once blond mane now stringy and gray. His eyes, deeply sunk into his face, suggested sleep was not something he often enjoyed. Purple robes flowed behind him as he glided towards the kneeling men, heads bowed. The King, smiling, took hold of each man's arm and raised them up together. Gorm was disconcerted by the strength of his grip. Cearl stared at them for a few seconds, smiling, then released his vice-like grip and returned to his chair.

The King peppered the men with questions about the small village of Kirkland. Without warning, Cearl switched from friendly interlocutor to stern inquisitor.

"What exactly occurred in the Three Decker Inn, such that two of my soldiers were both incapacitated?"

Eusibius nervously looked to Gorm. The younger man swallowed and began his speech.

"Sire, I merely asked this farmer about his son. Suddenly the whole inn seemed to come alive with peasants bent on protecting the boy. Why, I'm not sure. It's true the peasants overwhelmed us, but there were so many and they were so highly agitated, your Highness. We were lucky to have escaped with our lives."

"What was the cause of this great agitation? Certainly a simple farm boy was not worth risking their lives."

Gorm gulped and nodded in agreement. He continued with words well-rehearsed. "Even from the first day I was at Kirkland, I have heard of rumors of a boy who had unusual ways with animals. A boy who met the White Deer. Well, I had to ask his father about it, your Highness. I felt it my duty. It was this question that created the fracas."

The King looked long at Gorm, weighing the soldier's words carefully. An eyebrow was slowly raised as his head tilted forward.

"When, exactly, did the villagers tell you about him communing with the white deer?"

Lies have a life of their own, twisting and distorting reality, so the speaker himself becomes ensnared.

"Just after I arrived. It was all about the village. Again and again it came to my attention."

The King stared long at the man before he spoke again.

"So you questioned this farmer and the villagers rose against you. I had heard the peasant alone bested you, Gorm."

"Yes," admitted the soldier, "but only because he had angry men around him. Believe me, sire, many swords surrounded us."

"So why didn't you later arrest these malcontents?" The King's stare never wavered; Gorm had not yet seen him blink.

"Your Highness," offered Gorm cautiously, gulping to swallow his fear, "I thought getting this information to you was more important."

"You did? You took your time getting me that valuable information, Gorm. A few years by your own admission."

Gorm sputtered, but Cearl raised his hand, "It's of no consequence."

Pondering the fire, the King was silent for nearly a minute.

"This man, the boy's father. What is his name and what does he look like?"

Gorm hastened to a brief description.

"Larmack, your Highness. Tall. A beard."

"How old is the boy?"

"Thirteen, sire."

"Yes, that would be about the right age," the King mumbled.

"The boy's name?"

"Pen, sire," Gorm quickly answered.

"Pen," the King repeated, his gaze still fixed on the faint, red glow pulsating from the blackened wood of the fire. "Well, Pen, it's time we meet."

The King stood, towering over Gorm as he firmly gripped the soldier's shoulder.

"Gorm, you have done me a great service. This is important news. Eusibius, didn't you hear of this lad?" He directed his stare towards the older soldier, a great smile on his face.

Eusibius hesitated. An answer to the King's questions could bring rich rewards, but sometimes it could exact unsettling penalties. What to answer? How to best position himself? How best to stay safe, yet in favor?

"Sire, my work involves collecting taxes for your treasury. When fulfilling that task, conversation is sometimes harder to extract than the coin. I regret to say that I knew nothing of such a rumor."

His answer drew Gorm's surprised stare. He had assumed Eusibius would support his claim since they had agreed on the fabrication at the inn. Why would he not follow through with their plan? Gorm turned to face the King and noted uncomfortably the grip tightening.

"Gorm, thanks to you alone, I possess this information." As he leaned closer to whisper into the soldier's ear, his smile vanished. "But you knew of this years ago."

Gorm winced in pain as the fingers probed deep into his shoulder muscles. The smaller soldier leaned away, but was unable to break the grip.

"My orders in this matter are well known, Gorm. Any information about the White Deer must reach me immediately and yet you waited!"

He thrust a knife into the soldier's belly and wrenched it sideways as Gorm's eyes widened in disbelief. The soldier tried to pull away, but the King's iron grip held him in place. Pain replaced surprise as he collapsed to the floor. A moment later, a dark pool of blood surrounded the body, silent and still.

The King, breathing heavily, sidestepped the body and confronted an astonished Eusibius who stumbled backwards in fear. Cearl nodded his head and the two bodyguards immediately restrained Eusibius. He brought the bloody knife to the frightened soldier's chest, looked at the tall, trembling soldier, and slowly wiped the blade clean on his tunic. Returning the knife to its scabbard, he motioned the guards to release the man.

"Eusibius, here are my orders. Find the boy, and bring him to me. Do not, in any way, harm him. Do not alert his father. I want this done as discretely as possible. Before sundown tomorrow."

The soldier hastily saluted and strode as quickly as he could toward the door.

"Eusibius!" the King called. The man stopped and pivoted, afraid his heart's pounding could be heard.

"This mess here. Quite untidy and unsightly, don't you agree? Clean it up. And, make sure that you do it yourself. The staff shouldn't have to clean up your mess, should they?"

Not waiting for an answer, he left with his two body guards. The boom of the closed door echoed in the chamber and the hall stood empty except for the two soldiers. Slowly Eusibius walked toward Gorm. He stood over the body, recalling Larmack's last words to Gorm, "Try to hurt me or my own and you will die."

He began the grisly business of cleaning up the "mess".

CHAPTER 11

The lamb dinner was thoroughly enjoyed by all, though Songor was the only one who managed four helpings. After dinner, Mother Hebron and Larmack talked quietly by the fire while Pen and Liana went outside to be with the horses. Songor slept on the floor by the fire, snoring loudly. The two adults, smiling, spoke in a conspiratorial manner. A thirteenth birthday party for Pen was being planned. When the children were heard on the porch, Mother Hebron and Larmack drew apart and nonchalantly studied the sputtering fire. Larmack yawned and suggested it was time to return home. Songor was nudged awake and the three rode through the dark to their own farm.

The next day dawned particularly bright for Pen. This was his last day being twelve and he was allowed to spend it entirely on his own doing anything he wanted. In Mercia, at that age, a boy becomes a young man and he was going to make the most his last day of youth.

Larmack granted him Mirus for the day. Pen hesitantly asked if he might stay in the village overnight with Jack. His father considered the request. The boy had always been responsible and he would be a man tomorrow. As Larmack went out the door, he nodded his consent.

Pen rode directly to Thatcher's home, skipping his usual stop at Mother Hebron's. It was the earliest Thatcher had risen since the same lad woke him up nearly two years ago. When Thatcher finally made it to the courtyard, empty except for Pen, he watched the boy stretching. A warm smile formed on his grizzled face as he recalled his many lessons with Pen. Though technically not yet a man, he certainly fought like one. Thatcher had never crossed swords with a fighter as good as Pen.

"Well, young Pen, before we cross blades, let me show you a bit more about the knife."

After an hour of instruction, the two crossed blades. By noon, Thatcher stopped parrying with the lad and sat on a bench in the workout arena. Sweat streamed down his face and he breathed hard.

"I think, Master Pen, any more waging of war today will kill one or both of us. Probably me; I'm getting too old for this." Hands on knees, he rose slowly. "I have an early birthday present for you."

When Thatcher returned, he held a cloth bundle and offered it to Pen. The boy looked at the man and smiled, "Sir, you are too kind."

As he unwrapped the cloth, a small, shiny blade emerged. It was a bit shorter than most knives, but thicker and much sharper. An inscription on the side of the blade added to its uniqueness. Pen could not read, but he knew it was a foreign script. He handled the blade. It was unquestionably strong but surprisingly light.

"It was given to me by an old man who saved my life many years ago. It's made of a special metal forged only by elves. The inscription is right here, Pen." He pointed to the finely scripted words on the side of the untarnished blade. "Tis Elfin runes, lad."

Thatcher looked at the boy with a slight smile and a twinkle in his eye.

Pen laughed. "Elves? And I suppose a dragon was used as the forge fire? You always tell a good story, Thatcher. I admit that it is so beautiful that it could have been made by elves, if ever they existed. I have never seen a blade like this one. I will use my old scabbard here, but surely I will get one more suited to this knife's noble stature."

"No, Pen," Thatcher said hastily. "Take this here strap and leather sheath. Tie it onto your waist, like this." After tucking the knife safely in place, he helped Pen on with his tunic such that the blade was well hidden.

"Let no man see this blade, Pen. I mean this, boy. Perhaps I did embellish the story a bit, but it is a special blade. Some would rob you of it or maybe even kill for it. Show no one. I must have your promise on that."

Surprised by the older man's mercurial change in demeanor, Pen agreed. It seemed like an unnecessary precaution, but if Thatcher wanted it, he would comply.

"Let me tell you something more about this blade. This is true, lad. The old man told me that it would never break. I told you it was special, didn't I? He also said one more thing."

Though the house was obviously empty, Thatcher scanned the room and doorways and leaned conspiratorially toward his young charge. "Be careful when you first use it. The first time, it won't fail you in the task before you...no matter what."

Thatcher relaxed and spoke in a normal tone.

"At least that is what the old man said and I believe him, boy. Men like him don't lie nor tell stories. He owned it for many years and never used it. Nor have I. Choose wisely when to first use it, Pen."

The boy tilted his head, confused. He had never seen Thatcher this serious. He looked out the window; the sun had started its slow decline toward evening. He changed his mind about staying in the village, tempting though that was. He was exhausted from his practice and just wanted to rest in his own bed.

He thanked his mentor once again and walked outside to Mirus who was contentedly eating grass. The horse raised his head when Pen hopped into the saddle. He waved farewell to the old man and patted the gift hidden inside his pants. As was his habit, Thatcher watched the boy ride over the hill past the inn. He could make out the tall form of Eusibius on the inn's porch. No Gorm this time. Odd, as those two seemed joined at the hip. As the boy disappeared over the hill, Eusibius and a number of other soldiers walked down the porch, mounted their horses, and followed in the same direction. By this time, Thatcher had gone inside.

CHAPTER 12

Rider and horse were content with a slow walk home. For the first time, he noted the woods on one side, birds chirping, and on the other side, he smelled the rich, verdant fields of wheat, oats, and beans. He watched the distant forms of the farmers digging in the fields. A perfect day, he thought.

Suddenly, he heard the unmistakable cadence of hoof beats from the village. That could only be the King's soldiers, he realized with smoldering anger. Without regard for anyone, they would scatter the village folk off the road. Pen quickly directed Mirus off to the side of the road and waited. Seven horsemen charged around the bend. The soldiers came to an abrupt stop in front of the Pen.

"Ah, the farmer's boy," said Eusibius, looking up and down the empty road. Then focusing on the lad, he added, "Nice afternoon for a ride, isn't it?"

Warily, the boy nodded.

"Your name is Pen. Am I correct?"

He nodded again.

Eusibius took one final glance to his right and left. "Well, Pen, the King requires your presence and we are here to escort you. Come along, I know a shortcut through these woods." Having spoken, he motioned to one of the soldiers and Pen's reins were grabbed. To another soldier, he made a gesture with his head at the boy's waist. The soldier jumped down and unclasped Pen's old scabbard from his waist. Eusibius smiled at the boy's alarm.

"Wouldn't want you to accidentally hurt yourself."

After laughing at his own joke, Eusibius led the group down a well-trodden path through a copse of trees. Emerging minutes later, they intercepted the Tamworth road and followed it to the castle. The trip took the afternoon and nearly the entire night.

To enter the city, everyone had to first pass under a wide metal gate, held up by a stout rope. Two soldiers were posted at this gate. Without a word, Eusibius and his group walked past the checkpoint.

It was still dark, but a glow in the east marked the arrival of a new day. Eusibius chose not to gallop as he done on previous occasions. With so few people to scatter, what would be the fun? When they finally reached the castle, all dismounted, their horses tended to by servants rubbing their eyes. A soldier escorted Pen on either side as the group climbed the steps.

Mirus whinnied and tried to pull away from the stable hand. Pen looked over his shoulder and noted that the large horse, looking anxiously at Pen, stubbornly refused to go with the stable hand. Fearing the horse might be beaten, he wrenched free from the soldiers, turned back down the steps, yelling over his shoulder, "Wait. Let me calm my horse." Eusibius motioned for the soldiers to follow him.

Upon reaching the agitated horse, he patted his side, wet from the ride, and rubbed the soft nose of the great animal, calming him. As the horse nuzzled his master's neck, gaining reassurance, Pen whispered, "Go, Mirus, go home. Back home." He conjured an

102

image of the farm in his mind, patted the horse until he was calm, then walked back up the steps. The horse was led away be a stable hand. By the time Pen reached Eusibius at the top of the steps, there was a commotion below. The soldiers and the boy looked back to see the black stallion rear and wrench free from the stable hand. The horse galloped back along the street, now barely illuminated by dawn's early light.

Eusibius smirked at the lad.

"Seems you have little control over that beast."

Pen nodded. "Seems that way."

Once inside the castle, the group entered the central hallway cloaked in a soft red glow from the rising sun. Deeper inside, the rooms and passageways of the castle were well lit;   torches hung from the walls a few feet apart from each other.

Finally they came to the great hall. In contrast to the rest of the castle, he seemed to walk into a dark nightmare. At the far end, a fire was ablaze in an impossibly large fireplace. A chair faced the fire, its large back blocking the occupant from view. It was flanked by what looked like two large, black statues. As the small group approached the chair and fire, Pen saw that the statues were live sentinels. Tall, muscular, and bare-chested, the men stared impassively at the group. Their hands rested on the sword handles.

Eusibius raised his hand and the group stopped. The soldier grabbed the boy's arm and the two of them walked alone towards the chair.

"Stay here."

Eusibius walked around the large black man on the right. Facing the chair, he leaned in, and whispered something to whoever was sitting in it. Pen watched the soldier back away into one of the many shadows at the periphery of the great hall. A hand, loosely covered by a dark purple robe, stretched out. A bony finger curled, silently commanding the boy to come forward. With considerable trepidation, Pen slowly complied and found himself face-to-face with King Cearl.

"Thank-you, Eusibius. Take your men to the barracks, eat, and rest."

"Your Majesty," came a disembodied voice from the shadows. Pen heard the clanking spurs and the footsteps of the retreating soldiers. In the distance, he discerned the whining of the door opening and the solid, distressing thud when it closed.

All the while, the King's eyes were fixed on Pen. Except for the two bodyguards who were more like statues than flesh, they were alone. The only sound was the occasional cracking of logs in the fireplace.

"I am King Cearl, son of Jared, and you are Pen, son of Larmack. Welcome to Castle Mercia." The forearms protruding from his purple robe were muscular. His long gray hair hung haphazardly over his shoulders. Great haggard half-circles sagged under his eyes, completing an altogether alarming image.

"You must be tired now, Pen. Aldephi, fetch the guards. Instruct them to take Pen to his room. He can sleep there."

For the first time, he smiled grandly at the boy. Pen smiled back and felt he had made a friend.

"After you have rested, child, we are going to have a chat."

The guards, neatly dressed in fine red uniforms, escorted him upstairs. They shoved him into a large room with a canopy bed and fine linens. A table positioned before a mirror had a few implements upon it, one a brush with a few strands of red hair.

A table in front of the bed hosted a light supper for the lad and he devoured everything. He sank into the bed and before he could cover himself, was fast asleep.

When Pen woke the room was bathed in red, but this time announcing the onset of night. He had slept away the entire day.

He walked around the room. It was clearly a room for a woman or girl. A small anteroom was filled with dresses. Perhaps it was the queen's room? Was Cearl even married, he wondered? He lay on the bed again. There was a fragrance, slight, but somehow familiar.

The door to the apartment swung open and startled him as he leapt from the bed. The same two guards stood by the door. One of them inclined his head, indicating he was to follow them.

CHAPTER 13

Songor carried the large chair he had crafted into the main room. It was a simple chair, sturdy and polished. His thick hands lovingly caressed the smooth oak chair. Larmack patted him on the back.

"Oh, he will be surprised, sir. Mark me words. Mmm, Mother Hebron is sending us nice smells, ain't she? I might help her a bit…" The round servant waddled off to the kitchen, hoping for a snack to ward off his ever-present hunger.

Liana wore a white robe circled with a woven belt, dyed different hues of blue.

"I tried to pull him away from Thatcher, but he wouldn't listen to me. He is becoming more and more difficult!" Liana angrily slapped down the last silver spoon completing a formal setting at the rickety table.

"There. Done." She smiled approvingly before her frown reappeared.

"Now we just have to wait for him!"

"Well," Larmack remarked quietly, "it is his party, so if ever he can be late, today is the day."

"Yes, but to be gone all night and day! And with Jack! He could have at least stopped by to see me…and mother, of course."

"Of course," Larmack repeated with an amused grin.

The conversation was cut short by the sound of a horse's gallop. Everyone looked up expectantly. The door swung open and Thatcher peered into the room. Mother Hebron had come out from the kitchen, wiping her hands on a blue apron. Thatcher was obviously embarrassed as Larmack scowled at him. Looking sternly at Thatcher, Mother Hebron quickly intervened. "I invited him, Larmack. He didn't tell me he was going to be late!"

"I thought it would be a good thing to clean up first," Thatcher snapped.

Larmack looked at the warrior who taught his son how to use a sword. Resigning himself to the role of gracious host, he walked over to shake the man's hand. The two men were awkward with each other, but Songor filled the uncomfortable silence with amusing anecdotes about his own thirteenth birthday. Bored by the stories, Liana went outside to wait for her friend. From the kitchen Mother Hebron could make out some of what Songor was saying and often she would chuckle.

Liana rushed inside the door. "Pen is here!"

Everyone rushed outside to greet Pen as the great black stallion loudly galloped into the farmyard. The horse stopped in front of the house, Pen absent from his back.

"Well ain't that strange!" remarked Songor.

Larmack patted the Mirus finding him lathered with sweat. The animal was heaving, obviously exhausted.

"Mirus would never leave Pen of his own accord. He must have been sent here by him, but from where?"

They heard more hoof beats in the distance. Out of the blackness, Jack and his father, Griswold, appeared.

"Jack, where is Pen?"

"Dunno. Hain't seen him since yesterday."

In the distance, more hoof beats approached.

*

Pen found himself seated before the King who looked only at the smoldering fire. Without looking up, he queried, "Did you see the tapestries and engravings as you walked in?"

"Oh, yes, sire. They were quite beautiful."

"Did you see an engraving of a deer?"

Pen closed his eyes to recall. "No, your Highness, I'm sorry. I can't recall seeing one."

Cearl turned from the glowing fire to look at him, a slight smile on his thin lips. "You are observant, boy. That is good." He squinted his eyes, trying to see more clearly in the gloom. "Your eyes are blue, like your father's?"

"No, sire. My father's are brown."

The King tilted his head, his interest piqued.

"Ah… they must be the color of your mother's eyes, then."

"Don't know. She's been dead since I was born."

The King's own dark eyes opened wide now. He blinked and his gaze returned to the fire. *It's him.*

For a few minutes, Cearl casually probed Pen about his home life.

"You seemed impressed with the castle. How would you like to live here with me? We would be good friends, I assure you. I could teach you much…"

"Oh, no, sire. I could never live here. There's the farm, my family and friends…I would miss them too much. But thank you for the offer."

Cearl was annoyed, but he restrained himself. *Calmly now.*

"A pity. But we can still be friends, can't we? Yes, I thought so."

He chuckled while he watched the dying flames.

"Pen, I know this sounds odd, but some people have said that you saw a deer... a white deer. I didn't know such an animal existed. Tell me about her."

As he spoke, he glanced briefly at the lad. Pen was staring at him.

"White deer? I never saw a white deer. Never." Cearl was too observant and clever to miss the slight delay in his answer.

"Tell me, boy," the King commanded loudly, barely able to restrain his impatience, his eyes boring into the lad.

Cearl forced himself to speak softly. "Did she ever say anything to you, child? Some special word, perhaps?" He leaned over to hear what the boy was about to offer.

Pen hesitated. The white deer had told him to give the word to the man in white. Under the purple robe, the King was dressed in black down to his boots. He could not share the word with the King.

"No sire. She never talked to me."

Cearl noted the delayed response again. *The wretch was lying.* Unable to control himself any longer, he rose from his chair, causing it to crash noisily backwards.

"You think you can lie to me, boy? I can smell a lie and I smell one now. The truth, or you will long regret your folly."

Pen was terrified. Frightened as he was, he would not tell the King about his experience. He mustered all his courage, clenched his teeth, and stared back defiantly at the king.

Frustrated and seething with rage, the King went for his knife, but then thought better of it and released his hold. The boy's death would do him no good, at least not yet. He must be made to talk! He called for his guards. In the darkness, Pen could hear boots march across the floor and two men dressed in red materialized in front of the fire.

"Take this insufferable little monster to the dungeon. No one releases him except me. Understood?"

Standing above Pen who shivered with fright, the King gripped his shoulders. Bony fingers dug deep into Pen's muscles and shook him. "Now you will spend a few days in prison. No soft bed there, boy. No fire or comfortable chair, either."

As Pen was led away, Cearl paced in front of the fireplace, the fire now nearly out. He was so much like her. So much like my sister.

*

Pen was taken to the dungeon and pushed into a small cell. The door slammed shut with a distressing finality, and the clank of a large key made him shudder. The only light came through a small opening in the door. After his eyes adjusted to the gloom, he saw a dirty bowl near a stool in the center of the small cell and a large pail in one corner. All three objects exuded their own peculiar, revolting odors. The room itself was made of loosely fit rocks, and contained many gaps from which he could make out small, slimy, worm-like forms entering and leaving. He caught the quick movement of large insects scurrying further into the darkness. He heard a scratching sound coming from the darkest corner of the small room and shuddered again. Hesitantly, afraid to venture too far from his present position, he took one step to retrieve the three-legged stool. After Pen did his best to clean the stool, he sat down, elbows on knees, and covered his eyes.

CHAPTER 14

A world away, Larmack paced the floor in front of the fireplace. The riders who followed Jack and Griswold were farmers, led by Eldrick, who was quick to offer his thoughts to the worried father. "I'm sure it was Pen, Larmack. We saw soldiers pass by with a rider atop a great black horse. It had to be Mirus."

"And you say they went south?"

"Yes."

Larmack and Songor looked at each other. "The castle," Larmack mumbled under his breath. Songor nodded in agreement. For once, the great boisterous man was silent and unsmiling.

In the lull which followed, Songor shook Eldrick's hand and led the farmers, Jack and Griswold, to the door.

"Thanks to ye for telling us. We was worried when he dint come back for sup. We gots some figurin' to do."

"Songor," said Eldrick, "If there's anything we can do...anything. Pen, he's a special lad, he is. Just send us word and we be there, Songor. We be there!"

Griswold spoke up as well.

"We can fight, Songor. This can't go unanswered!"

Songor nodded, thanked the men again and watched the night swallow them. When he returned, Larmack was staring intently at the flame; the room was silent except for the crackle of the fire.

Thatcher broke the farmer's reverie.

"I still have friends in the castle. Folks who served with me. I can talk to them…"

Larmack spoke in a barely audible whisper. "Once before he robbed me of my happiness and I didn't act against him. This time nothing holds me back." He shook his head and closed his eyes. Mother Hebron placed her hand on his shoulder, but he shook himself away from her. He turned to her, his face dark.

"It's not consoling I need, woman. If you must mother someone, see to your own; Liana is crying in the kitchen. Leave me alone.

His words hung heavy in the air. Without lifting a finger, Larmack had slapped the woman and shocked everyone else. Mother Hebron coolly returned his angry stare. She knew grief and suffering could twist a person. The woman who was most like a mother to Pen quietly said, "Perhaps you are right, Larmack. Liana and I had best go home." She retrieved her sobbing daughter and left, not another word said.

Larmack's gaze returned to the flame's dancing patterns; he stood motionless before the fire. Somewhere in his jumbled mind he regretted his words, but at the moment, his anger outweighed his remorse. After a few more minutes of contemplation, he rose, brushed past the two men, and walked outside into the dark. The crickets heralded his passage toward the barn.

Thatcher and Songor exchanged glances and went outside.

"He be a hurtin', Mr. Thatcher."

"I know, Songor."

Thatcher, watching the shadows in the barn, spoke quietly. "I love that boy like a son."

A teary-eyed Songor looked back into the room at the chair he had spent weeks secretly crafting.

"I know, sir. Me too."

The two men waited and watched. Suddenly the barn door swung open. A tall form, determined in step, walked towards them. As Larmack emerged out of the dark, Thatcher saw he was dressed in the red of the King's uniform, a sword hung by his side.

"He was a soldier, working for the King, wasn't he?" questioned Thatcher, not taking his eyes off the approaching figure.

Seeing his master so attired, Songor answered with a smile, "You might say that, sir."

As the farmer moved closer, Thatcher barely recognized Larmack, as his heavy beard was gone. When he finally arrived at the door, Thatcher saw a long white scar formerly masked by the beard.

"Do you still have my back, Thatcher?"

The shorter man looked up in amazement.

"General Petronius!"

Dumbfounded, he shook the General's hand wondering about the transformation of general into farmer and back into general again.

CHAPTER 15

Twenty-five years earlier, at the age of seventeen, Petronius was made captain after saving the life of King Jared in a pitched battle with the raiding Angles. The king provided a few men and assigned him to the castle where his responsibilities were to protect the princess and teach the prince to use a sword. They seemed easy enough tasks, but after the first day, Petronius found out differently.

He was introduced to a demure eleven-year-old, attired in a simple but elegant light yellow gown. A shock of bright red hair cascaded over her shoulders. Princess Elen bowed politely, assessed the tall, handsome captain, and slowly walked to the door. Petronius turned to ask a question of the governess who nervously watched the maiden. As he turned, following her gaze, he saw the princess holding her dress up and racing through the door. Rushing to the hall, he caught a glimpse of her rounding the corner. The chase was on! He motioned for his squad to follow. Running through crowded hallways, weaving in and out of servants and ministers alike, the men followed the white slippers and the puff of yellow around one corner after another. It ended when Petronius watched her enter the great hall to lunch with her father. Her face was flushed from her giggling sprints. Poised for a moment at the door, she stared at the men, noted their heavy breathing, and smiled. The great doors closed behind her. Petronius, braced against the wall, slowly slid down to the ground, exhausted.

During the afternoon break, Petronius provided swordsmanship lessons to the prince. A few years younger than himself, Cearl was tall, strong, and insolent. Already adept at using the blade, he proceeded to engage the captain in a fierce one-on-one contest. The boy showed no restraint in using his sharp weapon and came dangerously close to cutting his instructor. Worried that one or both of them would be wounded, Petronius unleashed a few quick, complicated maneuvers and Cearl's sword was dislodged from his hand.

"How did you do that?" demanded the prince.

"Sire, when you attacked me the last time, you leaned a bit too far, so by feinting to the right..." And so the lessons began. Knowing he could learn new tricks, the prince listened carefully to the instructions and worked diligently to improve his skills. While the prince was more serious about his study, Petronius preferred the company of the less serious princess.

Over time, Elen disappeared less often. Sometimes, while no one watched, she stared at the young captain. "If only" thoughts played in her mind as she observed the unsuspecting soldier. If only I was older. If only I was prettier. If only... Whenever his eyes darted to her, worried she had run off, she would flush deep red—praying no one, especially him, observed her staring.

The nature of her position consigned her to a solitary existence. Other children of her age and status rarely visited. Consequently, she acquired a strong bond with animals. Within seconds she could calm the most agitated horse. In the woods near the castle, Petronius witnessed small songbirds swooping down to take bits of bread out of her hand. Some even perched on her shoulders, taking the tidbits more easily.

After a year of guarding Elen and tutoring young Cearl, King Jared sent Petronius to pay the ransom on Astible, one of Jared's most trusted captains. Two weeks later, Petronius returned Astible and the ransom money.

King Jared had aged gracefully by neither working too hard nor fretting too much. He warmly greeted the young soldier, linking his frail arm with Petronius' strong one.

"How did you do it, young man? Did they not require the money?"

Petronius allowed only a brief smile.

"No, they actually demanded more, sire. So I considered any arrangement between Mercia and the Angles already broken. Walls made from thin saplings are easily cut, sire. Also, prison huts are best placed in the center of a camp, not near the perimeter."

Realizing he had a gifted fighter, a loyal soldier, and a clever captain, King Jared relieved Petronius of his responsibilities at the castle and sent him on a number of dangerous missions. With each successful engagement, he was given additional men to command.

As Elen grew into her teens, she assumed additional responsibilities. Rarely did the paths of the princess and captain cross.

One day, after a rather boring luncheon with a nearby monarch and his obese, greasy-faced son, she spied Petronius leaving the great hall. Using him as an excuse to extract herself from the detestable pair, she hurried to intercept him. She called to him as she ran, nearly tripping upon her arrival. Petronius' strong hands reached out and steadied her.

"Aha! The sprite called Elen. How are you, girl?"

Seeing his tan, clean-shaven face up close, she flushed again. Having gained her balance, she lost her nerve as she stepped away from the man and cast her head downward. Allowing herself only briefest glance, she began to speak quietly to the floor.

"I think, sir... I think... oh, my!"

Not knowing how to best greet a soldier, she curtsied hurriedly, almost falling again. Red-faced, tears forming, she looked at Petronius and waited for derision or, at least, laughter. Silently she cursed her feet which always seemed to deliberately ignore her thoughts. It was an embarrassing affliction. Despite her training as a lady of the court, she suffered occasional mistakes in etiquette. Her stepbrother, Cearl, frequently criticized her. She looked up again at Petronius, waiting for the scolding, but he just stared at her, a warm smile on his face. Grateful he did not notice or perhaps care about her near tumble, she regained her confidence and continued her speech.

"I think, sir, you should address me as a woman and not a girl. I am of age, you know."

Fighting back a chuckle, he coughed.

"Is this a command or a request?"

She hurriedly shook her head.

"Oh, no, Petronius. A favor. An observation. Not a command. I would never..."

He interrupted her stammering with a graceful bow.

"Well then, m'lady. I am ever at the service of Princess Elen, a lady. I'm truly sorry if I offended you, Princess. Please accept me as your faithful servant from this day on."

All she could do was nod and back away from him, bumping into one of the columns in the hall.

"Thank-you, Captain. I accept your apology."

She turned and walked away quickly.

A day later, intent on visiting Cearl to help him with his swordplay, he again ran into the princess, literally. She had careened around the corner in a most unladylike fashion and crashed into him. Apologizing profusely, she then pulled him aside and begged for his attention.

"Petronius, I have just learned that a young maiden is being forced— oh, I can't even say it. Petronius, it's terrible. I must help her."

Puzzled about how he fit into this situation, he cautiously tilted his head and raised his eyebrows questioningly. As the princess tried to catch her breath, he interjected.

"Find a place for her in the castle. She should be safe here."

"Hardly safe, captain. There are too many old men intent on assisting young women in not so valiant ways. No, she must be part of my staff— then she would be safe."

"Then you must hire her."

"No, Petronius, no! My father already complains I have too many ladies-in-waiting. And, Cearl always chides me about it. I can't ask for her, I can't. You must."

"Me? Princess, this is no concern of mine. A captain doesn't speak for a princess. No!"

"But, just yesterday, you said..." Her eyes watered and she looked away. He must have been mocking me. Why should he care about me?

Petronius shook his head slowly and closed his eyes.

"All right. I will do what I can, m'lady. Give me a few days."

A great smile erupted on her face and she clapped her hands.

"Oh, fine Captain, thank you so much!"

The fine captain smiled at her. A flush came to her face and she broke the gaze.

"I must be going," she mumbled and quickly disappeared.

Petronius continued toward his appointment with the prince.

Mercia, with its rich farmlands, was strategically placed in the center of northern England. As such, it was often a target for conquest. The next day news came to the capital that a large army from the Middle Angles was moving toward Tamworth. Jared mobilized all able-bodied men to meet the challenge. Over the next two days, as increasing numbers of men grouped in and around the castle, captains began organizing them into battle groups. Then, one by one, the groups moved out.

Elen watched the men leave, looking for that particular man who had failed to say goodbye. She saw him astride a great black stallion, leading a few other horsemen and a least a hundred foot soldiers out of the castle. She saw a white bandage on his jaw and worried he must have been hurt. She watched him leave through the gate, not so much as a look back towards her!

After a long and tiring cry, she rested the head with red hair on her forearm, wishing a certain man had noticed her. A knock at the door roused her. She opened the door and a young girl smiled up at her.

"Elwyth, how did you get inside the castle? Wait, did he harm you again?"

The girl smiled.

"No. No, ma'am. Hain't hurt a bit. Not one bit. The king, he sent for me. To be your maid, ma'am." She executed a perfect curtsy which irritated Elen, as she herself hadn't yet mastered the maneuver. But a smile edged out her frown.

Petronius, she thought. He did what he had promised. Amidst all his work, with war imminent, he somehow found time to speak with the king and arrange for this poor girl to be assigned to the princess. Elen was, at once, contrite. She looked once again at the long line of men marching into a war from which many would not return. When will I grow up?

The war did not go well for the Mercians. More battles were lost than won. Desperate for some resolution to the conflict, King Jared attacked the Angles hoping one last battle would decide it all. Unfortunately, being old and somewhat foolish, the king was killed in the battle. The Mercians had suffered another defeat—their worst yet.

Cearl assumed command of the army and faced discouraged captains, all but one willing to concede the war to the Angles. That one was Petronius. He confidently spoke to the leaders and slowly raised their spirits. He outlined a battle plan playing on the overconfidence of the enemy. One by one, they saw hope for a final victory. When morning came, the men, though tired, were ready for another bout with the invaders.

The battle was hard fought on both sides, but the Mercians, avenging the death of their king (a point Petronius had made to every battalion), fought harder. The plan devised late at night unfurled perfectly in the light of day. The Mercians won a major battle.

At nightfall, after securing accommodations for his men, Petronius walked into Cearl's tent where he found the prince drinking wine. Cearl offered some to his guest.

"Good fellow, the wound has nearly healed. No hard feelings, I hope?"

Petronius rubbed the fresh scar on his jaw, a gift from Cearl in their last practice session. Cearl put his goblet down and took the captain's arm, a mannerism reminiscent of the former king.

"Petronius, I am going back to Tamworth. Mercia needs a strong king now and I intend to be that king. But we are not done with the Angles. I want you to take command of the army."

Petronius was aghast.

"Sire, please, I am young and inexperienced. Choose Astible or even Glock; let them head the forces."

Cearl looked at the man not yet aged a quarter of a century.

"No, dear friend. They were both willing to concede. It was you who inspired the captains and the men. You won the battle. Petronius, I need you at the head of this army. Be my general."

There were more protests from Petronius, but Cearl would have none of it. Petronius knew the young prince well enough that when he decided something, he would not change his mind. Reluctantly he accepted the generalship. The next day, Cearl galloped back to Tamworth to secure himself as king while Petronius led his army eastward.

*

Five years later, Petronius returned to Tamworth. The heavy burden of responsibility was etched on his face, robbing him of his youth. But today there were no frowns of worry. The last war against the Northlanders had been concluded successfully and he was back. As he casually rode through the busy streets, he smiled at the vendors hawking their wares, and nostalgically breathed in the dueling aromas of baking bread and pungent spices. He stopped a moment and listened to the din of negotiations, discussions, and shouts. At the steps of the castle, he dismounted the great black stallion and handed the reins to a waiting soldier. The general climbed the steps, two at a time, nodding at a number of ministers and soldiers. He walked purposefully to the great hall. The guards smiled as they opened the great oak doors.

Beams of light from slotted windows lit various groups of people: ministers, merchants, and soldiers conversed in many tightly knit groups. Near the fireplace, he could make out the shaggy blond mane of his former student, now King Cearl, gesticulating to a group of men by the table. Standing at the other side of the throne, surrounded by supplicants trying to gain her attention, was a tall woman. She wore a simple white gown with a green belt encircling a slim figure. The light from one of the windows conferred radiance to her hair rivaling the flame in the great fireplace.

Petronius was shocked. Could that be the same gangly girl he left behind five years ago? Princess Elen was turned toward the king, watching the proceedings, doing her best to ignore the long-nosed little man who was pointing to a young girl standing behind him. Reluctantly she looked at the bedraggled female, thin and wearing only a tattered robe. Even from a distance, Petronius could see Elen's own beautiful face frown sadly. A withering look was turned toward the man to whom she spoke few words, nodded her head, and motioned him away. Seeing the anger of the princess, the girl looked at the floor, trembling. Elen stepped towards her, whispered something in her ear, and smiled. The girl put her hand to her mouth, then grabbed Elen's hand and kissed it. The princess gently extracted herself as she pointed toward the back of the room. The young girl walked toward a small door in the rear of the great hall, smiling gratefully as she looked back at her patron. Petronius smiled. It was quite likely another servant had been added to the retinue of the princess.

The young general strode toward the brother and sister, cordially acknowledging her and kneeling before the king who graciously raised him up and hugged him before introducing him to some of the ministers. Petronius politely bowed to the men, but his eyes kept straying to Elen who was standing uncomfortably close.

Normally, when business matters were discussed, she excused herself from the tedium, but this time, she remained. Unabashed, she stared at her former protector. Whenever he looked up, she smiled at him. He quickly looked away, for some reason unhinged by her attention.

King Cearl had many questions about the campaign.

"Petronius. Petronius!" the king yelled, rising from his chair. "Are you listening to me, man?"

"Yes, sire. Sorry. Ah, the mines in the Northland…"

Cearl, his hands planted squarely on the table, bent his head and shook it angrily, his blond hair flying wildly. Looking up, he said, "That we talked about five minutes ago. Where have you been?"

Where had he been, wondered Petronius. Under a spell, no doubt. No woman (and he knew many) had ever had such an effect on him.

Forcing his gaze and full attention on the king, Petronius resolutely finished the interview. When finished, he looked for her, but Princess Elen was gone. After taking his leave, he was sorely tempted to seek her out. Now that would be a far more interesting interview. But he would not insinuate himself into her life. She was of the noble class, he the son of a merchant. While she was beautiful, an unsightly scar disfigured him. She was young, barely two and twenty and although he was only six years older, he knew he looked older still. No, he would not seek her attention only to be ridiculed by their differences.

He hurried through the castle and crashed into the very person he was determined to avoid.

She looked at him and beamed.

"General, we meet again. Rather violently, but how delightful. I was worried we might not have an opportunity to chat." She impetuously grabbed his arm and led him to a bench away from the busy walkways. Her hand was soft, nothing like his large, calloused hand.

Pulling him down to sit beside her, she asked about his campaign in the North. Petronius just stared at her. Soft red hair cascaded down her shoulders. Her skin was still adorned with a few freckles which he thought were perfectly placed. And, a man could all too easily drown in her eyes, so deep and green they were.

Elen meanwhile labored on, trying to extract a sentence, a phrase, or even a word from the general who remained mute and staring.

"I heard that you were surrounded by the Northlanders and broke free. How did you manage that?"

"My men." He answered.

"Your men…" she repeated, gently turning her head, hoping to extract a bit more information.

"Saved me."

"How fortunate for all of us… they saved you?"

"Yes."

"Ah, that explains it then." She nodded with a confused, half smile. "And the Black. How is your great stallion? Was he injured in the war?"

"Fine. Small cut. Healed."

With a bemused expression, she leaned back.

"You certainly don't bore people with too many words, do you, General?"

"No—I mean, yes. But no." Petronius could go no further with this interview.

"My pardon, Princess, I have to go." And with that, he abruptly left. Shocked by his sudden departure, Elen stared at his retreating figure.

Petronius almost ran down the stairs onto the courtyard. He called for his horse and a soldier went to fetch the stallion. Irritated and worried that she might come out of the castle, he yelled, "Be quick about it, man." He paced nervously back and forth as the soldier ran to the stables. A minute later, he mounted his horse.

No, he must not talk to this woman ever again. So, he galloped away from the castle, not daring to look back. His departure was noted by only one, a maiden with red hair who sullenly watched his departure from her chamber high above.

*

The maintenance of his army brought Petronius back to the castle often. He and Elen met frequently, if only briefly, and he remained tongue-tied in her presence. One day, after an interview with the king, she intercepted him in the portico of the castle.

"Your Highness, Princess Elen."

She laughed. "One appellation will be sufficient, general. And how are you today?"

"Fine."

In their meetings she had noticed he always turned to show only the right side of his face. Today she would play a game with him. She quickly stepped sideways to face his left side. He turned quickly, keeping her to the right. Slightly crouched like a hunter, she slowly circled the man to get to his other side, a smile on her face. He frowned, circled with her to prevent it. As she played her game, she peppered him with questions to distract him. Answering tersely, he continued the tireless positioning. Members of the court stopped to watch the spectacle. Seeing they were being watched, Elen stopped—forced once again to fix on the right side of his face.

Exasperated, she asked, "Why won't you ever let me see your left side, Petronius?"

He stared off in the distance and sighed before turning to face her.

"That side is scarred, your Highness."

She paled while her hand moved to her mouth.

"Oh, General, please forgive me. I had no idea. I would never..."

Now, it was Elen who was tongued-tied. She grabbed him by the arm and pulled him into a hallway which suffered little traffic. She faced him head on and slowly raised her hand to the left side of his face. He pulled away, but she shook her head and looked intently into his eyes. He braced himself for her touch as her fingers stroked his face, gently caressing the long, white gash. Not moving but clearly unsettled, Petronius closed his eyes tightly.

"You mustn't be ashamed of this scar, Petronius. It is part of you."

She stopped her actions and waited for him to open his eyes.

"I am so sorry I embarrassed you. I had no idea that you were so sensitive about your scar. I was playing a silly game and not thinking of your feelings."

Her beautiful face showed a visage he never seen— concern for him. Her eyes started to fill with tears. She turned away mumbling, "Forgive me."

Petronius was quiet for a few moments as he watched her wipe her eyes.

"I'm fine, Elen. There is nothing to forgive."

She blew her nose in a most un-princess-like manner, then turned to look at him. Cocking her head quizzically, a smile returned to her face.

"So, have we finally dispensed with 'her Highness'?"

He laughed for the first time in her presence and her smile widened.

They walked together to the stable.

"And how is the Great Black, General? Still strong and fast?"

One of his men brought the steed out and Petronius affectionately rubbed the great beast's ear.

"Yes, strong and fast and intelligent. More than once, he turned me away from death."

She patted the horse and rubbed his sleek black hair.

"You are a good horse, Black." She stared directly into the eyes of the animal. "Thank you for serving us and saving your master."

As Elen pressed her cheek against the horse's neck, he watched her stroke the horse's side, gliding softly over his many scars as she had so recently done the same for his.

"I will tell you a secret, Princess, but you must not repeat it to anyone. Indeed, if I share this secret with you, only three will know it."

She nodded her head eagerly and placed her hand over her lips. Petronius smiled at her gesture as he spoke.

"All refer to him as the Great Black, but that is not his name."

The tall man looked at his horse lovingly.

"He is Mirus, m'lady. Mirus. It is my name for him, spoken only when we are alone."

Balanced on her tiptoes, she hugged the horse's neck. Mirus closed his eyes and nuzzled her shoulder.

"Mirus," she whispered in his ear. Then she turned to Petronius. "Who is the third party to the secret?"

He smiled and pointed to the horse. They laughed as Mirus whinnied.

A few weeks later, while inspecting the armaments in the castle, he turned and almost collided with one of the Princess' maids running between ministers, soldiers, and common citizens in the crowded hallway.

"Pardon, sir. I be seeking you. The Princess, sir. In her chambers."

Petronius, head down, walked as though he was going to the gallows. A man who had faced death countless times and led men into battle was now petrified. Talking to her in the hallways was difficult, but possible; indeed, their last conversation was quite enjoyable, thought Petronius. In her rooms... alone. No, his tongue was twisting nervously already. She knew the effect she had on him. She was deliberately embarrassing him. With warriors, fear became anger in a heartbeat. The closer the pair came to the Princess' rooms, the stronger his resentment. How dare she drag him from his appointed tasks! He was the army's general, the defender of the Mercia!

The door opened, he stepped in. She sat by the window, looking out, huddled under a white wrap. She stared out across the valley, toward Cross Fell Mountain. She looked up; a weary smile fought through a face heavy with worry and fatigue.

"Thank you for coming, General," she said weakly. "Please sit down," she requested, pointing to a chair across from her.

"I'd rather stand, your Highness."

Princess Elen cocked her head, puzzled. She sighed and stood up.

"As you wish, General." Closer to him now, he saw tears in her eyes.

"What I have to say to you must stay between us, General. You are the only man in this court whom I trust and the only man, I think, who might help. May I count on your discretion and your assistance?" She stood before him, hands unfolded, beseeching.

Noting her obvious distress, his icy anger had quickly melted, replaced by the iron-willed devotion of a friend and protector.

"You have that and more, my Princess."

The Princess smiled her appreciation. "May we sit?" she asked hopefully.

"By all means," answered Petronius, the General of the Army, and the defender of Mercia.

The princess looked out the window as a cloud momentarily blocked the sunlight, casting a pall over the room. Turning to face him, eyes now brimming with tears, she began choking back sobs as she talked.

"I have a man servant… who supplies the castle with fresh fruit and other condiments. He is a kind man and has always spoiled me… by bringing me the sweetest fruit he plucks from the orchards or gardens. A few days ago, he gave me a red, most delicious apple. I told him… I told him it was the best I had ever tasted. He got it from a traveling peddler who claimed it came from Cross Fell Mountain. He is simple in the head, General, and he decided to go there himself to retrieve more. He was caught, Petronius, by the King's men." She put her head in her hands and wept.

Cross Fell Mountain was cursed by King Cearl ever since his unsuccessful hunt for the white deer a few years before. His precious arrow lost somewhere on that miserable plateau, he forbade any of the general population to set foot on the offending mountain. Until the deer was slain or the arrow found by his ever-searching, ever-growing band of huntsmen, the mountain was off-limits to peasant, merchant, adventurer, and even castle staff, upon penalty of imprisonment. More than a few curious peasants were already locked up in the dark, damp dungeon below the castle. Now it seemed one more would be added to the unfortunate group.

"Have you talked to the King?"

"Yes," she sniffed, "But he is unmoved by words…" She continued with a wry laugh, "…or tears." She dabbed her eyes with a scarf. The princess looked out the window at the mountain, far away.

"Ever since Cearl visited that accursed mountain to kill the white deer, he has changed."

"Then I will reason with the king."

"You know him, Petronius. When he sets his mind, no one can move him."

The General continued in a firm voice.

"Hark to what I say, Elen. You just have to make sure the reason's good enough to change his mind. I possess those reasons. Trust me."

Like his men, she felt inspired by his firm, confident demeanor. Hope replaced despair.

"I do trust you, Captain." She laughed at the mistake she made with his title. "Apparently I still see you as the man who patiently put up with me as a child and who was always there to care for me whenever I stumbled and fell; my apologies, General Petronius. You have more important duties now than handling a silly princess."

For a moment his brown eyes locked onto her green ones. Love can sometimes be read in a stare, but both were too new at the game to see the obvious in each other. After a few seconds, both looked away, equally embarrassed.

The General broke the uneasy silence. "Tell me, what is the servant's name?"

"He goes by Songor."

"Songor. All right. I will talk to the King."

With that said, he rose abruptly and left.

As Petronius walked toward the great hall, he thought about what he must do to save an innocent man. His position as general was his only bargaining chip. Now he was ready to play it, but not just because of the princess. Since his return he well noted the fear and despair that pervaded the kingdom

I have been silent too long.

The great hall was not as busy as it was a year earlier when Petronius had returned from the Northlands. Cearl slouched in his throne and watched Petronius stride into the room. Slightly disheveled and without smile or greeting, the King told the servants and guards to leave. He brought his goblet of red wine to his lips and looked over its edge at the General.

"My able General, so seldom do you visit. Business or pleasure?"

"Business, sire."

"How sad for me. I miss my old friend. You taught me the sword, remember?" The King laughed. "Do you recall the time I bested you with the sword, right before the war with the Angles? You taught me well, Petronius, perhaps too well. We crossed swords for well over an hour that day, practicing and playing. Then it became more serious. We both knew that it was going to be more than a lesson, didn't we?"

Petronius well remembered that day.

As though he was watching an enemy warrior, Petronius kept his eyes on the King.

"Rather an unsightly mark I left on you, dear fellow."

"Sire," Petronius said, "you are the best swordfighter in the land. Better than me, at least."

"Yes, Petronius, better than you." He glared at his general. Then he put down his goblet and smiled.

"But, let's return to... business," he slurred.

As he sat back comfortably on the throne, his hands hanging languidly on the arms of the chair, he maintained eye contact with his former teacher.

"What is so important that you summon your King to an interview?"

The man was drunk and angry, thought the General. This had to be done carefully or he would not only lose his influence with the King, he may lose his rank as well. Indeed, he could even end up beside poor Songor in the dungeon. Just stating facts, he related the story the princess had shared with him.

"Seems you have more connections with the royal family than your job description suggests, General Petronius. I had no idea that you were a confidant of my sister," the King parried.

Looking straight into his dark eyes, Petronius' riposte was quick. "Sir, I am not a confidant of your sister. Your father assigned me as her protector years ago, and in that capacity, she sought me out."

Cearl smiled slyly. "Of course, General. You acted only as her friend."

"Yes, your highness. As I am your friend as well, I trust."

The King smiled as he looked at his general. He picked up the goblet again and brought it to his lips, slowly sipping the red wine, studying the general. It was time for a feint.

"This is a messy business with that servant. On one hand, I would like to make an exception to placate my sister. But, if I show weakness just for her silly whims, then others, more powerful, may presume upon me in ways overstepping...their job descriptions. That would make things nasty, wouldn't it, General?"

Indeed, it's getting nasty now, thought Petronius. Perhaps he should concede this match of words and retreat until another day, when the King was sober. No, just as the swordfight long ago went too far and had to be finished, so had he now gone too far with this battle of words. But this fight he would win.

"I would not call a man's imprisonment, a silly whim, sire."

"That is where we differ, General," the king responded coldly.

His head lunged a bit toward his king.

"This man did no great wrong except to favor your sister with a piece of fruit from Cross Fell Mountain. Foolish? Yes. Criminal? No. Sir, in all matters have I served you. I do this out of loyalty and respect for your wise and considerate leadership."

The King nodded, accepting the flattery easily as all men in power do.

"One of your decisions was to place me at the head of your army. I presume you did this because you thought me an able leader."

The King nodded again.

"I believe you are a just ruler, but putting this man in the dungeon is not just. The penalty does not fit the crime. Have him serve in the army, away from eyes, ears, and tongues in the city. I will make a soldier out of him far away so that he can serve you on the battlefield. You gain three things by doing this: the gratitude of your sister, a new soldier, and...." The King's face darkened.

"And?" the King demanded in a voice devoid of any passion, his eyes boring into the General's.

"And you retain your general." Petronius met his stare and refused to look away.

Just as in the swordfight so many years ago, both men knew a real fight was upon them, an even more deadly one than the battle they fought years before with swords. The King said nothing for a minute, his eyes locked with those of the general.

Finally Cearl's face erupted into a great smile.

"A brilliant solution, Petronius. I can make my sister happy and not appear weak to those who would want to undermine my rule. The dungeons are overcrowded so we can relieve that stress a bit. Once again, you have done both our country and me a great service. Thank you."

The King stood up and wrapped his arm around the General's shoulder, walking him slowly to the door.

"Make the necessary arrangements, my worthy General. Take the poor man out of the prison. The guards will undoubtedly come running to me afterwards, but I will set them straight, be assured of that."

He finished the meeting by saying, "Go, now, my General, and free us from injustice."

Petronius left. As the door closed behind him, the King's smile disappeared. He learned two things from Petronius: he was in love with his sister and, more importantly, the man was now more a danger than an asset. He dared to use his position to compromise the King's authority!

Popular as Petronius was, it would be difficult to remove him from the army.

Later that evening while he still pondered the problem, a guard from the dungeon hurriedly informed the King that the General had removed the newest prisoner.

The King looked shocked and slammed his fist upon the table, frightening the messenger. "How dare he? I will certainly talk with him about it."

The guard bowed and hastily retreated from the great room.

After he left, the King smiled again. Not only was he a better swordsman than Petronius, he also was better at castle politics than the naïve general. Within minutes the busy mouths would be chirping about how Petronius overstepped his bounds in taking a convict out of prison. That should temper his popularity a bit, thought Cearl. A few more mistakes like that one and the King might just solve his problem most easily. He would just have to be patient.

After he freed Songor from the dungeon, Petronius reported back to the concerned princess.

"I left him with one of my captains. By now he should be fitted with a uniform and on a horse to Port Logan. I have a reliable group of men there. They will hide and train him. He will be safe, I promise you."

Tears of gratitude welled in her eyes. She knew full well what this must have cost the General. Bowing her head, she whispered, "I don't know how I can ever repay you for this kindness."

"You're...er...no trouble..." he replied, his tongue once again having lost its abilities. Without his voice as an ally, his eyes retreated to the floor. "Is that all, my Lady?"

Hoping the conversation might have gone farther, she sighed and said, "Yes, General. And thank you again."

After leaving the princess, the General admonished himself. Why did he keep punishing himself? This was not a romance. This was simply an officer fulfilling his duty. That is how she sees it, you old fool!

*

A year passed. Petronius and Elen met officially a few times, but she no longer detained him with conversation. Worried she had hurt her friend with flirtations regarding his scar and weighed down with the knowledge he gave up so much to secure Songor's release, she behaved in a strictly proper manner. Petronius interpreted the growing distance between them as a natural process. Clearly she had grown weary of him. A number of young nobles from adjacent realms visited Cearl, but most of their attention was directed toward the beautiful red-haired princess.

Meanwhile other problems surfaced for the General. He knew the King was paranoid about the power he held and, more to the point, the power he didn't hold. In particular, he was alarmed by the growing influence of the church of Jesus. His strongest followers worshipped the old gods of war, not this new god of peace. The church was also blackened by its association with the White Deer. So, it was no surprise he restricted the activities of the church. Petronius was shocked, late one night, when he found out how ruthless the King was in dealing with the new church.

"General...General." The captain gently shook the sleeping man. Petronius groggily rested on his arm, looking at the man.

"Sir, I thought you should know. The Baron and his men surrounded the convent during the night. They just broke down the door, and there are screams coming from inside."

Petronius jumped out of bed, shouting orders to the men within earshot. In just a few minutes, a dozen horses were galloping out of the camp, Mirus and Petronius far ahead of the group. In their dust followed hundreds of foot soldiers, trotting at a demanding pace.

He and his men galloped straight to the temple. Jumping from his horse, Petronius pushed through the Baron's guards at the door and started ejecting the disorganized militia scattered throughout the temple. Down one hall, he witnessed one of the Baron's men roughly handling one of the nuns. Grabbing the man by his tunic, he tossed him down the hall. As he continued moving toward Mother Hebron's office, he yelled over his shoulder for one of his men to escort the weeping woman out of the convent.

When he reached the inner sanctum, he heard a noise. Looking inside the door, he saw the heavy form of the Baron covering one of the maidens. Grabbing him by the collar of his tunic, he roughly pulled him off. The General faced the Baron. Angered to the point of killing the man, the most he allowed himself was a gratifying punch at the smirking face. The Baron fell, clutching his broken nose, trying to stanch the bleeding.

The Baron and his men were pushed outside. The General gave orders to his men and then he took the woman whom the Baron had raped to the only safe place he knew, the rooms of Princess Elen.

Meeting Elen in this way was different than before. She was his ally now, a confidant. He spoke freely and easily, then left to secure safe passage for the girl.

Perhaps this would be the last brutal act of Cearl. His madness centered around the White Deer. By throwing out the Christians, he had effectively destroyed the cult of the White Deer. Petronius hoped for change, but was not optimistic.

Returning to the city a few weeks later, the general rounded a bend and almost ran headlong into a white horse carrying a purple-cloaked rider. As he calmed the great horse, the dust settled and Petronius looked over to the other rider, making sure he was not unseated. At that moment, the rider turned to face him and threw back the hood, unveiling long red hair. He paused, his heart pounding both in fear of having hurt her and having her so close to him.

"Princess Elen, my apologies."

Finally gaining control of her horse, she laughed. "Do you always ride so fast, Petronius, or are you on some special mission?"

"No...I mean yes," he sputtered. There it was again: his inability to speak to her. He paused and took a deep breath, his eyes never leaving her face, drinking in the vision like a man dying of thirst. Slowly, speaking his words carefully, he answered. "What I mean is, no, I am not on any mission; I am just returning to camp. And, yes, I do ride this fast, at least when returning to the castle."

"And why is that? Are you so eager to see the King?" she queried with a twinkle in her eye.

"No. The King and I rarely speak. I have too often suggested he take a more lenient course. My counsel is rarely requested and never heeded."

Her face lost its mirth as her green eyes fixed on him and tears welled in her eyes. "I am the reason for the rift between you two. I am so sorry I brought this upon you, dear friend."

Dear friend, he mused. At least I have that, he thought with sad resignation.

"You mean the trouble with Songor? No, that is only a small part of the problem. The huntsmen, the new laws, the terrible manner in which he handled the Jesus people...I could go on, but those alone are enough. It was different years ago. We were fighting for our survival, he and I..." He stopped himself and put his head down, recalling a past when the future looked so much brighter than the present. "That seems so long ago and so much has changed."

Tacitly they rode towards the city in the cool shade of the tree-lined road; both were quiet. She broke the silence and murmured, "I like it when you talk with me, Petronius."

Petronius, who had been stealing glances at her, thought for a moment. "Sometimes I find it difficult to be around you."

The princess looked at him. "If it is difficult, it is because of the way I acted. I am sorry for seeming cold or acting silly, General. I have always had the greatest regard for you."

She added in a choked voice, "I just haven't shown my regard for you."

"Regard? What do you mean by it?"

The conversation, so much desired by her, was now going too far. If she spoke again, she would surely regret her words. The frustration of these last two years, being so close yet so far from him, trumped cautious judgment. Her eyes filled with tears as she stopped her horse and turned toward him.

"I mean, General...these months have been hard on me. I missed you greatly. I mean...I mean..." Whispering, not daring to look at him, she confessed her deepest feelings. "I mean...I love you."

Shocked, Petronius pulled Mirus back.

Her head turned quickly, seeing his reaction. A hand went to her lips.

"Oh, what have I done?"

She spurred her horse forward and galloped off towards the castle.

Petronius was dumbfounded. She loved him! He leaned forward and Mirus knew immediately what to do. In half a moment the two were one, galloping after the princess. Within seconds he caught up with her and grasped the bridle of her horse. He guided them to a grove of maple trees.

Dismounting Mirus, he stood beside the princess, her hands still covering her face, sobbing. His hands about her waist, he gently lifted her down to the ground. She kept her face hidden, but the crying stopped as her body heaved with great gulps of air. Gently he pulled her hands away.

"Open your eyes, Elen."

Her eyes cautiously opened and through the film of her tears, she stared into his eyes. His hand went to caress her cheek. She pulled away, but he shook his head and gently touched her face. He didn't need to say anything. She realized then his eyes had been speaking to her all along.

"Oh, Petronius!" And she fell into his arms.

He pulled her close again and they kissed, softly and for a long time. Mirus looked on. He whinnied, trying to get their attention. Their lips reluctantly separated, but they remained embraced, her head on his chest, both turned to the great stallion. The horse nodded his head and whinnied again suggesting a wisdom they lacked far too long.

*

Cearl detected the subtle change in the relationship. With hooded eyes, he watched the interaction between the two lovers. He worried about this possible union of sister and General.

Only the army was outside the full control of the King. Most of the soldiers were devoted to Petronius, and the general population nearly worshipped the man. Despite that and, indeed, because of that, Cearl believed he must be removed. But how?

One night while alone and brooding in the great hall, Cearl hit upon a plan. Devious in design, its goal utterly evil, it particularly delighted the King.

The treaty which Petronius had secured with the Northlanders created a lucrative trade between the two countries. But there were a few farmers who grumbled about the occasional encroachment of the horses and cows on some of their fields.

Amplifying these complaints in a meeting with his vassals, Cearl easily gained a decree stating the Northlanders had broken the treaty. Consequently, the King declared, the grasslands were once again off-limits to the Northlanders. The announcement confused and stunned the general population and angered the Northlanders. The clouds of war were once again forming between the two countries.

Cearl considered how Petronius might react to this crisis. If the Northlanders resumed their raids to secure the grasslands, then something had to be done by the general. But what? The king knew the general was a reluctant warrior, choosing battle and death only as a last resort. Indeed, he might refuse to march into Northland. The king smiled as he rubbed his hands together. Then the General would be branded a coward and insubordinate. Cearl could imprison him without annoying objections from nobles or common folk.

Or he might try to quell the war cries from the north by trying to broker a compromise. That would be best, contemplated the King. The Northlanders were not a forgiving people, and it was Petronius, after all, who promised the grasslands to the Northlanders. If he or any of his staff dared to venture into that rough country, they would most likely be killed. That was Cearl's most ardent wish: a dead Petronius could serve him well. It could be a provocation for a war of conquest.

Of course, the General could do the unthinkable... lead his men against a nation he should have defeated years ago. Even that act would tarnish his reputation.

No matter what, Petronius would no longer be the greatly admired General. In a few weeks he would be in prison, dead, or leading good men into an unpopular war.

The King laughed aloud at his clever plan, the sound echoing eerily through the empty chamber.

*

A day later, Petronius and Elen walked into the stables at the castle. The stable hands quickly retreated after Petronius frowned at them, one eyebrow raised.

"You mustn't go, Petronius." Elen's soft face pressed against his chest; she hugged him closer still as though the fierceness of her embrace alone could keep him from this folly.

In the absence of any response, she listened to his steady heartbeat. *Will I ever hear it again?*

"You know he wants you to go, don't you?"

Holding her tightly but tenderly, Petronius looked away and stared out the window, watching heavy gray clouds form, foreshadowing a storm. "Yes, I know. But, you've not seen war close up, my love. It's ugly business, I can tell you that. My men, Bruder's men, and others will die. If only I can stop this madness..."

"Then take the army with you; protect yourself."

He laughed. "You sound like one of my captains, years ago." He loosened her embrace, gently prying himself from her grip. "I think I know this man Bruder. I have a plan; it just might work."

Elen knew that his mind was made up. The prospect of war within weeks or perhaps days was weighing heavily on the country. Wiping away tears, she pressed into him. Putting her

143

hands on his chest and pushing up on her toes, she kissed his lips. Her eyes glistened with tears, but her voice was forceful.

"Promise me you will return."

He hesitated. He could see her neck muscles strain as she pulled on his tunic, bringing his head down just a bit.

"Promise me, Petronius! I can't bear life without you!"

"I can't, Elen. I can't."

The tall man, dressed in his general's uniform, walked quickly from her, not wanting to prolong their agony. With one fluid motion, he leaped onto Mirus and hurried the great beast down the path. She watched as he disappeared down the street, her tears now unabated.

*

Petronius rode through a rainstorm, rivulets of rain water on his face washing away his beloved's tears. His path: a straight line to the Northlands. News of his brave effort passed from noble to soldier to peasant.

Along the way, people came out to watch the General ride toward what most considered to be certain death. Shielded from the downpour, standing in the threshold of open doors, mothers wiped away tears while fathers hoisted young sons onto their shoulders to see the great man. Veterans who served under him offered to ride alongside him, willing to share his fate. Petronius shook his head and resolutely rode on through the rain and into the night.

The rains ceased as he entered the rich grasslands, now in grave dispute. Hours later, the sun high, he entered the dry, barren hills of Northland. He had already traveled this wide, sparse valley years ago with Thatcher. Unlike that time years ago, no brown-clothed sentinels marked his progress. As he emerged from the hills before twilight, he reached the jumble of huts that served as the capital. An angry, loud mob waited for him. He pushed through the growling crowd, ignoring the imprecations of the lean men and women about him. He stopped in front of the steps of Bruder's modest castle and stared at the King, surrounded by a field of brown tunics. Bruder's men glared at him with undisguised hatred, made more fearsome by the wild red designs that covered their faces. They were ready for war.

In stark contrast to his men, only a bushy black beard adorned the King's face, his eyes studying the tall man before him. The General didn't seem any older than the last time they met, but he was somehow different. He seemed more content. Bruder considered rumors he'd heard about Petronius and Mercia's Princess. She was sister to the King and that was bad, of course. Nonetheless, all reports from his spies in the south spoke of her good and kindly ways. That must be it, he thought. The man was in love! Yet Petronius, general of a powerful army, regaled by his countrymen as a hero, was willing to throw it all away to come here. A strange man, thought Bruder.

After Petronius dismounted, Bruder spoke loudly so that all could hear.

"So, the great Petronius deigns to visit our humble land. Look around you, Petronius. Do you see fatted cows and strong horses? No? Ah, that is because the grasslands have been taken from us. The grasslands you promised, Petronius. Hah! A sham! What do you seek now, great General? Do want to take the food off our plates and have us starve as well?"

"We must talk, King Bruder."

Bruder flashed a smile and pointed at the man before him.

"The great Petronius wants only to talk! Our food is safe!" Laughter followed.

"Then talk, great Petronius."

"We must talk alone, Bruder."

The crowd grumbled, enjoying the exchange. Bruder looked at Petronius, debating whether to slay him outright or listen to him first. The man was a living contradiction, he thought.

Then crossing his hands abruptly, he glared at his people.

"Silence!"

He angrily surveyed the crowd, his eyebrows high and eyes wide, daring anyone to complain. The crowd, which moments before had been bubbling with an undercurrent of restlessness, was silent. Bruder turned and walked toward the castle gates as Petronius followed.

Seated on a rickety chair in a large room, Petronius waited until the servants finally left them alone. Checking over his shoulder to make sure no one was behind him, he carefully explained to Bruder that the King alone was responsible for this heinous decision.

"Think Bruder, why would he do this? Why would he bring our two countries to war again?"

"Because he is a foolish man?"

"He is no fool. He has brought hundreds of mercenaries into the country, under the flag of the Huntsmen. They do his bidding and in the most brutal way. He has increased the size of the Royal Guard, against my advice, I might add. He cowed the nobles such that none dare to question his decisions. If he demands their militia, they will most certainly obey. If he says "to war", he can easily marshal over five times the forces you faced before. He is no fool, Bruder."

"We would all fight him to the death...man, woman, and child."

Petronius sighed, momentarily closing his eyes.

"That is exactly what I am trying to prevent...your extermination and the needless death of so many of my soldiers."

But the King would have none of it. He stood up and walked around the room, expostulating, angrily punctuating words with his finger.

"You promised me the grasslands...you, Petronius. And on your word, I agreed to peace."

Petronius looked straight at the King, absorbing his wrath without changing his expression.

"You are right. But I can't change what the King has done. I can only try to prevent needless bloodletting."

Silent for a few seconds, Bruder's darkening face conveyed his growing frustration.

"What do you offer to secure this peace?"

"Very little."

"What do you offer, Petronius?"

"Just my advice to beware of war, Bruder."

"You are the fool! That is nothing! Something must be given to us. You broke the treaty, man. What do you have to offer? What, Petronius? You must have something!"

Petronius was quiet.

Bruder looked at him and then realized the truth, his eyes widening.

"You came here to offer yourself, didn't you? To sacrifice your life for peace."

Seconds passed as the two men stared at each other, one impassively, one in wonder.

Strange, strange man, this Petronius. Willing to give up so much. But why?

"All right, general. Perhaps your blood can quench our thirst for war. As you may have already guessed, my people don't like you very much. It is possible your death might satisfy them." He called for his guards. "Take him to the prison house."

Before he was led away, Bruder faced the General. "Sleep well, great Petronius, for tomorrow I will kill you."

With that said the King walked off and Petronius was led to the prison house.

In the single room hut, crudely constructed of large rocks roughly fit together, well outside the castle, Petronius wearily sat down on the ground and waited.

Night, as it often does, conjures memory while it diminishes hope. He weakened. Perhaps he could still sneak out. Slowly, softly he crept to the door. Amazingly, it was not secured. He opened it a crack and looked outside. There was no guard visible in the dim, gray moonlight. To his amazement, he saw Mirus eating grass right beside the hut. He sensed a trap. He watched a long time for some motion. After an hour, he realized no one was watching nor guarding him. Bruder knew no one could catch him once he was atop Mirus. The King was giving him a way out. All he had to do was mount his horse and gallop off. But, if he left, what chance would there be for peace? Petronius slumped in the center of the cell. When he closed his eyes, he saw Elen.

Two soldiers came for him late in the morning and he was escorted to the front of the castle. There he was led through a crowd of natives, talking, laughing, and sharing beer and cheese, as they looked at him with curled lips. The guards escorted him to the King on the castle steps. Bruder was now formally attired, wearing a long brown robe, rimmed with a faded yellow band. A crown, with a few jewels missing, was on his head, his black hair sticking out wildly and his beard matching that same wildness. When Petronius reached the King, high on the steps, the crowd quieted. The guards turned him around to face the mass of people. He heard Bruder begin his speech behind him.

"Here stands before you Petronius, General of Mercia. Years ago, he was our sworn enemy, killer of our good men."

The crowd angrily jeered.

The King raised his hands to quiet the mob. "But the war ended and he gave us peace. And we believed him, didn't we?"

The people yelled their agreement. Some shook their fists angrily at the General who stood ramrod straight and looked out over the crowd to the distant hills whence he came, his face holding no expression.

Bruder waited for the noise to settle down. Then he walked down the steps and strolled among them, the people opening up to let him pace.

"Then what happened? The treaty was reneged on by the Mercians."

His hand went to chin as if pondering a thought.

"Yet, Petronius came to us unarmed, unprotected. Do you see his army at his side? Did he come here armed with a sword?" Confused, the crowd murmured "no".

"I think this a brave act."

Some in the crowd agreed with the King. A shout rang out. "Murderer!"

The source of the accusation was a gray-haired woman standing a few rows back. As the King walked towards her, men stepped aside.

"Yes, he killed and directed others to kill." Bruder spoke to her but all could hear. "As I did too, old woman... I killed and ordered others to be killed, if you remember."

He continued, his hand on her shoulder. "War is an odd thing. Men kill other men with whom they could have shared mead. Mothers lose their children, as you lost yours. Yet when some of the prisoners were starving in the pen, you fed them, didn't you, mother?" She put her head down.

He shook his head up and down, staring at her.

"Yes, you did, old woman, I saw you. And after your son was killed. As I said, war is an odd thing."

Then he cast his gaze upon the people who now surrounded him, and yelled into the crowd.

"So many things confuse me," he admitted. "Did you know the decision to go back on this treaty was not his? King Cearl alone has done this evil thing."

"Yet who comes to stop the war? The nobles? The King?"

There was absolute quiet.

"Without the protection of his army, without a sword by his side, he comes to us to stop a war Mercia would win."

There were some protests regarding this last statement. The King let the protestations die down, with eyes closed, his head shaking slowly left and right. "Oh, yes, my people. We would lose. Mercia has many more warriors, better fed horses, and an arsenal far deeper than ours. They would win; make no mistake about that. But here comes this man, knowing his country would win and probably enslave us, yet he comes to stop the war. Why?"

Bruder squinted his eyes and rubbed his chin once more.

"This is the question that I have asked myself again and again...why would he do this foolish thing? Coming here, knowing that we may kill him. It is very hard to understand."

He shook his head, then shrugged.

"I'll tell you a secret, my people, known only to a few of my most trusted warriors. My orders last night were to let him escape."

There was a roar of disapproval.

"I know, I know, I shouldn't have done that. But I wanted to test him. He was not guarded. His horse, the swift Black was right by his hut. He could have escaped. But he didn't." Here he paused again. Then he looked at the crowd and asked, "Why would he not flee, knowing death awaits him in the morning?"

Bruder walked up to the woman who, moments before, called Petronius a murderer. "I think I know." He then looked directly at the old woman; as he spoke he seemed to be speaking only to her, but he was heard by everyone. "Because he wants no more sons dying needlessly." The woman returned his stare.

The King returned to the steps and stood beside Petronius.

"I don't know what you see before you. A murderer? Maybe. A great warrior? Unquestionably. But, let me tell you what I see."

With one hand on the shoulder of the prisoner he said, "I see not a nobleman, a lackey of Cearl. No, what I see is a noble man."

He looked at his people and then raised his voice. "We all want vengeance for our starving animals. Starving because of a broken treaty. But how much food will be gained by killing this man? None. Killing this man won't bring back our dead..."

Silence.

"Ah, what do we lose? Only this one man, this brave, noble man who comes to us to help, at risk of his own life..."

Then shaking his head, eyes closed, and waving his hand as if to brush away a fly, he sighed.

"But, I speak too long on this matter. He has been condemned to die. Only the people can overturn such a fate. So, it is up to you my people. Let me hear what you desire."

He walked down the steps pulling Petronius by the arm. Stopping in front of the woman, he said, "What say you, mother? Do we kill this man?"

She looked at Petronius and saw the scar marring his otherwise handsome features and the lines of worry etched on his face. His eyes looked off in the distance, still showing no fear, no concern, no acknowledgement his life was hanging in the balance.

"No," she whispered as her head dropped.

"I'm sorry, mother. I didn't hear you."

"No!" She repeated more loudly, glaring at the King.

"But, you called him a murderer."

"No. No! No!"

As Bruder scanned the crowd, pointing from one to another, the same answer came back..."No". He stopped, raising his arms in question to the crowd. The same murmured reply came back to him.

Surrounded by his people, Bruder turned to the General. "We commute your sentence, great Petronius. But, as is our custom, you are shunned from this land. Return to it at penalty of death. Tell your King we will not graze our animals on the land given to us years ago nor will we raid that land. We seek no war."

Bruder left him alone in the midst of the crowd. In an instant, his horse was at his side. Petronius mounted and slowly made his way through the Northlanders back to his home.

As he returned through North Mercia, the people watched, waved; some ran out to touch him. There would be no war; Petronius had achieved a miracle. When the news reached Tamworth, the nobles met and without advice or consent from Cearl, sent the General a note of thanks for his efforts on behalf of a grateful nation.

The King was not quite as happy as the rest of his countrymen. In one of the darker recesses of the great hall where no outside light penetrated, he paced back and forth growling under his breath about this unforeseen turn of events. Instead of weakening Petronius, he had only made him stronger, even more of a threat. How could he rid himself of this man?

Cearl's great problem was solved not by evil machinations, but simply by the love of man for a woman. The day after his return, Petronius formerly requested Elen's hand in marriage from her brother, the king. He also gave the marriage as an excuse to resign as general. Cearl's response was quick. He kissed his sister and hugged his future brother-in-law. An hour later, he led them to the balcony overlooking the courtyard. There, his arms linked with each of theirs, he announced the betrothal and resignation of the General. All three smiled to the cheering crowd.

The two were married within a month, with all the pomp of a state wedding. As a wedding present, the King gave them a large house with a retinue of servants just outside the walls of Port Logan, far from the hub of power. Of course, the staff he appointed would report to him about any visitors, conversations, and strange purchases. Elen insisted Songor be added and Cearl reluctantly approved.

As days turned into weeks and weeks into months, the King realized Petronius had no designs on the throne. The General, once greatly feared by both armies and kings, was now battling weeds and pests as he struggled to make his modest gardens grow.

No longer tongue-tied with Elen, he talked with her whenever he came in from the fields. A picnic under the great oak tree in their front yard sparked memories of his boyhood and he rambled on about the visits to the woods outside the walls of Tamworth. While resting in the sitting room, servants scurrying about, he sometimes related his experiences on the battlefield. Elen's grip around his arm tightened as he casually described near death scenarios, so common in his past life.

After supper, in the cool of the evening, she read him stories about the heroes and maidens of the past, their adventures keeping him on the edge of his chair, intently listening to every word. Sometimes he would simply watch her, marveling over her sublime beauty. He was intoxicated with her nearness; his face perpetually bore a silly smile.

But there was sadness as well. For a year they had been trying to have a child, but Elen could not get pregnant. Sometimes he witnessed a melancholy demeanor when she gently stroked babies' soft faces. In the darkest part of the night, when she thought him asleep, he heard her cry softly. It ripped him as no sword ever could.

Cearl visited often, bringing presents for both Petronius and Elen. He would always ask when he was to be an uncle. Elen would answer with lowered eyes, and Petronius would tell him, "soon".

One bright fall afternoon, Elen greeted her husband and showered him with kisses as she pulled him into their home and shut the door, the servants sent away for a holiday. Walking backwards up the stairs while holding his gaze, she led him into the bedroom, and closed the door. After they made love she told him that she was pregnant. Overjoyed, he tenderly brought her to him. Again they enjoyed the private dance of love.

The next day Cearl happened to be visiting and he asked when he was to be an uncle. Her eyes beaming, she clasped her hands together, and cried, "Very soon, brother, very soon".

Cearl insisted his own physician tend to her during the pregnancy and even procured an excellent midwife who counseled and attended her daily. The presence of the midwife turned out to be a godsend to the young woman as the pregnancy was unusually difficult. Despite the frequent pain, Elen always managed to smile. She tried to keep up with her few duties, but the midwife wisely counseled her to relax and rest.

A few weeks before Pen's birth, Elen experienced excruciating pain lasting for a day or two, followed by relief for a few days. The cycle kept repeating itself. Both midwife and doctor assured her that this was normal, but the anxious husband noted the glances shared when Elen looked away. His continual attention to her and his own fears caused his personal hygiene to suffer as his clothes were rarely changed. Often he forgot to shave and a rough beard formed over his face.

Pen's delivery into the world was difficult. When contractions started in the afternoon, a nervous husband immediately sent for the doctor. The baby was twisted sideways in the birth canal making a normal delivery impossible. The doctor did not come, so the able midwife did what she could do to secure the successful birth of the child. Pen came into the world complaining loudly. The mother lay bleeding profusely and very pale.

Though she knew life was ebbing away from her, the smile did not leave her as she watched her sleeping son. It was she who named her son, Penda, the same name as Petronius' father. She looked over to her husband, lying beside her, knowing he would be a good and gentle father.

A few hours after the birth, greatly fatigued, her smile finally departed as she kissed the baby on the forehead. The once beautiful face was now drawn and haggard. Her green eyes rose from her son to the father. Her voice was weak, but determined.

"Don't let Cearl hurt him. Keep Penda safe. Promise me, Petronius."

Tears in his eyes for the first time in his adult life, he nodded. Then with one final look at her child, her eyes closed and she slipped away.

Petronius sobbed and rolled to the floor still touching an arm of his beloved. The midwife hearing the commotion entered the room and gently pried the sleeping baby from the dead mother's arms. For an hour, he cried as the once warm arm turn cold. Then wiping his face dry, he looked at his beloved Elen one last time and stood.

At that moment Cearl burst into the room, purple robes flying behind him and wide-eyed, looking at the bed. The errant doctor followed. Seeing his sister prone on the bed, he cried out and rushed to grab her hand. Feeling it cold and seeing her lifeless, he retracted. She was his last link with sanity and now she was gone. Suddenly he pulled out his knife and plunged it into the heart of the doctor. He watched as the man slipped to the floor in a growing pool of blood.

"He claims that he was attending a sick friend and not at home. True or not, he pays the price for not being loyal to his King," Cearl said through clenched teeth. He turned to the Petronius. "The baby?" he inquired hopefully.

His grief now spent, Petronius viewed the King with obvious contempt. Surprisingly, he wasn't outraged by the murder he just witnessed. Indeed, he could have done it himself.

He stared coldly at his brother-in-law. "You planned this, Cearl. Acting like the loving brother, but waiting for a chance to hurt us. I have seen you do it too many times to others. As far as I am concerned, you killed Elen. Except for a promise made to my dear wife, I would kill you right here." With that he grabbed a gray cloak, went to the adjacent room where the midwife was caring for the baby, gently took the child from her, and left the house. Cearl, ironically blameless in this terrible matter, just sat in a chair looking at his sister's body. As the room grew darker, his heart grew colder.

Petronius called for the stable boy to retrieve his great warhorse. Astride Mirus, he walked the horse slowly from the barn, the stride of the horse gently rocking the child to sleep. His mind still on the tragic death of his wife, he wiped away more tears.

After he passed the gate to the estate, he heard hoof beats behind him. Fitting the sleeping infant inside his tunic, he pulled his sword and turned to face the rider. It was not the King, but Songor.

"Ye be needing help, sir, and I'm ye man," Said the portly servant-soldier.

"I need no help from you or anyone. Leave me and my son alone." "Sir, begging pardon, but I canst do that. I owe a debt to ye and a bigger un to the Princess…" The large man choked up. "And if I canst be let to help, sir," he continued sobbing and wiping his nose with his sleeve, "then you might as well use that sword on me right now." The tears, unchecked, rained down his face.

Petronius saw Songor's deep sorrow: his body racked with continual sobs, his head down. This man had always been respectful, almost reverent with his wife, always talking far too much to him (and everyone else who came within shouting distance); Songor was her most beloved servant. Petronius put his hand over his eyes, trying to fight back a new flood of tears. Successful, he passed his hand hard over his bearded face. Then he slowly replaced his sword and reached over to grab the man's arm. "All right, Songor. You come with us."

"Thank ye, sir." His voice still shaky from crying, he had regained some control as he trotted beside Petronius. Down the road, barely lit by the dawn of a new day, traveled the two men and baby.

CHAPTER 16

Now, on his porch, thirteen years later to the day, General
Petronius recalled his wife's words: "Keep Penda safe."

Well, he would, no matter what, even if he had to tear the
country apart. His sword hanging down from his side, he put a
hand on each man's shoulders. "Let's go inside, gentlemen. We
have plans to make."

Songor blustered as they walked into the living room. "Ye was
always a great planner, sir. 'Pon my word, you knew what the bad
guy was athinken 'fore he did. Then you…"

Petronius raised his hand to stop the chatter of his servant and
bade the two men to sit at the table across from him. He scratched
his face, somewhat itchy from the rough shave, and frowned.
"Well, let's first consider what our opponent has…" he began, "the
enemy has a well-fortified castle, approximately two thousand well
trained fighting men, five times that number if needed, the ability
to hide Pen anywhere, virtually limitless funds, and the knowledge
an attempt will surely be made to rescue him."

Both men nodded in agreement, waiting eagerly for the plan.

"While we," he continued, "have three old soldiers, two of whom are out of practice, and one who is considerably out of shape."

He looked at Songor with a frown.

"Have I fairly stated the strengths and weaknesses of both sides?"

Both men nodded, their eyes expectant.

"A plan won't suffice, gentlemen; we need a miracle!"

A quiet despair settled in the room. The general stared at the fire, thinking. Thatcher stared at the table, bewildered. Songor, his brow furrowed, looked right and left repeatedly, perplexed.

"What sort of miracle, sir?" asked Songor seriously. The other two looked at Songor who patiently waited for an answer. Thatcher shook his head and Petronius opened his mouth to explain, but gave up.

The old general turned to Thatcher. "The friends you have in the castle. Reliable?"

"Yes sir. There are a few who I can trust."

"I have one or two as well," replied Petronius with a smile.

"One, in particular, Astible, is still a captain, I hear. Impressive since the baron has put so many of his own in positions of power." Petronius said. He looked sideways and toward the ground, nodded, and returned his eyes to the men in front of him.

"Thatcher, tomorrow you will ride to Tamworth. Well, today as I see the sun is beginning to rise. I will give you a list of men, you gather yours as well. Most important, are they willing to help us? I mean with their swords and lives? Also we need information. First and foremost, where is Pen? How is he guarded? Finally, I need uniforms, as many as you can get us. Meet me back here in two days."

Thatcher left as Petronius turned to Songor.

"Ride into town. Any man who will ride with Larmack, enlist them. This is important... each must bring an extra horse. Also,

Songor, speak to no one that the general has returned. Keep it a secret. Two days, Songor. Bring the men and horses back in two days."

Songor didn't understand why Petronius wanted the horses, but he nodded in agreement. As far as keeping a secret, he could do that. He had for thirteen years. Yes, he could keep a secret. He lifted his great body out of the chair and stomped toward the door.

Songor lingered by the door, clearly unsure of himself.

The general saw the doubt in his eyes.

"What is it?"

"You sir, you will stay here?" Songor knew Petronius had always been a man of action, a man who led his army into battle, a man willing to take chances for others. And now with his son kidnapped... .

The general walked over to his devoted servant and grabbed his arm. "The passion is past me, dear friend. No, I won't stay here. The rescue is going to be tricky, though I am confident of our success. But I think it wise to make sure that we all live after we rescue my son. Now go."

Relieved of his worry, Songor galloped off towards the village while Petronius leaped onto Mirus and, as the sun broke over the fields, rode into Markwood forest.

At the same time, nearly a hundred miles away, Pen woke to a tickle on his lips and quickly brushed away a large insect. He jumped up and brushed off his entire body. The dim gray light illuminated far too many creepy-crawlers as they scurried towards the dark, raising the hair on the back of his neck.

The events of the last few days flooded his memory: the kidnapping by Eusibius, the long ride to the castle, his meeting with King Cearl, and being placed in the dungeon. He also remembered trying to stay awake.

How much time had passed, he wondered. It must have been at least a few hours as Pen was cold, damp, and hungry, very hungry.

Looking once again at his surrounding, he wondered whether he should continue protecting the white deer with his silence. If he shared the word with Cearl, would that really endanger the animal? Head in hands, he wished he could do just that, but he couldn't. Something was deeply wrong about the king's request. He couldn't state exactly what bothered him, but telling him felt so wrong.

CHAPTER 17

The fog sat heavy over Larmack's farm. The muffled sound of heavy thumping preceded the materialization of horses and men out of the swirling mist. Leaning forward on horses, eyes strained to find the familiar lines of house and barn, but those shapes had been swallowed by the fog. Twenty mounted men, each holding the reins of an extra horse, watched Songor penetrate the gray mass and disappear. Seconds later he emerged out of the fog, his face tense, his eyes darting right and left.

"No one be there."

In the opposite direction from Kirkwood, the road announced the stuttering hoof beats of more hard-riding equines, still obscured from sight. Songor and a few of the farmers drew swords as the rest of the men apprehensively looked up the road. Thatcher burst through the fog, two packhorses behind him.

"Where's your master?"

"Don't know, sir. We be back but seconds ago."

The men on horseback ambled to and fro, staying within clear sight of each other. All had one thought... if the King found out about this meeting, they would be trapped. All had one question, where was Larmack?

Another set of hoof beats was heard behind them. Horses and men turned. Just as they feared, a red tunic sliced through the haze. As the men turned their horses away, a voice arrested their retreat…a familiar voice…the voice of Larmack.

"Hold, friends!"

The farmers turned and saw a tall, confident officer with the voice of Larmack only.

"My apologies, gentlemen. My route took me a bit farther than yours."

The astonished villagers milled around the soldier who, upon close inspection, was indeed Larmack. Thatcher reported that Pen was in the dungeon, news which both worried and infuriated the father. He also said there were many troops still loyal to the general.

Thatcher took out his knife. With one smooth motion, he sliced through the rope that held the bundle on the back of the first horse he led; a pile of uniforms fell.

The man who was once Larmack smiled at the haphazard collection of red tunics and black pants.

"Good work, Thatcher. That should be more than enough for our purposes."

He wheeled Mirus around to face the farmers.

"Gentlemen, my real name is Petronius. My apologies for my disguise all these years. To protect my son, anonymity seemed best. Now, however, things have changed…"

All recalled the incident at the inn when the farmer had subdued the impudent soldier, Gorm. The strange incident a week earlier now made sense to the men.

"Let me explain my plan; we have no time to spare. Entering the castle under the cloak of darkness would be the most clever way to rescue Pen." The General's eyes seemed to lock on each man, making them feel as though he was focused directly on them. "Cearl is no fool. He will have more troops about at night. So we must rescue Pen during daylight when the chance of success is greater."

The men worriedly look at each other. Farmers against trained soldiers?

Petronius smiled.

"Don't worry, men. We will go in wearing the uniforms Thatcher was kind enough to gather. And it won't be a farmer saving his son, it will be a general requesting a prisoner."

Petronius continued. "The King has always been secretive. I am sure he has not told his soldiers why there is a heightened alert. They will watch for either a wild father demanding his son or a few peasants sneaking into the castle. Either way, the soldiers will be on the lookout for farmers, not soldiers."

"My officer's uniform still commands respect and I know how to give orders," Petronius said with a smile. "Some, like Thatcher, may even recognize me and that will work to our advantage. What we tell officials is that I have come to extract the prisoner to take him to the King. And I have a squad of how many?" He turned to Thatcher.

"Here and there, nearly forty, General."

"We won't need that many to accompany the likes of a "dangerous villain" like Pen. A squad of eight should suffice. Four soldiers from inside Tamworth and four others from this group. Once we extract Pen from the dungeon, we will simply march out of the city gates."

He selected Eldrick, Griswold, Songor, and Thatcher.

"I want you four to find uniforms in that pile to fit; Songor, just do your best."

Moments later, the transformation was complete. Alongside General Petronius stood four uniformed soldiers.

"Thatch, the other bag."

The short man leaned over to the second pack horse and knifed open a second bundle; more red uniforms fell to the ground.

"Now, the rest of you need to join the army."

The milled through the clothes, picking red tunics and black pants. Petronius discussed his plans as they dressed.

"Once we are safely outside the city walls with Pen, we will all meet by the edge of Tamworth forest where we will split up and head in different directions. Soon enough the King will figure things out. You five men," he motioned to the ones on his left, "will take your horses in the direction of Port Logan." He pointed to other clusters of men. "You take yours to the south toward Angles, and you towards the wasteland between Mercia and Wreocan. At intervals each of you will switch horses. The large number of tracks may confuse the soldiers. They will think there are more of you."

One of the farmers stepped toward the front of the group.

"Larmack, we came to help Pen. Why we be riding from you? Makes no sense."

Petronius darkened and his eyes narrowed, a piercing stare stopped the man from continuing. Then he sighed as he closed his eyes and slowly shook his head. These men weren't soldiers.

Patiently, he explained, "The King will follow us with his cavalry. What set of tracks do they follow? They will have to split up and that will make them fewer in number and more cautious which means they'll move more slowly. We need all the time we can get."

He looked at the man who was nodding with understanding.

"Once each of you has switched horses three times, mount the best of the horses and scatter the rest. Then meet up with the rest of us."

Another man interjected a question.

"Where would that be Larmack?"

"Oh, yes. Sorry. We will meet at the entrance to Markwood Forest."

"Then where do we go, Larmack?"

Petronius smiled.

"Why, right into Markwood Forest, of course."

The villagers nervously looked at each other.

"Think about it men. The one place that they would not expect us to enter into would be that forbidden forest."

"Larmack, I mean General Petronius, sir. There be good reason for that," offered Eldrick. "Them woods is haunted! And even if you get past the dark part where monsters lie, in the center be the green men, and they don't take kindly to strangers."

Others nodded their heads in agreement. Petronius tightly clenched his jaw. God help us, he thought, would these men ever take orders properly?

"Let me worry about Markwood. Just make your way there to meet us at the crossroads beyond the inn."

He paused a moment, studying the men who'd been his neighbors for over twelve years. *They are farmers, not soldiers. But they are brave and steadfast. My plan might just work.*

"Once we have cleared through Markwood Pen, Songor and I will travel to Northumberland. They have no love for Cearl and we will be safe. Probably safer than you men. My thanks to you."

He cleared his throat.

"From now on you are my soldiers. Songor and all of you: don't give a hello to anyone. Thatch and I will be the only ones talking inside or outside the castle. Understood?"

The men nodded in agreement.

"Now, let's go get my son."

CHAPTER 18

Petronius, dressed in his red uniform and gray cloak, entered the city with his squad. Guards at the gate unremittingly stopped wagons, riders, and walkers from entering or leaving the city as they checked for weapons, contraband, or hidden men. Clusters of patrolling soldiers passed through unchallenged, as did Petronius and his men. Once inside the gates, the group dismounted. Eldrick stayed with the horses.

Petronius, with deliberate smugness often associated with officers these days, looked at the people about him. Some wore robes, but their black boots gave them away as soldiers. Without being obvious, he noted the troops secreted on the rooftops, a bow occasionally sticking out. There were more safeguards in place than he had anticipated.

They stopped in front of the castle. At the top, by the door five more men waited. Seeing the General, their eyes widened and smiles appeared on otherwise stern faces.

After reaching the top of the stairs, he shook their hands. "Thank-you for your help, men. I am in your debt."

The tallest of the five, a gray-haired, wiry man who seemed more suited to a game of dice in front of a warm fire than a swordfight, replied, "I served under you in two wars, General, and I'm proud to serve you now. We all are." The other men nodded.

Petronius remembered this man.

"Thank you, John. Where are the others?"

"They stay here, General. Best we have men in the King's service so we can better know what he plans. But they are ready to leave if you need them, sir."

Petronius nodded, looking at the steady stream of soldiers, merchants, and ministers going up and down the stairs leading to the castle. His eyes rested on the soldier.

"John keep watch outside. I don't want any surprises when we return."

Turning to the rest of the men, he gave other instructions.

"We are going to get a prisoner from the dungeon, men, under the pretense of taking him to the King. Thatcher and I alone will speak."

The General walked quickly to the main door, his men following. Once inside busy hallway, his step did not change. Younger soldiers stepped aside, giving wide berth to the officer. But older soldiers looked on in astonishment, recognizing Petronius with his signature scar. They leaned toward one another, whispering, pointing, wondering.

The walkway to the dungeon angled downward and with every step, the darkness grew. An unsettling odor grew as they penetrated deeper into the dark, dismal surroundings. Finally, the bold little band reached a door with a grill mounted on it. A single torch illuminated it in the surrounding blackness. Thatcher pounded on it, and the grill slid back as a sweaty face came to the opening.

"Yeah. Whatta ya want?"

"Open this door under orders of the King!"

The man hurriedly inserted keys and the door groaned open. He stepped aside, unsuccessfully attempting to pull his trousers as they sagged below his ample waist. Another man, who lazily reclined on a cot, rose quickly. The uniforms of both were soiled and unkempt as was their hair.

"The General will escort one of the prisoners to the King, a boy by the name of Pen. Now, release him to us immediately. The King is impatient!" Thatcher said in a commanding voice.

The guard who greeted them leaned toward Thatcher and spoke in a conspiratorial manner

"Sir, I have me orders, you see, straight from the King himself. Only he can release the child. I must see orders, sir. Orders from the King. You understand, sir."

Petronius, who had been silent, turned to the guard.

"In the absence of the King's writ, I am able to take the prisoner."

The man looked up to the General for the first time.

"Begging your pardon sir, but you hain't been seen about for a long time. I got me orders, sir."

The General looked down at the man, one eyebrow raised and a menacing stare pinning him to the wall.

"You don't tell my men what or how something is to be done. And you damn well don't tell me "no" or "maybe" either! Do as you have been ordered or, by the gods, I will have you on the other side of these doors. Now get that prisoner!"

Without further hesitation, the guard fumbled with the keys and opened a nearby door, his shaking hands delaying the task. An order from an angry general certainly carried more weight from the one he heard a few days ago from the King's messenger.

Pen, who had heard the commotion outside his cell, was already standing by the door.

As Pen was yanked out into the dim light of the anteroom, he looked at the calloused hand pulling him. He saw a small white scar he had seen dozens of times before.

He looked at the face of the beardless, tall soldier holding him. It was his father! He started to ask questions, but his father gave him a look that silenced him. Definitely his father, he thought. Looking at group which filled the room, he noticed Thatcher and Songor also attired as soldiers. They certainly acted like soldiers handling him in a not-so-gentle manner, each roughly grabbed an arm, dragging him along.

"Get going, boy!"

Thatcher's words were as gruff to him as they had been to the guards.

They walked back through the long, narrow, underground corridor, past the soldiers watching proceedings in the great hallway. As the squad made its way through the large lobby, a captain noted the group leaving the castle. That was odd, he thought. Why take the prisoner outside the castle when the King was in the great hall?

"Follow them," he instructed one of his men, "but do nothing to alarm them." He ran up the stairs toward the great hall.

Once outside, Petronius looked at John, who was casually leaning against one of the columns. He shook his head: no alarm, no unusual movements. Eight men and a boy went down the steps.

Pen was not sure what was happening, but he did his best to improvise, acting the part of a prisoner. Merchants and laborers averted their eyes; it was not safe to be too inquisitive about the King's business. A few heads popped up along the rooftops to check the procession. To see a prisoner escorted by a troop of soldiers was certainly not unusual and they slinked back down out of sight. As the band neared the city gate, with Eldrick and the horses in sight, Petronius felt confident they would make it through without being detected. His ruse had worked perfectly.

The sun was setting and they would be on their way, far from the castle, in a matter of minutes.

Suddenly a yell came from behind. Soldiers were running toward them with drawn swords. Someone further back yelled something, but the noise from the crowds of men and women around them muffled the words. Petronius, sensing rather than hearing the commotion, looked back... a group of soldiers was running their way. The soldiers at the gate turned and watched the commotion. Their heads cocked, listening, as a voice rose out of the swirling noise of the city.

"Stop those men! Imposters!"

Petronius and Thatcher simultaneously pulled their swords quickly slashing the king's soldiers in front of them who were just a bit slower. Groaning bodies were scattered on the ground in a matter of seconds. Another group of soldiers drew their weapons and blocked the gate. As they looked right and left, they did not know whom in particular they should stop, so they stopped everyone. Once at the gate, Petronius motioned for Thatcher to cut the rope holding up the gate. Three of the King's soldiers moved to stop Thatcher, but Songor and two other soldiers crossed swords with them. Thatcher commenced a hacking motion, working through the thick rope.

Other soldiers ran toward the disturbance, but were uncertain whom to attack. The confused soldiers turned toward Thatcher and started the fight there, attacking Songor and his companions. Clearly the ropes that held the gate should not be cut. Except for a few doors connected to interior rooms, this was the only exit from the walled city.

Weaving through the shouting soldiers and fighting men, Eldrick unobtrusively maneuvered the horses outside the gate.

Pen cringed as a group of the King's men rushed toward him. Before he could even think about what to do, his father was in front of him. Swords were crossed with one soldier and suddenly the soldier was down holding his arm. His father turned to a second soldier and a moment later the soldier was on the ground holding his stomach and groaning. It all happened so quickly, just like the night at the inn. Others moved around him, warding off the attackers. Seeing the fracas at the gate, more soldiers rushed from the outside and now fights broke out near the gate. Occasional arrows, aimed at Thatcher and Pen whined through the air, and added to the bewildering disorder.

The fighting was not as fierce as it could have been. The younger soldiers were reluctant to engage the older ones. They recalled nights in the camp when there were wrestling matches. Invariably those gray-haired men, now lacking some teeth, won every tussle. They didn't fight fair, these veterans of two wars; sneaky tricks invariably broke arms or fingers.

What was worse, they didn't seem to care if they lived or died. No, these were not men to challenge without many behind you or hard drink inside them.

Though a few of Pen's escorts were wounded, all fought fiercely. On the ground lay many writhing or still bodies of the King's men, visual proof of the younger soldiers' concern. Unfortunately, the number of the King's men grew, and with greater numbers their confidence grew as well.

Pen saw a discarded sword on the ground and reached to pick it up, but he could not grip it because he was shaking. Then someone bumped him away from the sword as a few of the King's men pressed forward. He looked about at his rescuers, all engaged in fights, and prayed no one saw him unable to retrieve the sword and help.

Thatcher yelled that the rope was nearly cut. Petronius ordered his men to rush the growing number of red-clad soldiers grouped outside the gate. There was a sudden and furious swinging of swords as red-on-red clashed outside the gates. Here, where no bodies yet littered the ground, the King's forces were more determined and seriously engaged the rescuers.

Thatcher successfully severed the last coil that held the heavy gate and it began its slow descent to the ground. The King's soldiers refused to follow him, willing to pass the fight to their comrades outside the gate. Startled, Pen rolled under the gate. He saw Thatcher crawl quickly and swing legs out of the way of the iron prongs that secured the gate to the ground. As he tried to get up, he was seemingly pulled back down...his cape was impaled by the gate's sharp points. Pen raced back and reached down to pull it out, but it was stuck. Soldiers began to move in, sensing an easy kill. Thatcher smiled at the boy and freed himself by simply unhooking the cape at his neck.

Three soldiers closed in on Thatcher and Pen; the boy searched the ground for a discarded blade, but found none. A tall form materialized beside them...his father again. A fourth man joined the soldiers as they attacked. Sword met sword, men grunted, and the skirmish was over. Petronius and Thatcher downed two men, wounded another, and the fourth decided retreat was his best option. The brave band (two hobbled with wounds, two others carried away), were now faced with a ring of about twenty red tunics directly in front of them. Many more of the king's men lined the walls of the castle above, stringing their bows.

CHAPTER 19

The other farmers, hidden in the woods, had one of their party survey the castle opening from the top of the hill, watching for the return of Petronius and his men. When he saw the fight begin, he hurried back to his friends.

"There be some fighting by the gate!"

Griswold climbed onto his horse.

"Then help them, we will."

Some of the men mounted their horses, but most were reluctant. One man, still unhorsed, looked sullenly at the large man atop his brown, shaggy steed.

"What we know of fighting, Griswold? We ain't even got weapons!"

The heavily muscled blacksmith controlled his horse as it pranced. Griswold pointed toward the road.

"Don't know nothing about fighting, Harold, nothing. But I knowed sumtin' about owing and I owe this to Larmack. He be a friend, and a good neighbor."

Griswold turned his horse around and galloped out of the woods and toward the wild fight below. The few on horseback followed behind.

The man on the ground watched them leave. He kicked the dirt. "Damn stupid, blacksmith!"

He got on his horse and raced to catch the group well ahead of him. The man beside him shrugged his shoulders, climbed on his steed, and followed. The remaining men joined the group rushing to aid Petronius and his men.

Galloping down the hill, the long stream of men actually gave the impression they were many more than just fifteen. They yelled and screamed as some menacingly waved their free hand, having no weapons. The soldiers surrounding Petronius and his men were confused. They weren't sure whom they were attacking and who was now attacking them. As the uniformed farmers charged into the fray, their horses bumped both friend and foe as they scattered soldiers in a dozen different directions.

The rescue party mounted the horses retained by Eldrick. Other horses milled about and Pen quickly mounted one. Arrows swished past the men as numerous archers released their missiles haphazardly into the fray. Eldrick slapped the flanks of a few confused horses and got them moving out. Petronius mounted Mirus and quickly raced to the front of the group as they galloped over the hill and down the valley until they were out of sight.

The thundering swarm of horses and men reached a fork in the road; reins of the free horses were exchanged quickly and a group of five raced away. A few miles later Petronius' party reached the outcroppings of a large forest. He waved one group to the left and another to the right. Petronius and the rescue party made their way through a few trees and bushes to a third road. Then they galloped off.

The sun had nearly set by now. In the lingering light the few farmers and merchants who still remained on the roads would be hard-pressed to declare which group had Pen.

After another mile, Petronius stopped and motioned for all the men to dismount. The General checked each man for wounds. Only one would require stitches; it still bled profusely. Eldrick brought out some ointment and covered the wound; Thatcher took out a needle and thread.

"This may hurt a bit, John."

"Aye, get on with it, Thatch."

In a few minutes, the ugly gash was sewn tight. The men mounted their horses ready to spur them back to a gallop. Petronius raised his hand to stop them. Then he led them slowly on the road to Markwood Forest as the red sun was pushed down by the black night.

Meanwhile, behind the gate, a new rope was secured and the gate was slowly raised up. In that short time, darkness had settled, but the eager mob of cavalry milled around, prepared to follow the men who freed the boy. Cearl had reached the front, yelled at the men. "Wait, you fools! You can't chase them in the dark. You, get some torches! When you leave here, don't go galloping in the dark! You would probably kill yourselves and, more importantly, you might lame the horses. You can't catch them tonight. But tomorrow..."

And so the King's orders were carried out. Messenger pigeons carried terse notes to the corners of the kingdom, hundreds of red soldiers marched out to reinforce garrisons, and a large squad of cavalry followed the tracks of horses by torchlight.

A red web was slowly cast out from the capital.

CHAPTER 20

In those dark days, when King Cearl ruled with an iron fist and a merciless heart, Markwood Forest suffered the most. Searching for the white deer, huntsmen killed many animals and wounded others. But, evil can create monsters. The larger animals hid only until an opportune moment presented itself for vicious attack. Unfortunately, the animals did not discriminate and attacked any lone human who entered the forest. Teeth would rip and claws would slash, leaving a bloody mess for the villagers to find. So fierce were the attacks that the village folk believed they had to be the work of supernatural fiends rather than wild animals. Terrible legends were born of this violence.

Deeper in the forest a worse monster lurked, far more dangerous than any animal. Man. The Green Men, in particular. Fugitives from the oppressive laws enacted by Cearl, they were as angry and mean as the animals. Any soldiers or nobles who ventured into the heart of Markwood found themselves targeted by a storm of green arrows and most were killed. Only a few managed to escape, their cowardly retreat deftly framed into a heroic saga by the time they reached safety. The humbler folk who found themselves in those dark woods experienced only their own fear as their passage through the heart of the forest normally occurred without incident.

Petronius intended to lead his men, unfortunately dressed as soldiers of the King, into that sinister region.

The farmers who rose early to tend the fields near the great forest could honestly report only soldiers had passed their way. A red cape covered Pen, so he too looked the part of a soldier. Petronius reasoned that such bands would soon not be an unusual sight.

Though the morning was not cold, the farmers in Petronius' small group shivered in the dim light of the dawn as they saw Cross Fell Mountain silhouetted in the sky, a stark reminder of how close they were to Markwood.

By mid-morning they finally reached the line of trees that walled in the forest. While waiting for the other groups to return, the farmers talked nervously as the horses eagerly chewed the grass near them. Petronius did not bother to hide his men. Even if they met a band of soldiers, Petronius figured he could bluff his way through the situation. If not, he still had seven experienced soldiers and two burly neighbors, healthy and able with a sword. Hoof beats announced the arrival of riders and round the bend came the red tunics. They hailed their comrades: five farmers returning from their diversion toward the coast. Minutes later, another group arrived. Moments after that, the final group joined the throng. After some backslapping and friendly jokes, the men noted Petronius had turned Mirus around and was slowly leading them into the forest. They were no longer jovial.

Once they entered Markwood only a subdued green light filtered through the thick canopy of leaves and a disconcerting coldness enveloped them.

Petronius looked back toward the anxious group. "Stay on the road. Stay together. Whatever you do, control the horses so they don't bolt into the woods."

The horses smelled danger and were agitated as they fought against the reins. Only Eldrick's leadership kept the horses together.

As they went deeper into the forest, the reassuring light from the entrance disappeared.

CHAPTER 21

At that same moment, just outside the city gate, a hundred or so snorting horses carrying hard-looking riders milled about. These men wore no uniforms and were of various sizes and shapes, some with long, unruly hair, some with none. Some were pale like moonlight, some dark as a moonless night. All had one thing in common though: their eyes...flat and expressionless, but ever watching. These were the infamous huntsmen. They collectively turned their attention to a young captain who was obviously nervous about being so close to group. King Cearl yelled into the face of the man: "What do you mean you couldn't find the path? How can you not track so many horses?"

The captain, his face mottled from dirt and sweat from riding all night, explained. "We could track the path, sire, but there was more than one, and many, many hoof prints along each." Then he explained how each path led to a different location, a different possible route for the escaped band. "I split up my men and they followed each as far as they could, but no riders were seen. They moved fast, sire."

The King shook his head angrily. This nuisance would take more time. He turned back to the captain.

"All right. The coastal city is by now well guarded, as is the border region in the west. But the border in the south is a long one. Take your men and set up patrols." To another captain with a band of cavalry, he commanded, "Go to Port Logan and fan out to cover all the roads in. Petronius has friends in Logan."

He turned to the odd assortment of stoic men who had remained stationary like grim statues: the huntsmen. They had no leader, but there was one feared even by the huntsmen: Narl. His word was law and disobedience meant death. Of average height, he was heavily muscled with scars covering most of his body. His face was well proportioned, even attractive. In fact, he took pride that no mark marred its handsome features. It was to Narl that Cearl spoke.

"Find them. If you must, follow them into any country and bring them back, alive or dead."

Narl asked, "Into other countries? Such action might be taken as an act of war."

"Just go, man, and do as I told you!"

Narl's only acknowledgement was to turn around and urge his horse into a gallop. The other huntsmen followed. Cearl watched the different groups leave the castle. He turned back to the castle and stopped. He looked at the captain of the guards, besides the huntsmen his most feared force. Cearl mumbled to himself, the captain tilting his head to better hear him.

"Or they could be going through Markwood to the northeast. More dangerous for them to be sure, but Petronius is crafty and now desperate. And, he lived in Kirkland."

He grabbed the captain by his tunic and brought him close.

"Take your men and find out if they traveled along the road to Markwood. Follow any tracks. Check with the villagers in Kirkland. They won't talk to you, so disguise yourself and listen."

The captain, already frightened by being so roughly handled, quickly shook his head in agreement. Cearl released the man, pushing him away. Then he returned to the castle.

CHAPTER 22

White knuckles held reins tight. The road was littered with weeds underscoring its infrequent use. Occasionally a fallen tree had to be hoisted out of the way by straining men who nervously looked about as they quickly completed their task. Unlike most forests serenaded by the distant chirps of birds, there was a disturbing silence. Even the wind was absent; not a leaf was fluttering. It was as though nature held its breath, waiting. The long line of red snaked slowly through the forest.

Gray forms burst out of the forest. A pack of unusually large wolves raced around the rear horse, snapping jaws just missed the flesh of the frightened animal. Thatcher held tightly as his horse kicked and moved to avoid the snarling animals. His sword nipped one of the beasts and the animal limped back into the woods, snarling over its shoulder. One of the soldiers near the rear pushed his horse at the wolves; his sword held out at his waist, ready to slash down at the attacking animals. The wolves slinked back into the forest.

The men moved on, swords drawn in readiness.

A terrible, deep growl thundered near the nervous band. A frightened horse carried a startled farmer into one of the smaller paths to the side. Soldiers fought with their steeds, trying to force them to follow. There was a great snarling, a terrified whinny, a man's scream, and then stillness. Two of the soldiers finally gained sufficient control of their animals to start down the trail.

Petronius pulled Mirus across the path to block them. The soldiers would be trapped if they ventured into the narrow confines of the woods. Whatever had brought down horse and rider could and would just as easily bring down one or both of them. Petronius shook his head. He recalled a desperate ride just two days earlier when he raced the great black along this same stretch of road, chased by an impossibly large bear. Only the speed and dexterity of the great horse kept them from being torn apart.

"Back in line."

After walking in an ominous stillness for an hour, the men heard the distant sounds of birds. The normal sounds relaxed the men, and swords were eventually returned to scabbards, weary arms gratefully relieved of the burden. The forest seemed less dark and men added to the cacophony of sounds with conversation and laughter.

Pen had not yet spoken to anyone. During the slow, dark walk the night before, silence seemed best. In the early light, he was greeted enthusiastically by nearly all the Kirkland men...a wink from Thatcher, a great smile from Songor, Griswold slapping him hard on the back...all except his father, who kept looking ahead.

His father raised his hand and stopped the group at a small clearing for a much needed rest. He posted guards, assigned a few men to tend the horses, and then sat underneath an oak tree so he could watch the road. Pen crouched beside him, picking up a few blades of grass.

"Sir, I am a bit confused. First soldiers kidnap me and I don't know why, then the King keeps asking me about the white deer and I don't know why, he puts me in prison and that wasn't fun at all and again, I don't know why." He took a deep breath.

"Finally I find out that father is Petronius, a legend. My father! You, sir! And I certainly don't know how that all happened. Now we are here in Markwood Forest and..."

Petronius did not take his eyes off the road ahead. "I know you have been taking sword lessons from Thatcher, but have you also been taking speech lessons from Songor?"

Pen smiled for the first time in days.

"No, no lessons from Songor. It's just that I am so confused."

Petronius finally turned to face his son.

"There is much that we have to discuss, Penda. Unfortunately, we don't have the luxury of time right now. You know there is danger behind us. Know this as well, son... it is all around us. And I don't mean the animals or the green men."

A quick look around and he returned his attention to the boy.

"Right now, the King believes you might be a threat and that makes this place dangerous for you."

"If it is dangerous in the forest, then let's leave!"

"By this place, Pen, I mean Mercia."

Pen's eyes opened wide.

"We are leaving, Mercia, son."

This was his home...his country. They couldn't leave!

"You know now my real name is Petronius. What you don't know is that your mother was Cearl's sister, Princess Elen. Pen, King Cearl is your uncle. You have royal blood in you, lad. That makes you a threat to him."

His mother was a princess? The King, an uncle?

Confused he tightly closed his eyes and shook his head trying to jar ideas into order. He was still coping with the notion that his father was General Petronius.

"But you never owned a weapon," he blurted out in frustration.

191

"I never showed you my weapons," Petronius corrected. "I kept them locked in a trunk in the barn. Weapons have always been a part of my life, Pen."

Petronius looked over the forest again, checking to make sure that all was well. He turned to Pen again.

"You said that he asked you about the white deer. What did you say?"

Frowning, he eyed his father. He had told the King nothing, but somehow Cearl knew the truth. His father had better know the truth as well.

"Nothing, sir. But he knew that I saw her and he knew...he somehow knew I talked to her." Pen lowered his head and plucked a few more blades of grass.

Petronius looked at his son, incredulously.

"You were that close to the white deer? You spoke with her? When?" he asked in a whisper.

"Oh, years ago, sir. I was only eight or nine. I met her in the forest."

"Son, you should have told me this before."

Pen looked down again. "I know, sir. I am sorry."

"Had I known this then, we would have been long gone from this land. Cearl must think you are the Chosen One."

Petronius shook his head.

"This is going to be even more difficult, now."

He continued to scan the road and surroundings.

"Cearl may be my uncle, but I don't like him."

Petronius nodded in agreement. "Well, that makes two of us, son. I don't like him either."

The boy went back to plucking blades of grass. Petronius continued to stare at him. His son had seen evil for the first time. Already the boy had enough fear to last him a lifetime.

"It must have been difficult for you...with him and in the prison."

The boy could only whisper. "It was terrible."

Petronius felt the inescapable pain of a parent whose child is hurt. Despite the mutual embarrassment, he hugged his son. Releasing the boy, the General rose abruptly. He pulled Pen to his feet and rested his hands on the boy's shoulders.

"I won't lie to you, son. We have a tangled knot. We must keeping working until it unravels. Right now, it's best to keep moving. We will talk more later."

The group mounted their horses and continued their slow, careful journey through woods with small animals skittering about, the former silence filled with the chatter of squirrels, birds, and insects. The noise of the animals seemed like a talisman against the dangers of the forest.

They camped that night in a large, peaceful meadow which opened to the sky, now speckled with stars. After their harrowing trek through woods, it was welcome respite. The horses were roped off into the center of the clearing, contentedly eating the thick grass. Guards were posted. Petronius sat near the fire, hands folded. Songor sat beside him, his hands unconsciously rubbing a loudly growling stomach.

"Did Pen tell you about the white deer?"

"Yes, sir. I don't think the King be liking that."

"You're right. He'll follow us, Songor. He won't rest until he has the boy."

"He hafta go through me, he will. And I be a big 'in to go through, master," Songor declared defiantly.

Petronius smiled wearily and patted his friend on the back.

"There's somethin' else, General. Something' rolls around in my head. None been with her for such a time…sixty yars, maybe. Pen, he must be special."

Petronius abruptly stood and walked into the darkness without a word to his servant. Songor was mildly surprised. He be a general agin. 'Spect thinking and talking don't be together.

Songor yawned, looked at the stars above, leaned back on the grass, and immediately fell asleep.

CHAPTER 23

The stars twinkling over the meadow shined above Kirkland village as well, though their light was diminished by the presence of torches, an uncommon occurrence for the little village. The events of the last few days deprived the villagers of their normal bedtime at sunset. Pen's kidnapping and daring rescue and a band of soldiers entering Markwood created more news in the last few days than the last several years put together.

After the exhausted villagers finally dispersed a few women separated themselves from the rest of the villagers and walked to a cottage, warmly lit by a fire burning in its hearth. Upon arriving, all were positioned in a half circle in front of Mother Hebron. She sat on a chair, hands folded neatly in her lap while listening to the reports.

After the last report, she sat quietly for a few minutes.

"This much is certain," she began, "By now they know Pen and Larmack escaped into Markwood forest. Tomorrow the King will know as well."

The silver-haired lady stared into the fire. So now it begins. The war she expected and dreaded would soon be upon them. Had

Petronius returned? They could use a leader of his caliber. No, it had to be more hopeful fancy than fact. He disappeared years ago after his wife died, and no one knew where he'd settled. She turned once again to the assembled women, all in blue cloaks.

"Many horses were purchased few days ago by Songor. My guess is our old friend Thatcher is behind the scheme, as only he would have that kind of money."

She stared into the flames again. Thatcher had to be the one behind this. He loved Pen nearly as much as she did. Over the years she had gained a grudging respect for the man. He was an excellent teacher and, except for occasionally imbibing a bit too much ale, possessed no bad habits. Though she would never tell him, she valued his counsel. Indeed, she wished he were present now.

"Thatcher and Pen will need our help, ladies. Take whatever horses are left. Steal them if you must, but we must have enough for all of us. Tomorrow night we ride to gather the sisterhood."

The women looked at each other, knowing full well the import of the command: war!

"We will meet on the training field on the night of the full moon."

Ten women quickly left the circle. The four that remained were offered chairs.

"Now, we must plan," she said calmly.

*

A mist hung over the forest, leaving the superstitious farmers unsettled as they saddled their horses. Eventually all mounted, but none were eager to continue the trek. Petronius eased Mirus to center of the group.

"If you stay on the road, you have nothing to fear. You will see fruits, but don't touch them. They belong to the green men. Stray from the road, steal their fruit, and you will anger them. You don't want to do that, trust me."

He smiled. "I promise you a hearty meal at the end of the day." Songor beamed.

The clearing well behind them, the forest walls loomed impossibly high on either side, just as dense as before, but now shrouded in an early morning fog. Bird chirps sounded from afar, but close by, bushes rustled and twigs snapped. Swords drawn in readiness, the men saw nothing.

The unseen sun warmed the forest as the mist disappeared, revealing a much broader view of the forest, more open and inviting. The few trees close to the path were fruit bearing, heavily laden with ripe apples and fist-sized pears. Songor did his best to resist temptation, but he finally succumbed. His hand reached up and he plucked down a particularly appealing apple. Holding his prize high in the air, he smiled at Eldrick who shook his head. Just as he was about to take a bite, an arrow passed through it and carried the fruit deep into the woods. He looked from where the arrow had come and saw only the green of the forest. Songor picked no more fruit.

Pen judged it to be noon, though he could see no sun, no sky even, just a dark, green world. It surrounds us, green everywhere! A small piece of the forest seemed to detach itself, and a large bush approached Pen. Startled, he shook his head and discerned a man wildly trussed with brush and leaf. Others emerged out of the wood holding bows, tightly stretched, with green arrows inserted. The men were clad in green clothes and their skin and hair was dyed green. As Pen looked at the long line of men on both sides of the group, he noted that they did not smile and they had their bow strings drawn tight with green feathered arrows.

Petronius yelled to not to resist. The farmers readily appreciated his wisdom while the soldiers were able, even eager to put up some fight. However, Petronius had commanded and they would obey.

A tall, thin green man suddenly dropped down from an overhanging branch, startling the Mirus.

"Well, the great General Petronius." He bowed gracefully. "Walking straight into a trap! Not something that happens every day."

As Petronius dismounted, he said angrily, "Stand your men down, Viridius, before someone gets hurt, you arrogant fool."

With that, the leader of the green men laughed and embraced the General.

CHAPTER 24

The camp of the green men was well hidden in a most peculiar manner. Weave through narrow paths and you arrive... and see nothing but trees all around. But, it is there, above. Looking up you would not see it as the intertwining branches and leaves act as a brown-green veil. But, take a vine near the largest tree and climb up. Just above the veil scores of roughly made tree huts appear with dozens of green men jumping from branch to branch, travelling along long, wide limbs, oblivious to the hard, unforgiving earth below them.

Petronius had followed Viridius even higher above the tree village. Though Petronius had been here many times, he still marveled at both the engineering feat and the dexterity of the green men moving about in their tree village. He turned toward the leader of the green man.

"Why didn't you let me through as we had discussed?"

Sitting down, calmly breathing, not a bead of sweat on his face, Viridius looked over to his friend. "Huntsmen were seen north of here. We were pretty sure they blocked the road to Lindsey. Seems to me your brother-in-law wants a family reunion."

Petronius looked away. He had been afraid of the possibility. "Another path through the forest, then. You owe me that much, Viridius."

The green man smiled at his friend. "Yes, I do owe you, Petronius. I'll send a few lads to find some deer path out of here. But those huntsmen know the woods; it might take some time. Why is Cearl so obsessed with you? This goes beyond his usual madness."

The man with the scar glared at him. "Just find us a way out. Don't worry about why."

*

Pen was petrified to be so dangerously high. He moved gingerly along a branch barely the width of his foot. He grabbed limb, branch, and even twig to give him the necessary steadiness to move along the narrow path. Suddenly he was gripped from behind. A green man roughly rotated him so that he could pass. Without word or smile, the green man hurried on his way along the tree limbs.

Pen, his face drained, as was his courage, wobbled and desperately grabbed a nearby vine. There were many vines on the trees, some deliberately looped on short limbs. His heart continued to pound wildly as he watched green men use the vines to coast from tree to tree.

He considered trying this mode of transportation. Why not? Anything was better than being perched so precariously. He gripped a nearby vine with both hands, took a deep breath, and jumped off into space. Tree houses, green men, and branches rushed by him. He swung almost to another branch but didn't quite reach it, swinging back to his starting point. The second time he pushed off harder and easily landed on the branch. Pen smiled.

He grabbed another one of the vines, loosely wrapped about a nearby limb and was off again. In this manner he gradually swung himself over to a ladder beneath a massive structure in the center of the tree village.

It was higher than any hut. Climbing an assortment of branches secured to the trunk of the tree, he made his way to a narrow promenade circling the building. The roof was bathed in partial sunlight which managed to peak between the few leaves and branches above it. Upon entering the structure, he found himself in a great hall, complete with a fireplace blazing brightly at one end and at the other, a long table filled with assorted fruits, breads, and cheese. A number of green men and some of his company jockeyed for position around the table. He heard Songor's booming voice and witnessed his old friend stack a plate high with food. Nearby his father talked to Viridius. The leader of the green men turned his head and saw Pen. His ever-present smile grew even larger.

"So, this is Pen, son of Petronius," he said jovially as he wrapped his arm around Pen's shoulder and led him toward the table. As they walked to the table, Viridius' smile vanished as he stared intently at Pen's face. His arm still around Pen's shoulder, he leaned in closer.

"I've seen your face before, young man. Long ago."

"I didn't see you, sir. I would certainly have remembered."

Releasing his hold he laughed deep and full. "No, you would never have seen me unless I wanted you to. Four, maybe five years ago, we watched you with the animals. Indeed, you have a way with beasts..." He winked at the boy. "One peculiar beast, in particular."

Before Pen could respond, Petronius had joined them.

"You have a special son, here, General. I spied him in the woods years ago. Surrounded by all sorts of animals. All sorts, Petronius."

"Seems I am finding out more and more about my son," replied Petronius, glaring sternly at the boy.

"Lad, you must be hungry. Help yourself to this feast." Pen needed no second invitation as he piled his plate high with an assortment of food.

His father was greeted by one after another of the green men, all former soldiers who served under him. While Petronius was thus engaged, Viridius eased Pen away from the table.

"You were talking with her, weren't you boy?"

Pen eyed the green man, but remained silent. The green man pointed to a nearby chair against the wall. Pen sat down and picked at the morsels in the crude wooden bowl.

"She came back for you, Pen."

Petronius nervously witnessed the green man's intense focus on his son. He tried to make his way to them, but former veterans intercepted him, and he was prevented from reaching Pen.

His arm linked with the boy's, Viridius lead him around the building. "Always walk after you eat, young Pen...excellent for the digestion." The green man patted his nearly non-existent stomach. As they walked, he talked about his time in the army and how he met Pen's father. He finished the brief story by the time Petronius caught up with them.

The green face wore a half smile. "That was how your father and I met," he said, smiling at the tall General. "Not a good beginning, eh?"

Petronius, now strolling alongside the pair, looked at Pen. "I should have killed him, son. How much trouble would have been avoided!"

Viridius unlinked his arm and put it around Pen's shoulder. His other long arm extended as he pointed at Petronius. "All he ever had to do was simply not save my hide that day!" Grabbing an apple from the table as they passed, he bit into it. He chewed the morsel slowly.

"You know, young Pen, these really are the best apples in the land. They are only found on the slopes of Cross Fell Mountain."

Pen looked quizzically at the green man. "You were a captain. How did you end up here, sir?"

Viridius broke his stare and grinned at Pen. "Well, that brings us to the last time your father saved me. This one he can't wiggle out of, Pen. He was made general by then... smartest thing that bastard Cearl ever did..."

Pen blinked at the word and Viridius noted his surprise. "I did not misuse the language, boy. There have been stories about the man. Some say he really was a bastard. He showed up in the court as Jared's long lost son. Who's to say? Jared took him in as his son, and that was that. Maybe there was no marriage for Cearl's mother. Again, who's to say?"

"He made things tough on many a good folk. I didn't like all them new laws, the new taxes, the new muscle...the huntsmen who pushed their way into the kingdom and then pushed the kingdom around. So, I spoke up about how certain things shouldn't be. Well, doesn't Cearl find out. He gives me the easiest job a captain can have...guarding the treasury. Puffed up, am I. This is an important job, young Pen. I takes it seriously. Next thing I know I am accused of stealing money from the treasury. So off to the dungeon goes Viridius. Not a nice place, the dungeon, but you know that pretty well yourself, don't you?"

Pen agreed with a nod, the smile momentarily gone from his face.

"Your father knew I would never steal. One of the tax collectors died soon after I was in prison. Your Dad found out how much money was missing from the treasury, tapped his own money, and puts the exact amount in this dead guy's trunk. Sends one of his captains to oversee the search of the man's house. Money is found, Petronius presents the information to Cearl, and I am out of jail."

Then he cocked his head at his friend. "Your father is poorer, and Cearl is mad."

Petronius grumbled. "I should have let you rot in prison."

Smiling at his friend, Viridius finished his tale. "Your father and I figured it was time for me to leave. I had already made up my mind I wouldn't be leaving the country of my birth, so I hid here in these woods. Cearl sent his huntsmen to find me, but I knew how to disappear. I dressed in green and changed the color of my skin, I did. Soon others joined me, and..." he grandly swept his hands.

"Every now and again, Cearl remembers I am here, and sends soldiers to find me. My men and I make sure only a few soldiers ever return to Tamworth. It's been five years since he tried to find me, and I think he found it better to forget me."

Petronius looked at him, a serious expression on his face. "Cearl will remember you now, friend."

"Yes. He'll remember us both, General."

CHAPTER 25

The table had been cleared of food, the flickering fire a smoky reminder of a once great flame. The torches by each of the two doors offered a modest light to the hall. Viridius yawned. "I have to make sure that everyone is tucked in. I know you folks might uncomfortable strolling in the dark, so rest in those cots over there." Three cots had materialized in the corner behind them.

Viridius patted Pen on the back, nodded to Petronius, and disappeared into the blackness. Soon quiet settled over the building. Except for Songor with his intermittent snoring, father and son were alone.

Pen was exhausted but he was having a difficult time digesting both food and information. So many questions bubbled in his mind, one more than any other, but he was afraid to ask.

Petronius was also plagued by an agitated mind, unable to rest. He sat down and stared at the fire, his spinning brain slowed down and allowed him to consider the myriad problems facing his son.

Pen had finally mustered up the courage to ask the question. Years before, he innocently asked his father about his mother. The questions tumbled out one night after dinner. What did she look like? What did she enjoy? Was she happy like Pen, or gloomy like his father? Petronius did not answer any of the questions. Instead, he got up from the table, walked out the door, and disappeared for three days. After he returned, no words were spoken about the incident, and Pen was afraid to ever ask his father about his mother.

Now he discovered that his mother was a princess! That was certainly nice, but princess or not, he didn't really know what she was like. It was a painful void in his mind, a missing piece to the puzzle that was now his life.

Alone with this man who barely resembled his father, this man who kept great secrets, he dared to ask again.

"You kept so much from me, Father. I'm not sure why you hid so many things from me, but now I need to know. You told me that my mother was a princess. Please...please tell me more about her." Petronius said nothing, rose and started to walk away.

No, thought Pen, not again! Startling them both, he yelled to his father. "I've been through so much, Father. I deserve an answer."

Petronius stopped, stunned by the forceful words from his son. He bowed his head, his hand momentarily covering his eyes, stanching the tears. He was right, of course. Petronius was not running from Pen's questions as much as he was running from his own memories. It hurt so much to conjure them again. It was time, he acknowledged to himself. He heaved a tired sigh, momentarily closed his eyes and prepared for the pain of remembrance. He walked back to his son and sat down.

After a moment of silence, he began. "You are right, son." He tried to find the right words as tears glistened in his eyes. "She was the kindest, gentlest person I have ever known. She was also a communicator, you know..."

And the two talked deep into the night, laughing and crying as Songor slept peacefully beside them.

The next morning, Viridius asked Pen come down to the ground with him. Pen was happy to comply.

"Things are starting to grow, Pen. My men say there are folks trying to get through the king's troop to get in the forest."

Pen looked around and saw a few new faces talking with some green men.

"You talked with her, lad. What did she say to you? This is important."

Petronius slipped down from a vine and landed near them. He interjected himself between the green man and Pen. Nose to nose, he angrily spoke to Viridius. "The boy just saw her. Don't read anything more into it.

Viridius returned the glare, his green eyebrows arched. "You know the truth, don't you, Petronius? The King is moving against us because of Pen, not you or me."

"Pen, get back to your hut. Now!"

Frightened, the boy climbed back up into the tree village.

Petronius pulled the green man aside.

"Pen is just a boy, nothing more."

Viridius shook his head. "No, Petronius. The deer came back for him."

"No!" yelled Pen's father. "He is my son, only my son."

"You can't change this, Petronius. Your son is the Chosen One."

Petronius grabbed the shirt of the green man and pulled him close. "Whether he is or isn't, if you keep saying it, people will believe and that is going to compromise our ability to escape the country, won't it? Help us get out of the forest as we agreed upon."

Viridius stood nose to nose with the General. He calmly responded to the hard breathing man holding him close.

"Can't accommodate you now, good friend. My men can't find a path out of Markwood that is not covered by red soldiers or huntsmen."

Petronius stepped away, shaking his head. He had been afraid of this.

"My spies say the King is gathering an army to invade."

The general, not the father, looked at the leader of the green men.

"We need to plan."

*

Songor looked out the window of the small hut. His head moved slowly from right to left and back again; a smile on his broad pink face.

"There goes another one, Pen. Just 'a gliding through the air, he is. Ah, these green men...they be so...so...what be the word? So...so, fine?"

Pen didn't respond. He was thinking about what Viridius had said... the deer came back for him. Why me? I couldn't even pick up a sword to help with my own escape.

"Songor, am I the Chosen One?"

Songor looked out the window but was suddenly quiet. Then he sat back down on the cot and looked at the boy.

"Ah...I can't rightly say. You've always been Master Pen to me. Hard to think the baby I held them tharteen yars ago could be me king. Can't see you as king, Pen. Just can't see you that way."

Songor scrunched his eyes into slits, his round face twisted in pain as he tried to think.

"I don't know much about kings, lad. But a king be strong and good. Cearl, he's powerful strong, but not good. You be good, goodest I ever knowed. But be you strong? I don't know if you be strong or not. But kings, they gots to be strong."

Now Pen looked out the window, afraid to face a man he had known all his life. "When there was fighting at the gate, I reached for a sword, but was afraid to take it. There was blood on the ground and people moaning and I was scared."

Songor waddled over to him and squeezed his shoulder. "Ah, don't worry none about that. Sword fightins' fer men. Ye not there yet, lad. But ye git thar."

Pen shook his head and whispered to himself. "Am I strong enough to get there?"

*

Viridius and Petronius were sequestered in one of the smaller huts all morning. When they emerged, Viridius called his people together on the ground. He explained Petronius and his band came to Markwood for temporary sanctuary before they slipped out of the country. Seeing Pen in the crowd, he motioned for him to join them. Red-faced, the boy stood beside the two men. Viridius laid his long arm over the shoulder of the lad.

"Now things have changed. The huntsmen are blocking any escape into Lindsey. The King will soon be coming after young Pen, here."

Alarmed but unafraid, the green men and women listened to their leader.

"I'm figuring the King will come into Markwood with hundreds of soldiers."

Viridius walked behind Pen and put his hands on his shoulders.

"Why? Why is the King bothering about a mere boy? I'll tell you. The boy has talked with the White Deer."

They waited, not even breathing now.

"The King invades because he is afraid of Pen, afraid he might be..." he looked over at Petronius who looked away angrily.

"Afraid Pen might be the Chosen One."

The whispers rippled through the crowd. Finally it was spoken. The Chosen One.

Viridius placed himself between Petronius and Pen. "You've seen new men coming into camp. There are more, many more making their way toward Markwood. To fight under Petronius."

The green man raised his bow.

"Now is the time to fight. Now, under Petronius. Now is the time to follow the banner of the White Deer."

Green bows were raised with yells.

Viridius motioned for silence. The green men all looked to their leader.

"Petronius and I have decided that we can't stay here. Tomorrow we leave for Bangor Hill. There we will set up defenses against the King and his men. There we will fight Cearl for our freedom and the freedom of our country!"

After another resounding cheer, loud and long, Viridius held up his bow as he leaned toward Petronius.

"Well, you have your army, such as it is: at least two hundred of the best bowmen in the country! Think we can stand off the hundreds Cearl will send against us?"

CHAPTER 26

The next day Petronius met with the handful of men who had helped free Pen. Thatcher, Songor, and a few soldiers were directed to gather any willing veterans who had served with the General. Eldrick was to surreptitiously enter Kirkland to enlist as many able-bodied peasants as possible to join the rebellion. The remaining soldiers were directed to find out what they could about the army's movements. All the men still had on the uniforms of the king so, one by one at night, it wasn't difficult to get out of Markwood.

Petronius went to meet with the Earl of Longham, an old friend. He hoped he could persuade the Earl and other nobles to join the cause.

The following morning, Pen and the green men were engaged in moving armaments, food, and other essentials from their tree village to the ground. Materials were then loaded into carts to be carried by the few remaining horses along the narrow path to Bangor Hill.

Muscles and patience honed on the farm, Pen was a tireless worker and never complained. His face, however, betrayed worry and frustration. Late one afternoon after working since dawn, he stood by a fully loaded cart ready to be moved to Bangor Hill, and rubbed his sore muscles. Viridius, carrying a large bag over his shoulder, patted him on the back.

"You have been working hard, Pen. Come, walk with me."

The pair followed a path so thin only a snake could easily travel along it. Far from the tree village, they emerged into a small meadow, the grass tamped down smooth. It was the training ground for the green men.

"I've heard your sword skills are considerable." Viridius reached into the bag and brought out two wooden swords. "I pride myself in being somewhat skilled with the blade. Shall we cross blades, Pen, son of Petronius?"

Pen weighed the sword in his hand and swung it quickly a few times. He smiled as he looked at Viridius. It had been days since he traded blows with Thatcher and he sorely missed the exercise.

The two men traded strikes for a few minutes, neither gaining an advantageous position, but both probing the skills of the other. Soon, Viridius found himself being beaten back by the lad. The tall green man saw an opening and lunged. It proved to be a trap as Pen sidestepped the blow and brought his blade down flat on the man's wrist, smacking out the blade from Viridius' grip.

Viridius winced in pain, holding his wrist. "You are good, young man. Very good. As good as your father and he was one of the best."

The green man massaged his wrist. "How are you with the bow?"

"Passable, sir."

Viridius reached into the bag again and withdrew two bows and a handful of arrows. He pointed to a nearby large oak tree, the figure of a man hewn into the trunk. "See, if you can hit the chest."

Pen notched an arrow, pulled the string back, took aim, raised his bow slightly, and released. His arrow ricocheted off the tree high above the target.

A few seconds later, Viridius loaded his bow and released the missile. The arrow hit the middle of the target. Turning to the boy, he smiled. "Perhaps I can help you with archery."

Viridius trained the lad as he explained how to gauge bow strength, distance, and wind deflection. Before night pulled up the blanket of stars over the forest, Pen regularly hit the target. The rising moon lit their way back with Viridius telling him stories about his youth in a wooded area near Lindsey.

The next day Pen worked only in the morning; all the necessary supplies were now on the ground. After lunch Viridius and Pen went out to the training field one more time. Upon entering the meadow, Viridius stopped and cast his eyes across the barren field, his face frowning.

"I don't think I will ever see this place again, Pen."

The green man blinked his eyes, darted a look at Pen, made a move to stretch, and rubbed his eyes as though he was waking. He clapped his hands together.

"All right, young man, one more bout with the swords!"

They parried for a few minutes, but Pen once again bested the older man. He brought the blade to the man's throat, stopping the contest. Viridius laughed and shook his head.

"My friend, you are better than your father!"

They sat on a log near the opening that led back to camp. Viridius seemed reluctant to leave so he told some more stories of his youth. When Pen next spoke, it was so soft that Viridius had to lean down to hear him.

"Sir, were you ever scared to fight?"

The older man looked down at the boy, easily divining the problem. He answered after a few seconds, his words casual, but his message as sure as the arrows from his bow.

"Well, let me tell you. Any man who says he is not afraid is either lying or crazy. So, yes, I get scared. Once, when I was a bit older than you, I ran from some soldiers who were annoyed we were stealing their horses. I ran, but my two friends stayed and fought. Never saw them again. I lived; they died. Maybe if I stayed and fought, they would have lived. Maybe I would have died."

"I got back to stealing horses again. Me and another friend stole horses from the same soldiers! What were the chances of that? We both stayed and fought. Held 'em off too, for a while. Then two other soldiers came."

Eagerly the boy prodded. "Did you fight them all?"

Viridius smiled. "Oh, no...we ran then, young Pen. We ran faster than ever before. Sometimes being scared is a good thing. We got away."

The green man stood and the boy followed. As they walked toward the table being filled with food, he continued. "I still get scared, Pen."

"But you fight."

"Yes, to save a friend. I won't ever leave a friend behind again."

Then he smiled at Pen.

"Guess that's what happens; we fight to save each other, and all of us are scared. Folks just don't show their fear, Pen."

They talked no more as they walked through the milling green men. Before they separated, Pen turned to Viridius. "Thank you, sir... for everything."

The green man put his hand on Pen's shoulder. "When next I fight, I want you at my back."

*

Pen and the remainder of the green men arrived at Bangor Hill late the next day. Petronius had also just returned from his conference with the Earl. Longham promised help, but only if they were successful in a major engagement with the King's forces. Viridius was angered.

"No," argued Petronius, "it is the correct response. He must first ensure his men are not dying for an impossible cause. Going against King Cearl is a deadly business. We have to prove ourselves first, Viridius. At least five hundred men will join us, if we can survive the next few weeks."

"That is the question, of course," remarked Viridius wryly. "If we can survive the next few weeks...without the support of the Earl."

The next day, Petronius supervised the construction of the defensive works at the base of the hill while Viridius organized a makeshift camp at the top. Pen resigned himself to simply unloading the carts.

Late in the afternoon, Thatcher returned with over two hundred veterans, most out of practice, some weighed down with too many years of farm cooking, but all willing to serve under their beloved General. A day later, Songor added another hundred former soldiers in much the same condition. Eldrick easily found nearly fifty men in and around Kirkland, all willing to fight, but most of those he brought did not own a sword nor did they know how to use one.

With the new recruits, the rebel army had tripled. Petronius made Thatcher, Eldrick, and John, one of the soldiers, his captains. Songor was given a small detachment of about twenty men. Viridius was captain of the green men. Petronius assigned Thatcher to immediately put the farmers through intensive sword training.

Men trickled in, darting into the forest between patrols. These recruits warned the rebels that the King was marshaling an army to attack Markwood. But they also said many in the kingdom were voicing dissent and sometimes expressing discontent in more physical ways. Cearl dispensed additional troops to all villages and the two cities.

Thatcher met with Petronius one afternoon. "Sir, there is something you need to know... about Mother Hebron."

The General eyed his second in command quizzically. "Go on, Thatch."

The short, gray-haired veteran could not look the General in the eye, the ground apparently a safer audience. "Well, sir, I've been meaning to tell you, but things have been busy around here. Getting those veterans and all. Then training them farmers..."

"Thatcher. Now!"

"I've been training them, sir. Hundreds of 'em."

"Who?"

Thatcher related his association with Mother Hebron and the blue-robed women. The General listened, slowly sitting back in his chair, dumbfounded.

"So, they be tied to the White Deer, sir. Some be sisters from the old church. Some just women folk. And Mother Hebron, well she leads them."

The General was quiet for a moment. "I've no doubt with which side this group would be aligned, but I don't know how we can use them. Should we use them? Tricky problem, Thatch."

The "tricky problem" was shelved the next day when word came to the camp that the king's forces were finally on the move. Cearl put Baron Glock in charge of the formidable army. With nearly a thousand well trained troops from the Tamworth garrison, five hundred of the Baron's own militia, and over five hundred of the King's Huntsmen, Baron Glock jauntily left the capital headed toward the dark forest.

CHAPTER 27

Time had always been the main problem for the rebels. Time to gather more troops, time to properly train them.

Surprisingly enough, the Baron gave them exactly what they needed. Never one to arrive too quickly to work or danger, there were frequent stops for refreshment and rest.

A week passed before the Baron's men finally spied the lazy curls of smoke from the homes of Kirkland.

The Baron realized this would be the last chance to get a drink and dinner for a week or more. Seeing a peasant woman in front of a cottage, he stopped and inquired about where to find such a combination in Kirkland. Mother Hebron stared at the Baron. Showing no sign of recognition, she smiled broadly, briefly cited praise of the Three Decker Inn, and pointed towards it.

Without thanks or acknowledgement, the Baron steered himself in that direction. She called after him, "I will see you again, sir."

As he rode away, he yelled back at her. "Not likely old woman."

Mother Hebron watched as the Baron and his officers climbed the slight rise in the road. She mumbled under her breath as soldier after soldier passed by her house, "Oh, I will see you again, Baron Glock."

As the Baron and his officers entered the village, roving bands of the black-suited militia were already looting various stores. A few officers of the King's troops tried in vain to stop the plundering. Seeing the Baron at the head of the column, the officers pleaded for intervention.

The Baron puffed out his chest and rode up to the largest group of marauding soldiers. "Stop that now, men," he ordered loudly. Leaning down to them and speaking so only they could hear, he added, "We can return in a week after we clear up this mess. Perhaps dally a bit with some of the women folk, eh?" He winked. "Back in line for now. Work before pleasure, lads."

The men smiled knowingly; the Baron was just as eager to plunder and rape as they were. Willing to wait, they put down their booty and returned to the main body of the army bivouacking just outside the village.

The night the Baron arrived in Kirkland, a daring plan was devised by Viridius and Petronius. By dawn the next day, nearly two hundred green men were positioned high in the trees along the forest road.

Off to a late start after noon, Baron Glock sauntered to the head of his troops, a small scouting group in front of him. Passing through the dark woods, the uneasy soldiers looked right and left at the impenetrable green surrounding them. They were nervous about the unnatural silence and their imaginations were excited by the stories of the vicious animals and dangerous green men who lurked within the woods. But after a few hours of uneventful passage, the men relaxed.

Suddenly arrows rained down on the long line of soldiers. Dozens were wounded or killed. Red and black scrambled to find cover. They looked into the woods and saw only green. Where to attack? What to attack?

Such indecision did not accompany the huntsmen as they dismounted and darted into the woods on either side of the attack. Gliding from tree to bush, they quickly but carefully infiltrated the green surroundings. The green men were not there. Knowing both the skill and cruelty of the huntsmen, Viridius wisely ordered his troops back to the village. The men traveled swiftly and silently using vines to propel them above the searching huntsmen.

The attack was only a pinch, but the Baron's army was put on notice that these were hostile environs. The column now moved more carefully through the forest as scouts checked the path ahead and huntsmen plodded through the underbrush, screening the army on both sides. The Baron felt he could be of better use positioned safely in the center of the long column. So guarded was their subsequent march that it took them three days to reach the clearing in the center of the woods. Precious time was again bequeathed to the rebels.

Less than a day's march from the rebel base at Bangor Hill, the Baron decided to set up camp in the large clearing. Within hours the quiet meadow was transformed into a noisy camp.

Ostentatiously overseeing the building of his defensive works (though not giving much advice) the Baron tarried there for two days. He would have stayed longer had it not been for the King's messenger requesting that he present, in one week's time, either the body of Pen, dead or alive, or his own body instead. The next morning found the Baron frantically organizing his troops to resume the march.

When the Baron's army finally reached Bangor Hill, the rebel force numbered fifteen hundred able-bodied men, positioned on or about Bangor Hill. The Baron's force, recently strengthened by one thousand of the King's own guards, boasted a force of nearly three thousand troops.

Meanwhile, the country held its collective breath from Tamworth to Port Logan to Kirkland to dozens of small villages dotting the countryside. Any news, reliable or suspect, became the coin of the day. Skirmishes were exaggerated into major battles. From inn to hearth to chance meetings on the street, citizens weighed the information and painted a dozen different pictures of the war. There was one common thread, however: the upcoming battle would be of paramount importance in the struggle.

On an overcast summer morning, the Baron's troops slowly aligned in front of Bangor Hill. Sensing imminent battle, Petronius gave final instructions to his officers: when to press forward, and, more likely, when and where to fall back.

After the captains left the meeting, Pen approached his father outside the command tent. "Sir, please let me help. You know that I am capable with a sword, and I've practiced the bow, and…"

"No, Pen, this is man's work now. Furthermore, we have to protect you, son. Stay with the rear guard by the corral."

His eyes filling with tears, Pen turned and started walking away.

Petronius, a master at reading men and thirteen-year-old boys, realized how utterly useless the lad must feel. An idea caused him to raise his eyebrows. "Pen, wait! I almost forgot…"

The tall man ducked back into his tent. He returned with a sword, nicked and tarnished, but still a formidable tool of death. "This was my first sword as a soldier. Not the prettiest, I admit. I am not even sure why I kept it, but it's yours."

The boy looked at it almost reverently. His father's old sword!

The General placed his hand on the boy's shoulder. "Do as I say. Stay with the rear guard. You and your men may still see action this day. I hope not, Pen, because it would mean that the battle favors the King. If it comes to that, your command may be our last hope." With that Petronius mounted a large white horse and was off to the front line.

The General's words, "your men", was all Pen heard. He was given a command! With renewed enthusiasm, he joined a hundred or so farmers milling around a few horses in the makeshift corral. He looked at the men, most of whom he knew. He gave orders tentatively, and was astonished the men actually listened to him. Soon he had them positioned and ready should any of the enemy break through during the battle.

He eyed Mirus in the pen. The great horse was agitated and confused after seeing Petronius ride off. His body pressed against the fence, snorting in frustration as he rushed right and left, looking for the General.

Pen stepped inside the enclosure. He walked alongside Mirus and calmed him. The horse swung his head over Pen's shoulder in a forlorn gesture. Pen hugged the animal, trying to reassure him.

"Looks like we are both destined to guard duty, faithful horse; I because I am too young, and you because you are too old. But, maybe we will surprise them, eh?"

Mirus bobbed his head as if in agreement. Suddenly a rhythmic clanging of the shields could be heard. Pen and Mirus turned their heads toward the sound. The battle for Bangor Hill was beginning.

CHAPTER 28

A few minutes after the pounding of the shields began, the sharp clangs of crossed swords, punctuated by inarticulate cries, could be heard. The battle erupted all along the broad base of the hill. Noise seemed to be everywhere. As minutes dragged into hours, wounded men made their way to the medical tent. As he patrolled the rear area, Pen noted the green grass under the tent was now speckled dark red. He looked into the tent, but quickly looked away. Discarded limbs and dead bodies made a ghastly pile in one corner while the rest of the area was filled with wounded men grimacing in pain, sometimes crying. All the while bloody surgeons worked frantically to save lives. The boy never looked back into the tent.

He walked from one detachment to another, checking on the status of his men. After talking with a few men at the corral, he walked toward another group of soldiers when an arrow rushed past his head and embedded in a nearby tree with an unnerving sound.

Pen crouched down behind the tree looking for the assailant, but saw no one. After that, he ran zigzag paths to avoid being hit.

Other arrows cut through the air, yet he still saw no red or black uniforms. He guessed some of the huntsmen made their way through the thicker part of the forest on one side of the hill. Not knowing the enemy's strength or position, he was unwilling to attack. He positioned some his men behind carts so they would be ready to repel a possible attack from that direction.

Meanwhile, the battle was not going well for the rebels. The Baron's forces were more diminished by losses, but their greater numbers easily absorbed this attrition. Eventually they broke through the outer wall on the lower slope and threatened the shorter inner wall, near the top of the hill. Though the green men's arrows took a toll on the approaching soldiers, too many arrows stuck harmlessly into shields of the approaching army.

While Pen fully recognized gradual weakening of the front line, he could not help. The huntsmen had finally shown themselves and were darting through the woods, using the trunks of trees as protection as they came closer. A steady rain of arrows from deeper inside the thick green effectively froze Pen's men in their positions. Fortunately, Songor showed up with a dozen men to help protect the hospital tent.

A rush by a score of huntsmen threatened the infirmary. The men crouched behind the wagons did not witness their advance. Songor and his men met the huntsmen and stopped their progress, but more huntsmen joined the engagement and pushed them back.

Seeing the attack, Pen called for a few men behind the wagons. The small group charged into the melee as a dozen isolated fights took place in front of the infirmary.

Pen engaged a short man, heavily muscled who, with both hands gripping tight around the handle, swung his sword wildly. The haphazard attack disoriented the boy and he backed off as the little man kept lunging toward him. The man's head was clean-shaven and shined like a helmet. His diminutive stature was compensated by quick, sword slashes high, low, right, and left. The boy parried the blows as best he could. Gradually he was backed against a large tree trunk.

Pen was frightened. This was nothing like fighting with Thatcher or Viridius; there was no polite holding back of dangerous strokes... this man meant to kill him! Pen countered one of the strokes with a move Thatcher had taught him just a few months earlier. Pen and the small man stared at each other for the first time, both surprised by the adroit maneuver Pen performed. Then the months of training took over and he automatically performed the myriad of moves Thatcher had drilled into him. The huntsman backed off a bit. Pen began to swing his sword with more confidence using some of the more aggressive combinations he had been taught. Soon he not only effectively defended himself, but pressed the attack upon the huntsman. Several times the man was wide open to Pen slaying him, but Pen was strangely worried about harming the wild, little man.

A series of strokes finally brought the man down to the ground as Pen's sword was pressed against the man's throat. The boy ceased fighting, as this was when his opponent should have politely conceded to Pen. Instead, the man swung his leg under Pen's and Pen tumbled backward to the ground. The man jumped up and lunged at him with a knife. Before he could bring his raised hand down upon the boy's chest, a sword flashed near the boy's head and plunged into the man's stomach. The huntsman screamed and fell over holding his stomach. Horrified by his close call with death and witnessing the man's death throes, Pen scrambled backwards. A hand grabbed him from behind. Pen looked behind him and saw Songor standing there.

"You all right, young master?" Songor asked concerned.

"Now I am, Songor." He looked around and saw the field cleared of huntsmen. Songor's men had pushed the huntsmen back into the woods. Many of the brave farmers were down and bleeding. One, at least, was dead. Only a few huntsmen were down, apparently subdued by Songor's more experienced veterans who looked into the forest, awaiting another attack.

Pen was disgusted with himself. While he spent time being afraid to hurt his opponent, his inexperienced men had suffered. Before he could punish himself for his lack of action, another assembly of huntsmen, much larger in number than before, charged their position.

He fought with one man who was tall, his body fully tattooed with odd designs. Another huntsman downed one of his men and the two huntsmen doubled up against the boy. After exchanging few strokes with both men, Pen gradually stepped back. The tattooed huntsman pressed aggressively toward Pen, his sword raised high to deliver a deathblow. He stopped mid-swing, eyes widened, and fell face down. An arrow with a blue feather stuck out of his back. Other huntsmen fell from arrows shot from somewhere in the forest. In a few moments the huntsmen had all but disappeared, replaced by blue-cloaked forms gliding from tree to tree, securing cover and firing arrows at the retreating enemy. Pen didn't know who the blue soldiers were, but he was thankful they were on his side.

Over his shoulder he saw the Baron's black-suited militia climb down over the inner wall and attack a group of new recruits, mostly farmers, led by Eldrick. Pen assumed the rear was secured by his unexpected allies, gathered his men, and sprinted to the front.

As he ran to engage the Baron's men, he noted the blue-robed wraiths turned their attack toward the front. The Baron's men engaged the farmers, but looked to the side at a new attack…a relentless and deadly rain of blue-feathered missiles.

Pen and his men met the black-suited warriors in a flurry of action. He clashed with his opponent, handling him easily and quickly. A wounded body rolled on the ground holding his shoulder. Three other black-shirted militiamen intent on revenge replaced the soldier. He did his best to parry the blows, but he had to give ground as he found it difficult and dangerous to engage three at the same time. One of the men fell straight back, an arrow with blue feathers protruded from his chest. Pen struck another man and wounded him. The third started to run away. A blue-cloaked archer, right beside him, strung a blue–feathered arrow. An instant later, the third man was dead on the ground.

As he watched the last man fall, he turned to thank his savior. The figure turned toward him at the same moment and unfurled the hood covering her hair. As light brown curls bounced out from their former confinement, he stood face-to-face with Liana.

She looked at him and smiled. "Hello, Pen. Did you think that we learned to bake pies from mother on all those mysterious get-togethers? Silly boy."

She darted from him and scampered up the wall that had been secured by Eldrick's men, and returned to her lethal work. He looked around at the other blue-robed silhouettes; many had removed their hoods. They were all women! Pen shook his head in wonderment. Pen mounted the wall beside Liana.

He saw Thatcher's men press the retreating line of the Baron's men. More and more blue-robed women lined up along the inner wall, raining death upon the enemy. Pen watched the panorama for a few seconds: the Baron's men running away from the slashing swords and the deadly missiles, the red soldiers desperately trying pull together their fragmented line, the Baron and his officers galloping back into the forest. Seeing the Baron flee, the reds followed.

The battle was over…the rebels had won.

CHAPTER 29

As Pen jumped back inside the compound, he noticed the blue-robed women had transformed from warriors into caring nurses, tending to the wounded rebels. One lady seemed to be directing the other women. Though he could not make out the face, he recognized the mannerisms. He came up behind her and tapped her shoulder. Mother Hebron cried in surprise, tilted her head, and held out her arms to the boy. Before he could protest, familiar arms wrapped around him. She sobbed, a sound he had never heard from her. He reassured her by hugging her and patting the small woman on the back. Wiping her nose, she looked at him.

"Oh, how glad I am to see you're not hurt. And your father, where is he?"

This last question rocked Pen. Somehow he never considered his father could be one of the many bodies littering the ground. He abruptly pushed her away and frantically scanned the battle field. Where was he? Relieved, he saw his father carry Eldrick through an opening in the inner wall, probably en route to the medical tent.

"He's over there, Mother Hebron."

"Oh, no!" she exclaimed, thinking that the bearded Eldrick was Larmack. Leaving Pen alone, she ran to the pair. They reached the tent before she finally caught up to the long-striding General. She leaned down to look into Eldrick's face and saw that it was not Larmack. Casting a glance at the officer who had carried the farmer, she recognized a face from long, long ago.

"General Petronius!"

The General gently laid Eldrick on a cot and turned to the woman beside him. "Mother Hebron...how thankful I was to see you and your women."

She gazed at him, dumbfounded. "So, you have returned. I know we need to talk, sir, but I am looking for a friend of mine, a farmer. He is tall and has a heavy gray beard. Have you seen him?"

"No, I haven't seen him, but I know he is quite safe and unhurt."

"Pardon me, sir, but I need to see him for myself." She frantically looked through the tent, ignoring the rebel leader. As she turned to leave the tent, the General restrained her. He smiled at her, a rare expression for both Larmack and Petronius.

"I hope you were not too offended by my poorly chosen words on the night of the party?"

She looked at the man, confused.

"All those meals you served me in your home and you don't recognize me? Mother Hebron, I am truly hurt." She looked more carefully at the General. Her eyes grew wider as her hand went to her mouth.

"Larmack... you were General Petronius! All this time, you were General Petronius."

He nodded his head and shrugged. "Regrettably so, ma'am. I apologize for the deception. I had to be careful."

She shook her head. "No, no! There is no need for an apology. Now I fully understand... so many things. Why the General disappeared, how Pen came into my life. Everything. How blind I have been!"

"Not blind, dear lady. Trusting. Things are not always as they seem."

She looked at him with a twinkle in her eye. "Funny, I told Pen the same thing, long ago. But, those words could now serve you as well."

Now it was his turn to look at her quizzically.

"General, you don't recognize me, do you?"

"Of course I do. You are Mother Hebron. The leader of a fine army of women warriors." He looked over the many women who now attended the wounded and dying. "And, apparently, leader of a good many nurses, too."

She held a lock of her fine white hair. "Seventeen years ago, it was blond. Does the name Mary help?"

He looked at her and his gaze became more intent; his eyes widened. "You were the sister in the church!"

She nodded. "One and the same. Changed my name too, Larmack. I too was afraid of being found out by the King."

He reached down and hugged her. With arms wrapped tightly around her, he whispered in her ear.

"Dear lady, you saved my son, years ago. You saved him today, as well. I owe you."

She stepped away and looked up at the farmer she had known for thirteen years. Were those tears filling his eyes? She wasn't sure.

Looking around at the broken bodies in the tent, the smile left her face and she noted seriously, "I think it will take both of us to save Pen again."

He squeezed his eyes and drew his fingers across them. There remained no evidence of any emotion. "You're right, Mother Hebron. You, I, and a great many more people and... a plan."

The General left, yelling commands to his soldiers.

Larmack was gone forever. In his place, a General shouting orders.

When the bodies of the dead and wounded were counted, the rebels estimated the Baron had lost nearly five hundred men. Though the smaller army suffered considerably fewer losses, everyone knew someone who was killed or badly maimed. Even with the addition of four hundred blue-robed female warriors, the rebels were still the inferior force.

After a somber supper, the captains met in the command tent. Standing around a large table, they looked at Petronius who studied the crude map.

"We were lucky today, sir," observed Thatcher, a bloodied cloth wrapped tightly about his arm.

Petronius had been engrossed with the map laid out in front of him. He looked up, first at Thatcher, then to the others.

"Yes. But, it wasn't just luck. You trained the men well. They didn't break line without a command. The defensive works gave us an advantage as well. We will have to repair that wall quickly. Most important was Mother Hebron's help...I couldn't have planned her entry into the battle any better."

Petronius looked back to the map. He pointed to a rough sketch of the Baron's camp. "The Baron is here. I am sure he is securely surrounded by all of his men."

There were a few chuckles. The General looked up at his officers. There was no smile on his face. "Fortunately he can't know the extent of our losses or the size of our force. That ignorance will discourage him from attacking too soon. Unfortunately, he will get reinforcements. Thatcher..."

Having already informed the General, Thatcher shared with the other captains that his contacts in the castle reported the King was planning to send more reinforcements to the Baron.

Petronius nodded and continued his assessment. "The Baron will wait until he has those men at his side before he attacks us again." A harsh, humorless laugh escaped the General's lips. "No one can call the Baron impetuous."

"Presently we have an edge in only one category and that is our artillery." He nodded to both Mother Hebron and Viridius. "Otherwise, the enemy has a stronger cavalry and better foot soldiers and a greater number of each."

Viridius asked the question which hung in the air: "How can we get more men, Petronius? Won't the Earl come now?"

Petronius shook his head. "We have to secure Markwood Forest and we can't do that yet. There may be other men from the countryside, but getting through the patrols and the woods is increasingly difficult. By the way, how did you ladies manage to get past the soldiers?"

She smiled and pulled up her hood. With a forlorn face, she closed the cloak tight about her face, looking like a kind grandmother. Speaking in soft feminine voice, she replied,

"Why, we are but helpless women. We can cook, clean, and lend a hand in so many ways to you poor soldiers." She batted her eyes.

Petronius smiled. She threw back her hood and switched to her more business-like voice.

"Of course they were hoping for more than just cooking and cleaning, so they let us through. Once in, we went off road to gather our weapons; they were hidden in our training grounds that happened to be in Markwood. Then we trekked toward Bangor Hill."

"Viridius, why didn't you tell me?" asked the General with a stern stare.

"Sir, they be just women. I had no idea…"

Mother Hebron glared at the green man and, seeing her fierce face, he decided silence might be his best, perhaps his only, defense. Before the lady in blue could take aim with acerbic words, a lowly farmer saved Viridius.

"Sir, what about them Northlanders?" asked Eldrick limping to the table from where he sat nursing his wounded leg. "They have horses and warriors… and better horsemen than the King's men. Might even us up with cavalry."

Petronius ruefully shook his head. "No. Let's just say they might be more easily persuaded to fight against me than for me. I was the one who made the treaty and they haven't forgiven me for breaking it, even though that was Cearl's handiwork. I have a death sentence on my head from Bruder himself. No, don't expect help from that quarter. Let's leave them out of our plans."

And so the talk went on. By the end of the meeting they all knew the problem: they needed more men to even the odds, but no one knew how or where to get them. Pen left the meeting depressed. Again, as a mere boy, he was pretty much ignored in the war council. And why not? What could he offer?

CHAPTER 30

The next morning found Songor and Pen chopping down trees for the resurrection of the outer wall. Songor wiped his brow with the back of his hand. He briefly pondered the height of the sun and figured it was high enough for him to take a break, so down he sat on crossed legs.

"Whoever thunk war be farm work?"

Spying a curving road leaving the forest and across some grassy knolls, Pen asked, "Songor, where does that road lead?"

"Northlands, young master."

"They talked about them last night at the meeting. Are they good warriors?"

"Aye, lad. They be good, very good. Best riders around too."

"I've heard so many stories about my father. I know they all can't be true. But one was that he went alone into their country during the war with them, and came back, unharmed!"

"Well, no. Maybe yes. Cearl told him ta take the army and knock 'em Northlanders around a bit. But your Da', he made the peace." Songor shook his head, frowning. "He is a brave one and stupid, I say. Oh, I love him, master Pen. I owe me life to your Da'. But brave and stupid is he."

The squat man, his bald head beaded with sweat, took out the cloth again and wiped himself dry.

"He gets on Mirus and rides off. People seen him go and figure him dead. Yet out comes he, three days later, looking like he just doan gone for a hello trip to a neighbor."

"What happened?" Pen asked.

"They just let him go. They be mean folks, them Northlanders, but maybe they like brave, stupid men."

Pen was quiet, thinking about the Northlanders. Strange people to like...what was it his fat friend said? Brave, stupid people.

Songor slowly raised himself up. "Well, back to work, master Pen."

The meeting that night found the group going over the same ground as the night before. The group knew two things. They didn't have enough men, and the Baron would soon be getting over a thousand more. In the next battle they would be outnumbered even more than the previous one, even with the "fine lassies" who Viridius complimented as often as he could.

Pen slipped out of the tent as they continued the meeting. He glumly sat alone at one of the campfires that dotted the encampment. Aware of the problems facing the rebel force, he also realized he was the cause of the war. He felt both guilty and helpless.

Liana saw him and sat down beside him quietly, just waiting.

"Liana, everyone says I am the Chosen One. All of these people are fighting for me, some giving up their lives or getting terribly hurt. Well, I don't feel very chosen at all. Maybe I am what I am...a thirteen year old boy that just saw a deer. I'm not the one, Liana."

Liana remained silent for a few moments. She watched Pen angrily poke the fire with a stick, sparks bursting from the agitation. She said softly, "You are a foolish boy. How often have I told you that?"

Pen's head went down dejectedly. Her arm reached out from her cloak and she gently turned his head, her gray eyes locking onto his blue ones.

"You are the Chosen One." He started to look down again, but she forced his head back. "I've thought it might be true for such a long time. Now I am sure. Why? Because you don't believe you are."

They held each other's stare for a few moments. Embarrassed by the intimate contact, she released her hold on his chin and looked at the fire.

Recently, Liana had a knack for both confusing him and exciting him at the same time. He looked down at her and watched her flick a few strands of hair over her ear. The firelight revealed an attractive profile with large eyes and a small nose. She really was quite beautiful, he thought. Turning to speak to her friend, she was startled to find him intently staring at her. She blinked nervously, but plunged ahead with her speech.

"Pen, the White Deer wouldn't have chosen someone vain and self-important. She would have chosen someone just like you...kind and considerate...not sure of himself."

"Well, I am certainly not sure of myself now!" His gaze returned to the fire.

"Are you sure of that?" she asked.

He nodded absentmindedly, then tilted his head and grinned at her. She returned the smile. It was wonderful when she smiled, precious because it was so infrequent. Her pretty face was just inches away from his own. She turned to watch the sparks fly up from the flame as Pen continued to stab at it.

"I feel so helpless. I bring nothing to this effort...no wise advice like my father, no battle experience like Thatcher, no

237

warriors like Mother Hebron." He looked at Liana, seemed mesmerized by the flames licking about the stick.

"You were magnificent in the battle, Liana. I think you saved my life."

She pulled herself away from her reverie.

"Yes, I most certainly did," she replied pertly, her jaunty demeanor returning. She winked.

"Don't worry, Pen. Somehow we will win this war, and you will help. I'm sure."

In one fluid movement she lifted herself off the log, leaned closer to the boy, and kissed him on the cheek. A second later, she walked away.

Pen looked over his shoulder and watched her. The blue robe billowed out covering what he knew was a slender body. Odd, he thought, she walked very fast, almost running.

He felt his cheek where the warmth of the kiss lingered. Hmm…he had never been kissed by Liana before. In fact, no girl had ever kissed him. Just like Liana to try shifting his focus from despair to…to what? Delight? He smiled as he gently touched where she kissed him.

She was such a good friend. Still another person who helped him, he thought ruefully.

Still agitated, he walked towards the corral. Along the way he saw two grizzled veterans who Thatcher had brought in, sitting on short stools outside their tent; they nodded to him as he passed. He overhead one of them say to the other, "Petronius' son."

A few steps later, he saw a farmer whom he recognized and said hello. Compared to the men in uniform, he was dressed in little better than rags. The farmer smiled in recognition and went back to sharpening his sword. He was still just a boy to these men. He felt both offended and relieved by this realization.

He was determined to somehow help. These men and women, these friends and neighbors, deserved more than just a boy meandering sullenly about camp. He had to do something. Just what that something was, he did not know…yet.

Seeing Pen lean on the fence, Mirus walked over to his young master. Apparently he was having a difficult time sleeping as well. He patted the neck of the black horse. "We both feel left out." The horse whinnied.

It was fine to believe, like Liana, that help would come to them just in time, but he knew from the meetings they were both surrounded and outnumbered. The situation was dire; he could hear desperation in their voices. They needed more warriors and soon.

The Northlanders certainly could not be persuaded to help their former enemies. Well, reasoned Pen, we were not their enemy; it was the King. So, we have a common enemy, the boy reasoned. He recalled something Thatcher had said about one of the wars when Mercia allied with Lindsey to fight the pirates: "The enemy of my enemy is my friend."

Just having Cearl as their mutual enemy was not enough, thought Pen. What would they gain by helping us? We could give them land, the very land they wanted years ago. That might entice them to join us. Unfortunately, only the King could give such a gift. He stood still as his eyes opened wide. But if I am the Chosen One, I will be King and I could give it!

A daring, perhaps foolish plan shaped itself from the tangled ideas floating in his head. He hoped Songor was right about the Northlanders liking "brave and stupid" people because he seemed to be in that category right now.

He thought hard for a long time, absent-mindedly stroking the great horse, past the time when the lights from the meeting tent were extinguished, past the time when weary captains checked their guards and retired to their respective tents.

It just might work.

He went to his tent and retrieved his father's sword. In the heavy darkness of the predawn, with only a few distant birds stubbornly suggesting day was close, Pen returned to Mirus. He patted the horse, offering him a bite of apple. Once done, the horse gently sniffed in Pen's pocket, hoping for more. The boy smiled and held the horse's head in both his hands.

"I know you are confused, great horse. Father doesn't ride you into battle anymore. Seems that people view you and me as pretty useless in this war, Mirus. Let's prove them wrong. You are my horse now and the perfect steed to help me." The horse whinnied his agreement.

"Quiet now, Mirus. You carried me as child, then as a boy, old horse. Can you now carry me now as a man? For tonight, we have a man's work to be done." The horse nodded his head excitedly. Pen grinned at the auspicious sign. He saddled the horse, hopped up, and eased the great beast through the camp. Then he and Mirus burst out of the fort.

As he charged past the line of trees recently decimated by the axes, he was in the open grasslands and on his way to Northland. Yells came from two of the Baron's horsemen as they spurred their horses after Pen and Mirus. A fierce, short chase ensued. Already forty feet behind Pen and Mirus, they could not catch up with the giant black shape that ran into the great blackness of the night, disappearing. By the time Pen and Mirus had gained the path to the Northlands, the pursuit had stopped.

At first, the two soldiers were going to alert the captain that someone had managed to get past their station. But, recalling the fate of others who had failed in similar tasks, they decided that it was more prudent for them to report a deer had startled them. Better to suffer the laughter of their peers, than the penalties of their superiors.

Meanwhile, Mirus continued to run hard along the path. After stopping and listening, Pen slowed Mirus to a walk, patting the horse on its neck, still listening. There was no pursuit. The horse was breathing hard again, he noted. But Mirus kept nodding his head as great blasts of air exploded from his nostrils.

When Mirus had sufficiently rested, Pen urged him forward at a pace sufficient for the task. Night traveled west and the world turned pink with the dawn. Rolling hills displayed lush grass and wild flowers, with a significant spattering of trees. Pen figured that this was the contested region between Mercia and the Northlanders. This was the same land that he, as king, would give back to them.

By mid-morning, the gentle hills behind him, he entered a rocky, barren area... the Northland. The path simply disappeared on the stone-studded surface, so he walked along the river, a path Mirus had traveled many times before.

CHAPTER 31

As they rode between the two steep valley walls, Mirus snorted and shook his head. Pen patted the horse's neck and looked at the top of the ridge.

"I know, boy. We're being watched."

The valley widened into a barren brown-red wasteland covered with rugged weeds and a few stubborn bushes.

He heard galloping from behind, turned his head slightly, but decided not to look back. He did not want to show fear or even curiosity. Suddenly another horse, as large as Mirus, paced beside him. The horse carried a warrior with worn woolen pants and a tattered brown tunic, Pen, his heart pumping hard, kept his gaze straight ahead. A minute later another warrior appeared on his other side. Pen and his two escorts stared straight ahead without acknowledging each another. Then he heard the hoof beats of more horses behind him, and he could not resist looking. At least a dozen warriors and horses of all sizes and colors followed with more galloping down the hills on both sides. He noted that all of the brown-shirted warriors were covered with red tattoos of wild designs.

Pen and his escort were buffeted by a strong wind from the west. The hills gradually disappeared as though blown away by the constant, fierce wind. Now they rode on a wide plain covered with splotches of green where horses and cows intently searched for tuffs of grass. As they passed crude huts, curious women holding thin children lined up to watch the procession, their eyes riveted on Pen, but not smiling. A large structure, ancient and decrepit, now more a large pile of rocks and boulders than a castle, stood before him. As he and Mirus approached, a half ring of horsemen stood behind a tall bearded man standing on the ground in the center of the path. Though he was also outfitted with a brown tunic, he had no tattoos. His beard was bushy... black with strands of gray lending him the distinction of age. Of average height, he was heavily built with no evidence of fat.

The riders stopped in front of this man whose dark eyes bored into Pen's. Dismounting Mirus, he patted the horse and whispered reassurance into his ear. Turning he faced the leader who had to be the infamous King Bruder. The man's arms were folded, feet apart, a scowl greeting the boy.

"Greetings, King Bruder. I am..."

Bruder uncrossed his arms and waved both hands back and forth rapidly, silencing the boy.

"I know who you are. You are Pen, son of Petronius... Petronius, our sworn enemy. Do you think us ignorant of happenings beyond our land?"

"Sir, I..." again Pen was interrupted.

The King waved his hands again, silencing the boy. "Did I give you permission to speak, boy?"

"My apologies, King Bruder, but I was..."

Again the hands waved "Why is it you always speak of "I"? "I" this and "I" that. Do you only think of yourself, boy?"

Unbalanced from the verbal attack, Pen blinked and shook his head. "I..."

The King started to wave his hands still again, but Pen continued loudly. "I am here to discuss an allegiance with you."

The King stopped waving his hands and looked at Pen. A hush came over the crowd. "By whose authority, child?"

Pen confidently spoke well-rehearsed words.

"By my own, King Bruder. I am the Chosen One and soon to be king. My people need your help now. For that help I am willing to concede certain lands to you."

Bruder looked at the lad, astonished and then laughed. The King quickly swiveled his head, raised an eyebrow, and leaned into the boy so that their faces nearly touched. "You are no king! You don't even have hair on your face, boy. And, from what my spies tell me, you and your father will never have a chance to make you king. The Baron is setting up his forces to attack again and he is even stronger."

Bruder smiled with some satisfaction seeing Pen upset by this news. Before the boy could recover, he motioned for his guards.

"Take him away." As the bewildered Pen was held firm by two of his men, Bruder tapped a finger hard upon his chest.

"Tomorrow, I will kill you, Pen, son of Petronius."

CHAPTER 32

After Pen galloped off, the rebel guards reported to the captain in charge. The captain immediately reported to the General. At first Petronius worried that a traitor might have defected to the enemy. This could have disastrous consequences if the deserter gave their strength and disposition, which was weak and disorganized. When Pen and Mirus were found missing, an even more serious threat emerged. Petronius sent Thatcher with a few men to search the region just outside the outer wall. Just after dawn they returned with grave news.

"We followed his path to the river, sir. Some sort of pursuit but only for a short distance. No one followed him into the grasslands."

"He was riding toward the Northlands?" Petronius asked incredulously.

"Looks that way, sir."

Petronius turned away. He divined Pen's plan. The son was trying to get men the father couldn't. Sensing the General's agitation, Thatcher left. Petronius gripped the table.

"A foolish venture. Now all is lost."

Minutes later his officers arrived. Petronius turned to face them.

"As you know Pen left the compound. He told no one where he was going, but it seems that he travels the Northland, perhaps to request help."

Some looked at the ground, fearing the worse. A few merely shook their heads in disbelief. Songor started to leave.

"Songor!" Petronius called sharply. "Where are you going?"

The portly man's face, no longer able to mount any sort of smile, showed only sagging folds of despair.

"To fetch him back, sir. He's our boy, ain't he? I aim to get him back," came the muffled response as he wiped his nose with his sleeve.

Petronius walked to Songor and gently pried him away from the tent flap. The tall man, his own eyes glistening, put his hand on Songor's shoulder. "No," he said softly, "It's too late for that dear friend. Were it not, we would ride together."

Songor stumbled back inside and collapsed in a chair near the General's cot. His hands covered his face, as he quietly sobbed.

A messenger burst into the tent. "General, there's an army forming in the valley below us…a very large army, sir," the man said breathlessly.

He snapped out orders to his captains. They ran from the tent, hurrying to set their men or women into position. He turned to his old servant in the corner. Songor had stopped crying. Now he stared dumbly at the ground. Petronius walked over to the man and patted his back. Songor looked up, his eyes still filmed with tears.

"The best decision I ever made was letting you come with me on that terrible night when Elen died. I could ask for no better companion."

A face so different than ever he had seen on the servant now faced the General. Great sorrow hangs far too heavy on those who are simple and love life.

"I be worried about our boy, sir."

"I know you worry as much as I do. But if we fail today, Pen returns to his death. Do you understand, Songor?"

Head down, Songor nodded. The red-faced man, a halo of white hair crowing his head, wiped away his tears, heaved himself up and stood as tall as he could, though considerably shorter than the General.

"What be ye orders for me and me men, sir?"

Petronius smiled. Fiercely loyal, dedicated to protecting Pen, and determined to do his best, Songor would never fail him. "Secure those woods from the huntsmen who are sure to come through. Use both your men and Pen's." With that said, Songor ran to his men, nimble on his feet for a man so large. Petronius continued giving commands to his other captains, all the while his heart heavy.

CHAPTER 33

The boy was pushed into a small room where he spent the rest of the afternoon and early evening. It was called the dungeon, though it was on the second floor, not underground. It was dry, not damp, and well lit, not dreary. He sat down on the stone floor and considered his plight. After some reflection, he conceded his plan was not going as well as he hoped.

After the sun set, his cell door was abruptly opened by a warrior. Pen was escorted into a larger room where the King sat alone behind a long stone table. He gave no greeting. Food was served. As soon as the platter was placed between them, the boy started eating. Amused by the boy's gusto for this simple offering of bread and cheese, the King could not help but smile.

"You eat well for a boy who is about to die."

Pen mumbled some unintelligible words. He raised his hand, looked at the King, carefully chewed the food in his mouth, swallowed, and took a draught of water. He began again.

"Pardon me sir, I haven't eaten anything in over a day. I figured if I am about to die I might as well eat and feel good now. Or, if death were not my plight, then I would need the nourishment for the trials before me. Either way, this is really good food, sir. Thank you."

Bruder stopped trying to hide his smiles, but tempered his good humor with unsettling words.

"Oh, you will die. Make no mistake, child, you will die." He paused, folded his hands on the table.

"I have but one weakness, Pen, son of Petronius, our sworn enemy, and that is my curiosity. Tell me what you offer if I help you."

Pen wiped his lips clean and swallowed the last bit of food in his mouth.

"You," he said solemnly, "I can give nothing."

The King frowned and Pen hastily added, "But for your people, I am prepared to give the grasslands."

"They should be already ours. Your King broke the treaty."

"Yes, I know. But, when I said I'd give you the grasslands, I meant to give it entirely to you. You will be in charge of that region and the Northlands."

"What else?"

"My protection. If anyone threatens you, they will find me at your side."

The King laughed. "I would feel so safe knowing that you would protect me."

"I would protect you, Bruder!"

The smile disappeared and the King's face darkened.

"Don't speak of me as your vassal! I am a King, boy."

"But I will be King," Pen shot back. "And I keep my word. I will protect my people."

"For the dubious honor of becoming part of Mercia, you want us to fight for you?"

"Yes, I want you to help us now and pledge your loyalty to me. You will be one of my most trusted nobles!"

Bruder looked at him, astonished. He leaned across the table, all mirth gone, his eyebrows pierced in a most menacing stare.

"You come into my kingdom, asking for me to help you win a war you will surely lose. Then you honor me by demoting me to one of your nobles? Surely you are joking."

"Not at all." Pen squinted his eyes as he had seen his father do a dozen times. He leaned into Bruder.

"You need me as much as I need you. When I rode in, you know what I saw? Most of your cattle were thin. You need the grasslands; I can see that. And, we both know that if Cearl is allowed to vanquish us, he will certainly turn on you. Together we can beat him, but separately he will certainly beat us both."

"What do you know of us or how we fight and defend ourselves? You presume too much, boy, and you know too little."

"I know famine and poverty when I see it, Bruder."

Angrily the king snapped back. "You know nothing! I am still king and I will be addressed as such! What is it about you and your father that you so eagerly seek death?"

"You didn't kill my father... King Bruder."

The King pushed up away from the table. "I should have! Then I wouldn't have had to face the impudent requests of his son. Finish your meal. It will be your last. Tomorrow you will die."

The King stomped out. After a few minutes, the guards came back and returned Pen to his cell.

Once more sitting on the floor, he continued to worry that this plan, hatched in the middle of the night while he was distressed, without the advice and consent of the captains or at least Liana, might have troubling weaknesses. He tested the door. It was not secured by a lock, but rather by a rope with an impossibly large knot. He could use the knife Thatcher had given him to cut it. The knife which would never fail the first time used. He reached for the knife, his grip around the handle. If what Thatcher told him was true, he could only use the knife once and have guaranteed success.

In the dark of the night, just before morning, we are at our weakest, often faced with our deepest fears. It was then that Pen heard the whisper... cut the knot and travel on to Lindsey. No pain, no death. But his escape would not bring Bruder and men to the battlefield. Without their help, his people could not survive the Baron's forces. He must stay here and somehow convince Bruder to help him. So, he lay down and went to sleep.

CHAPTER 34

The crowd formed early in the morning just outside the gates of the castle. Waiting for the prisoner, Bruder stood with one of his captains.

"I need to test this boy, Warshock. Let's see what he is made of. I want you to fight him with swords."

The warrior, taller than the King, groaned. "Bruder, he has no beard; there is no contest to be had."

"Yes, but his courage must be tested. I will declare it a fight to the death."

"King, don't ask me to kill this child. I am no executioner," the warrior pleaded.

"I know, Warshock, I know. Try not to kill him but press him hard. I must have a way to measure his mettle."

"As you wish." Shaking his head in disgust, the warrior stepped into the crowd. Bruder called to him.

"And Warshock! Try not to get yourself killed either."

The crowd percolated with anticipation. When Pen was escorted out of the castle doors, the noise abated. As the lad was led to the King, the crowd quieted and all heads leaned a bit closer to hear. One way or another, they would be entertained this morning.

Tall warriors formed a large circle, fifty feet in diameter. The King was at the far side of the circle and Pen was left alone in the center.

Bruder took a few steps toward him. "You slept well, Pen, son of Petronius, our sworn enemy?"

"Very well, King Bruder."

There were some chuckles in the crowd.

"So you are ready to die, Pen?"

During the night Pen had already resigned himself to the possibility. Now he was past worry and fright.

"I am ready sir, if such is my fate. I would really rather like to delay the event for a good many years, though."

Laughter erupted from the crowd.

The King also smiled and said, "Well, sometimes destiny is in our own hands. I have a contest in mind. Are you good at swordplay?"

"Passable, sir."

"I have randomly chosen one of my men to cross swords with you. If you can kill him, I will spare your life and we will help you. Of course, if you lose, well, then it was just as I told you…"

"I know, sir. I will die."

Bruder frowned at the boy. He was not suitably distressed. He was so much like his father.

"Now, to make this truly interesting and show you that I am not a heartless barbarian, I give you a choice. You and your horse can safely walk out of here without any allegiance from us, or you can fight and gamble your life. What say you, boy?"

Before Pen could agree or dispute the terms, Bruder called forth his man. Pen recognized him as the man who first road beside him through the canyon yesterday. He was taller and more muscular than Pen. Indeed, he was taller and more muscular than any man he ever saw.

"What say you, boy?" the King asked curtly.

Pen gulped, hesitated and then answered in a voice far more confident than he was.

"I came for you and your men, King Bruder. I will stay."

A warrior stepped beside Pen, handing him Petronius' old sword. Warshock stretched his great frame and sliced his sword right and left through the air. He moved to the middle of the circle. They faced each other as Pen watched his feet and sword, and Warshock, smiling broadly, watched Pen's eyes.

They traded a few blows, testing each other's abilities. The smile vanished on the warrior's face as he attacked with a series of sharp, sudden thrusts that surprised Pen, who parried each blow effectively, twisting, turning, and rotating to meet the other man's downward stroke perfectly. Exclamations of shock came from the crowd. It was obvious Pen was no common sword fighter.

Slowly and warily the pair circled one another. Warshock attacked again with a different combination. Pen skillfully deflected each blow. He made a quick feint to his left; Warshock retreated. Pen did not pursue. The older man, sweating now and wanting the charade to end one way or the other, attacked again. The boy defended each blow. With blades hooked together, Pen leaned down and swept the other man's legs with his feet while he pushed the man's chest backwards. Warshock stumbled back, but braced his fall with his arms. He rolled to spring up as Pen struck the sword from his hand. Warshock found Pen's blade point pressed against his throat. The crowd gasped. The man and the boy both breathed heavily.

King Bruder yelled to him, "Kill him, boy, if you want my army. We serve only under warriors!"

CHAPTER 35

Pen looked at the man pinned by his sword. Any movement would have the sword piercing the soft part of his throat. Warshock's eyes held no fear. Pen thought, so this is the first man I kill.

Killing in battle is one thing. But, this would be murder, thought Pen. He would not do it. He drew back his sword and walked swiftly to Bruder at the other side of the circle. Swords drawn, soldiers surged around their king.

"I won't play your game, Bruder. I won't kill this man," Pen said angrily. Then he raised his sword and threw it at the King who caught it by the handle.

"If you mean to kill me, do it now. Otherwise, I'm going back to my people and fight against our common enemy."

Pen stood still for a moment, giving the angry King time to use the sword. The lad turned and walked through the crowd to get Mirus.

The King yelled back at him. "Stop!"

Pen stopped.

"Turn around."

259

The King walked over to him and pressed the point of the blade into Pen's chest. Eyes fixed on Pen.

"Have you forgotten, child, that you will die?"

There was no approving noise from the crowd who were impressed with the boy as they had witnessed Pen's magnanimity with Warshock and his bravery in facing the King.

"Oh, yes, Pen, son of Petronius, our sworn enemy. You will die." He stared at the boy a moment longer, then lowered the blade, saying casually, "But not today and not by my hand."

Bruder had assessed Pen's mettle. He was a warrior, certainly...he had bested Warshock and that was no small accomplishment. The lad was unquestionably loyal to his people, intelligent (though brash), and...there was another quality hard to define...an inherent goodness. Though worried about his lack of experience, the King did not doubt his character. Bruder smiled to himself. He recalled he had assigned nearly the same description to Petronius years before.

Bruder looked at his people, ignoring the boy. "We will spare the boy. Cearl can kill him later."

His people were still quiet.

"I confess his death would sadden me. He is a brave one, this son of Petronius. We showed him death. He did not cry or plea."

He looked at Pen as he spoke.

"At first I thought him foolish, coming here and demanding us to fight for him as though he was already King."

The King paused for a moment, his head down, rubbing his chin. "But I thought on it more. When Cearl is done with the boy, he will surely come after us. If we fight, death or slavery will certainly be our fate."

His slowly scanned his people. "The boy was right. Divided we both die. If we join forces with the rebels, we could beat Cearl. It comes down to this: either we fight today with the Chosen One, or die tomorrow without him."

Bruder returned beside Pen and put a hand on his shoulder. "He has proven himself to me. This man before you is bold, wise, and a great warrior. Can anyone here doubt that? He is a man I can follow. He is a man I will follow."

Bruder waited for the murmurs in the crowd to subside. "I have made my decision. I will fight beside this man. I will fight beside..." here he paused for a few seconds as he looked at his people.

"...my king. But, that is my choice. You must make your own."

He turned to Pen and gave his sword back to him. Kneeling on one knee, Bruder looked up and declared, "I call you King and humbly pledge to serve you. I offer you my life. You have my unswerving loyalty from this moment on."

With that the King bowed his head. Pen was speechless. Bruder, with his head still bowed, whispered, "Tap me once on each shoulder, you damn fool!"

Pen did as he was told. Suddenly he heard a rustling from the crowd and he looked up to find every man, woman, and child bowed down before him. Again a whisper instructed him.

"Say something, lad, anything. Speak!"

Dumbfounded, Pen blurted out, "Let's go!"

After some confusion, the great tribe before him rose and chanted,

"Long live the King! Long live the King!" In the tumult that followed, with their hands locked and raised high together to the cheering multitudes, Bruder, smiling broadly, looked at Pen.

"Let's go? Couldn't you think of anything a bit more inspiring?"

Pen shrugged with a smile. "I don't know much about being a King,"

A stern look replaced the smile as Bruder replied. "Learn fast, sire. Learn fast."

That night blades were sharpened as well as other preparations for the march that would take place the next day.

Bruder, Warshock, and Pen watched women clear plates from the feast all enjoyed.

Pen turned to Bruder. "Sir, would you really have come with me if I had killed Warshock?"

Bruder laughed, wiping the foam from his mouth that remained after imbibing a particularly large gulp of mead. "No, of course not. You would have been dead a moment later. I don't want a king like Cearl and killing Warshock...well, that's what Cearl would have done. Much as I like Warshock, however, I was rather hoping you would have killed him."

Both Pen and Warshock were mutually shocked and both looked at Bruder.

"Why would you hope I killed him?"

"Perfectly obvious. This war could have been avoided. With Warshock dead, you would be dead. Then there would be no need to march against the King. That would have spared the deaths of many good men you see about you now."

Pen reared back and frowned. "But what about Cearl attacking you later?"

Bruder looked at him with raised eyebrows, shocked by his naivety. "It sounded good to you and to them." He pointed to the men carrying weapons and food to their horses.

"But it doesn't make sense, young Pen. After killing you, Cearl would have done anything for me. We would have been safe or possibly better off as he might have relented on the grasslands. Besides, why would he want this godforsaken land? No, killing you was, by far, the best way to go with this."

Pen closed his eyes and shook his head. He gulped, not sure if the answer to the next question was one he wanted to hear. "Then why didn't you just kill me?"

The great bearded man looked at him and smiled. "The great bearded man looked at him and smiled.

"Because Cearl is evil, my liege. I would rather die with you than live with him."

After a few minutes of silence, Pen asked, "Sir, why not leave now?"

Again Bruder looked at the boy, incredulously.

"You do have much to learn, your Highness. Two reasons. First, it is always good to look into the hole before you leap. I have sent some men ahead to scout the positions of the enemy."

Cutting an apple into slices, he offered one to Pen and Warshock. "Second, don't expect men to fight well when tired and hungry. Feed them and rest them and they will vanquish the hungry and tired. " He smiled as he ate a slice.

"Hopefully we will get there on time. But if we are too late, then we must be prepared to fight for our own lives. Either way this is best done on a full stomach and well rested. A young boy in prison imparted that wisdom to me."

He smiled as he offered Pen another slice. "Eat and go to sleep. Hopefully tomorrow you will not die."

Bruder patted him on the shoulder and went to oversee more preparations. Pen hoped that the preparations would not delay them past the time they could be of assistance to the small army defending a hill many miles away.

CHAPTER 36

In fact, that small army was desperately struggling to beat off numerous attacks from Baron Glock's men. The defenses that were set up, the expert directions from Petronius, and the vigor of the rebels, successfully thwarted the efforts of the soldiers and the huntsmen. Death was witnessed on both sides of the wall. When night's curtain finally fell on that bloody day, the drama ended, both sides of the wall respected the army on the opposite side. There was no great wave of optimism, no cheers of success, only bone-weary fatigue in the encampment and the grim knowledge that one more day of vigorous fighting would find the rebel force too exhausted and depleted to withstand the onslaught.

The General and his officers made desperate plans in the somber meeting. Everyone except Thatcher left to give final orders to the awaiting troops.

"You're thinking they might push us off the hill tomorrow, aren't you sir?"

"I'm afraid so. We simply haven't enough men. We may have to retreat through the woods and that won't be pretty. Most of the archers will get through to safety as they will be closer to rear, but the rest of us will be cut up pretty badly."

The shorter, muscular Thatcher, his face bristling with an unshaved beard, stood erect and saluted his general. "I'm at your back, sir."

Petronius looked up with a weary smile. "I know, Thatcher. If I had a dozen more like you, this affair would have ended differently. But," he put his outstretched hand on the shoulder the loyal captain, "alas, I only have one. For that one I am thankful."

Thatcher left. The General collapsed into the chair by his cot. For the hundredth time, he wondered about the fate of his silly, well-meaning son. Where was he now? Was he safe? Would he return in time for the inevitable retreat?

Deep in thought, he did not know Liana had entered the command tent. She coughed lightly to gain his attention. He turned and was surprised to see her. The last time they had talked was weeks ago at Pen's birthday party. He slowly rose from his chair to greet her.

"Yes, Liana?"

The girl remained in the opening of the tent; her lower lip was trembling.

"General... Petronius..." she began and rushed into his arms. Then she began to sob.

"Oh, Larmack, it was my fault. Mine. I am so sorry." Her hands went to cover her eyes as she cried.

He hugged her for a moment and then gently held her away to see her face. "What are you talking about, Liana?"

The girl related the conversation she and Pen had before he ventured into the Northland.

"I should have stayed and talked things over with him. I should have stopped him, Larmack. Oh, what have I done?"

The General sighed, recognizing she had been struggling with guilt for the last few days.

"Liana, dear child, this was not your fault any more than it was mine or your mother's. All of us have protected Pen over the years, you, perhaps most of all, but Pen is grown now. He makes his own decisions. None of us can stop that."

She teared up again and sniffed a bit. "You're right. He can be so stubborn sometimes. I just hope he's not hurt or...or..."

He hugged her again, tears forming in his eyes, and said, in a choked voice, "So do I, dear child. So do I."

In fact, Pen was quite fine and sleeping in one of the stone huts of the Northlander capital. He slept surrounded by over two thousand warriors who had just vowed to keep him safe at all costs.

The next day dawned with gray skies; a captain stirred the sleeping General.

"Sir, Songor needs you."

A minute later Petronius was beside his old friend.

"Sir, thar be many in the woods now. Seen 'em forming this morning. Huntsmen and reds, sir. The forest be blocked." Petronius grimaced. He told Songor to set up carts as a make-shift wall.

The news of their blocked escape route spread through the camp. The rebel army resigned itself to its predicament. Outnumbered, stretched physically to their limits and now encircled, they waited for the battle to begin. Knowing retreat was impossible, the men watched with as the Baron's troops grouped for an attack. Instead of fear spreading through the beleaguered camp, simmering anger settled in. The rebels were determined the Baron and his men would pay a dear price today.

The attack did not begin until high noon. There was no preliminary dashing and darting of cavalry trying to confuse and extract wild responses of arrow and spear, only a gritty onslaught of men in red and black attacking up the grassy slope.

Despite the heavy numbers threatening to overrun the walls, Petronius did not release his reserves, keeping them on guard knowing the huntsmen and other soldiers would attack from the forest. He moved along the outer wall effectively doing the job the reserves would have done, his presence raising the confidence and action of the men.

An hour later, dozens of ladders landed with a thud against the outer wall. Despite the best efforts of the rebels and the tireless fighting and leadership of Petronius, red and black tunics overran the front wall. The Baron's troops jumped from their newly gained position to the ground and the battleground shifted to between the inner and outer walls. Meanwhile, free of the deadly arrows from the archers, the King's men began tearing down portions of the wall. Fearing a rush by the Baron's massive cavalry, Petronius ordered his troops back to the inner wall and the encampment.

Then the huntsmen and the King's men pressed a rear attack. Petronius released the reserves composed mostly of farmers and merchants, to aid Songor. Pressed now on all sides, the rebels stubbornly held the shorter, interior line marking the perimeter of the camp. The arrows from the green men and blue women exacted a heavy toll on the attackers, but the number of effective fighters defending the inner walls was alarmingly reduced. Death showed no discrimination during the afternoon, men fell equally on both sides of the wall. Surprised at the vigor of the defense, the ever cautious Baron was reluctant to commit to a final charge.

Portions of the inner wall were torn down during the furious bouts between the king's men and the rebels. Those small holes were vigorously defended. Looking over the defenses from atop the wall, Petronius watched for an attack from the Baron, who still resisted committing the bulk of his army. He noted a large group of horses charging from the hills in the north quadrant where the wall had its widest opening. The General jumped down and grabbed a few men who slowly followed, running through the thick molasses of fatigue. These meager reinforcements would not be sufficient to stop the onslaught, he thought with deep despair. If they break through here...well, it would be the end. He led his small company of men to meet the Baron's militia who were already entangled with other rebels defending the gap. The militia backed away from the General's vigorous attack. A dozen men stood ready to face the onslaught of galloping horsemen, now starting up the long hill toward them. To his dismay he saw hundreds of horses approaching.

He looked more closely, puzzled. The men atop the horses wore brown tunics, not the red of the King's army. His frown changed into a grin when he saw that they were attacking the rear of the Baron's army and causing great havoc among the militia. Then he saw a great black horse, ridden by Pen, slicing left and right, a wake of fallen black tunics left behind. Petronius felt both pride and relief, a weight lifted from his shoulders, but he could not stop to enjoy these feelings for long. There was a battle to be won.

He turned to the men behind him and pointed to the surge of horses cutting through the Baron's army.

"Behold the Chosen One, leading Northlanders to help us. Let's greet him with our own steel. Push the Baron's men back!"

Finding that smoldering flicker of energy from deep within and having it fanned by watching Petronius charge into the midst of the enemy, old veterans and young farmers followed him and attacked.

Confused by the sudden rush into their center, the Baron's troops backed up. Why, they wondered were the defenders who were all but defeated moving toward them?

Viridius watched the great drama unfold, and quickly brought archers to the wall. "Fire deep into the back, lads, and keep firing."

Green men hurriedly strung their bows, angled them high, and released. Soon a rain of green arrows bit into unsuspecting flesh.

More and more rebels joined the attack in the front. The blacks in the rear looked left and right to see comrades pinned with green-feathered missiles, and behind them, the increasing volume of horses and men.

A few men started to run from the melee. Without the Baron or even a captain to rally the large mass of reserves, they backed up, uncertain. The trickle turned into a flood, men dropping weapons and fleeing back over the ground they had so recently secured. The Baron watched from the bottom of the hill in horror as the King's soldiers started to retreat as well, some actually running past him. A few seconds later, he joined the fleeing soldiers, soon leading them back into the forest, the dust cloud from his galloping horse his last order.

Seeing the commotion in the front, the huntsmen without even looking at one another, slowly backed up into the dark forest from whence they came; no need to expose themselves to full wrath of the rebels. They were willing to fight another day. The King's soldiers kept pressing the attack, but the rebels easily handled those few men.

Pen and the Northlanders wreaked havoc, hundreds were wounded or dead. Realizing they could not outrun horses, most of the black tunics threw down their weapons and raised their hands, yielding to the savage tribesmen on horses. Pen and Bruder quickly sped through the line making sure surrenders were honored. Petronius ordered several green archers to follow the Baron's retreating army, ascertain their strength, and find out where they were headed. He told Thatcher to arrange pickets outside the walls to be on the lookout for a sudden, though unlikely change of heart from the Baron. Having secured the battlefield, he scoured the arena, littered with bodies, searching for his son.

CHAPTER 37

Pen dismounted from Mirus, patted the snorting steed, and walked up the slope toward camp. Liana ran to meet him, and Pen gave her a great smile. She pushed him hard, almost knocking him down.

Grimy from the battle, hair disheveled, she yelled, "Don't ever do that again, Pen!" Her face was flush from exertion and the anger that had built up inside her.

"Do what?" asked Pen, stepping away, bewildered by her greeting.

She kept pressing closer to him, pushing him. "Don't ever go off without telling me! Promise me, Pen! Promise me!"

Still backing up, he responded quickly. "Okay, okay! I'm sorry Liana."

She lunged at him and he leaned away, expecting to be hit by her, but she hugged him tightly, her face buried in his neck. Pen was totally baffled now, but he wrapped his arms around the girl and held her tight.

"I was so worried, Pen." She quietly sobbed in his embrace. "Never again, Pen, never again. You promised," she whispered.

Suddenly aware of their intimacy with others smiling and watching, she pushed away from him, red-faced, but this time from embarrassment. Before either could decide on how to react next, Mother Hebron turned him around and embraced him.

"Oh, my boy, my boy! You're all right. You gave us such a fright."

He hugged her as he had hugged Liana. Mother Hebron was also crying. Petronius arrived and grabbed his son from the two women and hugged him hard, further embarrassing him. He, at least, did not cry.

"Pen, my son. I was worried you might be wounded."

"Sir, no battle wound could hurt me as much as you have now!" laughed Pen.

Petronius held his son at arm's length. "I thought I lost you, boy!"

"You did!" thundered a voice behind him. Petronius turned to see Bruder walk toward them. "A boy left you, but a man returned."

Red-faced and sweating, he went on to relate how Pen entered his country as his father had done years before. "The elder petitioned for peace and the younger demanded war, yet both were cut from the same oak."

Petronius could see the King was fond of his son. When Bruder told him that he allowed himself to be a vassal to his son, Petronius looked at his son, astonished. Before the battle, he considered him a boy to care for and mold into a man. Now he saw the man: brave, daring, loyal to his friends and family, and one worth following, apparently, as thousands of Northlanders followed him into battle. The Chosen One. A king.

He realized then this was not just an effort to save a son. It was, more importantly, a war to save a kingdom. He wondered if his earlier embrace might be the last between the two. He wasn't sure that he would be allowed to hug a king.

A wild assortment of people surrounded the scene as brown-shirted natives on horseback, blue-robed women holding bows, ragged farmers holding spears, gray-shirted veterans, and the green men, circled them. The chant started somewhere in the ranks, and as more heard the chant, they joined in and it grew louder.

"Penda! Penda! Penda!"

Pen walked toward his tent, patted on the back numerous times by men he knew only by sight. A familiar face greeted him at the tent.

"Jack!"

Now not quite as tall as Pen, but much heavier with muscles, the scraggly haired boy hugged his friend, picking him off the ground. Pen grunted uncomfortably.

"What are you doing here, Jack?"

"Doing nothing here now, but came to help, I did. Pa left me behind to handle the barn, but there be no more horses in Kirkland. 'Sides, Eric's pa took over Kirkland, he did. And Eric decided it was a fine time to pester me. So, off went I to join up. Just as well, Pen. Couldn't let my friend get into a tussle without me!"

He mussed Pen's hair. Pen looked around, slightly embarrassed by the action and then dragged his friend inside the tent, out of view. There they talked of friends and neighbors, the war momentarily forgotten.

*

Petronius called his officers together for the evening war council. Their exhausted bodies sagged with fatigue, but their eyes were bright and focused. Instead of frowns, his captains happily donned smiles, their voices bubbling with praise. For the first time, he had to raise his voice to divert their attention from the celebrations.

"First we must decide what to do with the prisoners. Thatch, how many are there?"

"Sir, the number is not yet fixed, but last count was some six hundred. That don't count the wounded…hundreds more, sir."

This was more than anyone could have guessed.

He turned to Bruder. "Maybe the Northlands could use them as slaves. Can we depend on your men handling them, King Bruder?"

Bruder shook his head. "Not likely. With all my men here, there is just enough food for the women and children left behind. Those slaves could end up enslaving my women!"

Viridius blurted out that he also could not handle the vast number of prisoners, but he surprised the group by saying, "Let them go, I say. How many would return to Glock? Men either fear him or laugh at him. Keep the reds though, as they would most likely return to the King."

After a long silence, Petronius looked at Thatcher. Both knew that prisoners usually ended up starving or dying from sickness. Of course, there could be a prisoner exchange, but, at this point, the enemy had no prisoners of their own.

Thatcher called them "the sheathed knife at our heart."

"They are going to die anyway, Petronius. Kill them now," Bruder said coldly with an expressionless stare. The words hung in the air, unchallenged.

During the lull while Petronius composed his thoughts, Pen spoke up. "We will not kill our countrymen."

It wasn't voiced as a suggestion, but stated as a command. All eyes turned towards him.

"I will handle the problem of the prisoners."

Many of the captains still saw the boy, not the man. Only Viridius and Bruder saw the truth. Gone was the uncertain boy, and in his place stood a confident man. For Pen, the play-acting with Bruder had become real.

Petronius looked at the man who would be king.

Petronius broke the stunned silence with a simple question. "What would you do with them?"

"I will handle the problem...my way. If I submit my plan to you now, we will be here all night. Let me handle it my way. It is late, and I am sure there is much to discuss."

Petronius looked at his son. He could see his son's eyes waiting for his approbation. Well, thought Petronius, if he is to be king, he must be allowed to make decisions...and mistakes.

"All right, Pen. Thatcher will give you men to accomplish whatever task you have in mind."

There were some polite protests from a few in the group, citing Pen's inexperience and the importance of the task at hand. Petronius raised his hand to quiet the group and then spoke sharply to his officers.

"Were it not for Pen convincing King Bruder to help us, we wouldn't be struggling with this problem, would we? Pen created the problem... thankfully... let him handle it."

With that said, Petronius went on to other matters. After the meeting, Pen told Thatcher what he would require the next morning. As Pen walked outside, he was warmly greeted by those with whom he was already acquainted, and eyed with wonder and admiration by others he did not yet know. He passed two soldiers sitting in a tent, and the men stood up and nodded at him. He passed a farmer cleaning his blade. The man nodded and said, "Sir." He walked back to his tent, walking on air.

CHAPTER 38

The prisoners milled around aimlessly inside a ring of armed guards. With Thatcher and a few guards at his side, Pen, now dressed in a dark purple tunic and black pants, elbowed his way through the ring of guards. A tight arc of prisoners formed in front of Pen. Thatcher and his guards were overwhelmingly outnumbered. The short man looked nervously up to some nearby trees. There, his bow already strung tight, Viridius and a few of his green men were hidden, watching the red and black uniforms swirl around the lad.

Pen at first appeared to be studying the ground, his face perplexed. Then he looked up, his forehead wrinkled, as though in thought.

"People say I am the Chosen One. Even if true, becoming king is difficult."

More loudly, he continued. "To win this war, to become king, it will take good, strong men...more than we have now. Good, strong men who will follow a good, strong leader."

The words that he had practiced the night before came together. His voice strong and confident, he continued. "You are here because the Baron betrayed you. He ran away. You all saw his cowardice."

He paused to look at the assembly before him. The sight of a boy speaking like a man transfixed the men. And, his eyes…

"Running away is something I will never do. Leaving my men behind is something I will never do." Pen paused again.

"Get to it boy, we ain't got all day!" The words were spit out of the grizzled face of a short, red-shirted soldier directly in front of Pen.

A voice from the back countered, "As a matter of fact, Marvin, you idiot, we gots lots of time. We ain't going anywhere soon."

A laugh rippled through the crowd. Pen smiled. He looked at the little man who tilted his head arrogantly, mouth firmly frowning.

"If I go too slowly for Marvin, it is because I am new at this and actually," he looked to the man who had joked with Marvin, "you are going somewhere…today. I am going to free you." The men started talking again, but Pen raised his hand for silence. "Hear me first. I am going to free you all, the walking, and the wounded when they are better. All I ask is that you consider my request."

His eyes scanned the attentive faces before him.

"I need men who will fight for me. You need a leader you can trust who won't desert you. I am that leader."

He looked down, his countenance heavy and sad.

"I have no love for war."

The men leaned forward, straining to hear every word. Raising his head to look at the assembly, his blue eyes held them as much as his words.

"I did not want this war, but I will finish it, with or without you. I want you to serve with me, so we can end this madness sooner, rather than later."

He looked at the men before him.

"Captain Thatcher will explain the details of your release. I am going to my tent. Those who choose to join, meet me there in one hour."

After Pen left, Thatcher stepped into the center of the arc and explained the terms of release. Then he abruptly left the men alone. The prisoners were elated and confused. Small groups formed and men talked, trying to decide whether or not to join the rebellion.

"The Chosen One? Hardly!" said one of the Baron's older militia. "Mark my words, fellows, he is a foolish boy who sets wolves free."

"No wolf here." stated another. "Me, I'm going home and staying out of sight."

"Not me!" responded Marvin. "You idiots forget the King. The King's gonna be madder than a wet hornet and his sting is a damn sight worse than the brown-nosing Baron. No going back home for me. Nope. I'm leaving the country, this ain't a gonna be pretty."

"No way I'm leaving my country," countered a younger red-shirted soldier.

"Me, neither," yelled a black-shirted veteran.

And so the talk continued. Some of the soldiers from the King's army left and walked out of the encampment. The bulk of the prisoners, however, mostly the Baron's militia, stayed, uncertain about what to do.

Two neatly dressed soldiers in black walked from the main group. Standing near them, but unseen by them, was Frederick, an older veteran. The one who wore a captain's cape said something about "killing the stupid kid". It was then the pair saw Frederick. They walked away, looking over their shoulders.

Frederick, who pretended not to hear the two men, did not follow them. He shook his head and frowned. Join him or not, he would never aim to hurt the boy.

Like so many others, Frederick did not know what to do. Soldiering was all he knew. It paid enough for him and family to live a comfortable life. He was no longer a young man, though. Not being an officer, it was just a matter of time before he would be out of a job; the Baron didn't like keeping any "old rags". He found himself slowly walking toward the tent where more and more soldiers congregated.

An hour later when Pen emerged from the tent, he was astonished to see hundreds of men standing there, ready to serve him. Most were young and discontented with the Baron and wanted to serve a new master. A few of the tunics before him were red...the King's men. Pen saw that Marvin was one of the men in the group.

"Marvin, I thought I was too slow for you?"

"You're slow, but my Pappy was slow when he slaughtered a pig. He always got the job done and done well. I 'spect you will do the same. Anyways, better than running round the countryside like a chicken with its head cut off. Figure it's better to die like a man than run like a chicken."

After the rebel officers heard how Pen had released some of the prisoners and allowed others to join the rebellion, there were numerous concerns expressed to Petronius in the next meeting. Pen, who added a black cape (compliments of Mother Hebron) to his purple tunic and black pants, addressed the group firmly. "Bruder, you could not take them, so where were they to go? Thatcher said they could not stay with us. And, you, Viridius, claimed most of the released men would most likely not join up with the Baron. Now the prisoner problem is resolved and we have nearly four hundred experienced soldiers. The rest will most likely go back to their farms."

The group was quiet, but many mouths hung open, stunned. Was he the boy who ran along the streets of Kirkland waving to everyone? Petronius smiled at the way his son had cleverly used their own advice in answering their concerns.

Before anyone could recover to offer objections, the General took command of the meeting. "Hopefully the problem is resolved. But a concern remains, Pen. These were the King's and Baron's men. Their loyalty is suspect."

Pen vigorously shook his head.

"Thatcher and I talked with each man. They have disavowed both the Baron and the King and pledged their loyalty to me. I gave them my word they could serve with me."

"I gave my word to your mother that I would protect you, son. Surely that counts too. I want two of my own men guarding your tent. Bruder, and myself will interview the men about what involvement, if any, they had in that nasty business with the Jesus Church years ago. I reserve the right to dismiss any of your men after those interviews. I want Songor and his detachment to watch over any drills you may have in mind for your men."

Pen reluctantly agreed and the meeting adjourned.

Pen followed Mother Hebron to her tent.

"Mother Hebron. Thanks for sewing the tunic and cape for me."

She smiled; he was still her boy.

"Purple suits you, Pen. Royal colors. You will be wearing it more frequently in the future."

"You said the purple cloth came from the Baron's tent. Was there any more of it?"

She smiled and walked over to a few trunks at one end of her tent. She opened two of them and pulled out reams of purple cloth.

"Just a bit left, Pen."

Pen looked at the two trunks. "I wonder if you could help me…" he asked as he pulled her close and whispered in her ear.

CHAPTER 39

Dirty and sweaty from the disorderly retreat through the forest, the Baron entered the great hall with some trepidation and, in the dim light of torch and smoldering fire, kneeled before the King.

The tall man with stringy gray hair rose from the throne with his two large bodyguards flanking either side. Six eyes fell upon the bowed figure of the Baron.

"Baron Glock, how goes the campaign? Good news, I trust?" Cearl inquired as he gently picked up his vassal to face him.

"Sir, the green men have been joined by the former priestesses, those of the white deer, and the Northlanders. The force facing us was too formidable for our attack…"

Cearl viciously slapped the man across the face knocking him backwards.

"You ran, you incompetent coward! Not once, but twice! You could have won both battles." The King pulled out his knife and the Baron tried to step away, but found himself restrained by the two bodyguards. The Baron's eyes opened wide with fright. He watched the blade as the fire's light colored it blood red.

With the knife pressed against the man's neck, Cearl whispered, "I could use this knife to express my dissatisfaction with you, Baron. It would be a delight to slowly, so slowly fillet you."

The blade cut into the Baron's throat, drawing a bead of crimson blood.

"And, I will, if you fail me again. Make no mistake, Glock."

He caressed the Baron's cheek with the blade, smearing the blood. Cearl gazed at the blade, reluctant to give it up, before he sheathed it.

He walked back to his throne and slowly eased himself onto the great chair. With a casual wave of his hand, the King motioned to the bodyguards to release the Baron. He slipped to the ground on all fours, his legs like water. He slowly gained enough control enough to rise from the ground, his heart beating wildly.

"Stay there, cur! The position suits you perfectly."

Pleased with the Baron's new position, Cearl continued. "Apparently I can't rely on you to rid me of a boy, a few women, criminals, and barbarians. So, here is what you must do."

Arms on knees, the King tilted his head down.

"I don't expect you to attack, even if you do outnumber them. Damn you, man! How could you have lost both battles?"

The King rose from his seat, reaching for his blade again, anger turning his face a deeper shade of red. He stopped, shook his head, and sat back down. After a deep breath, he continued.

"Block off all paths leading to the rebels. You can do that, can't you, Glock?"

Like a dog trying to please its master, the Baron rapidly nodded his head in assent.

"We must keep their force cut off from anyone trying to join them. That makes sense, doesn't it, Glock?"

The King's voice suddenly raised, his face once again turned red with rage.

"Doesn't it, Glock? Can you manage that, you bumbling fool?"

The Baron again vigorously shook his head in the affirmative.

Cearl continued in a calmer voice. "Good. When I have gathered an army, I will destroy the enemy. Can you contain them for a few weeks, Glock?"

"Yes, sire! Certainly, sire!"

"Fail me in this and I will personally skin you alive. I mean that literally, Glock."

The King took the knife out again and caressed the blade with his finger, his eyes, heavy-lidded. The King's eyes rose from the knife blade to look at the trembling man in front of him. The Baron held the stare, not in defiance, but in fear. He was afraid that if he took his eyes away, Cearl would fulfill his promise immediately.

Bored, Cearl stopped staring. He looked toward the hearth and dismissed the Baron with a casual flick of his fingers. The Baron started to rise.

"No. Crawl out."

The Baron retreated on all fours to door. It opened suddenly as officers and ministers stared in disbelief. Taking small, slow steps, they eventually stood before their monarch and orders went out to each man. After they left, Cearl dismissed his bodyguards, sat on his thrown, and contemplated the embers of the once great fire. The end game, he mused contentedly. It was, after all, his specialty.

CHAPTER 40

"That be the last of them, sir." Bruder said as he sank wearily in the chair.

"Wouldn't care to drink with all of them, General, but I don't think any were part of the rape and murder at the church."

"I agree, Bruder. And, for that…"

The guard outside Petronius' tent interrupted him.

"Sir, a former captain from the Baron wishes to see you alone."

Petronius looked at Bruder. He rose, nodded to the general and left. In a freshly washed uniform, a bearded man stepped in. He waited for the guard and bearded former king to leave and then he began.

"Sir," he began, "It's not my way to point fingers at my fellows, but what happened in the church was so terrible I feel it my duty to fill you in on some rather disturbing details." He went on to relate what he saw those many years ago. The General listened quietly while his posture became rigid and his face stern.

After the captain had been thanked and excused, Petronius ordered Thatcher to find one of the Baron's militia. An hour later, Thatch brought in an older soldier whose short hair framed a well-tanned face lined with worries. The man, of average height and solid build, walked with a light step as though he might suddenly spring in any direction.

He confronted the veteran with the accusations.

"Yes, sir," admitted Frederick, "I was there as I told you, but I did no harm to no sister or anyone else. Others did. But not me."

"Well, one of your own has accused you of raping at least one of the sisters."

"It's a lie!" cried the soldier indignantly.

"No, this is a man whose testimony I trust. I want you out of my sight. Leave the grounds as soon as you have collected your belongings!"

Frederick saw hatred in the General's fierce look, not to be overcome by reason or plea. Falsely accused and unfairly dismissed, the soldier stormed out.

Sitting on a stool in his own tent, he clenched and unclenched his fists trying to control his anger. Who, he wondered, would have falsely accused him of such a heinous crime? He had no enemies. In fact, he was generally well liked and respected. Eventually, he gathered his few belongings and marched out of the camp. He noted Karl, the officer who had furtively talked about killing the Chosen One, was watching him closely. Why would someone with whom he was barely acquainted take such a keen interest in his imminent departure? Perhaps, thought Frederick, the man suspected he was overheard. Yes, that must be it!

Now the pieces fit, but Frederick did not like the picture they formed.

Pretending not to have seen the captain's stare, he walked down the road until he was out of sight of the rebel base. Looking back and seeing no one watching him, he ducked into the forest. He worked his way back to the camp through the woods, hidden by the thick green underbrush. He settled between large tree trunks and thick, closely packed bushes. In such a place one man could be well hidden from the sentries. Also, he could easily see two tents: Pen's and Karl's. He settled down for a long vigil.

*

Pen drilled his guard from early morning to late afternoon in a field about a mile from the encampment. He wanted his men as well trained with the sword as he. A few days after Frederick was expelled, he presented the men with purple tunics that would act as their uniform. Mother Hebron and other ladies had matched the guard's long hours of practicing with long hours of cutting and sewing.

Pen stood before them, neatly dressed with his darker purple tunic, cape, and black pants. Smiling broadly, he raised his voice to the small army of men now wearing purple tunics.

"You are my guard, the Royal Guard, from this day forward."

After the training session, they returned to camp wearing the tunics. Other rebels, who were already upset over not being picked by the Chosen One, were incensed over this latest indignation. A few days later, fights broke out between the royal guard and other groups in the camp. Jealously had reared its ugly head.

One night while Pen chatted with some of his new friends in his tent, Jack came inside. Except for that one day when they so happily greeted each other, Pen had not spent any time with him. This was in part due to his new responsibilities in training the royal guard. His new prestige also attracted a higher social order of well-dressed men and attractive women with whom he spent considerable time.

"Pen, could I be a speakin' to you?" Pen was clearly agitated at the interruption and slightly embarrassed by Jack's worn clothes and crude way of talking.

"Sure, Jack. What's bothering you?"

Looking around at the unfamiliar faces, the shy boy leaned into his friend and whispered in his ear.

"Alone. Could I talk with you alone, Pen?"

Pen grimaced and shook his head in frustration, but ushered out the others. He was annoyed that the clumsy blacksmith's son had disturbed him and his new friends. The tone of his next question revealed his irritation.

"What is it, Jack?"

Jack couldn't bring himself to talk right away. He was clearly distraught as he paced back and forth in the tent. He bit his lip. Finally, his face strained, he rushed the words out before he lost his nerve.

"Pen, I been trying the sword. Know I ain't good, but I be tryin'. Thinks I could be part of your men? The Guard? Ye know I'd protect ye."

This peasant, one of his trusted guards? Impossible.

"Jack," he explained, "The guard is only for former soldiers, trained soldiers, not farmers...or blacksmiths."

Jack looked away. Obviously he couldn't be part of the royal guard. He should never have asked. He looked away as he spoke.

"Figured as much, Pen. Figured as much. Even told Liana. But, you know her."

He looked at Pen and smiled.

"Ye never can tell when ye might need some arm strength. I got that, I do."

Pen smiled, more from knowing the conversation would soon end than from recalling the strength of an old friend.

"Yes, you do have arm strength."

"Think on it. I'll help if ye need me."

"Sure, Jack." He led him out of the tent while his other friends reentered. As Jack walked away he heard laughter in the tent. He clenched his eyes tightly knowing he was the reason for their mirth.

ROBERT SELLS

CHAPTER 41

Power is a strong magnet, attracting all sorts of people. Young men and women Pen had never known introduced themselves and curried his favor with flattering words. Buoyed by his new fawning friendships, Pen believed he knew pretty much everything and wasn't shy about his dispensing knowledge. Early success can carry with it the seeds of self-destruction... Pen had become an obnoxious bore and an arrogant fool.

With so many associates eager to praise him and laugh at his witticisms, he had little time for his old friends. He no longer initiated conversation with Liana or Jack when their paths crossed. Instead, he simply avoided or ignored them. The friends from Kirkland, young and old, were surprised and disappointed.

Late one afternoon, taking a break from his own tasks, Thatcher watched his former student with some pride as Pen artfully demonstrated one move after another to some of his men. After his troops and the ever-present Songor left the field for dinner, Thatcher patted the boy on the back.

"Pen, my boy, you amaze me!"

291

Picking up a discarded knife from the ground, he looked quizzically at his old teacher. "Really? How?"

"How? My god, boy, you have made what was once a group of defeated soldiers into most able warriors, and they are devoted to you, boy. I can see that. Dag gummit, Pen, you have pulled off a miracle!"

The young man beamed at the old man's praise. They sat down on a log not far from the laughter and sounds of the camp, the evening meal just being served. Used to high praise from his new friends, Pen pompously expounded on his philosophy in bending such men to his will.

Thatcher, now first captain of the army, head bowed and finger tips together, patiently listened to the boy. He sighed, tired eyes closing, wishing the kind, unpresuming boy he knew months ago would return.

When Pen finally stopped, the gray-haired mentor spoke quietly. "Seems like my praise was unnecessary, Pen. You have much for yourself."

"Well, that is true, Thatch, I am doing well at a number of things," he said smugly, not recognizing the older man's subtle sarcasm.

Thatcher started to rise, but Pen pulled him back down.

"Stay awhile. I have a question to ask you."

Thatcher sat down slowly, but glared at the boy. Not only could Pen not hear rebuke, he could not see reproach.

"Thatch, you are the most able swordsman I know in this army. Well, except for me, of course."

Thatcher looked toward the camp and quietly replied, "Of course."

"You are respected by all, and no man would dare excite your anger. But, you must know that many wonder about your language...or rather, you lack of hard language. The other men...well...they color their language with words whose meaning

292

I can barely guess, but whose utterances often bring blushes to some of the farmers and most definitely all of the women. You never curse or use vulgar terms. I have long wondered why."

No one had ever asked Thatcher a question about his reluctance to use inappropriate language. Indeed, no one dared. Instead of staring at the lad with indignation, he bore a great grin on his face. Thatcher loved telling a good story and he had a particularly good one to tell.

"Hmm...this will take some telling, Master Pen." Thatcher readjusted himself on the log, preparing comfortably for a longer stay.

"After your pa quit the army, the Baron was my commander. He led about a thousand of us into the western barrens, near the coast, to handle some tribes raiding the villages in that godforsaken land."

Thatcher looked at Pen.

"Dagburn Baron had one of his girl friends in his tent and would do no moving. Nothing to do, so day and night were filled with stories about the elves who once lived in the nearby hills, or about the witches that might still. One of the lads talked of some sort of holy man. Seems these brigands, who harassed everyone else, were afraid of the old man. Weren't doing nothing anyway, so I packed some extra water and off I go to see for meself."

Evening brought a cool wind, and Pen wrapped his black cloak around him to keep warm. Thatcher, on the other hand, was quite warm from memories of a summer nearly twenty years earlier. He recalled the sun pressing down upon him as he walked his horse through the damp sand.

"Gosh darn hot it was! Saw a trickle of water coming down the cliff side. Got off my horse to fill me water bag. Good luck it seemed, but it really wasn't. That's when them gol darn tribesmen attacked me."

He shook his head. "Tried to fight them off, hurt a few, but they were too many. One of them clunked me hard on the head with some kind of stick. I fell to my knees and another stabbed me in my arm and my sword fell."

The older man pulled up his tunic sleeve and showed the boy the long, thin scar.

"A bit upset they were…I wounded a few of them…might have killed another one or two. Oh, they was mad, they was. Me just kneeling there waiting for death."

Thatcher stopped talking and the laughter from the camp turned both their heads. After watching the commotion below them, the older man continued his story.

"He appeared… an old man. Face all wrinkled with legs and arms more like bones than flesh."

Night had fully settled and Pen saw only Thatcher's silhouette, but the man's words filled his vision.

"He swung some sort of branch, maybe a staff. Bashed one of those buzzards on the head. Parried with another, and then struck the dagburn man in the chest with the end of the staff. Laid him out on the ground. He turned about in a circle, somehow knowing the third was creeping up behind him. Swung and hit that one smack dab in the face. The biggest came at him with a sword. Nearly stabbed him, but step aside, he did, quicker than I could ever move… quicker maybe than you, Pen. Jammed the rod into the man's throat and that man was dead, I'm sure."

Thatcher slowly rose from the log and started walking toward camp. Pen quickly followed.

"Takes me into his cave and fixes me up. I had the fever and the arm was puffed up. He was a healer this one. He took care of me, something good. Days I was with him. Whole time we was together, he never gave me his name."

Adjacent to the camp, the tall boy and the short man stopped under a willow tree, its branches hid them so that Thatcher could finish his story without interruption.

"He was always praying. He watched me one morning, just a' staring at me. Pulls something out of this dirty bag he always carried with him. Hands me a small package wrapped in fine cloth. He was the one who gave me the knife. You know, the knife I gave you? He's the one what told me about it being from the elves. I kinda didn't believe him, just like you didn't believe me, but he was a holy man, so there must be truth in it."

Thatcher looked at the camp, his stomach growling.

"He told me that stuff about using it. First time it saves you good. He never did use it for near forty years, but figured I might need it. Many times I could have used it, but I never did. Now you got the dang knife."

Pen smiled and patted his side, feeling the hard blade through the thin sheath.

"Before I left, I said to him that I owed him. What did he want in return for savin' my life? He says... and this I remember... 'I want nothing. Pay others, not me.' Strange thing to say, I thought, but I don't protest."

Then Thatcher started chuckling. "Well, Pen, I tried to get on my horse to ride back to camp, and I slipped off and hurt my wounded arm. Gosh darn, that hurt! Had a mouthful of bad coming out my lips."

"First time he heard me talk like that, he turned his head and stared at me, mad like. Then he spoke."

Thatcher's voice suddenly lowered in pitch and sounded menacing as he repeated the old man's words. "'Thatcher, let no foul words leave your lips ever again!'"

"'You mean I must stop cursing?'"

"He nodded. I was one of those colorful cussers, Pen. Were my trademark in those days. I owed him my life. So, I promised him

295

and I always keep my promises. From that day on, never did I utter any curse word."

They slowly strolled into camp. Men stepped aside to let the pair walk through. Pen noticed people did that for him these days. Pen glad-handed his new, neatly dressed friends, but barely acknowledged the tired, common soldiers who greeted him. Thatcher walked to a table to eat with some old veterans.

CHAPTER 42

Liana often came to the drills, supposedly to spend time with Songor, but she enjoyed watching Pen. He was too busy with his men and his new friends to ever walk her back to camp so she routinely walked back with Songor who, with a broad smile, was delighted escorting her.

One day Pen walked over to Songor who was plodding back to the main camp with Liana. He grabbed Songor by the arm. Liana beamed, thinking Pen would walk back with them.

"Beautiful day, old fellow, isn't it?"

"Pon my word, master Pen, it be pretty."

Pen looked back over the meadow. He swept his hand and said, "Peaceful place, here. You and your men can stop watching me."

With that said Pen turned on his heel without even a goodbye and started back to his friends. Songor watched him walk away and looked down at the ground, his face screwed up in thought. He yelled back at the retreating figure.

"Yes, sir, a great many tasks could find me. But, I best be here, a watchin'…"

Pen stopped abruptly. The Chosen One was not used to people telling him no. In fact, since the battle, only Petronius dared to challenge his authority.

From a distance of twenty feet, he yelled to Songor, loud enough for everyone to hear.

"That wasn't a request, old man. Don't come back here anymore."

Sure the exchange had ended, the boy resumed his walk. Songor was visibly shaken by the rebuke. With a tired expression, he spoke again to the boy's retreating back.

"I'm still worried a bit fer ye, Pen. Best I still watch."

Pen stopped. For a moment he was as still as a statue. He turned and marched back to Songor. The meadow was now quiet; all watched the drama unfold.

Pen lashed out. "You are countermanding my orders?"

He spoke slowly and carefully, not wanting to rile his young friend any further. "No sir. Just me be thinkin' watchin' be good."

"Then why won't you listen to me?" the boy asked, exasperated.

"I canst put words to it, sir. Something amiss, lad, and I thinks…"

"That's the real problem, isn't it, Songor? You thinking you can think. You don't know how to think at all. That's why you should follow orders. Now do as you're told!" Pen turned and stomped off.

"No."

Pen looked back. "What?"

Songor yelled his explanation. "No, said I. I speaks none too well, master, I give ye that. And thinkin' be hard for me…lord, you have me thar again. But, I says no."

Angry, he walked away. "You're a damn fool!" he spouted over his shoulder.

After Pen had left with his friends, Songor sat down on a log and rested his head on his hands, trying to think, his head shaking back and forth. Liana, standing behind the crumpled frame, gently rubbed his shoulder, her gray eyes ablaze at the retreating figure of her former friend.

In the evening the rebels would crowd around a few long tables, plying their metal plates with a lump of oatmeal, and if they were particularly lucky, a chunk of cooked venison. It was during this time Liana found Pen laughing with some of his cronies.

She roughly pushed through the entourage, scattering all the men except one talking with Pen. She stepped between the two and faced Pen. She had to look upward to make eye contact with him, and that added to her annoyance.

"I need to talk to you, alone. Now!"

She glared at the last man beside Pen. The man withered under her stare and quickly joined the others as chuckles welcomed him into the exiled group. Liana's reputation with a bow was as legendary as was her temper, and it was prudent to avoid both.

Alone, the full force of her anger was now directed at Pen. "I didn't say anything when you snubbed Jack, your best friend. That was stupid and thoughtless. Your choice, I know, so I didn't say anything."

Pen looked warily at the girl. She always had a way of needling him and she was certainly doing it now.

"I don't know who you think you are, but whoever you are, I don't like you. The way you dealt with that kind, wonderful devoted man was unforgiveable."

"He should have listened to me!" whined the boy.

"He should have listened to you? He should have spanked you! You had no right to speak to him that way."

"I have every right. I'm going to be king."

Her hands went to her hips and she leaned close into him.

"That means you have responsibilities, you imbecile, and one is to be considerate of your friends. That man cared for you as a baby, and protected you from harm, time and time again."

"You shouldn't be talking to me this way. What gives you the right?"

Her eyes widened. Then she squinted and pursed her lips.

"What gives me the right? The fact that I hugged you when you were scared in a thunderstorm, tended to you when you were sick, lied for you when you went off with Thatcher, and a million other reasons gives me the right to talk to you, you stupid, silly boy! You hurt him, Pen. That was wrong. And you hurt Jack, too, though he won't ever speak of it. What's gotten into you?" Arms folded, he looked away, ignoring her. Seeing him unmoved by her words, she turned and trudged off, pushing aside anyone who was even close to blocking her path.

Pen tried to look unaffected by the conversation, but he was only able to conjure faint smiles after his cronies gathered about him. Clearly distracted, he finally gave up any pretense of social interaction and shuffled away into the darkness away from the campfires' light. He kicked a branch out of his way, sending it toward a nearby tent. He was so irritated at her presumptions. His new friends never did that. Besides, Songor richly deserved his wrath. It was long overdue. He was embarrassed to acknowledge he knew the man. Songor, that ham-fisted simpleton! What could he do anyway? He certainly couldn't think. He wasn't at all good with the sword. And, if ever he were to actually try to help Pen, he would probably get himself killed.

Pen stopped walking. He knew Songor would die to save him. Songor was so fiercely protective of his young master that he would challenge the devil himself. He recalled a time when a rabid wolf had him cornered in the barn. Before the wolf lunged at the boy, Songor, without any weapon, ran to place himself between the snarling animal and the child. His broad presence and waving hands confused and delayed the animal from attacking. Moments later his father clubbed the animal to death. Songor sat on a bench shaking. All the heavy man could say was: "Oh, oh, oh." He smiled again remembering the scene.

Perhaps he overstepped a bit with Songor, he admitted. Still, Liana was out of line confronting him. Perhaps he should report her to Petronius. No, he realized his father would not do anything about this matter. He would just smile as he always did when they had these spats. He recalled the time Mirus had to push him into Liana to end one quarrel. He forgot what the disagreement was about, but he vividly recalled her laughter. He smiled. How rare and wonderful the sound.

He recalled, with another smile, both her level-headed guidance and mercurial temper. His dear friend. He stopped again and put his hands over his eyes.

The dam he had built in his mind burst as a flood of memories washed over him. Songor teaching him to cook and then burning a roast, but worried about adding too many spices. Afterwards, he and Liana ran into the woods, far away from the house and rolled in the grass with laughter. He recalled Songor's convoluted stories that somehow always ended funny; the fat man's laughter was contagious. He remembered fondly the fun he and Jack enjoyed fishing, never catching much because they too often slept. His good friends. They knew him, accepted him, and loved him before he was the Chosen One, not because he was the Chosen One.

Then he put both hands over his face as though he was trying to hide from some accuser. She was right. He was terrible to Songor. How could he have acted that way? He was terrible to Liana and Jack too. What have I become that I treat my old friends so cruelly? He recalled her words: "Whoever you are, I don't like you". He shook his head; he didn't like himself either.

He had been seduced by power, just like Cearl must have been years ago. The sweet, alluring, addictive wine of power...and only one sip changed him into this despicable person! What would happen to him when he did become king? Would he transform into what Cearl had become?

What else did Liana say? Being king means that you have responsibilities to all, not just the glib of tongue and the well-dressed. He knew that, but drunk with power, he forgot.

He looked back at camp, over to tables where food was still served. His eyes searched for Songor who was always hovering at the tables laughing, eating, and talking but he didn't see him. That was strange, Pen thought. Where was he?

He hurried back to Songor's tent and opened the flap. Sitting on his cot faced away from the door, arms on knees, head cupped in his hands, the great round form stared at the ground. The forlorn figure looked older and sadder. Tears flooded Pen's eyes. He wiped them away, and stepped inside.

"Have you eaten or were you just working up a good appetite, Songor?"

Startled, Songor looked over his shoulder and quickly rose. "Ah...Master Pen. No, me hunger is a wee bit today."

"That's not the Songor I know. Guess you've changed a bit, eh?"

Songor thought a while before he answered. "No sir," he replied, "Same me. Just not hungry."

Pen smiled. "Songor not hungry? What's the world coming to?"

The man looked at the ground. "Tis a strange world, master Pen. I canst always figure it."

A lump rose in his throat.

"Well, I could use a friend to walk with me to the tables. Could you help me with that?"

The large man looked up and slowly smiled. "Aye, lad."

As Songor passed him to leave the tent, Pen rested his hands on his broad shoulders, momentarily stopping him. For a long moment he looked down at the gentle man who guilelessly returned his stare.

"Songor, I wronged you today by saying unkind and untrue things, and I am deeply sorry. I respect you and your words. Please forgive my words."

Songor looked at the boy. "I knows ye meant no harm, Pen. Ye be under stress. All ye be. Songor understands. Maybe I should be more yessing, but I canst, sir. And I canst explain why. I just knowed is all."

"As ever you are too kind with your words and too generous with your forgiveness. Nevertheless, I will take both. As far as you knowing something is amiss, that's good enough for me. I trust your judgment, old friend and welcome your protection. Now let's go eat."

"Yes, sir; I'm powerful starved, I am. Me hunger is back! How about that? One minute I don't want a crumb and now I could eat a cow! Pen did I ever tell you the time your Pa and I didn't eat for an entire day? Well, Mother Hebron had this pie..."

Pen put his arm around the shorter man's shoulders and hugged him close as they talked and walked to the food tables.

*

Late that night, Pen sat alone by a fire when Liana plopped down beside him. They sat in silence for a few seconds.

"I don't know what happened to me, Liana. How could I have been so cruel to Songor?"

Looking into the flickering flame as though it contained the answer, she replied, "You thought too much about yourself."

Pen looked at her profile. The glow from the flames accented individual hairs curling from the rest that was neatly bound into a ponytail. She was, he realized for the first time, beautiful.

"You are so wise, Liana. And...and..."

He wasn't sure how to tell her she was beautiful. Besides how would she react?

"... so right. I have been thinking only of myself. I forgot the people who taught me important things...how to persevere...like Songor does with his cooking," he chuckled and then continued. "How to be true to your friends no matter what...and...and laugh, and so many other things. I forgot that others have wisdom too...even the large and clumsy."

Liana said nothing and stared at the embers.

"I don't want to end up like my uncle. How can I be a good king if I make these kinds of mistakes now?"

She turned to him, a playful smile on her face. "Well, you may not have to worry about that. We might lose the next battle. Perhaps you won't become king."

His anguished face turned toward her.

"Perhaps not. I'll tell you a secret, Liana. I don't want to be king anymore."

She studied him and saw he was struggling. The face she saw was not the carefree one she so enjoyed seeing every day in their youth. Nor was he the haughty youth who assumed pretentious airs and ignored old friends. His body has filled out with muscle and sinew, but his face was leaner and more lined than before. For a moment she regretted her harsh words to him. But only for a moment.

She covered his hand with hers.

"Pen, you will be king, a good one. And I will always be beside you...telling you when you are being an insufferable, silly boy." She winked at him. He smiled. For a few seconds, all was well. Then she rose, bade him goodnight, and walked back to her tent.

CHAPTER 43

Sobered by Liana's words, Pen talked less and listened more to both the richly dressed and the humbly attired. Late one afternoon, the sun low in the autumn sky, Pen saw Jack unloading barrels from a wagon.

"How are those sword-fighting skills, Jack?"

The sweaty boy looked straight at his friend, as he wiped sweat with the back of his hand.

"Probably not good enough for the guard."

He went back to unloading another barrel from the wagon.

"Well, perhaps I could teach you a few moves. Might make you a better fighter."

Jack looked at his friend through squinted eyes, burning from sweat.

"I already be a pretty good fighter, if you recall. I could wrestle down any of the Baron's men."

"I never doubted your fighting ability, Jack. I just don't know how many of the Baron's men are going to lay down their weapons so you can wrestle with them."

The two friends looked at each other. Jack burst into laughter and slapped Pen on the back.

"Ye got me there, Pen. 'Spect, you're right. Well, if ye think you can make a sworder outta me then give it a try."

A day later, a broad shouldered young man augmented the royal guard. Throughout his life, he would remain incredibly strong, ever the good friend to Pen, and a far better blacksmith than sword fighter.

CHAPTER 44

The country was like a snarling dog barely controlled by the firm grasp of its master. Cearl realized the new army had to come from the garrisons stationed all across Mercia and the dog would soon have to be unleashed. The autumn's colors burned away the leaves and the brown earth awaited both snow and battle, the delay of both puzzling the rebels.

Exhausted from a particularly strenuous day of drilling his men and meetings, Pen retired early. As though some magic spell had been invoked, the entire camp chose that crisp, dry autumn night to sleep early and deep.

After the last few stragglers, laughing over a joke, left the campfire, the center of the camp was empty except for the guards Petronius had posted to protect his son. They quietly murmured outside his tent, trying to stay awake.

In the ink-black darkness of that moonless night, a figure slowly approached the tent next to Pen's. Yet another offspring of the night glided toward the other side of Pen's tent. Engrossed in their whispered conversation, the guards were oblivious to the deadly shadows. The first figure moved silently toward the two men. Within seconds, both guards were motionless on the ground.

The tent flap opened and closed. The second figure followed quickly. As the flap was opened a second time, the light from the camp fire illuminated a blade plunging down toward the heart of Pen. The strong hand of the second wraith intercepted the blow and a furious scuffle ensued. Pen woke, jumped from his bed to grab his sword.

Sleep could not hold the old servant in its embrace when his boy was in trouble. Somehow Songor knew and in seconds, the stout man burst into the door, torch in hand. Men ran toward the tent, their torches revealing a grisly scene in front of the Chosen One's tent. Both guards lay dead; blood still flowing from neatly placed slits in their throats. Petronius pushed through the crowd and entered the tent. To his immense relief he saw his son in the corner, Songor beside him, both with their swords drawn. Two men, dressed in black, were wrestling on the ground. The General pulled the men apart.

Petronius did not recognize one of the men in black, still wildly lunging at his enemy, barely held back by two stout men of the Royal Guard. When he turned to the other man, he was shocked to find it was Karl, the captain who informed him of the unsavory behavior of the man who Petronius kicked out of camp weeks before.

Karl spoke quickly. "He came back and killed the two guards, trying to kill the Chosen One." He breathed heavily from his exertions.

Still straining against the strong hands of three soldiers, a voice erupted from the other man also in the black uniform of the Baron's men.

"Lies, all lies. He killed them. He's been planning this for a time. I've been watching him."

Petronius now recognized the man. He was the one dismissed due to Karl's charges of rape. What was his name? Frederick, recalled Petronius.

Petronius picked up a knife from the ground. It was dry. He reached for Karl's knife, still in his hand. Yanking it from him, he inspected it carefully. Blood stains.

Karl wrenched free and bolted out of the tent. A saddled horse stood close to the tent. The man broke through astonished bystanders and reached the horse, jumping quickly on its back. Before he could spur the steed away, an arrow burrowed into his back. His arms arched backward and he fell to the ground. Liana, standing outside Pen's tent, slowly lowered her bow. Petronius nodded to her.

The General walked back inside the tent and motioned for the soldiers to release the man. Frederick angrily shook his arms free. His black, tattered uniform was flecked with leaves and dirt. Petronius looked at the bedraggled soldier before him.

"What happened to you, man?"

The veteran brushed off his uniform and glared at the General. "Watching out for your son!"

Flicking a leaf from his shoulder and brushing his pants, he continued. "I overheard him talking about your boy, the day after the battle. He said something about killing him, but I thought it was mad talk after losing a battle. When I was kicked out by you General, he looked at me strange like and then I knew. Bastard set me up. Either I walk away like you told me to or figure how stop him. So, I hid, waited, and watched. Saw him change back into his black uniform this evening and figured he was going to kill the lad tonight. Came down to stop him."

Petronius looked at the soldier. He was much thinner than Petronius had remembered him. The man risked capture and sacrificed his well-being to watch over his son.

"I owe you an apology and a debt of gratitude. How can I reward you for the services you have rendered me and my son?"

"The apology I accept, sir. As far as a boon, I don't need or want one." He spoke fiercely. He squinted his eyes a bit and rubbed his chin. His haggard face allowed a smile.

"Well, I could do with some food, sir, and maybe a place to sleep tonight. Getting mighty cold at night now."

Petronius nodded to one of the captains and left the tent.

So Frederick came back into camp. After a short discussion the next morning, Petronius, Thatcher, and Pen all thought Federick would make a worthy captain of the Royal Guard. Working closely with Pen, the two quickly became friends. One of Frederick's first assignments was to choose two new guards to the task of protecting Pen. Jack insisted on being one of them and the new captain thought his fierce loyalty would compensate for his mediocre skills with a blade.

Little Marvin spoke up. "Damn General gave the job of protecting his child to the wrong men. Stronger than bulls, they were, but they couldn't tell a freck from a fickle."

Pen, who was watching the proceedings, couldn't help but smile. In fact, he didn't know a "freck from a fickle" either. He was fairly sure Frederick didn't either.

"Well, sir, my pappy always said if you want to catch a rabbit, then you gotta use a dog. Well, sir, I be as good a dog as any."

Frederick and Pen looked at each other. Both burst into laughter.

Jack and Marvin became the chosen one's bodyguards. They never spoke a word while on duty at night. Marvin had acute night vision or incredibly sensitive ears, as he pulled his sword in readiness whenever anyone came near the tent. Jack always followed the lead of the smaller man and his large sword was a sufficient deterrent to friend and foe alike.

CHAPTER 45

Finally the king had decided securing the villages and the cities was not as important as putting down the rebellion by brute force. Thousands of soldiers had already collected at Tamworth and the number was growing each day.

Good news followed the bad. From the west other news came in by carrier pigeon. Coming soon, bringing some friends. Petronius knew it came from the Earl. He prayed Cearl would stay his hand until the Earl arrived.

As the days lengthened into a week, the rebels speculated as to why the King did not move against them. None save Songor guessed the real reason for his delay. Unfortunately, try as he might, he couldn't properly explain his apprehension.

Eight weeks after the last battle for Bangor Hill, the crisp coolness of early November yielded to the sun's warmth. The royal guard had haphazardly discarded both their wool tunics and swords all over the training field while they rested close to the camp during the noon break. Pen was close to the center of the clearing, conferring with one of his men.

An arrow hissed through the air nearly missing Pen. Before he fully registered they were under attack, another arrow hit the shoulder of his companion. As Pen crouched down, he pulled the man down with him. Other arrows whistled harmlessly overhead.

The woods on the far side erupted with the charge of hundreds of huntsmen and red-shirted soldiers. In a few seconds, the running men would be able to push their blades into the Chosen One.

Pen raised himself up and pulled his companion along, but the man had fainted from the pain. Pen heaved him onto his shoulder and slowly made his way back to his men.

Now the Royal Guard would have its first test. Out of the forest charged an army of highly trained and ruthless mercenaries coupled with the King's best soldiers. The formidable force was superior in number and far more experienced in dealing death. The men of the Royal Guard knew the lethal force before them. They could have retreated to the woods, leaving Pen to his fate. Instead, most unarmed, they raced to pick up swords and meet the onslaught.

The clash was fierce. With their greater numbers and vicious attack, the attackers pushed the royal guard back. Pen, having dropped off his companion in the questionable safety of the rear, led the rest of the men to help their comrades. The entire Royal Guard was now engaged. Rallied by his presence and determined to protect him, his men traded blow for blow, slash for slash, and death for death.

Having the advantage of greater numbers, some of the huntsmen raced behind the line of battle to drive into their rear. Their maneuver was almost completed when they met an enraged Songor and his men. Songor fought like a man possessed, running headlong into huntsmen, yelling and screaming, his sword a blur. Songor's unfettered passion momentarily confused the deliberate and careful mercenaries. These practiced killers recovered quickly and slowly, deliberately surrounded the wild, yelling man.

Pen saw the predicament his old servant created for himself. Leaving the center of the line he ran to his friend and yanked him back inside the slowly shrinking circle of troops. Now the rebel line had been outflanked. Pressed on all sides, the end was near. Like wolves circling a wounded prey, the huntsmen were ready for their final attack.

Narl had fought near the middle, hoping to engage Pen, a wake of dead and wounded bodies behind his steady march. Catching Pen's attention, Narl pointed his sword directly at the boy, smiled, and slowly walked toward him. Any of the guard in his way was quickly dispatched. Pen turned to face him and Narl's smile broadened.

Two forms materialized by Pen's side: the large, muscular body of Jack, and the fierce looking, but smaller Marvin. Narl kept moving as other huntsmen came to his side.

The thundering footfalls were heard, before the horses and their brown-shirted riders were seen. Acting as one, the huntsmen retreated and disappeared into the wood. The red tunics followed their lead. Narl stopped moving towards Pen. Growling like a dog when its food is taken, he too turned and ran toward the thick trees.

Bruder and his men followed the huntsmen to the edge of the thick undergrowth and then stopped. The Northlanders were brave, but not foolish.

When numbers were counted, the toll on the guard was heavy. Nearly half were killed or wounded. But, amazingly, even more huntsmen and soldiers littered the ground. Pen had taught them well.

Pen walked over to his portly protector who was still breathing hard from exertion and trembling a bit. Pen touched his friend's shoulder and gripped it firmly.

"Seems you were right to stay close to me, good friend."

Songor, his face flushed, stopped shivering and looked at Pen. Relieved he was unharmed and between gasps for breath, he spoke.

"This were... what I be speaking. I knowed the King... was slow so sumthin' had to be fast. Sum thin' was coming... I knowed, young master, I knowed it. But in here." He pointed to his head.

"Me thinking don't always come out here." He pointed to mouth.

"I will never again doubt what you think here," Pen said, rubbing the stout man's ring of hair, "nor what you speak here." Pen pointed to his mouth.

"But, most importantly, I will never doubt what you feel here." Pen smiled as he tapped Songor's heart.

CHAPTER 46

After the unsuccessful assassination attempts, a frustrated King Cearl called his general and captains into the great hall. With considerable trepidation, the group mustered in the dark room. The King looked at his men, his black eyes boring into one man after another.

"By now you all know the boy still lives." He shook his head and continued, "Why do I have to always be the one to bring these trifling bothers to an end? Fortunately, your king has a plan."

"Baron Glock, you know where to position your men, I presume."

The Baron quickly shook his head yes.

"Then leave now and get your men in position by tomorrow. The rest of you, prepare your men for a march. Tomorrow we move toward Bangor Hill!"

A day later on that same Bangor Hill, Petronius found out the Earl of Longham was finally on the move to join them with other nobles and nearly four thousand soldiers.

Unfortunately, good news is usually short-lived. A farmer galloped into the camp. Petronius and his officers gathered around him. "They march now, General. Thousands, sir. I've never seen so many soldiers! They march well south of the forest."

South, wondered Petronius. Why south? Why not directly toward Bangor Hill? Petronius called for his officers to meet him in his tent.

As the officers gathered, another scout talked to the General. After nodding to the man, he stood facing the group, his hands braced on the table. The group stopped their excited chatter when they saw the General's grim face.

"Earlier this afternoon, my spies reported the King has at least ten thousand marching under his banner."

"My god," exclaimed Thatcher, "he must have emptied all the garrisons in the country!"

"And tapped into the militia of the nobles still loyal to him as well," offered Bruder.

Viridius was unperturbed.

"Let them come, General. With the Earl's men and our defenses, we can surely blunt his attack and then go after him."

"Cearl moves well south of the forest," Petronius repeated.

Viridius looked puzzled. "That's odd. It will take longer to get to us."

Petronius motioned to the rider behind him. "This scout tells me the Baron's men are reforming northwest of the forest."

Viridius was more confused. "He's given up Markwood and the east position?"

Bruder spoke up. "The Earl and the nobles are moving east, trying to join us, Viridius."

The green man's eyes got larger. "But, that means Longham will be trapped between the King and the Baron!"

Bruder nodded. Petronius' head was already studying the map. "We have to help Longham."

Mother Hebron spoke up. "But then we give up our defenses, Petronius."

The General wearily closed his eyes and shook his head. All too well he knew that. Petronius marked an X on the map and looked at the group.

"We must help Longham. We can't let a friend fight wolves alone."

Petronius continued, looking at Mother Hebron. "We need the Earl's men. The King has ten thousand men. That number does not include the Baron's men, which are at least four thousand, nor does it count the thousand huntsmen who lurk somewhere in the woods...they haven't been accounted for yet. No, we are woefully outnumbered without the Earl's men. Not all of our men are as well trained as the enemy. Our defenses are good, but not enough to balance their superiority in men and experience."

He pointed to the X he had marked on the map. "This place here is Charney Field, isn't it Thatch? It's about halfway between the Earl and us. If we move now, we can meet up with Longham and attack the Baron. If we can knock him out, the next battle will find the two armies better matched."

Leaving behind campfires stoked by a few soldiers, the army left Bangor Hill in darkness. By dawn the army was miles away from Bangor Hill.

The huntsmen watched the procession from afar. Narl smiled. Cearl's plan was working perfectly.

Early the next day, a lone officer of the King galloped toward the long line of the rebels, all stopped to watch the rider pass. Catching up with Petronius, the rider shook his hand. It was Astible, Petronius' faithful captain from many years earlier. Considerably aged, with white hair and a larger girth, he was, nevertheless, a welcome sight. All this time Astible had passed useful information to the rebels from the capital. Now he rode alongside Petronius, willing and wanting to share his fate.

Charney Field was a wide grassy plain backing up to the northern panhandle of Markwood Forest. As Petronius came to the crest of the hill overlooking the land below, he saw, to his immense relief, the army of Earl Longham nearly four thousand strong, fully armed and positioned for battle. He sighed and smiled, a great weight lifted from his shoulders. By making a bold decision in giving up his defensive position and acting quickly, he had both saved the Earl's army and significantly augmented his own. Petronius moved his army toward the field but saw no jubilation from the ranks of militia facing him. The men remained rigidly in their positions, aligned for battle. Not sure what was happening, Petronius gave orders for his army to halt. From Longham's camp came the Earl, three horsemen, and a cart. They stopped halfway between the two armies and waited. This is very odd, thought Petronius. He called for Thatcher, Bruder, and Pen to join him and the four rode toward the Earl.

The man who faced the four rebels rode tall in the saddle, at least as tall as he could be, since he was only a bit taller than Thatcher. His face, normally pink, was red from exertion or anger, and covered with a curly gray beard. He could have been a jovial grandfather, but his face was stern as though ready to rebuke unruly children.

Petronius stopped his warhorse a short distance from a man he had known for over thirty years and remarked wryly, "Earl, I don't know whether you are with us or against us."

"Nor, do I, General. Nor do I."

The two men stared at each other, once friends. Now what, wondered Petronius? What was going on here?

Without any explanation, the Earl leaned back in his saddle, reached toward the cart, and unfurled a covering. Underneath was the long decayed carcass of a deer; what little hair remained was unquestionably white.

As Petronius looked at the remains in disbelief, the Earl filled in the details. "Two days ago, with our army already marching, this was delivered. The King claims he killed the deer long ago. He argues since there is no deer and there can be no Chosen One. So, Petronius, it looks like I am not fighting for the new king as you led me to believe weeks ago."

Petronius fixed his eyes on the skeptical Earl. "Think, Longham, think! It doesn't make sense. The King has never been shy about boasting of his hunting skills. Why not show the country his kill years ago? Why now?"

Longham shrugged his shoulders. "Who knows? This whole thing about the Chosen One is rather far-fetched. The Chosen One, a child? Indeed, your child, Petronius. Rather convenient I would say."

Petronius flushed red with anger. "You know me better than that," he growled.

The Earl looked away.

Petronius asked a question to which he already had the answer. "So why did you continue, if you had doubt?"

"We may be able to redeem ourselves in the King's eyes," the Earl responded.

Petronius realized he might have trapped his own army between the Earl's army and the Baron's army with the King's army not far behind. It became clear how he got away so easily from Bangor Hill; the King wanted to get his army out in the open and in the middle of three armies all larger than his own. Now all was lost. His hand on his sword, he turned toward the Earl.

"Is there any way that we can convince you that this..." he pointed to the cart, "is a sham?"

The Earl looked at tall man who once was his good friend, and then at Pen.

"Perhaps."

CHAPTER 47

How wonderful the word "perhaps". The general relaxed a bit and listened.

"You know how Kings were chosen by the White Deer…proof was always needed. Whenever a noble had supposedly been chosen, he was required to recite just one word to one man. A secret word…known only to one other person, the Listener."

Petronius nodded.

"King Jared, Cearl's father did not know the word; apparently the White Deer was not that specific in his dream," observed the Earl with obvious sarcasm.

"King Cearl…well, he claims to have killed the deer, so it is unlikely that many words passed between them."

Petronius interrupted. "The line of listeners was broken long ago, Longham."

"Not so, Petronius. Before Cearl's father assumed command of the country, the deer chose the previous King. The word whispered to the Listener was correct, but, old as he was, he died shortly thereafter. The King chose a new one, a strong man of pure heart.

The King whispered the secret word to this man. So was born a new Listener."

Petronius shook his head. "Longham, it was over sixty years ago. That Listener must be long dead by now."

"He lives still, Petronius. On the western edge of my land are the barrens, a wild land inhabited mostly by wild Picts. In that land, a holy man lives who is both revered and feared by the people of that godforsaken land."

Longham paused a moment and looked back at his army. "He is here now, with my men. He knows the secret word. He is beyond reproach, Petronius; he is the Listener."

"So, you expect my son to know that word?"

"If he is who you claim him to be... then, yes."

Petronius twisted in his saddle to face his son. "Pen, did the deer ever share a word with you, a secret word?"

Pen thought for a moment. "Yes, sir, I know the word."

Petronius sighed with relief. "All right, Longham, let's go settle this."

"Only your son and you, Petronius." The general nodded in agreement. The Earl and his men started to steer their horses back to their troops. The old cart with the carcass followed. Sham or truth, all would soon find out.

Thatcher rode up in front of Petronius and looked into the General's eyes as he yelled over his shoulder to the Earl. "I go as well."

Petronius looked at the short man blocking his path. "No, Thatch. Just me and Pen."

"No sir. I go as well. I'll have your back, General."

He had been with Thatcher long enough to know he would not back down. A lump formed in his throat. How did he deserve such loyalty? He looked at the Earl who watched the exchange.

"Longham, what say you?"

The Earl raised his eyes to the sky in frustration. "By Odin! Let's get on with it!"

Turning to Bruder, Petronius whispered, "Return to the troops. If we don't return, prepare for an attack."

Thatcher, Petronius, and his son trotted alongside the Earl as Bruder galloped back.

After the entourage reached the Earl's army, an old man slowly stepped out of the crowd of gray-shirted warriors. He was bent with age, wrinkles embedded within wrinkles so that he more resembled a long, stringy raisin than a man.

Thatcher gasped, drawing the attention of the men. He coughed and looked away. After the men turned back to the ancient one, Thatcher leaned over to Pen and whispered into his ear, "That's him. Oh my gosh, that's him."

"Who?"

"The man in the desert, the holy man who saved me. That's him."

The Earl got off his horse, walked to the man, and spoke into his ear.

"Holy man," the Earl intoned loudly, "Penda, son of Petronius, claims to be the Chosen One. As such, he should know the secret word."

The old man limped toward the three rebels, using the stout rod as a cane. The Listener's tall frame was draped in a weather-beaten robe that barely covered him. He smiled at Thatcher. He stared a few seconds at Petronius and nodded to him. Finally his eyes rested on Pen. As though commanded, Pen got off Mirus and walked toward the ancient.

The old man had not taken his eyes from the lad. Pen met the gaze and did not look away. Finally, the holy man broke the silence with a voice surprisingly deep and strong.

"So he thinks he knows the word? Come to my ear, boy." A gnarled finger beckoned Pen.

He walked to the old man and stood beside him. The fate of a nation hung on the memories of an old man and a young boy.

The old man leaned forward, looked slyly at Pen and whispered, "Tell me the word, lad."

Pen hesitated. The color drained from his face, he looked helplessly at his father. "I can't, sir."

CHAPTER 48

The Earl and his officers slowly pulled back, hands on swords, whispering to one another. The words, "sham" and "pretender" made their way to Petronius, who was for once without a plan. Thatcher pulled close to his general, his sword immediately drawn.

The Earl's soldiers had positioned themselves to close off any escape. Sensing the tense atmosphere, the horses moved back and forth, nearly rearing. Only the old man and Pen remained fixed, staring at each other as though secretly communicating.

The old man, leaning on his staff, asked the boy, "Did the deer tell you something, anything?"

As though commanded, the horses stopped their agitated motion. The attention of everyone, including the horses, was once again riveted on the conversation.

"Yes, sir. Her name, sir. But I wasn't to repeat it to anyone, save he in a white robe. And yours, sir, is certainly not white."

The man looked at the boy, his squinting eyes carefully measuring him. A smile broke out through the lines in the face. The ancient one recalled a time, long ago when he was a respected captain. He was called by the old king, blind and near death. For over an hour the dying king told of the legend of the White Deer. Finally he brought the captain's ear close to his mouth and whispered the secret word he had heard from the deer forty years earlier.

The king asked for a servant to bring a pure white robe to the bed. The servant laid the white silk robe upon the bed and left. The old king, his breathing now labored, held the hand of the captain.

"I don't know why, but you must be sure to wear this white robe whenever there is a supplicant to check. A white robe for the White Deer." Those were his last words.

All these years, thought the old man; he had not forgotten. All these years he had kept the white robe close to him at all times. He pulled off the bag on his back. Undoing the strings, he removed a clean, pure white robe and with a flourish, donned it.

"Speak the word to me, Penda, son of Princess Elen and General Petronius."

Pen leaned forward, paused a moment, and whispered, "Angelus".

Though Pen returned to his upright stance, the man remained leaned over as though still waiting for the word. Pen was about to repeat the word thinking that the old man did not hear him, but the white-robed figure slowly rose, standing taller than the boy. Tears streamed down his face from eyes closed. When he opened them, he looked at Pen and said loudly for all around to hear, "He is the Chosen One."

After the two armies merged together with considerable backslapping and warm greetings, the Earl and the General conferred about their next move. Scouts for both armies told the pair that the Baron, afraid of the developing situation, had long ago retreated toward King Cearl and his army. The two leaders decided to abandon their plans to engage the Baron's retreating army.

Instead, the Earl ordered his provision carts to be unloaded for a feast. The celebration went long into the night.

Thatcher left the celebration and the dancing flames of the great fire in the center of the camp. He walked toward the forest where he last saw the old man. In the gray light of the full moon, Thatcher could just make out the old man crouched under a tree, his back to the camp. Coming up quietly behind the old man, Thatcher was about to introduce himself when the man said, "Hello, Thatcher."

Amazed, Thatcher kneeled down beside the man. He watched the old man slowly chew on a walnut. "How did you know it was me?"

After the old fingers extracted the meat from the last nut, frowning, he turned to the warrior. "I have to tell you the secrets of the Listener?" A smile followed.

"Who else could it have been? Longham and Petronius are sharing old memories of better times. Pen, a fine lad, was here an hour ago. He will make a good king. Who else could it have been? No one else is curious enough and brave enough to talk to an old man such as me."

Thatcher smiled. He had forgotten the conversations the two shared so many years ago in the cave. He was impressed with the man's wisdom even then.

"I did what I promised." Thatcher wondered if the Listener even remembered the promise after twenty years.

Finishing his last nut, still crouching, the old man stared off into the night. "I know you did."

Thatcher tilted his head and wrinkled his forehead in puzzlement. A half-smile formed on his face. "All right, you have me again. How did you know I kept my promise?"

The man picked up his staff and raised himself up with a groan.

"You never left Kirkland these last ten years, my friend, but others did. Your name came up often, all over the country. Your fame has spread...even to the barrens. People talked of a sword master who taught the blade and, more importantly, how to live.

The man who never loses a fight and never curses. You are well known, Thatcher. To be sure, you are feared by some, but respected by all. I know you kept your promise, my son."

"Well, I'll be danged!"

The old man's laugh was deep and melodious.

CHAPTER 49

The two armies set up camp in the great region known as Charney Field. A difficult place to defend, thought Petronius. It's only natural defense was the thick extension of Markwood to the north.

The King's large army lumbered around the great forest giving the rebels a few days to dig trenches and mound dirt into crude walls, considerably shorter than the well molded structures on Bangor Hill. The rebel camp, however, was a magnet for hundreds of new recruits who came from every direction. Petronius and Astible did their best to supply weapons and training, but clearly their ability in battle would be more tied to their enthusiasm and numbers rather than their skills.

The King and his army arrived three days after Pen was formerly declared the Chosen One. By afternoon a sea of red troops faced the smaller rebel force. Seeing the King's army arrayed neatly in red lines, the black uniforms of the militia substantially adding to the menacingly large force before them, many of the new recruits questioned their judgment in joining the effort.

Petronius, on a large white horse, casually trotted in front of his troops. He stopped and talked to the men in the ranks, his horse's backside facing the enemy as a silent snub. Seeing the calm visage of the famed General Petronius riding before them, all took heart, especially the new recruits. Though outnumbered and lacking experience, they had the best general.

Pen then thundered in atop the great black horse, Mirus. While the King's force glowered, a cheer went up from the entire rebel army. Resolve replaced indecision, confidence replaced doubt.

In the war council that night, Petronius told his captains the battle would probably not occur the following day.

"Post the necessary pickets and watch the King's line, but let your men rest. That is exactly what the King is doing for his men after their long march."

The final battle was near. The rebel army ended up numbering a respectable ten thousand, but too many were hobbled together into questionable fighting units. The King's army numbered nearly fifteen thousand, but nearly all experienced in battle, certainly better trained and, at least in the case of the huntsmen, more ruthless. Unbeknownst to both sides, however, the rebels would have help from one unexpected source.

CHAPTER 50

As Petronius had sagely predicted, the battle did not happen the next day. Nevertheless, sleep was a rare luxury enjoyed only by Songor and a few others. Disturbed by strange dreams, Pen had been up since dawn pacing back and forth in his tent. When he entered his father's tent, Petronius looked up and his heart dropped. Over the course of the last few months, he had witnessed his son change from a carefree boy to a man burdened with fear, concern, and perhaps guilt, lines of worry etched forever on his face.

Pen slumped in a chair, facing Petronius.

"Father, last night I had the most peculiar dream. I was again in the secret meadow of the White Deer and she was by my side. In my dream, I was as clothed exactly as I am now, in this purple tunic."

"Just the dream of a young man with far too much responsibility placed upon him, Pen. Pay it no heed, son."

Pen persisted. "The dream was very vivid, sir. Not like a dream at all, really. More like a memory of something. The white deer

331

kept urging me to listen to the forest. What could she have meant, sir?"

Petronius was mildly annoyed, impatient with this distraction from his battle plans.

"I don't know. Check with the holy man."

Pen nodded to his father and walked into the bright sunshine of the crisp morning. Instead of joining the Royal Guard, he made his way toward Markwood Forest. What did she mean, listen to the forest? Passing a few isolated trees, he reached the edge of the green wall and stopped, his head cocked. All he heard was the wind rustling the leaves and branches.

As he began to walk away, a thought insinuated itself in his mind. It startled him. The thought was not his own. Something about the rich smell of the forest. Smells he never had sensed and never could... on his own. He stopped, relaxed, and closed his eyes again. He listened, not to the forest, but rather to his own mind. Still, he heard the soft murmur of the leaves, rustling in the late fall breeze. Wait, no. There was another thought...a whisper. Not so much heard by him as simply known by him. It was not a well-defined thought which invaded his mind, but it was certainly there. Then he sensed other thoughts...many, many other thoughts.

Pen kneeled down, bowed his head, and closed his eyes tightly in concentration. He blocked out the sound of wind and leaves. He focused on those tiny, almost imperceptible thoughts filling his head.

He was somehow able to untangle one from the many and examine it. There, he had it! Waiting to help. He separated another thought. All to give. And another. The deer commands.

A flood of messages flowed into his mind. He opened his eyes and jumped up. He knew what the White Deer meant. Quickly he ran back to Petronius.

Bursting through the tent flap, he interrupted his father, standing over the map, in a meeting with some of his captains.

When the General looked up, he saw his son doubled over, heaving deep breaths from his long run. Petronius sighed, and shook his head in frustration.

In gasps, he told his father of his discovery. "I know...what the dream...was trying to tell me. The animals...will fight with us tomorrow."

"The animals? You mean the horses?" asked Petronius. "Yes, of course, that goes without saying, son..."

Pen shook his head wildly, still struggling with his breath. He explained in gulps of words. "No, not the horses...all the animals of the forest...all of them...they will join the fight tomorrow."

Petronius rolled his eyes and looked at his son again. Had Pen buckled under the strain? He waved the captains out of the tent. Before they left, he admonished them, "Not a word of this to anyone!" They nodded in agreement, equally concerned about Pen.

After the captains exited, he turned to his son. "Are you out of your mind?"

"They will help, I know it!"

As Petronius closed his eyes, Pen realized what he said was rather incredible. He had to convince his father.

"You know how I am with animals. Remember when I told you that the cow was sick from eating the wrong grass and you changed the field and it got better? That wasn't just intuition or idle guessing. That was me hearing its thoughts. Remember what Mother Hebron told you...I'm a communicator."

Petronius looked at his son. He knew this to be true. Elen had the same ability, but this was different. This was somehow communicating with animals unseen, wild ones at that. No, this had to be more desperate hope than reality.

"So you heard from the animals that were going to help out tomorrow. Maybe the squirrels are going to throw nuts at the huntsmen?"

"No, not squirrels. Actually, I don't know what type of animals sent the messages. Father, listen to me. This is important. They are out there waiting, ready. Hundreds of them, ready to fight with us."

"And you can, of course, communicate back to them? You can control them?"

"I think so, sir. I didn't try that yet, but it makes sense to me."

Petronius leaned over the table, looked down, closed his eyes, and shook his head. He walked quickly around the table. Impatient with his son, Petronius roughly pulled him by the arm and led him out of the tent. The pair walked through the crowded camp with men sharpening weapons and officers yelling. As they approached the woods, only a few soldiers were seen and their attention was on the forest, looking and listening for sounds of men. Petronius stopped far from any guards, just short of entering the thick woods. He waved his hand toward the trees.

"All right, Pen. Summon your animal army."

"It might not be wise to call them all, sir, but let me try to call a few."

Pen closed his eyes. The thoughts came back and he could now easily discern them. He grabbed a few strands floating in his mind and did his best to send a return message. The forest remained quiet. He squeezed his eyes shut tight, his forehead wrinkled with the effort. A minute passed. Nothing. He opened his eyes and looked toward the forest, seeing no animals.

"I'm sorry, sir. I can't do it," Pen said dejectedly.

Seeing his son's anguish over his failure, Petronius' anger diminished. He put his arm across his son's shoulders. "Don't worry about this son. It was nothing more than a nice dream."

Father and son started to walk back to camp when they heard a low growl behind them. Turning, they saw a large, gray wolf, about twenty feet away, looking at them as it nervously paced back and forth. Another wolf came out of the thicket, a bit further away.

Petronius slowly began to pull out his sword, but Pen gripped his father's forearm.

"No, Father," he whispered, keeping his eyes fixed on the two animals, "I called them."

From another area of the forest came a black bear. Two deer appeared. Though wary of each other, the animals continually looked at Pen as though they were waiting for him to speak.

"I think I should tell them to go back into the forest, Father. They are uncomfortable being out in the open like this."

His astonished father dumbly shook his head in agreement. Pen closed his eyes and one by one, the animals returned in to the forest.

"You can control them!" Petronius blurted out as they left. "How many are there, Pen?"

Pen thought for a few seconds. "I don't know, but in my mind there are so many little thoughts that they make quite a din in my head. Hundreds, Father, maybe thousands."

The General thought for a moment. "I think that we may have the perfect way to use them, Pen. Let's go back. We must hold another war counsel to introduce our newest allies."

CHAPTER 51

The sun, not yet completely risen, cast shades of purple and pink on the horizon. Petronius mounted his large white horse. Mirus looked at the general, puzzled. Petronius rode over to the old horse. "You carry my son, old friend. Take care of him as you have so faithfully cared for me." He scratched the horse's ears, patted him, and left. The horse followed the retreating figure with perked ears perked, hoping for his old master to return.

Pen, witnessing the exchange, went to Mirus.

"Well, Mirus, it's you and me again." He patted the horse's neck and leaned to his ear. "I promise you, faithful horse, we will be in the thick of battle today." Mirus whinnied excitedly, and nuzzled his young master.

As the rising sun pushed away the black night, the Earl shivered in the cold and led his militia to the right side of the line. He passed the old man hobbling in the same direction, braced by his rod. Waving his troops along, he pulled up his horse to talk with the ancient one.

"Stay behind the lines, old man. You have played your role and played it well."

The old man pushed up on the rod, stood tall and squinted at his sovereign. "Not likely, Longham. This is my battle, too."

With that said, he limped along with the troops toward the battlefield. Longham shook his head. Who can order around a ninety-year-old warrior? He galloped to the head of his troops.

Behind the long line of Longham's militia, the blue-robed sisters, on slightly higher ground, formed a tight square.

Petronius was momentarily alone in the field, birds swooping down here and there. Behind him, the brown-shirted cavalry led by Bruder slowly formed. Further back, the green men packed close together under Viridius. Commanding a slight rise between Longham and Petronius was Thatcher and an odd assortment of determined farmers and merchants, all well trained. Scattered among them was a cadre of former veterans, men who had served with the General in the past, all in gray uniforms. As ever, Pen was well in rear, but this time with the purple uniforms of the Royal Guard. Over three hundred new recruits, barely trained and all untried, were attached to his command. Hopefully their numbers would compensate for their lack of skills. Indeed, it was uncertain if their choice would be to follow him or run the other way.

Over the rise, into view, came line after line of red and black.

Intermingled with the incessant beat of the shields, orders were being shouted, sending men and women scattering. Finally, the pounding stopped and the orders had ceased. An absolute quiet enveloped the camp. Suddenly the loud roar of thousands of screaming men echoed across the battlefield.

The two forces clashed in the tall grass between them. For over an hour captains juggled footmen, cavalry, and archers to gain advantage. The battle line ebbed and flowed. It was a stalemate of death in the tall, green grass.

Near noon, Cearl gave his signal to the huntsmen. Out of Markwood Forest charged over one thousand of the most able warriors on the great battlefield. They raced toward Pen and his men. Pen stood as tall as possible on Mirus and looked to his father. Petronius lifted his hand and lowered it straight down. That was it! He yelled to his men who had turned to face the onslaught of the huntsmen.

"Turn this way, men, we move to the front. Now!"

The men were puzzled. Out of the woods, two hundred yards away came a relentless force, yet they were turning away from the horde which would attack the unprotected underbelly of the army. Confused, but obedient, the Guard quickly advanced to the front. Not wanting to be slashed by the huntsmen, the new recruits in the rear more than kept up with the veterans in the front.

After he waved his men forward, Pen delayed a moment with his head bowed, concentrating. Absorbed with his task, he ignored the racing huntsmen drawing closer and closer.

The huntsmen slowed down, confused there was no one with whom to fight, except one sole rider, his head down, on a great black horse. Narl had no hesitation; smiling he marched quickly toward Mirus and Pen.

A cacophony of noise suddenly sounded from behind. Large animals of every type burst from the forest at a full run. The huntsmen were quickly enveloped in a flood of snarling wolves, growling bears, yelping foxes, and charging deer with pointed antlers. The men turned to fight the animals. It was mayhem between man and animal. Frustrated, Narl watched his quarry trot away toward the front. He ducked as a wolf leaped over him.

If Pen's troops could outflank the King's army, the battle might be won. Without being told, Mirus sprang into a gallop and Pen burst in front of his men, leading the Royal Guard into fray, the inexperienced troops still at the rear. The presence of the Chosen One lifted the spirits of the other soldiers and the front began to slowly move in favor of the rebels.

Cearl immediately recognized the seriousness of the situation. Leading his cavalry, the King quickly insinuated himself in the midst of the faltering front, wreaking havoc with the great sword, Elinrod. Either out of fear of the King being so near or just good training, the red line held firm, and the crisis was averted. Cearl directed a large mass of his army to knife through the inexperienced troops following Pen. Bewildered and unsure, they scattered, leaving Pen and the Royal Guard effectively cut off from the rest of the rebel force. Cearl's masterful counterstrike blunted the attack of the rebels and put the Royal Guard in jeopardy. A circle of red began to constrict around the Royal Guard and Pen.

CHAPTER 52

Nor was the battle faring well on the other side of the rebel line. After a morning of continual fighting, Longham's militia weakened, pressed hard by the better-trained soldiers of the King's army.

The rebel archers, led by Mother Hebron, were exacting a terrible toll on the King's men, and in large measure, this accounted for the Earl's initial success. But the Baron and his black-clad militia had managed to outflank the Earl's troops and were now attacking the blue-robed archers on their flank. The woman slowly retreated up a gentle slope, shielded by the occasional tree. Hand-to-hand combat had already begun, eliminating their effectiveness as archers.

Mother Hebron shot an arrow at a rushing man, his sword held ready to strike, and brought him down just three feet in front of her. The action was so close now that her bow was useless. Just as well, she thought, feeling the contents of her quiver; only one arrow remained. She debated whether to string the arrow, but a black-suited man charged her, and she discarded the bow while smoothly pulling out her blade. She swung about and clashed swords with the warrior in black. This was not good, she thought.

*

Cearl saw the Earl and his men slowly retreat. If he could take the Earl out of the contest, his men might lose their grit and determination. Over the din of the battle he yelled to his two black bodyguards, pointing to the Earl.

"Kill that damn traitor Longham."

Off they walked with long steps, double-edged axes cutting a thin line into the rebel troops. Within minutes they reached the Earl, his men retreating from their bloody axes. The Earl, however, stood his ground and parried their strokes as best he could, but they were too fast and too strong. Longham was knocked to one knee and stunned by a blow on his shield from one of the black giants; the other raised his axe high to deliver the coup de grace. Out of what seemed like empty space, a hard wooden staff was buried in the black man's chest throwing him off balance. The Listener, standing as tall as his enemy, turned to the other bodyguard and swept his feet with his staff, bringing him crashing down. With a vicious swing, he hit the man's head. Skull cracked, the great black man was still.

The old man helped the younger one up. "Seems I still have some use, sire."

The Earl smiled, looked alarmed, and pushed him aside. Instinctively, the old man jumped out of the way to avoid the swinging axe of the other giant. The Earl, still unbalanced, tried to slice the arm of the black bodyguard but succeeded only in nicking him. It was enough to cause the giant to release the axe. The giant used his other hand to pull out a sword. The Earl could not recover his balance in time, but the ancient brought his staff up to protect them from the slicing blade. The strength of the savage swing splintered the wood. The sword was raised again. The Earl brought up his blade to blunt the attack, but the giant black bodyguard knocked the sword away. Smiling he raised his sword at third time to slay the defenseless Earl when the boney body of the old listener plowed into the man. The great black man did not budge; his sword hand knocked away the old man as though he was but an annoying fly.

Thatcher materialized and the two parried back and forth. Ducking under the deadly arc of the man's blade, Thatcher rose up as he plunged his blade into the chest of his assailant. After dispatching the bodyguard, he quickly turned away to pick up the old man who had fallen on the ground. Longham, still on the ground, yelled.

Somehow the black giant had not gone down. He swung his sword at Thatcher's back. The old man whirled Thatcher away from the blow, but, in doing so, he took a deep cut. Thatcher regained his stance, shared a few clanging blows, and deftly plunged his sword deep into the stomach of the King's bodyguard. The great giant fell, writhing in pain. Thatcher wanted no more resurrections so he jabbed his sword into his heart and the giant lay still. He kneeled beside the old man who had saved his life yet again. The Earl walked painfully over to the pair and kneeled down on the other side.

The weathered face, tough as leather, was frozen with pain. "Ah...it seems I die now, Longham."

He grabbed Thatcher's hand and whispered, the deep wound taking his breath away. "My name...my name is Markos. Tell it in the stories, Thatcher. Markos the Listener. I want to finish my life with my name."

With that he sighed, closed his eyes, and his head dropped back.

Thatcher gently rested the head on the ground and released the hand, murmuring "Markos."

He looked up the hill and saw the Baron and his men attacking the sisters. Without a word, he ran to them. The Earl watched, but didn't follow. He started to gather his men, trying to rally them.

*

The encircled Royal Guard was hard pressed. The perimeter of the circle found the men entangled in one-on-one combat. While Pen was fighting from atop his horse with one soldier on his right, another unseen red soldier on his left attempted to strike him. Seeing the man approach, Mirus reared up and discouraged him from the attack. Pen, unseated by the sudden movement, fell from the great steed and hit his head on the ground so hard he blacked out. The King's soldiers saw the prostrate figure and realized their opportunity for fame, fortune and victory. They rushed in for the kill.

*

Mother Hebron had effectively handled two men who attacked her; one lay dead and the other was wounded and stumbled off, holding a bloodied arm. Most of her blue-cloaked women fared worse. Some lay wounded, a few dead. She ordered a full retreat and turned to join her maidens a short distance away, a line of blue archers growing slowly in the rear. As she ran near the large oak, she was slammed into its trunk from behind. Her sword knocked loose by the blow, she reached for her knife, but her wrist was caught and turned; the blade fell harmlessly on the ground. She found herself turned and pushed up against the tree by none other than Baron Glock.

"Well, what have we here? Leader of the blue archers, perhaps?" the Baron inquired, his sword pressed sideways against her throat.

"You are a bit too old for me, woman. I like 'em young. What do they call you? Mother Hebron? Still you have a pleasant face and a fetching figure, that's for sure. The battle is won. All right,

I'll honor you by making you an exception. Maybe we might play a bit here, eh?"

Mother Hebron, unafraid, looked at the Baron whose hand steadily worked up her robe. "You don't remember me, do you?" she asked calmly, ignoring his vulgar groping.

"Oh, dear lady, I am sure that I would have remembered you." His free hand under her robe started to trace the outline of her body.

She stared coldly into his eyes. "The temple; you raped one of the sisters. Now do you remember?"

He stopped his offensive actions, looked at her quizzically, and then smiled. "Now I do remember. The same pretty face. Of course. What was your name? Sister Mary? We would have had even more fun had that impertinent general not hit me. Now we can remedy that loss. Sorry, dear, no time for pleasantries."

"Indeed," she said and slowly slid her hand to her quiver, withdrawing the one remaining arrow. Without hesitation and with lightning speed, she plunged it into the neck of her assailant, her face screwed into an unsightly sneer.

The Baron's eyes bulged. He dropped his sword and tried to take the arrow out, but her hand remained firmly attached to the shaft. Their eyes met, his in terror, hers in grim satisfaction. Blood gurgling from his mouth, he fell to his knees. She kneeled beside him, her hand still firmly on the shaft, wiggling it a bit.

"I told you we would meet again."

He looked at her in shock and pain.

"Sorry, no time for pleasantries, Baron."

She pushed him down with her foot. She picked up her sword and ran to join her sisters.

*

Pen lay on the ground unconscious. The King's men, swords drawn, approached the fallen lad. A single blow now would end the battle. All that stood in their way was an unruly large black horse standing protectively over the boy. As the soldiers cautiously approached, Mirus bucked and charged around in a circle about his fallen master, careful not to step on him, but effectively keeping the soldiers at bay. A few of the men were pushed aside by the large bulk of the animal, while its hooves spiked others. The approaching swordsmen were wary of the creature, but the unconscious prize spurred them forward. Clearly they would have to dispatch the horse first and the boy second. The swords and spears that would have found Pen's body were now focused on the horse. Cut after cut pierced the great horse, yet he toiled on, refusing to let anyone inside his circle of protection. Eventually however, the blows had exacted their toll on the great beast. After numerous slashes and piercings, Mirus' strength gave way and he stumbled on his front legs. He tried to get up, but another sword slashed one of the rear legs, severing tendons. Curled around his young master, he frantically kicked his front hooves to discourage the men from hurting Pen. Another sword pierced his neck and the great horse's head fell to the ground.

The precious minutes gained by the efforts of the horse allowed Pen's guard to battle their way to their fallen leader. Marvin, screaming at both friend and foe, put himself in front of the boy. Others stepped over the fallen horse and shielded the still unconscious lad.

Mirus, weak from his wounds, looked over to the boy. He tried in vain to nuzzle Pen. Then blackness.

A moment later, Pen gained consciousness and found he had an excruciating headache. The noise, at first seemingly far away, grew louder and louder. He opened his eyes and saw his men fighting with the reds. Leaning for a moment on one knee, shaking his head, he grabbed his sword, pushed up and entered the skirmish. His men, seeing him fight, felt relief and pushed the King's soldiers back. With Pen's blade added to the battle, the King's men were quickly scattered.

Pen turned to mount Mirus only to see his horse punctured with bloody wounds, prostrate and lifeless. Frederick was beside him. "He died protecting you, sir." Another surge of emboldened red soldiers attacked the group. Pen turned to face the onslaught. There was no time for grief that afternoon on Charney Field.

Petronius looked in the direction of his son and saw him surrounded by a red sea and desperately fighting the tight confinement. His first inclination was to break away to save him, but he was securing the center. If the rebel troops collapsed here, the battle would be lost. In vain he looked for a captain to help Pen. Spying Songor, he caught his attention and waved to him, urging him to come nearer.

*

The Baron's men pressed up the slight incline, even though the archers were once again exacting death with their arrows. It would only be a matter of minutes before the valiant women would be once again engaged in hand-to-hand combat, greatly to their disadvantage. The next charge found the front few women, including Liana, throwing down their bows and bringing out their swords. The women were being beaten back.

CHAPTER 53

Hurrying to join Petronius, Songor pulled away from the confused entanglement at the front line. As they raced behind the thin line, his five remaining men found it difficult to keep up with the portly man. Songor was pressed by one man, but somehow managed to wound him and the man limped away. His men engaged, Songor alone pressed toward Petronius. Suddenly, standing before him was the tall, lanky form of Eusibius, grimy and disheveled from the business of war and death.

"Ah, the dim-witted servant, Songor. A captain, I see! The General is that hard up for officers?"

The man laughed at his own taunts. "You know, dumb-one, you did get the better of me in the tavern. Now it's time to set things straight."

"Ye talk much, man. Do ye fight as much?"

Eusibius bared his teeth and lunged at Songor; the two crossed blades loudly. Songor was pushed back by the man's superior sword skills. The round man stumbled, but nimbly regained his balance. Unfortunately a moment was all Eusibius needed. With a series of quick movements, he flicked Songor's sword from his grasp.

Eusibius smiled at the unarmed man before him. "Yes, I do fight well, as a matter of fact. Any last words, fat man? Oh, and by the way, after you, I will go after that young friend of yours...what is his name? Pen."

Songor was silent.

Eusibius raised his sword to strike a deathblow, and Songor ran straight into his attacker. The slicing blade just missed cutting into Songor's considerable bulk. The subsequent collision brought both men to the ground, and Songor's arms wrapped tightly around the other man's chest. Eusibius couldn't move the long blade to strike his assailant and Songor would not let go. Instead he applied more pressure, both men grunting.

"This here dumb man won't...let...you...hurt...his...boy."

Muscles well-formed from years of farm work were hidden within the folds of fat. Those muscles kept squeezing until Eusibius' eyes bulged. The eyes filmed over, the body sagged, and out of the pocked-marked face, a tongue hung loosely. Songor pushed up, scrambled for his sword, and returned to the reclined man. He pushed him with a boot and rolled him over on his stomach. Eusibius was dead. Songor trudged toward Petronius. Finally arriving at the slight rise where Petronius hailed him, the loyal servant looked about, but could not find him. In the middle of the battle, the General had disappeared.

*

Petronius had directed his troops to fill the gaps created by fierce thrusts of man and horse in the King's army when a group of screaming red soldiers broke through the line and commenced a rush on the General. A clamor of metal on metal punctuated the din of the battle. In the furious skirmish, the General slipped to the ground as hostile swords lunged at him.

Petronius scooted backwards, deftly deflecting the swords jabbing at him. A green streak suddenly scattered the red tunics; it was Viridius fighting like a mad man. Petronius got to his feet and joined his friend.

"Well, it looks like we are even, Petronius," yelled Viridius with a smile. The two friends fought side by side, each downing a red tunic. As Petronius directed his attention to the next attacker, he saw Viridius holding off two.

Knowing his friend was not as skilled with a sword as he was with a bow, Petronius did his best to end his encounter quickly. Just as he wounded his antagonist, another took his place. Out of the corner of his eye he noted, with some relief, the green man had taken down one of his assailants and was finishing with the other.

Both men downed their opponents simultaneously. Viridius beamed a great smile at the General. He was about to say something when another of the King's men plunged a sword into his side. Viridius crumpled from the blow. Behind Petronius came more rebels pushing the King's men back. Petronius rushed to the side of his fallen friend.

Viridius had his eyes squeezed tight. He looked up at his friend. "Not a nick this time, Petronius. By Odin, it hurts!"

"I'll get you to the tent. Hold, Viridius, hold."

"No, my General. This is bad. We both know it." The green man, through the pain, smiled briefly at his friend. "You can't save me this time, old friend."

He gasped for air, but squeezed out a few words. "We're even, now, right?"

The tall man with the scar looked down, tears in his eyes. "Even, my friend…"

Viridius' face screwed in pain, his eyes closed tightly. When he opened them, he looked up at Petronius. His voice was faint and wheezing.

"You have a wonderful son. He'll be a good king."

His eyes closed, his face relaxed, Viridius died. The fighting now returned to where the general kneeled and he was immediately up. Petronius was engaged in a number of quick sword fights and backed up as two soldiers pressed him. A moment later, Songor was by his side diverting the efforts of one soldier and discouraging another from joining the attack on the General. Petronius was able to dispatch his opponent and Songor's antagonist wisely retreated.

Taking advantage of the momentary lull in the fighting, he yelled to Songor, pointing to where Pen and his men were still surrounded. "Go now and help Pen." Songor nodded and went to gather some men. Petronius plunged back into the melee.

*

The Royal Guard kept a tight circle, giving ground very slowly and always at a high price. Red-shirted bodies formed a crude outer circle. The King, seeing the object of the battle encircled and near, started a bloody path toward his nephew. Only a few rebels were brave enough to block the path of the flashing sword Elinrod. Those who dared quickly succumbed to the bloody blade.

A clear path was opened to Pen. For a moment, uncle and nephew stared at each other. Both recognized the battle and the war would end with their terrible reunion. In an instant, the strange link between them was severed. Songor and his men had finally reached their objective as they positioned themselves between the King and the chosen one.

The roiling mass of red and purple blocked Pen from reaching the King and Songor. Less than fifty feet away, all he could do was helplessly watch Cearl and Songor circle each other: Songor cautiously, Cearl with haughty disdain.

Songor well knew the King's skill with the sword. Nevertheless, he was determined the King would not get past him.

"I should have killed you years ago, gardener," said Cearl, his lips allowing an ugly frown to form. "I will remedy that error now." He launched a sudden attack on the portly Songor. The King's tall, lanky body moved gracefully around the stumbling captain. Doing his best to parry the numerous and frighteningly quick thrusts, Songor found himself backing up, deeper into the opening mass of red tunics who stepped away from the struggle.

Sweating profusely, his feet refusing to back up any further, his blade swung wildly at the King.

"Ye shant git by me. I won't have ye hurt me boy." With that Songor rushed the King, trying to end it with a collision of flesh as he did with Eusibius. Deftly the king stepped aside and back-slashed him in the stomach. Songor crumpled into a fetal position and lay writhing on the ground.

He knelt down and spoke loud enough for the suffering man to hear. "You die gardener, but know the same painful death awaits your precious Pen." Songor tried to strike out at the man with his bloodied hand, but the King pushed up and away. The large man gasped and then lay still. Cearl smiled and walked off toward Pen.

*

The animals were doing their best to tear into the huntsmen, but on the featureless ground of the grassy field they were at a disadvantage. The huntsmen had paired up, back to back, and started pushing the animals back into the forest. More and more animals were limping into the safety of the forest.

*

From his vantage point in the center, Petronius could see it all. The black horde of the Baron's militia encircled the remaining blue-robed sisters. Longham and his forces were hard pressed on the other side. The King's forces surrounded his son. At the rear was the gravest threat of all. With most of the animals wounded, dead, or occupied with other hunters, he saw some of the huntsmen slowly migrating toward one man, Narl. The General instinctively knew a deadly attack in the rear was imminent. Leaving the front in charge of an able captain, he ran to meet the huntsmen.

*

On the knoll, the blue-robed sisters were engaged with the Baron's militia. Liana managed to knock away the sword of one soldier, but another took his place. She was pressed with a second soldier attacking her. Both men were smiling, sensing a kill. Suddenly Mother Hebron was beside her and they fought side by side. The pair of soldiers backed away.

Other soldiers joined in. Now mother and daughter were clearly out numbered. Suddenly someone elbowed himself between the two females. It was Thatcher, short, sweaty, and smiling. His blade darted right, left, up, down as he moved quickly between the men. First one man clutched his arm, then another grabbed his leg, and a third fell down dead. Mother Hebron handily killed her single opponent and Liana held hers at bay until he saw that he was alone facing three deadly fighters. He ran away. Before he could make two steps, Liana's knife was in his back.

"Thatcher, you are a welcome sight," Mother Hebron declared during the brief lull in the fighting.

"Always glad to help, ma'am. Now, if you will excuse me, I have a bit of tidying up to do."

Thatcher's men stopped the black militia. The women, relieved from defending themselves with their swords, regained their bows and their well-directed arrows took a heavy toll on the enemy. One by one the black tunics turned and raced back to the safety of the King's soldiers. Trained and led by the Baron for many years, the militia was particularly good at retreat.

*

The animals had retreated to the woods, confused and licking their wounds. Weakened but still a potent force, the huntsmen returned to their original mission to gut the rebels from the rear. Petronius had extracted a nearby captain and nearly one hundred men to follow him and they turned to face the onslaught of the huntsmen. Walking through the cluster of individual fights, Narl saw Petronius. The General caught his stare and understood its meaning. He turned to walk toward the killer. Seeing the two antagonists coming together, nearby huntsmen knew enough not to challenge the considerable skills of the General nor deny Narl his trophy.

Narl, his bloody blade held loosely at his side, stopped a few feet in front of Petronius. "The legendary Petronius, just an old man."

"Old man…yes, Narl. Legend…no, I think not."

Narl wore no tunic, even on this cold day. The many scars on his body were both a record of his life and a deadly warning to others. His muscles rippled a bit as he slowly raised his sword. "I tried to fight your son, Petronius, but he ran away."

"I doubt that, Narl."

"They say you are best with the sword."

"Better than you, Narl, better than you."

With that the two men lunged at each other. Back and forth, they fought; skillful moves by both brought them to a virtual standstill. Narl ducked to avoid the slicing sword of a tired Petronius. The younger killer feinted one way and sliced the General's arm, a move a younger Petronius would have both expected and countered. His sword dropped as he grabbed his arm, wincing in pain.

"Well, the great Petronius is totally defenseless. What shall I do?"

*

In horror, Pen had watched the whole spectacle from Songor's cheerful wave to his abrupt collapse. He saw Cearl look down, then disappear for a moment, and reappear to walk away. Pen had no illusions about what those motions meant.

Something snapped inside the boy's mind. Love had been eclipsed by raw, ugly hatred. Even fear was pushed aside. He started walking purposefully toward Cearl. One of the King's soldiers raised his sword to fight Pen. The Chosen One's weapon moved with blinding speed and wounded the man's arm, sufficient to remove the man from both his path and the battle, but Pen plunged his sword into the soldier's heart, killing him instantly. Previously reluctant to kill, disabling wounds were now unacceptable to Pen. He thirsted for death. As he cut a bloody path toward his nemesis, Pen became death.

The Royal Guard fanned out in the wake of this destruction, protecting him on both sides. Seeing his flat stare and noting the swift, accurate blade dripping with red, few stepped in his way and quickly a direct path to King Cearl opened up.

Cearl, also involved in the business of death, sighted Pen making his way to meet him. He smiled. The boy makes this too easy, he thought. They closed the gap until they stood only a few feet apart: Pen breathing hard from exertion and anger, Cearl still smiling.

"Just you and me, nephew?"

"Yes, just you and me, uncle." Pen waved his men back. Cearl did the same.

*

After Thatcher left, Mother Hebron helped some of the other women fight off the reds. Most of the Baron's men were now falling back. Soon the King's men joined the retreat. Looking past the running men, her eyes widened, her worst fear realized. Well behind the King's army, a circle had been formed, half ringed in red, half in purple. In the middle was the tall form of Cearl slowly creating his own circle within the larger one. In the center of both circles was a familiar figure in black pants and purple tunic. Her boy started moving toward the King.

Mother Hebron looked frantically for Liana. It was unnecessary; a few feet away Liana watched the same spectacle. Both women looked at each other. Then they ran, trying to close the distance between them and the fight.

*

"A family reunion, isn't this? Your father over there, Songor, poor chap, messing the ground with his blood behind me, dead by now, and you and I, together at last."

"I mean to kill you Cearl." Pen spoke coldly.

"Oh, dear boy, you sound just like your father."

Behind the King, wild-eyed soldiers began to clank their shields with a steady beat. A growl started deep inside both men as they rushed together with a clash of swords. Some who watched claimed there were sparks as well. They fought with blade and muscle.

Evenly skilled as swordsmen, the King was shaken regarding the boy's skill and dexterity. Being taller and stronger, Cearl had some mechanical advantage, but Pen managed to neutralize this edge by staying out of range, except when he darted close with a series of quick, sure moves. It was a stalemate. Even though they were even, the King had one significant advantage unknown to the boy. Both breathing heavily from their fast and furious actions, they stepped apart, tacitly agreeing on a short break from the fight.

"Someone taught you well, Pen. I would say that we are about equal in skill. I may be a bit better, but that, no doubt is because I have had more practice…Songor, for example," taunted the King.

In anger, Pen, pressed the attack again. The King parried, backing up. He was laughing as Pen assailed him. Gaining some safe distance between them, the King shook his free hand to stop the rush.

"Stay your blade just for a few moments, nephew. We are nearly equal in skill, as I said, but not in equipment. Do you see this sword, Pen?" And, while watching the motions of his adversary, he stroked his blade, drawing Pen's attention to the detailed script on the side of the blade.

"The blade is called Elinrod. A special blade, it is, nephew. It may well be over one hundred years old. They say it was made by the elves. Not a scratch on it, even after this battle, even after all these years and so many other battles. Not a scratch. It can hack into a blacksmith's anvil without suffering a single mark. It can do the same to your blade if I strike hard enough and just the right way."

The King suddenly lunged forward and with mighty strokes backed Pen up. Pen had no choice but to block some of the shots with his own blade. On one such ferocious stroke, his blade suffered a serious crack and on the next it severed in two. Pen stood before him, defenseless.

*

Petronius, engaged in his own death struggle, did not see the predicament of his son. Instead, he looked at the sword facing him, still wet with his blood.

"Apparently you are not the best with the sword, are you General?"

Still holding his wound, the General, his face pale, shook his head. "No, I am not the best. My son is…"

"Ah, the boy who runs away. I will deal with him next."

Narl's eyes were wild with anger as he thrust his sword at the wounded man. Tired but still light of foot, Petronius stepped out of the way of the sword. Narl kept coming with broad strokes and quick jabs, each just missing the General. In frustration, the younger huntsman jabbed toward Petronius' wounded arm. For this simple action, the General had waited. Grimacing with pain, he grabbed the forearm of his assailant and pulled it past him. His good hand slapped the man's back and forced him onto the ground. This was the same move he had used on Gorm many months before. The startled Narl reached for his knife, but Petronius already had it under his throat. With a quick slice, it was over. As life left the cruelest huntsman of all, Petronius whispered in his ear, "An old man with old tricks, Narl."

He sprung up and was immediately surrounded by his comrades. The huntsmen near him didn't know what to do...Petronius had killed the best of them. All heads turned toward the great sound from the center of the battlefield...the steady beating of shields. Petronius turned and looked on helplessly.

*

The King circled, blade down, the tip biting into the ground inscribing a still smaller circle. He struck once or twice but without any real conviction; the boy jumped right or left to avoid the blows. The beating from the shields got louder. Pen's men started to lunge forward but the Chosen One waved them off again.

They were cat and mouse now and the cat was enjoying himself. Pen reached inside his tunic for his knife. He figured this was as good a time as any to use the weapon. Thatcher had better be right about the blade never failing the first time used. He held the knife in front of him so it could ward off the sword.

Cearl saw the short blade, stepped back and laughed. He pointed to Pen and spoke over his shoulder to his men, "Ah...here is the Chosen One, ready to do battle... with a knife!" The men laughed cruelly and continued clanging their blades against their shield in a steady and unified beat.

His sword pointed at the ground and, keeping his step in phase with the rhythm of the beating of his men's shields, he walked around the boy. Pen rotated, keeping him in view, his small blade held high.

"Oh, you are priceless, boy. But alas, it's time to end this family reunion."

Cearl swung sideways with all his might. The stroke was positioned such that Pen could not jump over it or duck under it. He brought his own small blade up to deflect the slashing sword. With all his strength and his vise-like grip on the handle, he pushed the hard blade over his head and Elinrod cut into the ground on the other side. With one fluid motion, Pen drew his knife backward into the King's side, slicing under his armored breastplate.

Cearl pulled back. He pressed his hand to his side and immediately pulled it back into view. To his astonishment he saw his own blood.

His quick movements made the pain of his wound come all the more quickly; the King winced. The wound was deep and Cearl knew it was bad, most likely lethal. As blood spurted through the gap, the King paled. If he was to die, he thought, so would this offensive child.

"You have wounded me, Pen. No matter. This ends now, nephew!" With that, he raised his blade to commence a final attack.

Pen prepared for the onslaught of what would be series of thrusts and strikes, all of which his short blade surely could not defend. With his sword raised to commence the attack, the King suddenly stopped. Why did Cearl withhold his blow, Pen wondered?

He followed Cearl's astonished eyes as they looked down to his chest. There, protruding from his chest and piercing through his armor, was an arrow with golden feathers. The King staggered and quickly put his sword tip down to balance himself as his knees began to buckle. He wobbled, still looking at the arrow. His eyes widened as he saw the emblem of the deer painted in white on the arrow's shaft. He started to fall back, into the arms of one of his soldiers, letting go of the sword. Elinrod remained vertical momentarily as Pen lunged for it and snagged the wavering handle.

The soldier who caught the King looked at the arrow and dropped the now lifeless form to the ground as though his hands were burnt. Backing away, he screamed to the men around him: "The White Deer! Tis the arrow with the deer upon it. The White Deer done kilt the King!" The news spread among the troops as a shockwave of confusion; the superstitious troops were greatly alarmed.

Pen's gaze shifted to the prize he held. Finally, he looked up at the red troops talking nervously, stepping back. Without looking, he knew his men gathered behind him. Now he had the weapon. Now was the time.

"The King is dead. I have Elinrod; onward men of the White Deer!" A great cry arose from his guard. They followed as Pen charged into the stunned ranks of the dead King's army.

Pen became even more deadly than before. Single strokes cut through metal and flesh with ease. The King's troops, confused by the sudden turn of events, fearful of the young warrior and his hungry blade, backed up slowly, some running away. Bruder and his cavalry, sent by Petronius to break the encirclement, arrived. Assessing the situation immediately, Bruder led his men around the fight and hit the retreating soldiers, not giving them a chance to reform. With that added pressure, the men in the rear either surrendered or kept running.

Pen continued his bloody march into the ranks. His men followed his lead and killed without mercy. The Royal Guard, smaller in number, could not be stopped. The great bulk of the King's army gave ground slowly, then quickly.

Pressed by Thatcher and his men and those deadly blue-feathered arrows, the Baron's men had already left the battlefield. The huntsmen, who had wavered about attacking the wounded Petronius and the determined, gritty veterans protectively grouped around him, saw the death of the King and the unmistakable start of a rout. Ever cautious, they pulled back slowly and melted into the woods. The General held his ground for a moment, and turned to join the front. The animals left behind were wounded or dead; those that lived were frightened and confused and did not follow the huntsmen.

Pen continued to deal death, trudging steadily into the red ranks facing him. Under the relentless pressure from Pen's guard and Bruder's cavalry, the leaderless King's army folded. After slashing one man's torso and quickly severing another's sword, Pen turned to a weaponless, cowering soldier kneeling on the ground, begging for his life.

Pen didn't care. He was about to strike him down when someone grabbed his wrist, stopping its lethal arc. He wrenched away and turned on his assailant, his mind seared with white, hot anger. He looked fiercely at the man who denied him another kill. It was Frederick. Guided only by his blinding hatred, he lifted his sword to strike him. Frederick kept his face impassive, speaking firmly to his leader.

"Tis done; they are surrendering, sire. The battle is over."

As though waking from a nightmare, he slowly lowered his sword and saw soldiers in red tunics lay down their weapons. As his rage drained away so did his strength. He leaned on the great sword to hold himself up.

CHAPTER 54

The setting sun eerily accented the havoc stretched across the great field. Pen, exhausted, slowly walked from the area where he had so recently led his men. Had it been minutes or hours since he had raised his sword of death, he wondered? He made it to the pivotal place in the battle, arriving at the body of Cearl who lay in the grass, dead and alone, the arrow strangely missing. Pen looked down upon the man who had caused so much pain for so many.

A soldier, part of a burial squad hastily assembled by Astible, stood beside Pen as he looked down upon the former king.

"Sire, what would you like us to do with him?"

Pen thought a moment. There would be no royal funeral for this creature.

"Bury him here. Deep. Leave no marker behind."

He took a few more steps and stopped for a moment, shaking his head as his thoughts swirled. Slowly the thoughts materialized into hundreds of different voices, all asking the same question. Pen smiled.

The animals had faithfully stayed by forest edge as they milled about, licking wounds, snarling at each other, but maintaining an uneasy truce. Pen had ordered them out of the forest and there they stayed. They had successfully neutralized the huntsmen during the battle, but at a dear price.

They wanted to return to the forest where the natural order of things would be restored, but had first made one collective request: before wolf would be set against deer, fox against rabbit, they asked to pursue the huntsmen who had for so long persecuted them. Pen consented, and the animals suddenly vanished into their dark domain. Throughout the night, distant screams sounded. They were not the screams of animals.

After communicating with the animals for the last time, Pen continued walking through the large, well-trampled field. Pen saw blue-cloaked women tending to the wounded and dying. The women played their role in the terrible battle, dealing death with the flick of a string, and they felt death's terrible bite as well. Now they were angels of compassion and care.

One of the matrons knelt beside a soldier, tearfully murmuring his last words. Pen saw he wore the uniform of the King. The color of it didn't matter anymore. It was getting too dark to tell the difference anyway, he thought. He looked in vain for Liana or Mother Hebron, but he could not see either and a cold pit formed in his stomach.

He retraced his steps of that bloody afternoon, looking for Songor's body. His search was continually diverted as men called out to him; he went to all who beckoned. Some he recognized, some he didn't. Some were rebels, some the King's men.

He made his way slowly through the terrible land which he, in part, had created. He, Pen, had killed so many in those mad rushes. This was his penance, he thought, witnessing this great agony on the field. For a moment, he leaned on the great sword.

A large, sweaty man ran to Pen and embraced him. It was Jack.

ROBERT SELLS

"Ah, Pen, I found you. We was worried about you. So many folks…" he remarked as he stepped away and looked at the bodies lying about them.

"I know," said Pen softly, tears filming on his eyes.

Jack looked at him. "Your Pa, he's fine, Pen. Cut his arm a bit when he done kilt Narl. My dad done get cut in the arm too. Liana she be fine. Spitting mad at not finding you, I can tell you that"

Jack's looked at his friend.

"You all right, Pen? You look strange, lad."

Pen laid his hand on Jack's shoulder. "I'm not hurt, Jack. Go back to my father and Liana and tell them."

Pen started walking away. Jack hesitated a moment, worried about his friend. But he did what he was told.

Pen searched the area where he last saw Songor but did not find his body. He silently prayed Songor's men had already carried away the body of the kind, clumsy, wonderful man.

Darkness now robbed the twilight of its meager light, but the many torches scattered over the battlefield allowed him to see the body of the great horse. Mirus had been left there on the ground, cuts covering his body, evidence of his final devotion to his master. Angrily he called to some of his men, still filling deep holes with dead bodies, to bury the brave animal. Pen could take no more. So many hurt and wounded to protect him. Pen's mind sent a final message of love to the faithful animal, but it was a futile gesture. Mirus was long dead.

Petronius, working his way through the battlefield, giving commands to his soldiers, saw his son beside the horse. He slowly approached and came up beside him. He lightly put his hand on his son's shoulder. Pen turned, plunging his head against the chest of Petronius, and started sobbing uncontrollably. Petronius, wincing, wrapped his good arm around him. General of an army, soon to be king of a nation, they were still just father and son.

EPILOGUE

The great hall was alive with scurrying servants setting the last plates on the long table. At the table itself chatting well-wishers and musicians tuning up added to the festive din. Over all this noise was heard the shrill voice of the steward, Nathan, imploring people to move out into the courtyard to join the others. The coronation was just minutes away.

The hall was infused with late morning sunlight; broad beams created fan-like shapes of gold in the long chamber. The cold stone walls were mostly covered with tasteful tapestry the capable steward had found in the one of the storage rooms. He was one of the few holdovers from the court of the previous king; he had to be retained since he was the only one who knew what door each key opened, and more importantly, what was in each room. Besides, he was harmless and efficient. Deathly afraid of the old king, he fawned over young Pen.

The tailor fitted Pen with a purple coronation robe rimmed with white fleece, his lanky body resisting the tailor's best efforts. Beside him two men laughed at the tailor's consternation.

"Leave it, man!" said the taller of the two. He had resumed wearing a beard to cover the unsightly scar marring his otherwise stately face.

Noting the man frowning, Pen added his voice. "You have done well, noble tailor. But, alas, he is my chief adviser and we both must acquiesce to his wisdom."

Begrudgingly, the tailor, pins in mouth, backed away and was hurried out by the fretful little steward. Eldrick, now in charge of the King's stables, turned to Petronius and said, "Before Nathan suffers a stroke, I must join the others outside. Pen, you do look regal!" The insistent little steward pushed him out of the great hall.

"I must take my place, son," said Petronius turning to face him. One arm hung loosely by his side, never to be used again. He put his other arm around the shoulders of the man before him. "I am proud of you. Your mother would be proud too." Then, as tears started to well in his eyes, he quickly turned. A stern look to Nathan made it clear that he needed no prodding or escort.

A commotion ensued at the door.

"I tell you, he said for me to be here and be here I will!"

Hearing the familiar voice, Pen saw Jack's large, well-muscled body easily push the guards aside. Dressed in a clean gray tunic and black pants, Jack could just as easily shoe horses with such an outfit as watch the coronation. Before swords could be drawn and anyone hurt (and Pen was not sure who would take the brunt of the damage), Pen rushed over and waved off the guards. He hugged the young blacksmith.

"Devil of a time getting to see you, Pen. Never seen so many folks. Got inside the castle knowing a few blokes at the door. But, getting in here…whew. Easier to shoe a just castrated stallion!"

Servants and various officials looked at the large, solid man talking so vulgarly to their king. Pen laughed and the looks of disapproval gave way to begrudging acceptance. The young king was strange in many ways.

"Kirkland? Tell me how are things in the village?"

"Much the same, lad, much the same. Me dad canst use his arm no more from that wound in the last battle, much like your father, I guess. So I am the blacksmith now. But business be good, much traveling through Kirkland now."

The large man smiled. "Some things have changed. Remember his high and mighty, the fat merchant, and his son Erik?"

"Hard to forget the richest man in the village and his son," answered Pen, touching his chin where the son hit him years earlier.

Jack smiled. "Well, not so rich, now. Eric and his father joined with Cearl, you know."

Pen darkened. "I knew that, but I granted amnesty to all."

Jack nodded in agreement, a twinkle in his eye. "Yup, you did. But folks in Kirkland didn't pardon them. Seems Erik's father's store had no one gittin' anything. Became the poorest man in the village. Moved out, they did. 'Course, they had a few words...nasty ones...with some of the folk before they left. Folks mostly laughed at them."

Pen looked at the ground. "I've been trying to get back, Jack."

"Oh, we all knowed that, Pen. You be busy. Doing good things. You be back and fishin' again with us soon."

Pen didn't respond. They both knew the days of their youthful frolicking were over... one assuming the responsibilities of a blacksmith shop and the other governing a kingdom.

Dwarfed by the two men, Nathan, arms folded, tapped his foot beside Jack. Jack smiled down at the little man.

"I guess I best be going... "

"Wait, Jack. Take a place with the Royal Guard."

Jack beamed. "Ah, Pen. That would be just fine, if I could. Just fine."

Pen motioned Frederick to join them. Clean-shaven and sporting sharply pressed black pants, purple tunic, and black cape, the older man smiled at Jack.

"One last addition to the Royal Guard, captain. Can you manage it?"

"Yes, sire. Should I get him a uniform?"

Pen looked at Jack who was wincing. The young king put his hand on the shoulder of the blacksmith and smiled. "No, I think he is fine just the way he is."

Frederick and Jack walked out the door together, talking and laughing as they merged with the sunshine.

Nathan was desperately trying to block another man from entering the great hall. The tall, broad man was attired nobly, sporting a well-trimmed black beard. The man simply picked up the steward and plopped him aside.

"Bruder? Bruder!" Pen cried and walked to greet him. "You arrived just in time!"

"The roads were filled with people still trying to get into the city and castle. It is a great day, my liege," said Bruder, smiling.

"I barely recognized you...what fine clothes you wear!"

"Ah, lad, I'm no longer the king of some wild tribes, but a noble of his majesty's realm. I must play the part." The tall man, smiling, bowed in a genteel fashion.

He leaned close to Pen's ear. "I know this might not be the best time to talk, but there is some trouble in the Northlands, sire. Maybe you can fit me in for a meeting after the party?"

Pen nodded. Bruder looked at the lad covered with the trappings of a king. "You have come a long way, my liege."

Pen smiled at his friend. "I still have much to learn, Bruder."

"You are doing fine, boy...I mean, your highness."

Bruder nudged forward a bit. From behind, the smaller Nathan was trying to push him out the door. The former king and the king-to-be laughed.

"I'd best be going now, Pen."

Nathan followed Bruder out, yelling over his shoulder to Pen. "Remember sir, when you hear the bell ringing... that is when you must come through the door." He closed the door and left.

The hall was finally quiet, though cheers and chants could be heard through the open windows. Speeches and such would take some time, he knew, so he reckoned he had many minutes alone. Alone at last. What a rare delight! Every day was filled with requests from various citizens and decisions to be made.

He was fourteen now. So much had changed over the last year. From delightful obscurity, he found himself the new focus of everyone's attention, whether a supplicant requested a favor, a criminal sought a pardon, or a servant asked direction. Instead of taking care of a few chores on a farm, he now had to set up a government. In the past, his birthday parties had involved close friends and his father…today his birthday was celebrated by a nation, his coronation adding to the celebration. So much had changed.

All his comrades in arms would be there with the sad exception of Viridius and Songor. Tears welled in his eyes recalling the ever smiling green man and the large, boisterous Songor, always first to laugh or eat. Poor Songor, he thought.

A door opened and a cloaked figure slowly moved in the direction of an unsuspecting Pen. The form stumbled; a chair skidded along the floor.

Startled, Pen turned toward the sound, instinctively grabbing Elinrod. Recognizing the hunched body, he rushed forward.

"Songor, you are still too weak! You were supposed to stay in bed," Pen scolded, gently propping him up.

"And miss this? Not me, young master. Ye canst do this without me. Just had to wait till that bossy Mother Hebron left." He said all of this with a smile, but the sweat and occasional winces told the sacrifice he made in just moving that short distance.

"She be a good lady, mind you, sir. A good, gentle woman is she. Always has been from when we put ye in her arms all them yars ago. And then she goes and fixes me up. Me who should be dead. Using them herbs and ointments and giving me bitter brew to drink. She saved me life sir, but ye canst do this without me, Pen and no man, no woman will stop me."

"No, I should have known better, my dear friend. Rest here in this chair. I have an idea."

As Pen left the great room, Songor slowly eased himself onto the throne, oblivious of its meaning and only barely satisfied by its comfort. The resting body was considerably less than the one that had worked at a farm just a year before. Cearl had left Songor for dead and only the skills of Mother Hebron could bring him to the living. His wound was so severe that he lingered between life and death for weeks. Pen, ever at his side, attended to his needs almost as much as Mother Hebron. One morning Songor woke up, alert to the world around him. Seeing Pen asleep on a chair beside his bed, he gently shook the lad's hand and asked him if he could help with anything. Pen laughed and cried for the first time since the battle.

Songor still suffered if he exerted himself too much. Pen hoped that his latest efforts would not compromise his unhurried recovery.

He came in with four of his largest guards, dressed in regal purple cloaks. He kneeled down beside the haggard shape. "You shouldn't walk anymore, dear friend. I will have you carried out on this chair, Songor. Do that for your boy, won't you?" Pen pleaded.

Hearing Pen refer to himself as Songor's boy brought tears to the old man. From his chair he reached out and stroked Pen's face. "Aye, master Pen. I will do just that," he whispered.

The four men gently hoisted the chair. The task would have been unthinkable before the great battle, but now, his body much diminished, carrying him was possible. Still insisting he could walk, they laughed affectionately as they slowly and carefully walked him out into the sunshine on that fine summer morning.

A great roar went up as the crowd saw him. Pen smiled, imagining his embarrassment over the cheering which accompanied his presence. He was greatly beloved by the population, his acts of bravery and sacrifice now legend.

By now, thought Pen, the Royal Guard, still wearing those purple tunics made nearly a year ago, will be neatly arrayed on one side of the steps with the blue-robed sisters, the order fully revived, on the other side facing them. Behind them would be the soldiers, adorned in brilliant red, Thatcher wearing the gray cape of general.

All coronations in the past had taken place at the top of the steps, but Pen insisted that he be crowned at the base. A large platform had been constructed so that the people could watch the proceedings. Serfs and freemen, farmers and merchants, men and women, parents and children: all crowded on the sturdy platform. Above them were more people filling the rooftops and windows. Pen snuck a peek out the window. It seemed as though all of Mercia surrounded the castle.

He strolled back to a smaller chair and sat down, his long legs stretched out, hands intertwined behind his head.

A voice came from the far end of the hall. "So this is the boy who would be king."

Pen turned to face the tall, lithe form of Liana adorned in the blue robe. No ponytail now, her long hair hung gracefully down her back. Pen was more shocked at her stunning beauty than her presence.

Recovering, he asked with a smile, "Shouldn't you be outside waiting for me?"

"Waiting for you? Me wait for you? Silly boy. I only do that in horse races with you!" she responded tartly.

"All except one," Pen reminded her somberly.

"Yes," she quietly acknowledged, her gray eyes locked on his, "all except one. Mirus was the best horse, Pen."

"I didn't deserve him, Liana. So many good men... and animals died for me."

Liana was quiet, knowing when to listen.

"I am sad sometimes when I think of the past. Of the losses..." his voice broke with what sounded like a sob and both were quiet waiting for him to gain his voice. "But mostly, I'm worried. Worried about all of the decisions I have made and will have to make."

"You, worry? I never knew you to worry."

He looked up at her, his grin matching hers as he recalled all the times he admitted his concerns to her alone.

"Pen, you will often make mistakes, but you will correct them. You are wiser than most men because you listen and worry. You are also the kindest man I know."

"But how will I know when I am wrong, Liana? Remember how I treated Songor before the great battle?"

She laughed. "Don't fret about that, Pen. I'll let you know."

He joined her laughter, a rare treasure for him alone, it seemed. It was like it was when they played together. Was it just a year ago, he wondered? The quick retorts, her insistence on what they would do, her wisdom, and the laughter. She was like a balm to all his wounds, physical and spiritual.

He realized Liana was remarkably beautiful. The few who dared to woo her were summarily pushed away. She was not a maiden aching for the arms of a man. She was already a woman, he thought, and destined to become a bride to the Jesus god, like her mother. Usually the nuns did not marry, he thought ruefully.

They sat together, barely touching, but the contact was somehow soothing. Pen's mind went back to the great battle. All these months after the battle, he had been plagued by a question, a question he was afraid to ask anyone except Liana.

"Liana, something has puzzled me: the arrow which killed Cearl. Of course, people say the White Deer killed the King, but I don't think so. I mean, how could she? I don't think she would ever kill. So, I wonder…who shot the arrow?"

He looked over to his friend and saw her staring at the flame, her face wrinkled in uncertainty. She turned to gaze at him, her eyes conveying both wisdom and love.

She began. "You deserve to know, Pen. But keep it our secret."

He nodded his assent.

"Long ago after Cearl had tried to kill the deer on Cross Fell Mountain, one of the sisters climbed the mountain and found the spent arrow. For many years it was hidden. I only found out about it a few days before the great battle…"

She stared back to the fire.

"Mother showed me the arrow and it was the finest arrow I had ever seen. In the right hands, the arrow would travel perfectly. She told me the arrow had to kill the King. Then and only then would the power of the White Deer be restored. The problem, of course, was getting an archer close enough."

Pen interjected. "But his armor, surely that should have protected him."

Liana smiled. "Yes, it should have. And it would have against any other arrow, except this one. You didn't see the arrowhead, Pen. Larger than any I have ever seen and jagged. We figured it would be able to penetrate the armor."

Her face strained as she returned to the flame and the past.

"We saw you fighting the King and rushed over, but we couldn't get close fast enough. When he broke your sword, I stopped..." Tears welled in her eyes as she remembered her fear of losing Pen. She stared back at the fire, the flames reminding her of shapes from the past...

*

"Liana, you aren't close enough! A little further." She tagged on her daughter's robe.

Liana angrily shook her hand away. "No, the King means to finish it now."

Liana took out the arrow from inside her cloak and notched it in the bow. Cearl had raised his sword. She pulled the arrow back. The wind, she worried, which way blew the wind? No time. She released the missile, praying God would guide its flight.

*

"It wasn't just me, Pen. I was too far away to make a sure shot. God or maybe the White Deer was watching over both of us that day. But yes, I made the shot."

Now it was Pen's turn to contemplate the fire. Without looking up, he whispered, "Thank you, Liana. You have always been there for me. Thank you."

She stroked his cheek softly, their eyes locked. "I will continue to be there for you."

Suddenly a bell started its rhythmic ringing. Pen heard it, looked up, and sprung off the chair. Liana fussed with his robe. "There, now you make a passable king."

They walked toward the door together as she put her arm in his.

"Liana, you know when I come out you will have to kneel like everyone else."

She unlocked her grasp and looked at him with disdain. "Kneel to you? Silly boy!"

The doors opened and the bright light of the day beckoned. They could see the long lines of purple and blue cascading down the stairs leading to the throng below. They both saw Jack, incongruous in his regular clothes, but his presence somehow right. Liana went quickly to take her place in line; another great cheer erupted from the crowd.

Pen took a deep breath, closed his eyes for a moment, and walked into the sunshine. When he appeared at the door, a great roar sounded. Some of his guards could not suppress smiles. As he walked out, there was a sudden silence and soldiers, nobles, guard, and subjects all kneeled to the future king. He looked over at Liana. She too kneeled, but looked up and glared at him. Then a smile, followed by a wink.

Looking over the sea of people before him, he said with the voice of a man, "Arise kingdom of Mercia."

High atop Cross Fell Mountain, the white deer slowly walked to the ledge overlooking the land below. Farmlands were turning green and the great forest seemed less dark. Villages dotted the great plain, but her sharp eyes discerned no people. In the distance, she imagined the castle and nodded her head. She looked over Markwood Forest again and walked away, confident she had chosen well.

ABOUT THE AUTHOR

Robert Sells has taught physics for over forty years. He has been a story teller for over 50 years, entertaining his children, grandchildren, and students. Return of the White Deer is his first public offering.

He lives with his wife, Dale, in the idyllic village of Geneseo, New York with two attentive dogs who are uncritical sounding boards for his new stories. He is intrigued by poker and history, in love with Disney and writing, and amused by religion and politics.

Learn more about Robert Sells
and his work at www.robertsells.org

11364961R00244

Made in the USA
Charleston, SC
18 February 2012